ABSOLUTION

Copyright © Paul Martin Midden, 2007. All rights reserved. No part of this book may be reproduced or transmitted in any form or by any means, electronic or mechanical, including photocopying, recording, or by any information storage and retrieval system, without permission in writing from the publisher.

Millennial Mind Publishing
An imprint of American Book Publishing
5442 S. 900 East, #146
Salt Lake City, UT 84117
www.american-book.com
Printed in the United States of America on acid-free paper.

Absolution

Designed by Lucinda Vessey, design@american-book.com

Publisher's Note: *This is a work of fiction. Names, characters, places, and incidents either are the product of the author's imagination, or are used fictitiously, and any resemblance to actual persons, living or dead, events, or locales is entirely coincidental.*

ISBN-13: 978-1-58982-418-8
ISBN-10: 1-58982-418-0

Midden, Paul Martin, Absolution

Special Sales

These books are available at special discounts for bulk purchases. Special editions, including personalized covers, excerpts of existing books, and corporate imprints, can be created in large quantities for special needs. For more information e-mail info@american-book.com.

ABSOLUTION

PAUL MARTIN MIDDEN

**To my wife Patty
and my daughter Kate
Blessings!**

ACKNOWLEDGMENTS

I would like to thank my editor, Wanda Morgan, not only for her attentive and conscientious work in trolling through the manuscript time after time but also for shepherding me through the mysterious process of bringing the raw material of writing to a finished product. I would also like to thank all the people at American Book who contributed to this process. I would like to thank the many friends and colleagues who read the work during its creation and immediately afterwards and who encouraged me along the way: Patricia Cashman, Pamela and Patrick Cacchione, Suzanne Constanz, Marjorie Cassidy, and James Schroeder. A special thanks to enthusiastic family members, especially Constance Hornburg, Mary Glasener, and Barbara Selecman, my sisters; my brother Ron; and my sister-in-law Diane. These people not only read the unwieldy manuscript but provided invaluable feedback in addition to encouragement. I want to give special thanks to Patricia Cassidy Midden, my wife, for being so kind when I anxiously handed her the first few pages of creative writing I have attempted since college. If her response in that instance had been less gentle, this moment may never have come. And special thanks to Kate Midden, my

Absolution

daughter, whose young life inspires me more than she will ever know.

And then there is the Catholic Church itself, a sprawling organization that focuses goodness in the world and strives everywhere to be worthy of her own exalted ideals. Particular thanks to the dioceses of Baltimore, Chicago, and Bismarck, which served as the unwitting background for this story. And to the many fine priests who labor in dioceses throughout the globe. For the good they bring to the world, I, along with much of humanity, offer sincere thanks.

To these people and many others, I want to express my gratitude and respect. The contributions of all were helpful; the limitations of the work are entirely mine.

Saint Louis, Missouri
2006

Part One

CHAPTER 1

Radko Slopovich did not have the kind of name most people associated with being a Catholic priest. Maybe in Eastern Europe, but here in the United States most Catholics thought of it as a slightly sinister name, more suggestive of a gang member or even a war criminal than a kindly man who might teach second graders their prayers. Nonetheless, Radko took pride in his name and his heritage, more so since he was part of the Roman church, not the Orthodox church of most of his countrymen. He thought that the name set him apart from others, something that appealed to his pride. He also thought it gave him some room to maneuver. So when he started his assignment in Chicago, he told people if they asked that he had tired of the East Coast and wanted to seek out humbler, more Midwestern roots.

The truth was that he loved the East Coast with its cosmopolitan ways, its rich cultural heritage, and even its hubris. He always agreed with the attitude he perceived in most residents of the original colonies: that they were the real United States, and that the states added after the Revolution were more like outlying prov-

Absolution

inces. Radko always felt lucky that his parents left the Balkans when he was an infant and settled in Maryland, where they raised him and his sister like good American children. Though his looks would have tagged him as a foreigner, his accentless English put everyone at ease that he was one of them, a true American. Radko had no memory of the Balkans, and his parents never returned with him to visit. So despite his appearance and the obvious foreign-born impression his parents made, Radko felt himself to be an American. He was granted citizenship when he was twelve.

He left Baltimore five years ago not because he didn't like it, but because his life had taken a turn that surprised him, delighted him, and gave him constant cause for worry. He thought Chicago, where he didn't know anyone and where he could easily find work in the sprawling church structure, better suited his purposes.

That was five years ago. During these years, Radko has been executing his priestly duties, as these were required by his influential if humdrum job in the Chancery office, and was pursuing what he came to think of as his real life without exposure. There were times when he got anxious about this, of course; but more often he was pleased that he had grown so skilled at living parallel lives, deceiving almost everyone he knew, and walking a tightrope so thin at times that he was sure it was only the grace of God that allowed him to do it.

Not that Radko put much stock in the grace of God. He had come to see himself as an intelligent but simple and honest man, not given to self-aggrandizement so common among clergy, especially office-bound politicos who dreamed of dying in possession of a mitered or even a red hat. No, Radko believed he had few illusions about himself, even as he pursued a career in an institution in which his faith had dwindled. He was enormously fond of the church he served and felt bound to it. It defined the context and texture of his life and was his road map for traveling through time. He loved its history, its liturgy, even its efforts to do good in the world. In fact, he could hardly imagine not being a part of such an enormous worldwide organization with such power, such breadth, and such reach across the globe. And not just in the West, but in the emerging countries: in Africa and even Asia, in Polynesia. It made his head spin just to think about it. But he saw himself as a modern man, perhaps even an intellectual, who had little use for the myths and folklore of Christianity. Despite his education and his pious upbringing, he could no longer make sense of arcane concepts like the Virgin Birth, or transubstantiation, or the Trinity, for that matter. Even the concept of God, something that Radko could allow, did not include a person with whom one was in daily conversation, especially not on the receiving end. He missed these beliefs, but he was a realist.

On the other hand, Radko saw the world through religious eyes. Wherever he looked, he was awed both by its intricate beauty and by its sheer immensity. Everywhere he looked he saw mystery and knew from his reading and studies that even modern science limited itself to probabilities and not certainties. He also knew in his heart that, if you strip away the mythology of religion, its basic values—of reverence, of mystery, of love—best described the core experiences of self-aware humans on the planet. His church always seemed like the biggest tent: the place where the rich diversity of life was reflected in a tolerant and accepting way. The details didn't really matter to him.

So his "doubts"—he didn't really think of them as doubts, just as the way things were—began vaguely in his formation for the priesthood and never completely abated. They didn't even change. He did not have an alternative explanation for how the world was or who made him or why he was made. He didn't think these matters were really knowable or even important and wondered at those Christians who seemed so sure of the view of reality they foisted onto others so insistently. The term "born again" made him wince; fanatical "defenses" of marriage made him nauseous; damnation of the different made him faint. Fortunately, in his work, he did not have to deal with those types of pastoral concerns. The way Radko

Absolution

saw it, he was just a guy doing his job as best he could. For himself, for his wife, and for his family.

Because of all the ecclesiastical artifices that Radko had trouble digesting, the hardest was celibacy, that quaint if perverse stipulation that the church had required of its priests for the past nine hundred years. One of the first things to go in the upheaval of the Reformation and one of the most staunchly defended institutions of the remnant Old Church, it remained a hallmark of the Roman church, which exulted in its celibate priesthood even through the many sex scandals that revealed the extent of its sheer unworkability. Because Radko did not see himself as militant, and because he was a man not without ambition, he elected not to protest publicly this lunatic requirement. And because he loved the church despite itself, he could not bring himself to abandon the priesthood. Nor could he ignore his desire—no, not only his desire, but his need—to be feverishly close to a woman, to love her in no way chastely, and to celebrate the children this fever spawned. To Radko, this was not so much a conflict as it was a matter of just living his life, juggling his needs in the most efficient manner possible, much as a single mother must work and still be a mom. Tough at times, but no question about the need to do it. No question at all.

Of course, were his unorthodox lifestyle to be exposed, he would have to face music he did not want to hear. But being simple and honest did not include being stupid, and Radko did everything he could to make sure that such exposure would never happen. Not to him; not to his wife; not to his family. It was for this reason that he came to Chicago, a big, tolerant city where it was easy to be anonymous.

CHAPTER 2

It was a bright Tuesday morning, and Radko rolled out of bed early for him: 7:30 a.m. His wife, Ursula, had already left for work, dutifully dropping the twins off at their preschool on the way. Though Radko envied his wife many things—her job as a teacher, her looks, her spirit, her courage, and her can-do attitude—one thing he did not envy was her schedule. Brought up in the old East Germany, Ursula was up at 5:30 and at school at 7:00, even though classes did not begin until 8:00. She was responsible to the point of being fastidious. School ended at 2:45, but she would not be home until at least 5:00, and often later if students wanted more of her time and her guidance.

After his morning ritual—shower, shave, dress in flexibly black clothes—Radko went to the kitchen for breakfast. As usual, the coffee was made, a bowl, cereal, and milk were on the counter, and the paper was opened in front of his regular chair. Radko sat down and did what he did most every morning of his life as an adult. He ate a leisurely light breakfast, drank his coffee, and read the paper. He loved these simple rituals; they made him feel connected to the world, cared for, and warm inside. He thought of Ursula and his eyes moistened. He loved her beyond words. And he was so hope-

Absolution

lessly sentimental that he couldn't even think about her without tearing up. It wasn't just Ursula; he had a whole list of moisture-producing names: Marguerite and Sergei, the twins; his friend Silas; his parents. He was especially lachrymose when he thought about sex. Just the thought of sex brought tears streaming down his cheeks and aroused him to distraction. This was sometimes bothersome, but he cherished his own sentimentality and could not imagine life without it.

After breakfast, Radko left for the office. When at home, he thought of the Chancery as "the office," and this was how he spoke about it in front of Ursula and the twins. He also spoke this way in front of their casual friends, neighbors, and others to whom they were not particularly close. Sometime during the fifty-minute drive downtown, however, his clerical identity asserted itself. He often chuckled because it was such a peculiar Jekyll-and-Hyde transformation, no less dramatic because it happened every work day, every week. Each morning, about halfway to work, he deftly removed his striped tie and donned a black and white collar over his starched white shirt. He mastered the art of doing this just as traffic began to snarl on the outskirts of downtown. After the change, he quite unconsciously started singing or humming a favorite hymn or whistling some chant he remembered from his childhood. This total immersion experience eased the gap, which he felt between being a publicly celibate priest and having a wife and kids. On the way home, he reversed this process in the same way, removing the clerical collar, replacing his tie, and humming popular, secular songs. Elvis and the Beatles were his favorite artists.

When he arrived at the office, he checked his mail, greeted the secretaries, and set about arranging his morning tasks. The support staff was always surprised to see Radko before ten, but he had good working relationships with them, and they didn't mind his "early" arrival.

Radko sat at his desk and looked out the window. The Cathedral sat across the street, and he had a good view. It was a handsome if not very impressive edifice, very unlike major cathedrals he had seen in Europe or even in America. It lacked the presence of St. Patrick's in New York or the scale of the Cathedral Basilica in St. Louis. It certainly did not have the size, grandeur, or price tag of that new monstrosity in Los Angeles. But Radko liked it, as it was of human dimension, worn and dear.

As always, he began his day by going through the phone messages. Nothing unusual here, he thought to himself. Mostly just phone calls from anxious or irritated people wondering how their annulments were coming. These marriage cases were one of the most tedious parts of his job as judicial vicar, but he knew that he had to maintain contact with these people. He had to call each one and assure them that their annulment was on schedule, even though it had been in an ecclesiastical court for two years. What a tough sell, Radko thought to himself. It would be a lot easier if the church left marriage to the state and simply focused on the sacrament. But that would not happen in his lifetime. The church has jealously guarded its authority over marital and sexual behavior almost as long as it had been in existence.

I can picture this, though, Radko thought, falling into a reverie. Instead of managing marriages, he could envision a time when the church just blessed them and when annulments, divorces, or other marital woes were managed by the state or the civil authorities. This would cut down substantially on the anxious and irritated crowd whom he spent most of his time handholding. Then people would only call upon him to bless them.

But that would be the distant future, if ever. For now, he had work to do. He took a deep breath and grabbed the phone.

Several hours later, Radko leaned back in his chair and stretched before he began to look through the mail that had just been delivered. As he flipped through the envelopes, one in particular caught his eye. It was from Silas, an old friend with whom he had studied in Rome many years before. He smiled and slid his expensive brass opener under the seal.

Absolution

Dear Radko,

I know it has been a long time since we've spoken. Life in Rome goes on pretty much the way it always has. I am sorry I missed you when you were here last; the demands of my job require frequent travel that is not always under my control. I do look forward to our next meeting.

The reason I am writing is that I heard your name the other day over lunch; actually, not my lunch, but close enough to some Cardinals on the Bishop Selection Committee. Evidently your name is not unknown on those interminable lists that the Pronuncio is forever drawing up. I just wanted to give you a heads-up and to encourage you to keep me in mind on your way to the top. Toiling in the archives has its rewards, but, well, we know bishops live better. All of this is very hush-hush, so destroy this letter after reading it.

Looking forward to seeing you soon,
Warmest regards,
Silas

Radko smiled. He always felt happy to hear from his friend Silas, but about being a bishop? Fat chance, he thought to himself. He did not think that he was suitable bishop material, but the thought of it made him smile. He remembered clearly a time when he would have salivated at the thought of joining that elite club. And Silas was right: Bishops do live better. But the thought of disassembling the life he had painstakingly constructed was too much to contemplate. A vague sensation of anxiety skipped along the edges of his awareness, then burst into a flash—he did not know what he would do if given a choice between becoming a descendant of the apostles or staying married to Ursula. It was not a choice he relished making, but ....

This is nonsense, he thought, tossing the note aside and reaching for the rest of the mail pile. Radko had some take on how these things worked; and while he was ambitious, his ambition lay primarily in maintaining the life he had. He had no desire to take on a highly public role in the church. Plus, he could not just dismiss Ursula and the twins even if he wanted to. Revelations about his personal life would not only sink his prospects for being a bishop but would also most likely result in his expulsion from the priesthood. After the sex scandals of a few years before, the church did not take kindly to unorthodox living arrangements, at least not in the USA.

Despite this stern lecture to himself, Radko could not stop fantasizing about what it would be like to be a bishop or what it would be like to be forced to make a choice. His vivid imagination ran the gamut from picturing himself as an acclaimed bishop heading a great procession to being unceremoniously driven from the priesthood—alone, unemployed, destitute. He had to chuckle at that last series of overblown fantasies. He believed Ursula would stand by him no matter what, and her strength alone would not allow their family to go down. She is stronger than me, Radko thought to himself; I can count on her.

Radko sat immobile for a few moments, thinking about the horrifying prospect that something might happen to his family. He didn't think he was worried so much about himself: he had made his choices. But the prospect of harm coming to his children, his beloved, innocent, cherished children, was unbearable. He closed his eyes and held his breath for just a moment. Never, he swore to himself.

By the end of the day, Radko was exhausted. More from his renegade fantasizing than from the actual work he did. It was after closing that he donned his coat and left the building.

Driving home, he could not wait to tell Ursula about the note from Silas. She would laugh, he thought, and help him play out his outsized fantasies over a bottle of decent Italian table wine. And then they would celebrate their being together the best way humans know of. He had to force himself not to exceed the speed limit. For a change, Ursula and the twins were already at home when he arrived. The twins looked up blankly from the television and mumbled hello before turning their gaze back to it. Radko leaned over and tousled their hair, annoying each one of them just enough to get their attention. He smiled and walked into the kitchen, where

Absolution

Ursula was making dinner. He walked up behind her and hugged her around the waist. "Guess who this is?" he asked playfully. "Could it be the Archbishop of Turin?"

"Maybe the archdeacon of Brooklyn," Ursula teased.

"Silas thinks not," replied Radko, "and you know Silas is seldom wrong," he added jokingly.

Ursula looked at him askance and said, "You know something I don't, Pére Slopovich?"

"Not really," Radko replied. "I did get a note from Silas today saying that he had heard my name being bandied about by a couple of two-martini cardinals from the bishop selection committee."

Radko stopped talking when he saw Ursula's reaction. All of a sudden, her look turned dark, eyes hooded and focused somewhere beyond him, blank expression, an eerie silence. More than just being quiet, it was a silence that commanded all verbal activity in the immediate vicinity to stop.

"What's the matter, sweetheart?" Radko finally asked. "Surely, you're not taking this seriously?"

Ursula did not respond. She was thinking of Silas, whom she knew and liked. But she knew him to be a shrewd, methodical man who was not given to dashing off funny notes across continents. If Silas took the time to write Radko about this matter, it was most likely not a joke or a pleasantry. It could actually be a done deal. In a few seconds, she flashed through Radko's options and her own. Marriage, separation, quiet divorce? How would this affect the twins? She didn't think she would be the first priest's wife to vanish. She also thought about the exposure risks, something that had become routine in their lives—the possibilities of scandal, the impact of this on the kids, the impact on her husband. She stood silently considering this breathtaking news.

In this same still moment, she reviewed her history with Radko in rapid panorama: how they met, how they became involved, how they talked of marriage, and then actually did it. The young Ursula had not been looking for a husband or a family; she had certainly not been looking for this odd living arrangement. The stress of living two lives did not impact her much—Radko was the religious one in the family, the one who wanted to see if they could cling to each other and not rock the boat of his publicly celibate, ecclesiastical career. It was he who suggested that they come to Chicago. She went along because she loved him, because they connected so well both emotionally and physically, and then because they had the twins. She gradually stopped thinking about what she came to regard as Radko's predicament, as his problem. She was a teacher, a mother, a wife. And she cherished her life.

Ursula blinked twice and focused on Radko. "What are you going to do?" she asked bluntly.

"What am I going to do about what?" Radko replied, more than a little irritated with her chilly reaction.

"You know Silas doesn't fool around," Ursula continued. "You know he was writing you for a reason." Ursula knew Radko to be an intelligent and educated man. She often wondered, however, how he could be so thick.

"I think you are jumping to conclusions, Honey," said Radko, trying to be conciliatory. "He does like to brag, you know, about how highly placed he is. You know that 'I'm just a lowly archivist' crap is a very thin veneer." For Christ's sake, Radko thought, the guy is in charge of the Vatican Collection. Lowly archivist, my ass. Radko wondered why Ursula could not see this. Silas, dear as he was to Radko, was just blowing his own horn. No harm done.

The matter was dropped because dinner was ready. Ursula called the twins, they protested, Ursula took charge, and then everyone sat down to dinner. Ursula busied herself with their education in appropriate dinner behavior. Radko ate quietly. The wine was decent.

After dinner, Ursula continued to be busy about many things: the dishes, the children, homework, correcting papers from her students. She had that stony Germanic look on her face that Radko

Absolution

knew read "Keep Out." Radko sulked, went to his small study, and turned on the television.

Radko hated these domestic squabbles, the little disagreements that blossom for no good reason into hours or even days of alienation. A waste of time feeling so separate, he thought, chiding himself for being so childish. But like many husbands, he thought his wife was being unreasonable. He also knew that it was something of a contest to see who broke the ice first. This experience was enough for him to reconsider his critique of celibacy. He knew that Ursula could hold out longer than he: she had a clearer sense of right and wrong and did not brook what she thought of as muddled thinking, especially about matters she deemed important to her family. Radko gazed at the images on the television screen, not really paying attention.

CHAPTER 3

Radko's mind wandered back to before he and Ursula first met. He was teaching an evening course at the University of Baltimore to make some extra money. That's what he told himself, although he really did it because he was lonesome and needed to fill his time with something, preferably something that involved people. He liked to teach, and he had some expertise in English, having done a master's degree some years before—pretty much for the same reasons, as he thought about it.

He thought about how he ended up living in an apartment alone, an unusual arrangement for a Catholic priest. He remembered how he had hated living in a rectory with two bitter older men whose devotion seemed to lie in doing as little work as possible. Out of frustration, he appealed for permission to live closer to his work at the Baltimore Chancery, and, to his surprise, obtained it without too much trouble.

Living alone was such a relief for him; he took to it immediately.

During those years, he was working as a canon lawyer: one of those members of a legal profession that was generally invisible to the general population. He practiced church law, preparing cases for ecclesiastical courts. Most Catholics, he thought, didn't even know there were church courts. Radko was sure that his job had a great deal more status in the past, say in the Middle Ages, but he was satisfied not to be a civil attorney. Church law at least had some compassion to it, and he hated the limelight. His small apartment was within walking distance of Baltimore Harbor, and he sometimes said Mass when he was needed to fill in for regular priests' absences. He had a few friends with whom he spent time. It was a quiet, simple life, but Radko was lonely.

He remembered the day that Ursula first showed up in his classroom—tall, blond, clear-eyed, and thirty-one years old. Pretty if not beautiful, she had a steady presence and a firm sense of herself that attracted Radko immediately. He was not in the habit of dating his students. He was not in the habit of dating at all. He knew to steer clear of any impropriety in his professional life, and he did not even consider asking Ursula out while he was her teacher. Well, he considered it, but he thought he could manage his attraction until the end of the semester.

Barely, as it turned out. As the days went by, he thought of her more and more. He tried to read her thoughts on her face or in her work. That was impossible. Ursula was hardworking and focused. She did not smile; she did not frown: she kept herself focused on her work and only occasionally asked a question or made a comment in class. Always thoughtful; always concise. Always right. Radko had decided that he would step out of role after the semester and ask her to coffee, at least. This was the only way he could quell his enthusiasm to get through the remaining classes. He thought the semester would never end.

Finally, it did. He planned his approach carefully. On the last day of class, he was returning the final essays. He had them stacked neatly on his desk in prearranged order. He said that he would give everyone a few minutes of feedback about their work and their final grade, and then each student could leave. Of course, Ursula's was the last in the pile, and when she came up to his desk they would be alone in the classroom. Radko was nervous but struggled to appear calm. As the students came forward, he became increasingly anxious. By the time the last few students were ready, he was sweating and his hands were beginning to shake. He had barely been able to speak to the two students before Ursula, and his voice was getting shaky. He knew as her turn approached that this plan was both transparent and foolish, and he just wanted to run away.

The fate of Radko Slopovich and Ursula Fliegendorf was sealed that very evening. For as she rose from her seat toward the back of the classroom, Ursula looked without smiling directly into Radko's eyes, and her gaze did not flinch as she strode toward the desk of the pale, trembling professor. Radko pushed the blue notebook across the desk to her with the A clearly marked on the front facing her. It was at that moment that Ursula broke eye contact, looked down at the notebook, and slowly returned to gaze at Radko. And then she smiled.

At the first sign of Ursula's lips curling into a smile, Radko's anxiety vanished. Without realizing it, he was smiling too and began congratulating Ursula on the good work she had done all semester. She thanked him for his well-prepared lectures and his thoughtful feedback; he in turn praised her steady and thorough work. "It is difficult at times for a foreigner, you know," said Ursula coyly. "I understand," said Radko expansively. Gaze and smile, smile and gaze. I love this about you; I love that about you, although neither could say that word at this point. As they approached the natural end of their mutually adoring conversation, it seemed the easiest thing in the world for Radko to propose a drink—coffee, perhaps, or a glass of wine along the Inner Harbor. Dinner would follow, overlooking the harbor lights and the boats coming and going. Baltimore may suffer from whatever urban problems are endemic to American cities, but that night, it was Paris.

When the semester ended, so did Radko's time at the University. He had decided mid-semester that he could not bear to be exposed to attractive women on a regular basis and harbor any

Absolution

hope of remaining a priest. It wasn't hard to stop teaching; it was, after all, only a part-time assignment based upon his availability. But leaving the University also freed him to make that dinner the beginning of a relationship such as he had never had before.

Because Radko had thought of being a priest throughout much of his adolescence, he had kept his distance from girls. It helped that his development lagged most of his peers and that he was naturally shy. He had never dated. He did not know the first thing about protocol or sex.

At the end of that first evening, Radko walked Ursula to her car. "Thank you for a wonderful evening," he said.

Ursula turned to face him directly. "And thank you, Radko," she said, and then she took his hand and took a step toward him. She leaned toward him and kissed him.

At that moment, all of Radko's education, all his spiritual training, all his work, and all his circumspection evaporated. He felt things he had never felt before and hadn't anticipated feeling. The intensity of his response appalled him. He kissed Ursula back as if he knew what he was doing. After a few moments, he realized he had forgotten where they were.

"Will you call me, Radko?" Ursula asked.

"Of course, I will," Radko replied.

"You will probably need my number," she teased.

Radko felt like an idiot. He reached in his pocket for a pen, which he had, and for a piece of paper, which he didn't. He wrote her number on his wrist like a middle-school student and tried to act as if this were normal adult behavior. "I'll call you soon," he said.

The truth is he would have called her later that evening if it hadn't been after midnight. Instead he lay in his bed like the lovesick puppy he was and replayed the evening over and over and over again. He had never felt such exhilaration, such joy, such love. He didn't fall asleep until an hour before his alarm went off.

And the next morning he hopped out of bed and sang himself through his morning rituals. His morning prayer ritual was a new experience. He did not feel guilty. If anything, he felt the power of love that church people are forever talking about but which he now realized he had never experienced. For the first time in his life, Radko was happy—truly, genuinely, easily happy. Not right or correct or learned, just happy.

Radko spent most of the day, a Friday, wanting to call Ursula. He called the number and got an answering machine. He called it again just to hear her voice. It must be her home number, he thought. Radko then realized how little he actually knew about this woman who opened the door to his heart. Did she work? Was she involved with someone? Was she an American citizen? He knew that she had been born in the old East Germany, but he didn't know when she came to the U.S. Then he thought: Is she Catholic? The prospect that she might be scandalized to be dating a priest dismayed him. Did she know he was a priest? He didn't wear clerical attire to classes at the University, and he tried to think back to see if his being a priest ever came up. He couldn't think of a time, but it made him uneasy anyway. In his mind, he and Ursula were already having a relationship, even though they had only had dinner once. Needless to say, Radko got little real work done that day.

The next few days were torture, after a fashion. His mood remained euphoric, but he got more and more agitated when he could not reach her. He was sure it was the correct number because of her voice on the recorder. He called it dozens of times over the weekend in hopes of finding her home and then just to hear that strong female voice. What if something had happened to her? Maybe she didn't want to talk to me? He tried to read, to watch TV, to go for a walk, but he couldn't get his mind off this woman who had become, quite beyond her knowledge, the instant center of his life. I have fallen off the deep end, thought Radko during passing moments of lucidity. I am a priest; I cannot date this woman or have a romantic relationship with her. Radko had never

Absolution

considered leaving the priesthood. He knew many men who had, and he understood that the job had certain stresses, but he liked it, and his education was not readily transferable to the non-church world. He threw himself onto his bed and wailed into a pillow.

Looking back to this time, Radko smiled. He might be angry with Ursula at the moment, but he knew there was no question of his attraction, of his love, or even of his devotion to her. It had happened so quickly, so decisively.

On Sunday evening of that lost weekend, Radko made yet another call to Ursula's number, and this time she answered.

"Hello," she said.

Silence. Radko was stunned; he expected to hear the by-now familiar voice-mail greeting.

"Hello," Ursula said again.

More silence and the line went dead. She had hung up.

Radko felt cataclysmically stupid. Love falls into his lap, and he instantly destroys the relationship he hadn't even known he wanted until three days before. He didn't know what to do. Do I call her back and act as if I were calling for the first time? Do I tell her I was speechless? He stared at the phone for five minutes.

And then it rang. Very few people called Radko, and it startled him. He jumped. Do I answer it? he wondered, still half mad with anxiety. Finally, an old habit reasserted itself, and his hand reached for the phone. "Hello?" he said softly.

"Radko?" Ursula said.

"Yes?" he replied.

"You called me," she said, not with a question but as a declarative sentence.

"Ah, yes, yes I did," Radko replied.

Now there was silence on the other end of the line. Then: "I see you called me twenty-seven times."

Radko felt the blush rising rapidly up his face. But then he heard Ursula laugh, and exhaled for the first time in ten minutes.

Paul Martin Midden

So this was how it began. Radko and Ursula began seeing each other on a regular basis—dinner, coffee, movies, late night phone calls. It was such a novel experience for Radko to be so open with someone. He told her things he didn't even know were important—things about his upbringing, his travels abroad, his friendships, his family. He loved talking to Ursula, who listened attentively He also learned a great deal about her. She came to this country with her parents when she was eleven. She was uncertain about the many details of leaving East Germany, but it was just before the Berlin Wall fell, and there was apparently danger involved. Her parents did not talk about it much and never shared with her the details of how they actually managed to get out. After an initially difficult transition, Ursula found American life agreeable. She loved the variety of new things, even as a child. She also loved how tolerant, open, and flexible her teachers were, especially after the stern taskmasters of her state-run school in Germany.

The one thing she never talked about was religion. Since she didn't bring it up, Radko didn't either. But as the weeks went by, he became more and more troubled and focused on withholding from her the fact that he was a Roman Catholic priest.

This anxiety generally followed his rising apprehension about having sex. When he saw Ursula, they would end up kissing and holding each other at the end of the evening, but he never went any further. There were many reasons for this. He didn't exactly know what to do, although he was so surprisingly comfortable touching Ursula he thought that might take care of itself. The real reason seemed to be that he felt he was withholding important information from her and was in essence being deceitful. He didn't feel right about becoming more sexual with her without being more transparent. Radko became so preoccupied with this topic that he thought of little else between their encounters.

Finally, and quite uncharacteristically, Radko decided that he needed to tell Ursula the whole truth. They agreed to go walking

Absolution

around Jones Falls late one afternoon. Radko thought the sylvan setting would help ease his anxiety.

"Ursula," he began, "There is something I need to talk to you about."

Ursula looked at him. "What, Radko?"

"There is no easy way for me to say this, so I am just going to say it directly. You know I have been growing very fond of you. I love spending time with you and I would never ever wish to harm you."

"Radko," Ursula interrupted, "What is it?"

"I am a Catholic priest," he said, biting his lip and looking away.

Ursula did not say anything. When Radko turned to look at her face, she was staring off into the distance. After several long minutes, she turned and looked at him. "A Catholic priest," she said, "The kind that don't marry." It was almost a question.

"Yes," said Radko, "the kind that don't marry."

What Ursula said then surprised and even shocked Radko a little. "Radko," she began, "I don't know much about religion. Surely when I was a child in East Germany it was not allowed, but even here, my parents never...." She paused, searching for the right word. "They never took me to church or went themselves. So does that mean you cannot have sex?" She was not quite smiling.

Radko did not know what to say. "Well, yes, that is correct," he began. "We are not supposed to have sex or get married." As he said this, a weight was lifting off his heart. He couldn't tell why; maybe it was just talking about it so openly after thinking about it for so long alone. "We are not supposed to have exclusive relationships with women."

Ursula was again silent. Then: "So you are not supposed to be happy?"

"No," replied Radko, "we are supposed to be happy, um, loving everyone." He started having that feeling of being stupid again.

"Oh," said Ursula, "I've never seen a priest up close before."

CHAPTER 4

As it turned out, Ursula really did not understand. She had a thousand questions. Who made this rule? What happened if a priest had sex? What was church all about? Why did he do it? When Radko tried to explain his faith to her, it was as if she had just heard the word for the first time. Oh, she knew what faith meant in its quotidian sense. She had a very difficult time, however, trying to grasp the religious signification of that term. It just did not make sense to her.

"So," she said over a glass of wine later that evening, "You believe—meaning that you think you know—that this man Jesus, who was a teacher, really did rise from the dead and then conveniently went up to heaven?"

"That is what the church teaches," said Radko. This was becoming his most frequent response to her many questions. It allowed him to clarify, or so he thought, without committing himself personally. But Ursula was a dog with a bone. "And you believe this? You think this is actually true?" she said innumerable times. At these times, Radko nodded and shrugged his shoulders. He did not feel very convincing. Not that he was trying to convince her. This may have been Ursula's closest exposure to a priest, but it was

Absolution

his closest exposure to—to what? a nonreligious person? an atheist? an agnostic? All of a sudden, the person, the woman to whom Radko had felt so close seemed a bit more like a stranger, an alien who did not quite speak the same language.

The truth was that Radko had never thought much about the convictions he was supposed to have and which he espoused publicly, except during those times when he was called upon to do so in school or later when he preached. He was now realizing that these things were hard to explain from scratch to a person who was not brought up with the same presuppositions about the world. He marveled at this: that a person could be so guileless, so honest and loving, without a guiding set of religious principles. He had always associated virtue with religion, and it seemed at times quaint and at times incongruous that a person of sound intelligence could find the association suspect or even fraudulent.

The conversation didn't end that evening. They spent the better part of that weekend going over it and over it. The more they did so the less clear it became to either Ursula or to Radko. He finally gave up and told Ursula flatly that he did not know what he believed anymore, that what he was sharing with her was what the church, the organization to which he had always been so devoted, taught to the billion souls under its care. Power in numbers, he thought.

On Sunday, Radko tried to explain his job at the chancery. But this raised more questions from Ursula's fertile mind, and Radko was too depleted to respond. "So you're a lawyer?" Ursula said at one point. "Yes," replied Radko, "I am a lawyer of sorts." Finally, he gave up and told her that he was confused and that he needed some time to sort things out. She looked at him sadly and hugged him close. "Not too long," she said. "I would miss you."

Radko left her apartment a defeated man. He felt that everything he had taken for granted for so long lay in ruins. It was not that he was such an orthodox guy. He had often wondered about the reasonableness of many of the church's teachings and even of the church itself. He knew much about the long and often sordid history. He knew that the sex scandals in recent years were not novel in that history. As he walked home, he realized he was afraid of doubt.

Doubt, he thought, would wreck his life. It would mean that he couldn't go on doing his job as if it mattered, acting as if everything the church did and said was correct, right, and reasonable. Radko recognized a big problem when he saw one.

Monday morning, after a fitful night's sleep, Radko went to work as usual. He charmed the secretaries with his usual oleaginous remarks. He fielded telephone calls with the same vaguely righteous aplomb. He handled his normal correspondence with a clear sense of purpose. Well, at least with a sense of task. Somewhere during the sleepless night before, Radko recognized that he did not have a solution to this big problem. Quitting the church and quitting his incipient relationship were equally bad things to his mind. In fact, that was all he was clear about. He didn't think he could abandon his calling or the woman he was already sure he loved.

At the end of the day, he took the long way home, walking through Little Italy. He thought that maybe that colorful venue would have a positive impact on his mood. He was wrong.

He felt that he had been wrong about so many things. Before he met Ursula, he thought of sex and physical love only dimly and usually only theoretically. He had somehow missed the intensity, the passion, the surety of the attraction he now felt. He had not factored these things into the equation of his life. He knew loneliness, but he was, after all, a celibate priest, and spending time alone was part of that life. He knew that; everyone knew that. But deep down he felt tricked, lied to, cuckolded. He was angry and did not know toward whom. No one forced him into the seminary. It was true that in his youth being a priest was highly regarded, especially in his immigrant neighborhood, but his parents had always told him that the decision was entirely his own, and he had believed them. They were proud of his vocation and proud that he had done

Absolution

so well for himself in the church; but there was no doubt in his mind that they loved him the way he was, that if he hadn't been a priest or even if he left they would still cherish him the same way.

The feeling he had was more personal than that. It was he who had been wrong, who had ignored parts of life that were too complicated and settled for things that were too pat. It was he who studiously avoided contact with women that would shake his neat and tidy little world of books and law and ponderous thoughts. It was he who had constructed this sterile world where all that mattered was work and what you did in the meantime was just pass time. Radko was angry at himself.

He pulled out his cell phone and called Ursula.

CHAPTER 5

When Ursula's phone rang, she barely heard it at first. She was bonded with her computer screen trying to learn everything she could about religion and about the Catholic church.

Ursula felt that she was visiting another planet. She recalled her stern German teachers mentioning religion in passing but only in the most unflattering and even contemptuous terms. They ridiculed it, really, and she had no reason to think they did not have good reason. It seemed born of superstition, like the quaint and charming stories of the old Roman gods: of some interest, but no one in his right mind could actually believe this. When she grew up in East Germany no one went to church, and when her parents landed in the U.S., she just did not pay any attention to the people who did. She never felt the need to pray or to worship; she never thought of seeking out a priest, minister, or rabbi. Moral questions were settled on the basis of common sense and simple justice, and being responsible just seemed like the best way to be. When she was anxious, she forced herself to relax. When her thoughts made no sense, she concluded that she was tired.

When she finally heard the phone, she glanced at caller ID: Radko. She quickly picked up the phone and said hello.

Absolution

"Can I come over?" Radko asked.

"Yes," Ursula replied, unable to read his intent in his voice. "Are you hungry?"

Radko smiled. "No...Yes... Don't do anything special. I'll see you in twenty minutes."

Ursula put the phone down and turned her attention back to the screen. She had been reading the Catholic Encyclopedia Online and found it rough going cross-referencing entry after entry. It seemed like arcane history to her, and it just did not pique her interest. She kept wondering what people saw in this stuff. After a few minutes, she closed her browser and headed to the kitchen to see what dinner might be.

In exactly twenty minutes, there was a knock on the door. When she opened it, she saw Radko with an expression she could not identify. "Are you okay?" she asked.

Radko did not respond. Instead, he walked into her apartment and turned to face her. He put his arms around her and looked into her eyes. He didn't smile or frown. He was as serious as if he were teaching his first class. "I love you," he said, and he burst into tears.

For the next two hours, Radko did something he had never done his entire life. He cried, he wailed, he said the unspeakable. He raged, he anguished, he held Ursula and thought he would die if she were to go away. He was hopeless and inconsolable. He was pretty sure he was losing his mind.

Ursula did not let him go. She held him, caressed him, told him it was all right. After a while, she stood up, still holding both his hands. She led him the short distance to the bedroom and guided him to the bed. There she gently pressed his shoulders to the mattress and lay down next to him, holding him close.

And then, for the first time in his thirty-eight years, Radko made love to a woman. Or rather, he participated in a sexual experience that was at once intense, joyful, and pleasurable as nothing he had experienced before. Afterwards, he fell into a profound sleep.

Some time during the night, he awoke with a start. For a moment, he didn't know where he was. He felt Ursula's presence next to him before he focused on the fact that she was physically there. He looked at her bare shoulders and felt her exposed skin beneath the covers. Memories of a few hours before came rushing back, and Radko felt the connection that had seemed to be missing his entire life. He listened intently to her breathing and watched her chest rise and fall. It was all so natural, he thought to himself, so basic, so right.

But so was the need to work, and Radko knew he had to get up the next morning. He was unsure about what to do. Should he let himself out and walk home? It was three a.m., he saw by the small clock next to the bed. Surely Ursula had to go to work in the morning, too. He didn't feel right just leaving. I could leave her a note, he thought. How cold, he countered to himself. In the midst of this quandary, he fell back asleep.

It was the smell of food that woke him as the sun began to appear through the window. He turned quickly and looked at the clock: 6:00 a.m. There's time, he thought with relief. Time to eat, he hoped, because, having skipped dinner last night, he was starving. He found his clothes, made his way to the bathroom, and then to the kitchen.

"Good morning, Father," said Ursula from the stove, where she was cooking eggs and bacon.

"Good morning, love," said Radko, wrapping his arms around her and kissing her on the neck.

Radko did not know what else to say that wasn't academic, philosophical, or just plain stupid. So he said nothing. He felt calm—very calm for him—and sat down and picked up the newspaper, which was spread out on the table. Ursula brought him a cup of coffee. He looked up at her and smiled. Is this what happiness is like, he wondered? She kissed him on the lips. I guess so, he thought.

Absolution

This entire experience seemed to Radko to be something from another reality. How could the simple joy of this be such a secret, he thought to himself. A secret to him, he realized, not to most people. As he perused the paper, he recalled the night before and remembered his ravings with some measure of embarrassment. Embarrassed or not, he felt preternaturally calm. No, more than calm: real, grounded. He felt his flesh-and-blood self, his animal self, his bound-to-the-earth self. And he loved it.

Ursula served breakfast in an easy, matter-of-fact way. "How are you?" she said as they ate.

"Good," Radko replied. "Unpotted, but good."

"Unpotted?" Ursula said.

"Perhaps 'transplanted' would be a better description." Then he turned serious: "Ursula, I feel I need to apologize for last night. I don't know what came over me. I didn't know I was so..." He searched for the right word, "...so desperate."

Ursula put her hand on his. "No need to apologize," she said. "I think this is all harder for you than it would be for a, for a, for a..."

"Normal person?" Radko offered.

"Well, for a person who wasn't so taken up with religion and all those mysterious things," Ursula replied. "Although for a—what do you call it, a celibate person—you did pretty well last night."

"We did pretty well last night," Radko said, squeezing her hand.

"Yes, we did," said Ursula, her eyes smiling.

Radko looked at her with adoration in his eyes. "I love you, Ursula," he said.

"I love you, Radko."

CHAPTER 6

The radical reorientation of Radko's life was not apparent to anyone with whom he had regular contact. This amazed Radko, who felt as if he had a banner across his forehead: CHANGED MAN. Nonetheless, he went about his work as if it were just that: work. He didn't talk to anyone about what was happening; he didn't quit his job; he didn't do anything different. Except see Ursula more and luxuriate in the sublime rabbit hole into which he had only lately fallen.

He especially loved Saturdays. After going to dinner, or a movie, or the theater on Friday evening, he and Ursula would make love late into the night. In the morning, they awoke naked and barely stepped out of bed. More lovemaking, but also more talking. Radko felt completely open with Ursula, something he had never felt before. Being naked with her reflected how truly open he felt with her. He prized this feeling above all.

They talked about everything. Since religious matters were so foreign to Ursula, Radko spent a lot of time filling her in on the details of his life and the culture to which he belonged. Ursula never really understood it, but she slowly came to appreciate how much it meant to Radko and how it had infected his whole life.

Absolution

Basically, she saw it as a cultural phenomenon: much the way she was formed in an officially godless culture, Radko was raised to believe that the church was the true path to happiness. She smiled when Radko had to admit that the happiness offered never really materialized until he encountered a casually atheistic female in ways that were supposed to be forbidden to him.

Ursula did not really think of herself as an atheist. She bristled whenever Radko referred to her as a "nonbeliever." She was not without beliefs. She believed deeply in herself and in her abilities. She also believed in people in general. She believed in the world and wanted to taste all that it had to offer. She also believed in greater things: intelligence, rationality, the ability of people to work things out; the basic goodness of most people. She did not pretend to be a philosopher, but she knew injustice when she saw it, and she abhorred it. She also believed in love.

Ursula did not really know what to do about Radko's passionate beliefs about religion. She saw how animated he became when he talked about certain aspects of his work and of the church. Even of the priesthood. His priesthood.

"So you love being a priest," Ursula said one Saturday morning in the fall.

Radko paused. "Yes," he said. "I do. I have a hard time imagining myself doing something else. I suppose I could, but Catholics refer to the priesthood as a call, an invitation from God. Hard to say 'no' to that. The truth is that this is how I experience it. I feel I am doing the right thing."

Ursula looked at Radko with some pity. She could see how torn he was between two things he loved. And even though she didn't understand the power of the other side, she experienced firsthand Radko's intense tie to her and his passionate devotion to it. If what he felt toward his religion was similar, he was in deep and troubling water. She felt wrapped up in him: not just special but loved in a real and compelling sense that was new to her. She thought she knew the real thing when she experienced it, and she was experiencing it. She clung to Radko the way he clung to her: wholeheartedly, without reservation.

And it was during this conversation, which went on over several weeks, that she realized that she might be pregnant.

CHAPTER 7

Ursula Fliegendorf was above all else a practical woman. She did not fear the prospect of having a child, but she did not know exactly what to do about Radko. First things first, she thought, so she went to her doctor.

"The answer is yes," Dr. Heidenberg intoned. He looked at Ursula tenderly. He had known her for almost twenty years, since she first came to the U.S.

Ursula did not respond. Dr. Heidenberg had great affection for Ursula, so he began laying out her options. "You do not have to pursue this to term," he said. "It's early in the process, and we could make it go away." He tried to put this as delicately as possible, but it was not in his nature to be circumspect.

Ursula still did not respond.

"Ursula?" he said.

Tears began to run down Ursula's face. She loved Dr. Heidenberg as a father. Or an uncle. She was embarrassed. "I'm sorry," she said.

"Ursula, my dear," Dr. Heidenberg said. "You don't need to apologize for doing what humans do most naturally. I just want to encourage you to think hard about what you want to do now. Hav-

Absolution

ing a baby would change your life, and you are single." Not single enough, Dr. Heidenberg thought, but he did not intend to lecture. Ursula had not mentioned the possible father. For her part, Ursula promised Dr. Heidenberg that she would think about her options.

She left Dr. Heidenberg's office awash in feelings. Despite her promise to the avuncular physician, Ursula could simply not see herself terminating her pregnancy. She loved Radko. She was pleased to be bearing the child of the first man she could say she unequivocally loved. More than pleased: honored. But Radko's life was complicated. He was a priest. He was not her husband, and it didn't look as if he would be. She had in weaker moments allowed herself to imagine the two of them married, but her hardheaded self soon took over to list the very real obstacles standing in the way of that.

But now that she knew she was pregnant, she knew the right thing to do. Common sense and simple justice. She had to tell Radko.

CHAPTER 8

It was not difficult to arrange a time to meet with Radko to discuss this. They saw each other almost every available moment. She decided that she needed time with him, so she decided to tell him on the next Saturday morning.

She awoke first that November morning and looked at Radko. He looked so peaceful, she thought, so innocent and, yes, naive. She was sure that was about to change.

Ursula had prepared herself for all possible reactions, or at least those she could think of. She thought he might be angry and leave her; he might be angry and insist that she abort the pregnancy; he might just be angry and rail at her. Would he get violent? Ursula thought not. She realized that he had never asked about birth control. It hadn't mattered to her because she had great faith in her diaphragm, the device that she had always used to avoid pregnancy. But, as she was learning, avoidance was not absolute prevention.

Radko stirred. Ursula reached over and put her arms around him. "Radko?" she said.

"Ursula," Radko moaned. And he moved toward her and hugged her body close to his.

"Radko," she repeated, "We need to talk."

Absolution

Radko opened his eyes and looked into hers. "Swell," he said. He loved talking.

"I'm pregnant," Ursula said.

Radko's eyes closed. Not once in the past six months had he given a single thought to the possibility that just slipped from Ursula's lips. He did not speak.

"I'm pregnant," Ursula repeated.

Radko opened his eyes. "And I, I presume, am the father?"

Ursula landed a knee in his stomach. "Don't joke!" she said.

After he recovered, Radko sat up in bed. "Are you sure?" he asked groggily.

"Yes," she almost screamed. "I went to the doctor on Wednesday. He confirmed it."

"You've known since Wednesday, and you didn't tell me?"

"I was waiting for the right time."

Radko scooted back under the covers and wrapped his arms around Ursula. "I love Saturday mornings," he said.

Now Ursula did not know what to do. She was being squeezed by a man she loved but with whom she was furious. "How can you make light of this!" she yelled.

Radko did not move; nor did he open his eyes. He didn't say anything. He was thinking. After a long time, he opened his eyes and looked at her from a few inches away.

"Ursula, my love," he began. "I am a priest who was lucky enough to meet a woman with whom I violated every rule by which I had been living my life. A woman with whom I fell is love so hard I am sure I will never recover. I am sure this business of your being pregnant will be trouble, but I have had nothing but trouble for the past six months. And I have loved every minute of it." He closed his eyes and continued holding her. He had no idea how this would turn out. He just knew he loved this moment, this Saturday morning.

Ursula lay still. She relaxed her rigid, angry body and let Radko hold her. She started to cry. "I love you," she said.

Radko didn't really know what he felt. He was not unhappy. He felt the naturalness of fatherhood. What does one expect, he thought, when one has sex all the time? He felt some apprehension, but he also felt certain that he and Ursula could work out whatever they faced. If anything, he was happy to have a challenge, a crisis that would move him and Ursula forward into a future about which he was anything but clear. Maybe clarity is overrated, he thought as he kissed Ursula deeply.

CHAPTER 9

In between telephone calls at work and paperwork and mail, Radko thought of little else but being a father. He was brimming with pride and only occasionally wracked with worry. He felt joy and pride from some primordial place within him, the one that Ursula had discovered and unlocked. He couldn't shake it. I can't really be happy about this, he thought from time to time. But he was. The fact that he was a priest, that he was supposed to be celibate, and that his career might be in the balance: these were vague worries that did not seem to impact his day-to-day life. He still went to work, did his job, and occasionally presided at Mass. Sinners are closer to God, he thought to himself, repeating something a spiritual director told him long ago. He didn't understand that statement at the time, but it had come into his mind often during the past six months.

For Ursula's part, she went into high gear and treated herself like a celebrity patient. She pampered herself; she exercised; she stopped drinking; she stopped smoking; she took naps. She read everything she could about pregnancy, especially in women over thirty. She was dismayed to learn that this was almost a "geriatric pregnancy". Even though that unhappy designation did not apply

Absolution

officially until she was thirty-five, she was close enough to be mildly insulted. She didn't feel geriatric or even her own age. She felt energetic and happy.

The shadow lurking beneath all this happiness was that stubborn but basic contradiction in Radko's life. He could not imagine abandoning Ursula or his child, but he also couldn't bring himself to resign the priesthood. He had always been taught and believed that a vocation was a call from God, and while he was rapidly shedding his long-neglected religious beliefs, he still could not face saying no to that thing deep inside him that made him feel that he was the person he was, that made him feel special, that defined his place in the world. He could not act as if it didn't matter. After all, for over two decades he had defined himself this way. It wasn't just a job or a profession. So he had long been taught, and so he believed. And felt.

Finally, it occurred to Radko that he could talk to someone. In the months he had been seeing Ursula he had gotten so accustomed to cordoning off that part of his life from the rest that the thought of telling someone the truth, the whole truth, seemed novel. It then dawned on him how "out there" he and Ursula had been, often going to public venues where he could easily have been seen. He blushed thinking about this.

But whom to talk to? He ran through other priests he knew and respected. Was it wise to talk to a priest? he wondered. Maybe he should see a therapist. But Radko wasn't depressed; he had a decision, or rather several decisions, to make. He thought about talking to his parents; after all, they would have to know sooner or later. He felt ambivalent about this. He had never gone to his parents for advice, at least not since high school. My sister! he thought. I can talk to Gordana.

CHAPTER 10

Gordana Slopovich Raminski lived in New York City. She had married a Russian immigrant who, like her, had been born abroad but had grown up on the eastern seaboard of the United States. Gordana and Radko had always had a peaceable relationship. They were far enough apart in years—Gordana was six years older than Radko—not to have felt threatened by the ordinary sibling conflicts that characterize children born more closely together. Radko was twelve when Gordana went away to college, something that thrilled their parents in theory but which they had a very difficult time with in practice. They were proud to send their firstborn to college in America, but Gordana was the outgoing member of the family. Even though she was seven when the family moved to the United States and therefore had to learn a whole new language, she took to it with relish. To her, Bosnia was a dangerous place where you could get hurt or killed for no reason. The U.S. offered her safety, freedom, and a larger stage on which to act out her vivid hopes and dreams. She was the one with many friends who always had a part in the school plays, who always had dates for weekend nights, who learned to drive as soon as she turned sixteen. Her departure upset

Absolution

the balance of the family, and she was sorely missed. Naturally, their parents turned their attention to Radko.

Radko did not need a lot of attention, nor was he accustomed to it. He was a good student; he didn't get into trouble. So when his parents turned their sad attention to him, he withdrew. He didn't know what to do. He also felt vaguely guilty for not being more outgoing, for not being able to fill Gordana's large shoes. The Slopovich household became a lot quieter after Gordana left.

For Gordana, however, leaving home was the adventure she had longed for. To move into that provisional adulthood that college offers with increased responsibility for herself and the freedom to do what she wanted: this had been her dream throughout high school, and she could barely contain herself. She felt no apprehension about those things that parents worry about and that afflict many college-age students. She had no desire for drugs, for promiscuity, for failure. She wanted to succeed in life, to win, to be part of that segment of the population that grew beyond its roots and forged new identities. She wanted to be a thoroughgoing and modern American woman. As a child, she had tirelessly practiced American pronunciation so that she spoke with no accent, overcoming the taunts of her peers when she first started school in the United States. She approached college and her subsequent career with the same tenacity and can-do spirit. She was unafraid of work and welcoming of challenge.

Her relationship with her quiet brother was always cordial and even at times warm. Both intuitively knew that they had come from different emotional planets. His bookishness contrasted with her instinct for action; his reflective intellectuality with her quick-witted reactivity. Radko and Gordana both felt fondness and respect for each other, but their actual contact had become infrequent in recent years, owing to all those things that collude to keep adult siblings apart: geography, divergent interests, work and family related preoccupations. Nonetheless, Gordana was happy to hear from Radko.

Paul Martin Midden

"Hi, Gordana," Radko said as she answered in that overly loud way that was so like her. He was nervous and trying not to show it. He knew he was dismal at this, but he could hardly blurt out the truth on the phone.

"Radko, how have you been? It's been months," Gordana replied with real warmth in her voice.

Radko decided on the direct approach. "Gordana, there is something I need to talk to you about. Do you have some time this week or next? I could come up for a few days."

Gordana was silent. This was not like her brother. "Is everything okay, Radko? Are Mom and Dad all right?

"Yes, yes; they're fine. Something has come up for me that I need some advice about. But I'm okay. I just need to talk to you." As he said this, his voice cracked, and he realized he sounded desperate. Tears came to his eyes.

Gordana heard it too. "Sure, Radko, sure. Anytime. I can change my schedule if need be. How soon can you come?"

Radko looked at his calendar. "I can be there Wednesday evening. Would that be okay for you?"

He deepened his voice, trying to make it sound calm.

"Sure, Radko. Why don't you plan on having dinner with Gavril and me? We can talk during or after dinner. And please plan on sleeping over. We would love to have you." This formality, Gordana hoped, would help tide Radko over till Wednesday. She had never heard him sound so needy.

"Thanks, Gordana. This means a lot to me. I'll see you Wednesday evening."

Radko put the phone down. He suddenly felt scared, and he realized that his hands were shaking and sweaty. He was not afraid of seeing his sister or even of telling her about his life for the last six months. He knew Gordana and even Gavril to be good, solid people who were favorably disposed toward him. He was scared because he had never regarded himself as an emotional person, as a person who could not control the sound of his voice or its strength

Absolution

or timbre. He thought back on that evening at Ursula's apartment when he wailed and cried in her arms. That frightened him, too, but it seemed part of a bigger process, like the scary and exhilarating experience of going down the big dive on a roller coaster. Plus, it ended with such an explosive sexual event that it seemed triumphant in retrospect.

This was different. He had never been a person to ask for something from anyone else emotionally. Or in any way, really. His parents had raised him and his sister to be self-sufficient, to rely on no one but themselves for what they needed. Life had always filled in the rest. He didn't know how he would feel about actually talking to Gordana or about changing this part of his life. He hoped he did not have to do it too often. When Radko went to bed that Monday evening, he prayed for the first time in a long time for the strength to get through what lay before him.

CHAPTER 11

Radko took Wednesday afternoon off from his job at the chancery and caught the 1:35 train from Penn Station in Baltimore to Penn Station in New York. He told his boss, Fr. Catsweiler, the Vicar General, that his sister had an emergency in her family and that he was traveling to New York to support her. This, he felt, was one version of the truth. The work culture at the chancery was not strict, and Fr. Catsweiler made no objection to Radko's unexpected but understandable request.

Radko waited impatiently for the train and finally got settled into a seat by the window. As soon as the train pulled away from the station, he began to feel relief. From what? he wondered. From the stress of doing two incompatible things at the same time? From Ursula? He didn't think he was feeling relief because he was getting away from Ursula. In fact, he wished she had gone with him. When they had talked about his going to talk to Gordana, Ursula was pleased.

"Tell me about her," Ursula had said.

And Radko did. He reviewed the entire history of his relationship with his sister in a way he had never done before with anyone, not even himself. As he talked, he realized how close he actually

Absolution

felt to Gordana, even though their lives had taken decidedly different paths. He felt a genuine bond with his sister and had from the time they were children. He had always liked her and respected her. He was more than a bit jealous of her outgoing temperament; but he knew she was different from himself, and he delighted in how she was. He hoped talking with her was a good idea.

Radko also told Ursula that maybe she should go with him. At this, Ursula hesitated. She was flattered to be asked to meet members of Radko's family, but she worried that this might be premature just now. She was also slightly embarrassed at being pregnant and unmarried at her age. Nonetheless, she thought it best for Radko to go alone and make whatever peace he could or do whatever he needed to do. Somewhat apprehensively, Radko agreed.

Now as he sat on the train watching the megalopolis go by, he contemplated the events that were developing in his life. His methodical mind reviewed what he knew so far: He had been lonely but didn't know how deeply. Perhaps he had even been unhappy and didn't know it. He met Ursula, who opened his eyes to an experience that was… what?… "unforgettable" at minimum. He searched for other words: "great," "deep," "profound". The much-vaunted and trusted power of words failed him in the face of the experience itself. The truth was that Radko felt he had been touched by God. Loved, singled out. He had never in his life been sure of what people talked about when they described God. He tended to think that mostly it was something they made up to feel better or to make sense out of things. Or maybe it was a way of having a conversation with one's higher self. He had heard from childhood about how God loved the world and the people in it. But those explanations were always complicated by inconvenient doctrines about hell and damnation. A loving God who sent people to hell never made sense to Radko, so throughout most of his life, he just didn't think about it. This was surprisingly manageable as a priest, he thought with some irony.

But now, well, he didn't know about the hellfire and damnation part, but he felt deeply in contact with himself and with the world. This did not seem bad. Or evil. He knew dating and having sex were against the rules, but it just didn't feel wrong. He could barely imagine not having met Ursula or being with her or even, and this perplexed him deeply, being the father of her child—their child. He did not know where this feeling came from, but it was clear to him that he could not simply shed it.

By the time the train pulled into the station, Radko was tired. Calm and clear, but tired. He found Gordana waiting at the platform.

"Radko," she shouted.

As if you need to shout, Radko thought to himself. He made his way toward her and wrapped his arms around her. "Gordana," he said softly, grateful to be in her presence.

On the way to his sister's apartment, Radko found himself not only grateful but also unable to stop talking. Gordana thought that perhaps Radko was ill or dying. This was not how he was with her, or as far as she knew, with anyone. He had always been reserved and proper; even more so since he'd been ordained a priest.

By the time they got to the station entrance, Radko had told her about Ursula. "I am in love with a woman," he said and looked at his sister stoically with no discernible expression on his face.

Gordana thought he made it sound like he had just been sentenced to prison.

"Does she make you happy?" she asked.

"Beyond words," Radko replied. He smiled and hugged his sister again.

Gordana didn't know what to think. She was not personally religious, although their parents had worked hard to raise them in their faith. She loved and respected her brother but thought his being a priest was a little too "last century" for such a bright, capable man. She never thought he seemed very happy in that solitary profession, but it was his life, and she tried not to interfere. So

Absolution

when she saw Radko smile, she was relieved. She had a disquieting sense that there was perhaps something else, but she dismissed the thought.

"What's her name?" she asked.

"Ursula," he replied, smiling too much. "I can't wait till you meet her."

This is serious, Gordana thought. Then she wondered why Radko was here. Was he going to tell her he was leaving the priesthood? Did he need money? She listened more intently.

"You're probably wondering why I came," Radko said, as if her mind were visible to all. "There has been a complication..." There have been a thousand complications, Radko thought; the pregnancy was just the last one of a series. He didn't know how to tell Gordana, so he just blurted in out: "Ursula is pregnant."

Silence. And more silence.

Gordana was thinking that Radko was in way over his head. She wasn't sure if she could safely recommend an abortion, given Radko's religious affiliations, although it seemed like the logical decision in such a situation. But Radko had not said anything about his vocation or his religion yet, so she continued to listen.

"I came to talk with you because I am torn," Radko continued.

What a relief, Gordana thought.

"I love Ursula and don't want to give her up. I even love that she's pregnant, which sounds a little crazy, even to me. But at the same time, I don't want to abandon the priesthood. I know you're not religious and that you probably have suspicions about my work as a priest, but it has always been an essential part of me. I don't want to do anything else, and even if I did, I'm not trained to do anything else."

Gordana's mind was swimming. This felt like the most serious and important conversation she had ever had with her brother as an adult. She felt the gravity of it, and compassion rose up inside her. She felt more affection for Radko at this moment than at any other time in her life. But she was also afraid for him. He seemed so young, so naive in these matters. After a while she said, "So you want to be a father and remain a ... Father?"

"I think so," replied Radko, ignoring the pun and sharing with Gordana what he had concluded halfway through his trip to New York.

"Interesting" she said and then directed him toward the subway. It was not like her to be quiet or not to have an opinion, but she felt she should be very, very careful.

For the rest of the evening, through dinner preparation and the meal itself and beyond, Radko spoke of nothing but how he was going to do two different things that were entirely incompatible. As the evening wore on and as the wine settled in, he became more and more certain that he could do this and do it successfully. Gavril applauded his chutzpah. Gordana fretted, mostly silently.

The next morning Radko woke up early and in a vibrant mood. It was snowing outside and Manhattan had a light dusting that made it look uncharacteristically clean. Just like me, he thought to himself, hopping out of bed and jumping into the shower.

When he entered the tiny kitchen, he found Gordana making breakfast. "Smells good," he said.

Gordana glanced his way and said good morning.

"Gordana," Radko began, just following his nose. "I cannot tell you how happy I am that you are my sister and that you were available to me to talk about this crazy situation. I feel enormously better." He poured himself a cup of coffee.

There was a tear trickling down Gordana's face. She turned to face Radko directly. She folded her arms. "Radko," she said, "I'm happy for you. But I'm also worried about you. What you were saying last night about remaining a priest and trying to raise a family: I know it can make sense in theory, but I'm afraid the reality is not going to be so easy."

Radko thought for several minutes.

"You know, Gordana, I understand your concern. And maybe I am just being stupid. But one of the things my religion—the relig-

Absolution

ion in which we were both raised—has always said is that hope is possible. And love is possible. I know what I am proposing for myself is improbable, but so was Christianity. So was the establishment of the State of Israel. So was our parents' escape from Bosnia. So was my meeting Ursula and impregnating her. She did use birth control. I think it is wiser to believe in what I want than to abandon my dreams out of fear. Even if what I want seems a little nuts."

Gordana did not argue. Good points, she thought to herself. As always, she did not place much stock in the religious part of what Radko said, but she could not deny that passion and belief could carry one far. It had done well for her. And she was glad to hear that Ursula had used birth control. Not foolproof, obviously, but at least one member of this couple had been thinking.

Gordana had taken the day off, so brother and sister spent the rest of the day doing Manhattan. They went to galleries and museums, did some shopping, had lunch, and enjoyed the many sights and sounds of that high-octane island. They talked a little more about Radko's situation, but not at any length. It was clear what he intended to do, and Gordana did not think it wise to try to stop him. Radko was an adult; it was his life. She promised herself that she would be there for him if, or more likely when, this situation exploded.

CHAPTER 12

Radko returned to Baltimore late on Thursday on the 6:20 train. By the time he got home it was after ten, and he picked up the phone and called Ursula as soon as he walked into his apartment.

Ursula picked up the phone on the first ring. She did not usually think of herself as an anxious or overly eager person, but this was the first time she and Radko had been in different cities since they started dating, and she was nervous. Silly girl, she chided herself.

"How was New York?" she asked as nonchalantly as she could.

"Good," replied Radko. "I have a plan."

Ursula hesitated. She had always thought of herself as independent, autonomous, self-contained. She had no ready explanation for the breathlessness she felt now in anticipation of hearing what Radko might say. "I meant, how was your sister?" she said after several moments' pause.

"Fine," said Radko, smiling. "And how was your day off?"

"Come over."

"On my way."

Ursula was in Radko's arms in fifteen minutes.

"I missed you," she said.

"And I you," he responded without hesitation, pulling her close.

Absolution

"Ursula," Radko continued. "I know this is not the time for what I have in mind to share with you, but I can barely stand the tension I feel. I love you; I want you to have our baby. I want to be with you." Long pause. "I also think I can stay a priest. Not here in Baltimore, but somewhere where I am not well known. Los Angeles, maybe, or Chicago. I can get a job at the chancery there and we can live out in the suburbs…"

"Radko…," Ursula said sharply. He stopped talking. "I love you too; you know that. But having a baby is a major commitment. I am flattered that you want to be with me. I want to be with you. But your staying a priest—I don't know how practical that is…" Her voice trailed off. "Even keeping the baby…"

Radko went numb. He had never seriously thought of Ursula not having the baby. As his perspective rapidly widened, he realized that it was, after all, her body, her baby, her life quite apart from his interest in it. He felt humbled and embarrassed.

Ursula felt his discomfort. She saw his cheeks redden. She leaned over to kiss him, but he stiffened. "Radko?" she said softly.

Radko did not respond. He looked down and let go of Ursula's hand. After a long while, he turned to her and said, "I need to go."

Ursula felt as if he had punched her. Fine time for a first argument, she thought. But both her pride and her good sense told her not to push any further.

Radko got up and walked out of Ursula's apartment. As he walked through the door, he mumbled something that Ursula did not hear. It was: "I have a lot to think about"

Radko walked out into the cold Baltimore night and headed home. Or rather, he started walking. He did not really care where he went. For the first time in his life, Baltimore seemed like the sinister place it was often portrayed to be in the press. He didn't care. He was angry, he was hurt, he felt like a fool. He had never been angry with Ursula before and didn't want to be; however, he could not deny that he resented the fact that she had the most important voice in this situation. He was bereft, filled with self pity, and confused as to what to do. He thought he had brought this situation to resolution when he thought about it on the train to New York. It seemed so clear. Gavril had urged him on; Gordana did not protest. He was a fool.

Ursula was shocked when Radko left her apartment. She wished she had heard what he said when he left, but she felt certain it was some version of "I need time." She was confused, angry, hurt. She also felt betrayed. If it hadn't been eleven o'clock at night, she would have called to arrange for an abortion and packed her bags and gone to another city without Radko.

Memories of past relationships flooded her thinking. She chided herself for this, knowing it was dangerous ground. From the beginning, she felt that her relationship with Radko was different, that he was made of sturdier and more loving stuff. That he would stay with her no matter what. And now that simple idea lay in ruins.

CHAPTER 13

Ursula did not dare to stay home from work on Friday. She knew it would be dangerous for her to spend too much time alone. She needed diversion, structure; something or someone else to think about. She reported to school as if nothing had happened.

After her initial, wrenching refocusing, she fell into the routine of the day. She worked extra hard not to be short with her students or to let her feelings show in any way. By noon she felt that she was on the right track; by three she felt like her old self. Almost.

When her last class ended, Ursula began slowly packing her materials for the weekend. She filled her briefcase and walked slowly out of the school. She was afraid of what the evening would bring. She had grown so accustomed to spending time with Radko that she couldn't remember what she did before she had met him. All the way home, she berated herself for giving up her life to a man, for surrendering her identity, her happiness, her life, for God's sake, to an idea of romance that she knew was childish. Her resentment grew as she approached her apartment.

Once home, she knew that spending the evening by herself was lethal. As soon as she dropped her briefcase on the kitchen table, she began calling people she knew. Friends, acquaintances; she just

Absolution

did not want to be by herself. She was even tempted to call old boyfriends but knew that was unwise.

After visiting with several answering machines, Ursula sat down. Get hold of yourself, she demanded. Then she remembered that she was pregnant. Oh, she thought to herself, letting this notion reenter her edgy consciousness. She walked to the refrigerator and opened a bottle of water.

After a while, she went over to her computer and started writing a letter.

My dearest Radko,

I don't know exactly what was going on with you on Thursday evening, but I want to you know...

Know what? Ursula thought. Then she continued:

that I have loved you more than anyone I have ever loved. And that I cherish the thought of having your baby. I also fear, my love, that this pregnancy is too much too soon for us.

I do not pretend to understand your work or your religion or the things that you value. I understand that your being a priest is important to you and that you do not want to abandon it. I can understand that as much as one can without being inside you.

What now, she thought? Tell him that I am responsible for my life and that he may or may not be in it? That it is my body, my baby, even though he contributed to it? That trust comes hard to me? She berated herself for telling him about the pregnancy in the first place. It would have been much easier to just end it without saying anything. But we had been so completely and hopelessly in love. Ursula hit the delete key and decided that taking action on her own was the far wiser course. She promised herself that she would call Dr. Heidenberg first thing Monday morning.

CHAPTER 14

Radko had taken Friday off, so he didn't have the luxury of diversion. He couldn't sleep; he couldn't eat. He fretted; he swore; he railed against the God to whom he had just lately been introduced. I cannot do this, he thought. He laid out his limited options: 1. leave Ursula and go back to being a celibate if unhappy priest. 2. Stop being the priest he was and marry Ursula and abandon the identity he had always lived as an adult. 3. Go back to the tattered original plan and try to convince Ursula that it was possible to do two mutually exclusive things at the same time.

Radko had to admit that none of these options shone very brightly as a realistic plan. He could not remember having such an emotional storm in his life. Is this why celibacy was supposedly better than what theologians patronizingly called "the married state"? He dismissed that idea. Despite the pain he felt, he knew that this dilemma was real, that it was natural. He loved a woman; how basic do humans get? he thought. Maybe he just didn't have the "gift of celibacy," as it was referred to in his training. Obviously not, he thought. The whole world seemed like a bad joke.

He picked up a piece of stationary and started writing.

Dear Cardinal Belinqua:

Absolution

With great regret I am submitting my resignation from the priesthood. It is my intention to apply for laicization at the earliest opportunity.

I could not be a happy priest. I fell in love with a woman for whom I would jump off the damned church steeple.

Radko chuckled for the first time in twenty-four hours. I guess I'm not ready to write this letter, he thought to himself. He tore up the paper he'd written and stared into space. What will become of my pathetic self, he wondered. He needed a break, so he grabbed his coat and left his small apartment.

It was noon, and Radko thought about what he could or should do. He was painfully aware that he had not called Ursula, and he felt like a jerk for walking out on her. But he didn't know what to say to her yet. He felt enormous responsibility for what had happened, and he could not bear to face the devastation he had wrought in his life, in Ursula's life, and in the possible life of his baby.

This was the part that was hardest for him. He could not bear the thought of Ursula's terminating the pregnancy. He knew it was ultimately her decision, but that child was as much his as hers, and it felt like murder—as his religion said it was—to end the possibility of its life. His life or her life: whatever sex that baby was, it was a person. A person he and Ursula had formed together. Even if unexpected, it was a life that existed apart from his or Ursula's or anyone else's. It was precious, holy; not to be ended because it was inconvenient. All humans are inconvenient.

Maybe I do believe in something, Radko thought. This felt like the bottom line to him. Ursula may not agree, but he would beg her to keep the child and bring it to term. He would support it by whatever means were necessary. He would have a relationship with it, love it, and cherish it forever. And if Ursula could no longer love him, well, she could certainly love the child they had together. For one of the few times in his life, Radko prayed earnestly. He prayed that Ursula would not destroy that baby.

But Radko also knew that he was avoiding a basic decision in his life. He felt like a coward for insisting that he remain a priest and somehow marry Ursula.

CHAPTER 15

Radko stopped at a diner in the Inner Harbor area of Baltimore. He remembered that he had not eaten since yesterday afternoon; and while he wasn't hungry, he thought it best to put something into his body besides torment. He sat down and ordered a hamburger, french fries, and coffee. He also picked up the morning newspaper which was on the rack next to his table.

Neither eating nor reading was of much interest to him, he found. Mostly he perused headlines that never registered in his consciousness. When his food came, he tried to eat but just picked at it. He would have burst into tears if he hadn't been in public, and he sat at his table wishing himself out of this impossible situation, much like the teenager he felt himself to be. Jesus Christ, he thought. Is this what people go through? Radko rapidly reviewed his life and realized that he had never throughout his forty years been in such a state of uncertainty, of turmoil, of raw pain. He was so agitated, he got up from the table, threw some money on the counter, and left the restaurant.

He had to see Ursula. She was the only one who could help him quell the distress within himself. He looked at his watch and headed in the general direction of the school where she taught. He

Absolution

had never been there and wasn't exactly certain where it was, but he thought he had heard the name before and believed it to be only a few blocks from the diner.

Fifteen blocks, he soon learned. After asking for directions several times, Radko finally saw the William Bailey Middle School sign in front of an undistinguished red-brick building with a red tile roof. He also saw what appeared to be the last of the students leaving the large central doors of the school, mostly shrouded in their winter coats. Radko look at his watch, trying to remember when school let out. What day was it? Friday. Early dismissal? he wondered. He thought of asking a student or a teacher if he could find one, but he just leaned against the street light and sighed.

After a few moments, he thought maybe he looked suspicious and thought it best to move along. He headed back toward his apartment, fighting off the chill produced by the dropping temperature. Halfway there, he realized he was standing in front of Ursula's apartment. He considered what to do. Barge in on her? Call her and explain that he just happened to be in the neighborhood? He shook his head and continued on his way.

When Radko got home, he threw himself onto his couch and grabbed the telephone. He held the receiver to his forehead for five full minutes with his eyes closed before he could bring himself to dial. Finally, with great effort, he punched the keys with Ursula's number.

Ursula saw the number on caller ID and hesitated. She was enormously relieved despite herself to hear from Radko, but she was afraid of what he would say. She was also afraid of what she might say. She took a deep breath and picked up the phone.

"Hello," she said.

"Ursula," Radko began. He felt a wave of relief washing over him. "I am sorry for walking out so abruptly last night. I just needed some time to think"

"And what have you concluded?" Ursula asked, sounding a little more annoyed than she intended.

"I need to talk with you in person," Radko said.

Ursula paused. She wanted to see Radko more than anyone else on the planet just now, but her fear deepened. "Would you like to come over?" The words fell out of her mouth.

"If it's all right with you, yes, I would like to come over."

After putting the phone down, Ursula went in the kitchen as much for something to do as to think about what she could prepare for dinner. She looked through her cupboards and her refrigerator. Nothing looked good. Her anxiety was too great to focus on food, so she left the kitchen and started straightening her apartment.

Fifteen minutes later, Radko knocked on her door. Ursula took a deep breath, opened the door, and saw a cold and shaken man on her threshold. Her heart went out to him.

"Radko," she whispered, wrapping her arm around his waist. "Come in."

Radko entered the apartment as if it were rigged with explosives. After scanning the room slowly, he looked at Ursula. This man is suffering, Ursula thought, her heart melting for her lover and friend. Radko put his arms around Ursula and held her close.

"This is all pretty intense for me," he began. "I have done nothing but ponder the possibilities since I left you yesterday evening. And I have only a little bit of clarity."

Radko proceeded to explain how he felt about their child and his or her well-being and how important it was to bring the pregnancy to term and how he thought that this should be the sole or at least the major consideration in any decisions they might make and how he and Ursula should build their relationship around the child and…

"Radko, stop," Ursula said.

She looked at him grimly, even though her heart went out to him. "Slow down," she said. "I don't know what to do about the pregnancy, but I am aware that we have some time to make a final decision." She sensed her earlier determination evaporating. "You

Absolution

don't look so good," she said finally. Radko looked at her for a moment and then ran to the kitchen sink and vomited.

CHAPTER 16

The next days were an intense blur for Radko and Ursula. They spent almost every moment together talking about the baby, the pregnancy, and the possibilities. They cried, they argued, albeit tentatively, since Radko had little practice or stamina for fighting with a woman, especially one he loved.

"Radko," Ursula said on Sunday morning. "I do not understand you. You really think that you can get a job in some office as a priest and we can live like a normal family? You really believe this is possible?"

"Yes," replied Radko. "Look," he said, "if the city is big enough and if I am transferring into a new diocese, it wouldn't be usual but it would be acceptable for me to have my own place. I have my own place now, and no one knows what I do or how I spend my time outside of work." He didn't say that he had often wished someone had.

This is lunacy, Ursula thought, wondering what it would be like to live her life with a big secret. "Catholics are everywhere," she finally said, thinking that this last gauntlet would help Radko return to his senses.

Absolution

"Most Catholics don't know there is such as thing as a chancery," Radko relied calmly. "Much less what goes on there."

Seeing the calm and believing look on Radko's face gave Ursula pause. She felt herself slipping into this concept, this notion that they could be happy together with Radko managing his career as a priest while keeping his family a secret from everyone with whom he worked. It still sounded improbable to her, but she had to admit that this came down to a problem for Radko, not necessarily or directly a problem for her. This would be his double life. He would just be her husband who went to work and came home. She would teach and raise the children. She didn't want to look too far out into the future, but she felt deeply connected to Radko, and this seemed better than ending their relationship. She sighed and nodded her head.

"So how do we do the marriage thing?" Ursula said.

Radko smiled broadly. He had thought about this. "I have a friend," he said.

And so it was that Radko and Ursula were married on December twenty-second of that year in New York with his sister and brother-in-law in attendance. Ursula invited a friend and colleague to be her maid of honor. Silas, a priest and a friend of Radko's who worked in Rome, came for the service and performed it ably with an eye toward ecclesiastical and civil jurisprudence. It was duly recorded in the county of New York, and Silas promised to keep the church documents private. All present went out for dinner that evening at Gavril's expense. Radko and Ursula spent their honeymoon in snowy Quebec City, luxuriating in the warmth of the Frontenac Hotel's Bridal Suite. It wasn't for several more months that they discovered that the child they had so thoroughly discussed was in fact a pair of twins. And it wasn't until April of that following year that Radko heard from the Archdiocese of Chicago about an opening in the Judicial Vicariate. After the school year ended, Ursula, now great with child, went house hunting in the far west Chicago suburbs, as far as she could possibly get from the downtown office where Radko was scheduled to begin working in September.

CHAPTER 17

When Radko awoke, the clock on the wall said 4:15. The TV was off, and he was covered in a blanket. His body was stiff from sleeping so long in the chair in his study. He thought of Ursula and smiled. She is angry and still takes care of me, he thought, feeling the same warmth he had always felt for the woman he married.

Radko could not get back to sleep and thought it best not to wake Ursula, who would in any case be getting up in about an hour. So he went to the kitchen and made coffee as quietly as he could. He fetched the paper and began reading. Same old nonsense, he thought, as he pushed the paper aside.

What was beginning to dawn on him was that Ursula may have been right. He remembered dismissing the content of Silas's letter with only a vague inkling that Silas might be trying to tell him something. Of course, Silas would never create a paper trail to write anything in a traceable form about Vatican politics. That would be indiscreet, and Silas was the soul of propriety. But he also had an ear to the ground and a huge fondness for Radko. After all, he agreed to marry them in a religious ceremony that was against all the rules of their church. So maybe Ursula's reaction was not so unreasonable. Maybe it was another instance of the damnable

Absolution

Germanic instinct for the jugular that was so much a part of his beloved wife.

How can I check this out? he thought to himself. He could call Silas, but it was unlikely that his friend would be anything but polite on the phone. He could e-mail him, but a cyber trail was almost as incriminating as a paper one these days. Radko thought of other men he knew in the Vatican bureaucracy. All acquaintances. All political. No one nearly so close as Silas. It was becoming clear to Radko that he had to go to Rome. He decided to call Silas from the office later in the day after he came up with some pretext to make the long flight to the Eternal City.

Making a plan energized Radko. He heard Ursula close the bathroom door and went to their bedroom to wait for her to come out. He startled her when she saw him sitting on their bed dressed in the same clothes he had on last evening. "Good morning," she said after she calmed down.

"Good morning, dear," said Radko. "Thanks for tucking me in last night." He hesitated. "I'm sorry about our disagreement. I thought more about our conversation this morning, and I think you may be right. I have to go to Rome to visit Silas and see if there is more to his message."

Ursula looked at Radko and kissed him on the forehead. "I, too, am sorry. That letter scared me, that's all. I can't fathom the prospect that something might happen that would hurt our family."

There was a sober silence between them.

Finally, Radko spoke. "I think if I can meet with Silas I can get a read on whether there is any serious likelihood that I would be named a bishop." He paused and then continued: "What makes me think that this is not so likely is that a man's character is a big part of the selection process. And no one around here knows me very well, much less knows about my character. I am only seen at work and occasionally at a parish. I don't even live in the Archdiocese although no one knows that at the chancery."

After this brief conversation, Radko and Ursula fell into their normal morning routines. The anxiety they both felt hung heavily in the air between them, but both went on in automatic mode.

As Radko drove to work, he thought of some reason why he might have to go to Rome. There were no formal meetings scheduled for the rest of the year, so it would have to be something case-related. He reviewed his current cases in his mind and finally thought that there was one or two that might justify his personal attention at the Vatican court.

He arrived at his office early so he could catch Silas in Rome before he left the office. He knew that Silas often worked past six o'clock in the evening, and Radko quickly calculated the seven-hour time difference. He thought it best to call around ten Chicago time.

Just before ten, Silas dialed the long series of numbers to Silas's Vatican office. A secretary picked up the phone. *"Buon giorno. Ufficio di Monsignor Ranke,"* said a pleasant male voice. Even though Radko has studied in Rome, he was still not accustomed to male secretaries. Probably a young priest, he thought.

"Buon giorno. Monsignor Ranke, per favore," replied Radko, grateful that he didn't have to bother with cumbersome translations. He knew that this man most likely spoke English, or at least enough English to negotiate this simple transaction, but he did not like unnecessarily troubling someone so important as the secretary to the Director of the Vatican Archives.

"Posso sapere chi lo desidera?"

"Si, sono padre Slopovich."

"Un momento, per favore."

Radko waited. Monsignor? he thought. It's about damn time. He was proud of his friend.

"Radko!" Silas shouted. "Good to hear from you. How are things in Chicagoland?"

Radko smiled. It was always good to touch base with Silas, a Chicago native himself.

"Fine," said Radko, "and yourself?"

Absolution

"Good, good," Silas gushed. Radko had a feeling he knew why he was calling.

"Listen, Silas," Radko began. "There are a couple of difficult cases that are going to require that I spend a few days in Rome, and I was hoping we could get together for dinner one evening."

"I certainly hope so," said Silas. "When are you coming?"

With that seamless and circumspect introduction, Radko and Silas made plans. Radko always admired Silas for his warmth and discretion. He did not ask after Ursula or the kids; he knew better than to risk exposure on a phone line. Nor did he allude to the letter he himself had written. As Radko hoped, Silas would be in Rome for the next several weeks, so he arranged to travel to Rome early the following week. He would leave on Sunday evening and arrive late Monday morning. He could see Silas that evening for dinner. He would also spend Tuesday in Rome on "business"—trying to find out what he could—and leave on Wednesday.

When Radko put the phone down, he had mixed emotions. He was glad he was going to see his friend and even glad to shed some light on the mystery he was facing. At the same time, there was something about Silas's tone that made him uneasy. It was too set, too convenient that Silas was available for the call, available to meet, available to take the next step that only he knew about. Enumerating the possibilities occupied much of the rest of his work day.

On the way home, Radko thought about how much he should share with Ursula. Keeping anything from Ursula seemed like a dangerous thought. He had always told Ursula everything, and he had no intention of changing that now. In his heart he felt an old feeling, one he was afraid of. He felt the pull of the miter, an attraction to the power that went with the office of bishop in the Roman Catholic Church. Bishops shared power with the pope himself; they were responsible for entire dioceses; they reported only to Rome. He thought back to the English Reformation, when the archbishop of Canterbury had a mistress who was for all practical purposes his wife. After the state took over the English church, he married her, although not much actually changed in their relationship.

But that was hundreds of years ago, and though it was similar in some respects to the situation Radko now faced, he did not have a king ready to sever the whole country from the church on his behalf. In fact, his only ally in this situation was his wife and his friend Silas. I hope they are enough, he thought.

CHAPTER 18

Radko didn't mind the long flight to Rome. He slept easily on planes and enjoyed the solitude that being in a crowded jet offered. He knew no one, and he was disinclined to talk to anyone. He had a good book and ordered a bottle of Alitalia's best wine. The food was passable, and he soon drifted into the trance spawned by the combination of eating, drinking, and the droning jet engine. He was physically comfortable but mentally troubled.

When Radko was younger, he did not think too much about being ambitious. He pursued every educational opportunity that came his way. This was how he was trained by his parents, who valued education above all else. He never seriously considered being a parish priest; it just seemed too tedious and unchallenging for him. On the other hand, he only occasionally allowed himself to think of rising higher in the church hierarchy. The Roman church took its hierarchy very seriously, and politicking for a job usually disqualified one for the higher levels. The whole process of selection was supposed to be guided by the Holy Spirit with precious little input from possible candidates. The first the selected person knew about his elevation to the episcopacy was a letter from the pronuncio in

Absolution

Washington, D.C., the pope's personal representative to the United States. That was the theory.

In practice, there were career tracks that increased the likelihood that an intelligent and prudent man could wind up in possession of a miter and his own See. Being educated in Rome was one of those. Knowledge of canon law was another. A third was working in a chancery office, where one's work and temperament could be observed by high officials in the church. When Radko thought of these, he recognized that he was qualified on all three grounds.

What did not qualify him, however, was the noteworthy absence of pastoral zeal. He did not routinely preside at liturgy on Sunday. He was not widely known among the priests of the archdiocese of Chicago. He had little contact with the day-to-day lives of most Catholics. It was this veil over his private life that allowed him to live with his family so comfortably. He was never public, never on TV, never interviewed by any of the media. He was not invited to preach at liturgies around the archdiocese. The only calls he got from other priests had to do with technical questions about canon law, and Radko had worked hard to give answers framed in the most neutral way. He never took sides in a dispute; he always supported the cardinal archbishop. He never gave any hint that he wanted higher office. Radko frowned as he thought about these things. This sounds like just the type of man they look for, he thought.

When his plane touched down at Leonardo Da Vinci airport, Radko was filled with anticipation. He was grateful to be in a place where he might get some answers and where his imagination did not have to run riot. He deftly made it through customs, aided by his Roman collar and black suit. He headed straight for the train that would take him to his room at the Hotel Columbus on the Via della Conciliazione. Once there, he threw down his small suitcase and phoned Silas at once.

Silas had been awaiting his call. With little fanfare, the two planned their rendezvous: Silas would meet Radko at the Columbus at 5:30. They could have a drink and then go to one of Silas's favorite trattorias for dinner at 7:00 p.m.

Radko glanced at his watch: 12:30 Rome time. Five hours til Silas's visit. Radko took a deep breath and decided to attend to the official business that was his cover story in coming to Rome. He did not suffer any jet lag or the usual fatigue of transatlantic travel. In fact, he felt energized and relished the prospect of moving forward in finding out those things that might well impact his immediate future. He started making the necessary phone calls.

The afternoon flew by. By four o'clock, Radko had completed his consultation with the appropriate authorities and had all the answers he needed to justify the trip. He was a little tired, but adrenaline kept his attention keen. He showered and poured himself a drink as he waited for Silas.

At five-thirty on the dot there was a knock on Radko's door. One of the many things he loved about his friend was his promptness and exactitude. He opened the door and greeted Silas warmly, giving him a hug and thanking him for being available. He offered his friend a drink, and they sat down facing each other in the smallish room.

"I am so glad that you were available to meet with me, Silas," Radko began.

"As am I, old friend," Silas responded, sipping his scotch.

Radko did not beat around the bush: "You know something," he said.

Silas hesitated, took a sip from his drink, and placed it carefully on the small table. "I think so, Radko," he began. Your name was submitted by the Metropolitan of your province to the Selection Committee. That in itself is not so unusual; your name has been on that list before. What is different is that a call came from the papal palace to express the pope's favor at the prospect of your elevation."

Radko froze. This was more serious and more decisive than he could have dreamed.

Absolution

Silas continued: "It seems that you have a friend in high places. After I heard about this call, I checked around—as discreetly as I could, mind you—and found out that Archbishop Mueller, your catachetics professor when you were here at the North American College, has been following your career for some time. He was impressed with you in school, and he has kept himself abreast of events in your ministry." Silas paused. "He was instrumental in your getting the job in Chicago."

Radko did not thaw. His mind was racing. How could he possibly have known? he thought. The job in Chicago? What else does he know about me?

As if reading his mind, Silas went on: "It appears that Archbishop Mueller understands that there is something... um... irregular about your life, but I don't think he knows exactly what it is. He apparently thought that intervening through his job at the Vatican was a way to signal the committee not to scrutinize your personal life too closely. He has the ear of the highest authorities."

Silas waited. He sensed that this was a lot for his friend to digest, and he sipped quietly on his drink, silently thanking God for Scotch.

"I'm flabbergasted," Radko said after a long while. "I didn't even think Mueller liked me. Or even noticed me." He thought back to the businesslike German priest who had been his catachetics teacher before going on to higher things. Radko always thought of him as, well, his catachetics teacher. Not a friend, not a colleague, not a potential future ally; just a teacher. And not a great teacher at that, he thought.

"I guess I need to pay a visit to the Archbishop," Radko said. He was wondering what in the world he could say to the man: Thank you very much, I'd rather not be a bishop; please do not say nice things about me to the pope; leave me alone.

More mind-reading: "I don't know what you would say to him exactly, Radko," Silas said. "He obviously sees something in you that he believes is good for the church. You may not know Mueller well, but he's said to be stubborn as a mule when he makes up his mind about something."

For the rest of the evening, Silas and Radko went on that kind of autopilot close friends develop, eating and drinking heartily at a small trattoria they had frequented while both were in school, catching up on each others' lives, asking about mutual acquaintances, and generally ignoring the tension Radko, and to some extent, Silas, felt.

CHAPTER 19

After Silas left, Radko sat on his bed sipping more of the Scotch that he and Silas had opened. He felt deeply the irony in his predicament. Any one of his peers would envy this scenario: a powerful bishop high in the Vatican nurturing his career, all but ensuring the mitered hat and probably a good-sized diocese. He remembered a time when this kind of possibility went through his mind early in his career as a priest. It seemed like a lifetime ago. He was acutely aware of how he had spent the past six years veering off in what now seemed a wild and perhaps foolhardy path that he thought at the time would bring him all the fulfillment he ever wanted: a respectable career, a close partner, children to love and who would love him. He knew it was unorthodox and canonically illegal. But it worked for him these past six years, and he valued the life he had. Now, the only prospect he saw for himself was to resign the priesthood quietly. To abandon the life he had so painstakingly nurtured. He was very, very sad.

He pushed the glass of Scotch away and stood up in the small hotel room. He thought of Ursula. Could they weather this? He thought they might. After all, he had asked a great deal of her to marry him under these conditions in the first place. At the same

Absolution

time, he felt selfish and full of regret for pulling her into a life she had not bargained for.

His training weighed heavily on him. What was the right thing to do? He felt the familiar pull of opposing forces: the love he unquestioningly felt for Ursula and his children and the fabric of his life in the church. Did God want this for him? To be pulled apart by two things that were both unmistakably good? Where was God in all of this? Did He really want him to desert the most magnificent and compelling experience of his life and live half a man buried in work? Questions abounded but no answer came from the silence. Disgusted, he flipped on the television to fill the empty space.

Radko's rumination percolated just beneath his consciousness as he watched lame Italian television melodramas. Mostly he suffered. He found himself tearing up at goofy soap-opera quality shows until he finally flipped the TV off and tried to go to sleep. The balance of the night was purgatory: not quite the hell of decided experience but a kind of limbo in which he imagined catastrophic outcomes. He was bereft and had no clear course of action.

By the by, morning came. Radko remembered how he used to cherish early mornings in Rome, where the light played on the magnificent architecture of that thrown-together city that had survived so much over two-and-a-half millennia.

At 7:00 a.m. the telephone rang. Radko was stunned: he had been feeling so cut off from reality, lost in his own unbridled cognitive machinations, that the prospect of someone else being out there did not at first register in his foggy and befuddled mind. Tentatively, he reached for the phone.

It was Ursula. Relief washed over him, and he felt the power his tie to her gave him.

"How is it going?" Ursula asked.

Radko paused. "Worse than I thought," he began. He tried to explain to her the ins and outs of Vatican politics and the mysterious role of Archbishop Wolfgang Mueller.

"Does he really have that much power?" Ursula asked.
"Apparently he does," Radko replied.
Long pause. "I'm scared, Radko," Ursula said.
"Me, too," he replied.

CHAPTER 20

Speaking to Ursula gave Radko a firmer sense of direction. I need to visit with Mueller, he said to himself, even if I don't ask him specific questions. I'll just be paying a courtesy visit to an old professor. If he's as supportive as Silas says, he will make time for me.

Armed with this frail sense of determination, Radko went to a nearby restaurant for a leisurely if strained breakfast to await a reasonable hour in Rome to make a telephone inquiry. He figured that to be about 10:30, and the time till then seemed too slow.

At 10:45, Radko went back to his room and reached for the phone to call Silas to get the Archbishop's number. Silas was predictably at his desk, doing whatever archival directors do midmorning, and he did not act surprised when he took Radko's call.

"Do you think it's a good idea for me to contact Archbishop Mueller?" Radko asked.

"I don't think it would hurt to touch base with him if he's in town," Silas replied. "You know how these guys are: very protective of their schedule and their attention. He may or may not see you." Pause. "But I think if he does have the time, he probably will agree to see you." Pause. "From what I hear, the Archbishop does

Absolution

what he wants to do." With this ambivalent statement, Silas gave Radko the number. "Good luck," he said.

"Thanks, Silas." Radko hesitated. What can I say? That he's been a big help? That I appreciate what he told me? "I may need to touch base with you again," he finally said.

"Anytime, Radko," Silas replied.

Radko put the receiver down and waited. When he realized that he was barely breathing, he picked up the phone and dialed the number Silas had given him.

He connected immediately with a male secretary. "Section for General Affairs," the man, no doubt a priest, said in answer to the phone ringing. Radko took this in for a moment. The "First Section" of the Secretariat of State was the second highest position in the Secretariat of State, the most powerful office of the Curia, or the bureaucracy of the church, just after the Secretary of State himself. It was always held by an archbishop. Radko had no idea that his catachetics teacher had gone so far.

"Archbishop Mueller, please," said Radko with all the self-importance he could muster.

"May I ask who's calling?" replied the man with equal or better self-importance.

"Father Radko Slopovich, Judicial Vicar from the Archdiocese of Chicago," wondering if this title even registered on the status scale.

"One moment, please," replied the secretary.

Radko was sweating. This is lunacy. Mueller probably doesn't even remember me, he thought, despite what Silas said. I was just another student. He had not rehearsed what he would say. Just thought I'd pay a visit to someone I haven't spoken to in twelve years? He would have hung up the phone if he had not given his name so officiously.

"Radko, it is so good to hear from you," said a different voice on the phone in heavily accented English.

"Archbishop Mueller," Radko stammered. "I was in Rome for some business and had dinner with Fr. Ranke last evening. He mentioned your name, and, and…I thought I would ring you up to see how you were doing." Radko despised feeling so foolish.

"I am so glad you did, Radko," the Archbishop replied. "Would you have any time today or tomorrow to have dinner?"

"Of course, Your Excellency," Radko replied with excessive formality. "Today would be fine. What time would be good for you?"

And so this conversation went, as Radko made plans to visit with an old professor to whom he had never given a second thought after he left school. When he finally put down the phone, he berated himself for some time for calling the archbishop so impulsively, with so little preparation. But then he began to feel the strength that came with facing a situation head on. He thought that visiting with the archbishop was really the only way to get a read on what might come his way from the Roman bureaucracy. He spent the rest of the day calling old acquaintances to see what he could find out.

CHAPTER 21

Radko was nervous when he went to the restaurant where he was to meet Archbishop Mueller. When he arrived, he saw the white-haired man seated at a table near the rear of the small establishment chatting with the waiter. He looked only slightly older than when he was Radko's teacher and seemed to be on familiar ground.

"Archbishop Mueller," Radko began, extending his hand to the tall, thin prelate. The Archbishop was dressed all in black, as was Radko. "When in Rome... ." he thought.

"Radko, it is so good to see you," the archbishop said. In fact, he seemed abnormally happy to see Radko, as if the two of them had been having a relationship all along and were separated by unfortunate events. "What brings you to Rome?"

Radko told the archbishop in a general way about the difficult cases he had to resolve with the Rota officials, those judges who hear appeals from the diocesan tribunal of which Radko was a part. It was standard empty talk that Radko had learned to do when he was studying in Rome, designed to fill the air with sound and convey a sense of conviviality but specifically intended to give no real information. Fluff.

Absolution

The archbishop listened patiently, as if he were genuinely interested. He asked Radko specific questions about the officials he met with in the Rota and if this person or that person were helpful. He asked Radko if he needed any help from him with these matters.

Radko paused when the archbishop made this offer. Top Vatican officials did not routinely put the prestige of their office behind routine business for no reason. Did the archbishop want Radko to be beholden to him somehow? Was he trying to trap him? Despite these internal questions, Radko smiled at his old professor. "Everyone was fine, Archbishop. I was able to clear the matter up in just a few hours."

"Please call me Wolfgang," the archbishop said.

Okay, Radko thought. I guess that makes sense. We're both adults. His suspicion deepened.

The balance of dinner was pleasant. The archbishop—Wolfgang—regaled Radko with stories of Rome. He was utterly unpretentious and even self-effacing. Not at all the serious and often boring teacher that Radko remembered from his days at the North American College. Why in the world am I here? wondered Radko throughout the evening.

Over after-dinner coffee, Wolfgang looked at Radko without speaking for several minutes with a look that Radko could not interpret: serious but not strained; calm but focused. Radko was about to open his mouth to reinflate the air with words when the older man spoke.

"Radko, my friend," Wolfgang began slowly, "I was delighted to hear that you were in Rome and even happier when you called me." Pause. "There is something I have been wanting to share with you for some time now." Longer pause, as Wolfgang sipped his espresso, as if uncertain about whether or not to proceed.

"As you probably suspect, I have acquired some measure of influence in the Vatican," he continued, seeming to select his words carefully. "There are a number of men with whom I have had contact over the years whose careers I have been following. Yours has been one of those."

Radko's chest tightened. He was struck by the straightforwardness of Wolfgang's words. Understated but revealing for a high Vatican official. His breathing slowed.

"I happened to be in the loop when you applied for the job in Chicago. I was working in the Rota at the time, and I thought it was a good move for you. A bigger stage where your uncommonly good sense could get a larger hearing. It turned out that Cardinal Masterson was in Rome around that time, and I was able to recommend you to him." The old man paused. "Please forgive my actions taken without your consent, but it was something that happened on the spur of the moment." He looked at Radko as if awaiting a response.

Radko nodded. He wasn't sure he could actually speak at the moment; he was filled with anxiety about where this conversation was going. This was not what he expected from the archbishop in charge of General Affairs of the Secretariat of State. Radko felt that his status was being elevated just by being in the presence of such a frank discussion with this important man. He could feel the muscles in his face begin to quiver. Breathe! he ordered himself. He opened his mouth to take in air.

"As it turned out," Wolfgang continued, ignoring the nervous signs Radko was emitting, "the cardinal has been pleased with your work. I saw him at a meeting in Washington just a few months ago, and we were able to converse about it." He looked at Radko and smiled.

"I don't know what to say," Radko finally blurted out. Once he began to speak, however, he was able to breathe more easily, if in fits and starts at first. "Archbishop Mueller, I am pleased that you think so highly of me. I am just…I am just…not accustomed to attention from men who are so highly placed. I am more than a little bit intimidated."

Absolution

The archbishop burst out laughing. For a moment, he was unable to speak. Finally, he put his hand on Radko's on top the table.

"My dear Radko," he said. "I sometimes forget that there are people on this planet who think I am important." He kept chuckling. "Forgive me. All I am saying is that I respect you and your good sense. Even your honesty about your reaction just now says a great deal about your value to me and to the church. Most people in your position would have tried to cover their nervousness and act as if everything were okay. We need more men like you in 'important' positions."

Then the archbishop called for the check and signed it, signaling for Radko that their dinner was over. He bade him a fond good evening and walked smiling out of the restaurant.

Radko sat back down. When the waiter came to check on him, he ordered an after dinner drink and another espresso. It was on the archbishop's tab, the waiter said to Radko when he tried to pay him later. He wouldn't even accept a tip.

CHAPTER 22

Radko walked back to the hotel in a state of confused clarity. He was confused about the Archbishop's—Wolfgang's—specific intentions. He felt he had gotten a very clear glimpse, however, of the political lay of the land in his own regard. It was very clear there were forces at work of which he had been unaware only hours before. He was not happy or unhappy. If anything, he was energized and cognizant of a need for time to digest this not entirely unwelcome news.

He had trouble classifying this experience. He felt he had been shown a slice of life in the church that he had only occasionally heard about. He felt that Wolfgang treated him as an equal and smiled inwardly when he thought of how the old archbishop had burst out laughing at Radko's confession. He felt he had some insight into how the man that he thought of as a dull catechetics teacher had risen so high in the church structure. He was charming, direct, and engaging. He was obviously focused on his agenda and unapologetic for it. Radko felt proud of Archbishop Mueller and proud of himself for making it through the evening without disabusing the old man of any myths he might have had about his former student.

Absolution

Radko thought of the church. He had to admit that in recent years he had paid a price for the life he had chosen. He began to feel a bond to the church he had not felt for some years and longed for it to be restored. It was for this reason that he loved the church—a good and holy organization, despite its checkered history, doing good and holy things. Here was the third most powerful man in the Vatican laughing at Radko's foibles as if they were nothing. How many secular executives do that? he wondered. In the church, politics were personal, engaged. He felt honored to be part of it.

But he knew that it was not something that included him the way it had at one time. When he recognized this, he felt sorrow. Not just sorrow, which was one thing, but also distance, which was quite another. Distance from the church and from an especially fervent early hope to be folded into the life of the church, to dissolve his personality into that worldwide fraternity of goodness and holiness. To be redeemed.

That was a long time ago, Radko thought. He had not had such thoughts for years; certainly not since his relationship with Ursula; but not even for years before that. His ministry began to turn dull and colorless not long after it started. He had lost sight of that early vision even before the work began to pile up and his relations with other priests in the diocese became hopelessly superficial. It was not until he met Ursula that his interest and ability to relate to another person was re-ignited. But that very restoration made tonight's revelations moot. He was not going to be a member of this fraternity much longer, much less a privileged bishop, however feasible that might be for Mueller and the others on the Selection Committee. He knew that the ultimate price he would have to pay for the restoration of enthusiasm in his life would be to abandon the priesthood and perhaps even the church he loved so dearly.

Oddly, Radko did not feel so sad or forlorn or distraught as he felt somber. He recognized the choices he made in his life with a clarity he had never experienced as an adult. This was not yet tragic news so much as it was how things were. He felt the heft and shape of reality and respected it more than at any other time in his life.

CHAPTER 23

It was not in Ursula's nature to be anxious for no reason; but, despite the fact that she had been talking to herself for four days, she had to admit she had plenty reason to be nervous. The last time she spoke to Radko in Rome he admitted that he was afraid. Ursula did not think that Radko would abandon her or her children, but she knew she did not really understand the complicated relationship Radko had with his work and with the church.

She thought back to the one time she saw him preside at Mass at a parish in a neighboring city. He did not want her to go, but she had never been to church, and she insisted. She sat in the back of the first church she had ever entered and took in the strange surroundings. Hard wooden benches, high ceilings, an altar. An altar! Just like the ancient Romans. She half expected someone to sacrifice a lamb or some other kind of animal on it.

Then Radko came out dressed up in what seemed like a Halloween costume: long robes with different symbols and colors on them. She almost started laughing but recognized that everyone in the large hall was taking this very seriously. He intoned various prayers and the congregation responded according to the text she saw in the paperback booklet in her pew. It reminded Ursula of

Absolution

some science fiction movies she had seen. Then Radko read a story from the Bible and began to preach.

Ursula was nervous for Radko when he began speaking, but she found his sermon very dear. He talked about love and how God accepted everyone, even and maybe especially sinners, and how important it was for us as Christians to accept and forgive each other and love each other as God loved us and how this would lead us to happiness in this world and God would take care of us in the next. Then he walked back to the altar and resumed the quaint ritual. Ursula breathed a sigh of relief, but she had to admit that Radko had done a good job with his talk, as far as she could see.

Ursula did not pretend to understand all that was involved in these goings-on, but she saw how respectful everyone was and how they greeted each other as if they were friends or at least acquaintances. It struck her as homespun and warm, but not as something she wanted to make a regular part of her life.

She also remembered the conversation she and Radko had about the children and whether or not they should be raised in the Faith, as Radko referred to it. As with most of these conversations about Radko's religion, Ursula learned to listen with a serious look on her face as she wondered inside herself what all the fuss was about. They determined in this matter to have the children baptized but not to attend Catholic schools or church. Because discretion was so important, they waited until Silas was in the United States on business. He came over to administer the sacrament while the children were still infants and completed all the paperwork. As with their marriage, he agreed to keep the relevant documents secret. It seemed to Ursula that Silas made all this stuff a great deal easier and wondered what Radko would have done or would do without him.

Ursula looked at the clock: 5:30 in the afternoon. Another two hours before Radko's plane would land. She thought of going to the airport early, but she detested sitting around O'Hare with nothing but a book between her and all those travelers. She had already taken the twins to the babysitter. They would be there until morning because she thought she and Radko could use the time without interruption to talk about his trip, to be together without the distraction of the kids.

Despite herself, Ursula could not help but think about Plan B. The one she would need if Radko decided to cast his lot with that damnable religion of his. Would she stay here? keep her job? move back East? She didn't mind the Midwest; she liked her job okay. For a few minutes, she let herself fantasize about life without Radko, without the stability she had attained over the past five-plus years. It made her too sad to think about it; she decided to go to the airport instead.

It turned out that Radko's plane would be arriving early. She got to the security station just as the announcement was made that Alitalia Flight #1703 had arrived at Gate 46. She was breathless from running to the concourse and from the anticipation of seeing Radko.

After what seemed like an inordinate amount of time, she spied him walking down the concourse. She waved until she caught his eye. He picked up the pace.

They embraced as soon as Radko entered the nonsecure area and held each other for some minutes. Radko didn't care about being seen. He was not wearing his clerical blacks, and he was very happy to see Ursula. They discussed the flight and other details of travel on their way to baggage claim and then to Ursula's waiting car.

Once inside the car, Ursula began: "I am dying to know what you found out," she said, true to her direct nature.

"Well," Radko said. "It looks like my name has indeed come up before the Selection Committee." He paused. "But more than that, my candidacy got a boost directly from a highly placed official in the Vatican. Very highly placed." He did not take his eyes off the road.

Absolution

Ursula did not take her eyes off Radko. Why is he not looking at me? she wondered. Out loud: "Are they going to make you a bishop?"

Radko hesitated and then took Ursula's hand and squeezed is softly. "Yes, it looks like they will," he said, glancing at her quickly.

They drove on in silence. Radko did not know exactly what to say, since his feelings about this whole matter were less than clear. Ursula was shocked and angry that Radko wasn't more decisive about his own intentions or desires. She was getting angrier and angrier that there might be any question in his mind about which way to go in this matter. So she felt not just angry, but sad, disillusioned. Nearing heartbreak.

"Radko," she finally said. "I understand that these matters are complicated and difficult for you in ways I do not fully understand." Understatement of the afternoon, Ursula thought to herself. She took a breath and continued: "But I need to know where you and I stand."

Sometimes Ursula wished that she were more demure, more patient and tolerant, and less direct. But she didn't think she had much choice about how she was. She turned her body toward Radko and stared at him stolidly.

Radko could feel her staring at him. He glanced toward her and said, "What do you want to know, Ursula? That there's any question about my personal or moral responsibility?" His voice was louder than he intended. He sighed heavily. "I can't be a bishop. I can't just leave you and the twins." He paused for a moment. "I don't even think I'll be able to remain a priest much longer." Toward the end of that sentence, his voice cracked slightly.

Ursula heard it, and her heart began to melt for her husband, a man who was so torn by powerful forces known only to him. She took his hand in both of hers. "I am sorry, Radko; I was frightened."

Radko then began to explain to her in as detailed a way as he could how the selection process worked. He also described his meetings with Silas and with Wolfgang.

"Ursula, it was as if Wolfgang knew my every move. I wonder how much he really knew about me. Silas said he was instrumental in my getting the job in Chicago, the one I have now. This came up in my conversation with Wolfgang, who acted like it was a coincidence." Maybe it was, Radko thought to himself. After all, he does mingle in august company on a routine basis.

Ursula listened intently. She was unsure of what to say, and she thought that this was something that Radko had to work out on his own. She thought he might be best served by a quiet but attentive audience. What she was sure about was that her anxiety had not completely dissipated.

CHAPTER 24

Archbishop Wolfgang Johannus Mueller looked out the glorious windows of his Vatican Office, beyond which he saw St. Peter's Square, where the late-afternoon sun was shining on the pigeons and tourists milling about. When he turned his attention back to his office, he beheld the equally glorious frescoes that covered the walls and ceilings of his large but sparsely-appointed office. Beauty upon beauty, he thought to himself with satisfaction.

Archbishop Mueller was waiting to place a call to Silas on his secure line. He wanted to compare notes about Radko's visit to Rome, but he was waiting until the secretarial staff was gone, both at Silas's office in the Archives and at his own office at the Secretariat. The two men shared an obsession for secrecy—true Vatican officials, Wolfgang thought. But both men also had layers of interest in Radko: they both liked him as a person; they both had professional ties; and they both wanted him to do some heavy lifting in carrying out a plot—no, not a plot, a plan—they hoped would eventually revolutionize the church.

Absolution

The plan was not too complicated, although it had required consistent effort on his part and on the part of the coterie of priests, bishops, and cardinals who were privy to it. Its goal was quite simply to rework longstanding and even ancient church teaching about sexuality and to counter the anti-sexual bias embedded both in the teaching and in the culture of the church. And to do so by building a network of secretly sanctioned marriages and other sexual alliances among members of the clergy. In time, this secret fraternity would grow to the point where its influence would make itself felt throughout the church in a way that could not easily be dismissed or outlawed. The reputation and the very functioning of the church would weigh in the balance. Not in Wolfgang's lifetime, perhaps; he did not care whether or not he lived to see the plan arrive at its ultimate goal. He did not think that practical or likely. It was enough for him to plant it, to see it grow, to foster it, and to know that it was safely in the hands of competent men and women to be safeguarded until such time as it could be made public. For the sake of the church Wolfgang loved, he hoped it would not be too long.

For now, his focus was on an obscure diocesan official from the midwestern United States who had, unbeknownst to him, played into the archbishop's plan perfectly. Wolfgang remembered Radko from his student days at the North American College. Wolfgang hated teaching catechetics, but he did so because he believed—rightly, as it turned out—that it would provide a boost for his career in Rome, giving him time to build the kind of contacts he wanted and needed.

Wolfgang reflected that Radko was not the only one who kept secrets. He thought back to his experience as a young *peritus*, or expert, during the Second Vatican Council in the mid-sixties. He had thought as the Council proceeded that the church would actually do what John XXIII intended for it to do: to open up the windows of modernity and allow fresh air to fill the aging organization that was steadily losing influence in the world. Specifically, that it would change its strict, nonnegotiable attitude toward the sexuality of humans and open itself up to a more modern, more sensitive, more scientifically informed, and more realistic view. He had been sure back then that clerical celibacy would become an optional matter and that a shift toward more acceptance of sexual variety would ensue. He was also sure that the divorce laws would be relaxed and that the millions of Catholics who suffered for years feeling alienated from the church would be welcomed back into the fold as full members, able to resume complete participation in the sacramental life of the church without suspicion or fear of condemnation. At that time, it didn't really seem too much to ask. The winds of modernity were blowing strong, and good Pope John was open to all manner of change.

He recalled his bitter disappointment when the good pope died and reactionary forces hijacked the proceedings of the Council, watering down the final documents and basically arriving anew at the status quo ante, with showy but unsubstantial changes in the church as a whole. He remembered returning to his university job at Tübingen appalled and depressed that so little was accomplished, just more words.

And what transpired in the following decades did not hearten him. He saw the church and its leadership drift more and more toward the right: toward the rigid, conservative, and even reactionary views he abhorred. Outwardly, he continued to manage his career, and he tailored his focus to whatever was in fashion. Intelligent but modest, even-tempered, and even meek by temperament, Wolfgang rose from one responsible job to another. Whereas outwardly he was compliant, obliging, and utterly supportive of whatever the church was doing, he was inwardly embittered as he saw legions of priests and lay people abandon the tradition in which they were raised because they could not countenance the irrational intransigence of church doctrine, especially regarding sexual matters. By the time he was appointed to a position in Rome, he was determined to do something about this situation.

Absolution

In the early days he was not sure exactly what he could do to remedy what he believed to be an outrage. But as he saw his career rise higher and higher, he realized how important it was to make himself palatable to the powers that be so he could position himself to make a difference. And that was precisely what he did. He bowed, he scraped, he suffered fools with apparent gladness. He was punctilious in his work and ingratiating with his superiors and tolerant to those beneath him. During many of these years, Wolfgang traveled the world and found that celibacy was not always so important to many in the less-developed sections of the planet. Also along the way, he identified intellectual stand-outs: men and women—although this being Rome, there were more men to be sure—whom he deemed not to be fools, but bright, resourceful, and caring people who wanted the best for their church. And who weren't too swayed by superstition and tradition.

In retrospect, Wolfgang's professional success did not seem very difficult, although he tended to forget the long hours he put in doing his job better than everyone else. But Wolfgang was also surprised to have gotten as far as he had. He wanted power and access; but he also wanted to remain in the background so he could subvert this odious strain of the tradition of the church from behind the scenes. But his ambition worked too well. Now he was widely thought to be the third most powerful prelate in the Vatican, and as such his behavior was highly visible. But it was, Wolfgang mused, a trade-off. There were the risks of exposure, but there was also unparalleled access to power—unquestioned access.

At first, he thought he should focus on a single, simple goal: perhaps doing away with mandatory celibacy for priests. But over time, he came to recognize that the celibacy rule came from a deeply rooted anti-sexual, anti-feminine bias in the church. He saw how, even though most Protestant groups discarded celibacy early in their reforms, it took additional centuries for that modest change to translate into a more mature appreciation of sexuality overall. It was only in the last century that some out-front Christian sects—

radical Anglicans, for instance—were allowing women to be ordained or homosexual unions to be blessed. He secretly applauded their progress, but he lamented the long, tortuous, hurtful process that was required to get to the point of basic acceptance of human diversity.

He also thought bitterly of the American and the European sex scandals of late last century and the early years of the current one. What did the church really have to say to those people who were victimized by priests molesting children, penitents, or married women? Did they believe that there were just a few bad apples in an organization that had a coherent and realistic approach to sexuality? That everything would be all right if people only had sex to produce children in church-sanctioned marriages? How painfully and disastrously naive, he thought. How destructive and disrespectful of one of the most joyous acts of which humans were capable. But to the old men of the Vatican bureaucracy—he still thought of them as old men, as if he weren't one of them—that was the single acceptable reason for sexual contact. Any sixteen-year-old knew better, he reflected.

To keep himself beyond reproach, Wolfgang dutifully lived his celibate promise. He had no mistress, no sexual contact of any kind. He knew that Rome did not get its reputation as the fleshpot of Europe for no reason, and he knew many men—high church officials—whose behavior varied widely from the ideal they publicly supported. Wolfgang thought that dangerous for him personally and a threat to his project to overthrow antique notions of sexuality.

On the other hand, he had had many circumspect conversations with officials and bishops from around the world, especially the Third World, who thought the Roman demands of celibacy and lifelong chastity were outmoded and who were generally unbothered by the rampant violations within their own jurisdictions. Early in his teaching career, Wolfgang spotted the most talented among his students and began to keep a discreet eye on them. He

Absolution

kept a very close watch indeed on Radko and others like him. He knew about Ursula and the children. He knew about the lengths to which Radko went to cover his tracks. But he also knew Silas, who was a member of the core group of...of what? Wolfgang thought. He hated the term "conspirators," but he knew that this was exactly what they were, the few dozen or so men around the world who were promoting breaches of celibate living so as to foment a rebellion against the ancient curse they felt hobbled the church in its true mission to preach the simple gospel of Jesus Christ. Conspirators we are, Wolfgang thought, and reached into the credenza behind his desk for a late-afternoon aperitif. It was nearly time to call Silas.

As he sipped his drink, he thought about the collision course Radko was on. Wolfgang was betting that Radko could not resist the pull of power and position within the church. He also knew that his bonds to his wife and children were strong. It would be a painful dilemma for Radko and Ursula to work out, but he had confidence that they would at least try to make it work. If not, it would set the plan back for awhile. Gazing out at the gathering darkness, Wolfgang wondered how much time he had left to nurse his little plan along.

CHAPTER 25

Across the time zones, Radko lay awake in his bed next to Ursula. They had spent most of the evening talking about the practical reality: that Radko would resign the priesthood and try to find some other type of job. Outside the church. Not much call for lay canon lawyers, he thought to himself.

What kept him awake was not that sensible plan. What tugged at him was how much his short trip to Rome had rekindled something he thought was long gone: that euphoria that comes with exposure to power. He was a little embarrassed even alone to recognize this in himself, but he could not help replaying his visit with Wolfgang over and over in his mind. He always came to the same delicious part: he treated me as an equal. He treated me as an equal! Please, call me Wolfgang...is there anything I can do?...the burst of laughter at Radko's confession of being intimidated. He felt the intoxication of relating as a peer to one of the most powerful men in the Vatican, and he loved it.

Maybe this is why people pray, Radko thought absently. He looked out his bedroom window at the dark suburban night. He turned toward Ursula and touched her head, gently caressing her hair. He had no doubt about his love for her. And he had no doubt

Absolution

about his love of power. The only person in this whole complicated scenario he doubted was himself.

CHAPTER 26

Back in the Eternal City, Wolfgang and Silas were talking on Wolfgang's secure line.

"What did you think?" asked Wolfgang. "Do you think he suspects anything?"

"No, I don't," Silas replied. "I think he believes that he will be made a bishop, and my hunch is that he will resign the priesthood before giving up Ursula and the children and before being humiliated in a public sex scandal." He paused and thought for a moment. "I think the next few weeks will be critical."

"If he leaves, it will be almost impossible to get him back into the priesthood, much less convince him to stand for bishop," Wolfgang mused. Then he continued: "It was my impression when I saw him for dinner that he was much more engaged than I thought. After I spoke with you, I expected Radko to be anxious and ingratiating. But I thought he held up pretty well. Despite himself, I think he responds to power."

Then the Archbishop looked at Silas. "Do you think it's time to bring him in?"

Silas hesitated. This part of the plan always made him nervous. "I think we will have to if he takes any steps to resign. I'll keep a

Absolution

close eye on that. If we need to move, I can get to Chicago on short notice."

Silas felt the palms of his hands moistening. It's almost time, he thought to himself.

"Thanks, Silas," said the kind archbishop. "Keep me posted as things develop."

"You know I will, Wolf," replied Silas.

CHAPTER 27

The next morning, Radko went to work as usual. He was groggy and irritable because he had slept so poorly the night before. On top of the normal jet-lag this made his morning commute a frustrating rather than a peaceful transitional time. In fact, he reflected that he did not feel as if he were transitioning. As he loosened his striped tie and replaced it with the clerical collar, he was angry and dispirited. What's the use of this charade? he demanded of no one in particular. What has it gotten me? A damned promotion! If he had been in a better physical and emotional place, he would have smiled at the irony.

But not today. He was tempted to walk into the chancery and resign, but he knew that this whole situation required more thought and more caution and more of all those things that got him into this mess in the first place. Radko thought, not unhappily, that getting involved with Ursula was the only risky thing he had ever done in his entire life. Sure it was followed by the construction of a lifestyle that was unique, but it was one that made abundant sense, given what he discovered to be valuable in his life. The truth was that he had everything he wanted—a woman he loved, a job he

Absolution

valued, and children. But now, all these delicately balanced things were at risk.

He and Ursula had resumed their conversation at breakfast, but it was mercifully brief because Ursula had to leave to collect the children and redeposit them in their preschool. Radko told her he had trouble sleeping, but he did not tell her about his thoughts as he lay awake replaying his Rome trip. She, on the other hand, still had an air of anxiousness about her. He knew there was more to talk about, but Radko felt he needed some time to sort things out. Alone.

That's right, Radko thought; I do need some time alone. He turned off the highway at the next exit and called the chancery to say he was not feeling well and that he was going to take the day off. Apart from a tinge of guilt for missing work, he immediately felt better, threw off his Roman collar, and headed north.

Radko thought to himself that he needed a neutral spot. Not a church place or a home place but someplace where he was not pulled in either direction. As he drove toward the Wisconsin border, he tried to think of a place that met these criteria. He wasn't sure why he turned his car northward, although this felt like the right direction.

As he headed up Interstate Highway 94, he forced himself to concentrate on the situation facing him. What did he actually know? As far as he could tell, he was sure that (a) Mueller wanted him to be a bishop; (b) Mueller had the power to make it happen; (c) there was no practical way he could become a bishop and stay married to Ursula—too much publicity, too much notoriety, too great a risk for Ursula and the children. This last item triggered a chill that Radko felt run through his body as his imagination threw the image of humiliating revelations about his beloved wife and children in the media onto the screen of his mind. Then he again forced himself to concentrate. (d) this process will take time. The church seldom moves quickly, especially in these weighty matters pertaining to leadership. And finally (e) if I want to avoid disaster, I will have to take the situation in hand.

A horn blast from behind him shook Radko out of his ruminating trance. He looked around and glanced at his dashboard and found that he was driving only forty miles an hour in a section of interstate where seventy was the limit and eighty to ninety the norm. He pushed his thoughts aside and accelerated to a respectable seventy-five. Getting killed on the interstate was one way out of this dilemma, he thought to himself darkly. He shook his head and concentrated on driving for the next twenty miles.

After a while, he realized where that voice in the back of his mind was steering him. It was Lake Michigan, that vast expanse of water that was for all intents and purposes an ocean that had the misfortune of being hemmed in by land. I suppose all oceans are, Radko mused as he exited the interstate and made his way to a secluded area of beach that he recalled from an unnumbered summer past. Safely alone on a short stretch of beach, Radko began walking toward the water and stared out at a sea that had no end.

The experience of ocean never failed to clear his mind and provide a perspective that was elusive amid the buildings and skyscrapers of large cities. Radko knew he was at heart an urbanite; he often felt uncomfortable being far from where the people were, where the action was, where the results of civilization held sway. But he also knew that after a while the urban environment made him feel boxed in. He was too vulnerable to getting caught up in what was happening around him. It was easy for him to feel swept away in the circadian rhythms of city life. He began to feel unbalanced amid the hubbub. His small suburban bungalow helped rebalance him. It was quiet in his exurban neighborhood, and he often felt that the relative silence salved his harried soul on a regular basis, but not on this day. It was that peaceful environment itself that now stood at the heart of the conundrum that confronted him. That awareness tempered whatever balm his family and his home

Absolution

normally provided. Despite all his efforts, his marriage to Ursula was at the heart of the problem he now faced.

The truth was that he did not know if he could even tell Ursula how shaken and infatuated and captive he felt to the call of power from Rome. From Mueller, from Silas, even from the disembodied church itself. He looked out at the bright sun blazing across the water of the lake. Was there really a God who was in charge of these things? he wondered absently to himself. Am I really a part of something where nameless, invisible forces have the power to move us around like so many little chess pieces? I don't think so, he countered to himself. This is just the part of the hand life is dealing me right now. I wish it weren't so; I just want to go on doing what I was doing. These thoughts did not hearten Radko, who could swallow neither the notion that there was a God who had it in for him nor the idea that he could handle this situation in a way where someone, including himself, wouldn't get hurt.

What concerned him now was what to do next. He rarely kept secrets from Ursula, and the thought of doing so now filled him with sorrow and self-loathing. A deeper voice encouraged him to talk to her honestly about this conflict in his life. He knew that this meant saying out loud something they both no doubt felt but had not yet stated: that their relationship was in the balance. I love you, Ursula, he said to himself quietly. I just don't know if I can do this. If I can resist the tug, if I can say no to the life that has been my heritage since birth, that I have been guarding so jealously. And I don't know if I can be worthy of you or if I can leave you. I am not even sure I can talk to you. He began to cry softly.

CHAPTER 28

Ursula's day was full of frustration. She worked hard not to be angry or short with her students, but they seemed to be dancing on her last nerve every time she turned around. By lunchtime she thought of going home, a thought that she seldom had and one upon which she had never acted. Taking her brown bag with her, she decided to go for a walk. The air was brisk, and the neat tract houses that surrounded the school seemed sufficiently bland to offer some hope of tranquility.

She could not put her finger on whatever it was that was disturbing her. She felt Radko's turmoil, but he had assured her of his devotion to her and to the children. She knew that it would be a big change for him to give up his job at the chancery and find a whole new line of work. Was he up to it? she wondered. Even if he didn't find a job for a long time, she was working and her job was by all accounts secure. She was liked by her colleagues and by her students even if they seemed less than cooperative today. She was pretty sure it was Radko she was worried about. She was pretty sure it was their relationship she was worried about.

Ursula knew that she could weather a lot. Radko could change his job and go through his emotional ups and down: those things

Absolution

did not bother her much. The nagging anxiety she had today was more personal than that. She was unsure if Radko really wanted to end his career as a priest. She thought back: what was it he said at the airport? Something about personal and moral responsibility? About not being a priest for much longer. These seemed like impersonal assessments to her. The truth was that she felt his distance all evening as they talked about it. The only time he lit up during their conversation was when he described his dinner with Mueller and how important he felt when this highly placed Vatican official petted him. Ursula smiled contemptuously when she listened to her choice of words. I am angry at Radko, she thought; I don't think he is leveling with me about how all this is affecting him.

Ursula had always stopped herself from saying much about Radko's career beyond taking his side in the occasional internecine office conflict he talked about once in a while at home. She did not think she knew much about it and, when she tried to learn, found the material turgid, boring, and needlessly mysterious. But she knew that the Vatican in Rome was where the power was and that something happened there that changed Radko. Not since their courtship had he talked about resigning the priesthood. But there was something else. He seemed inordinately moved by some simple gestures on the part of this Mueller, the archbishop who took him to dinner.

Does Radko want to be a bishop? she wondered. How could they pull that off? The archbishop of Chicago was regularly in the news and in the media. Whereas neither Radko nor his job ever came to the attention of the press, his boss probably appeared at least monthly in some newspaper article, local TV news broadcast, or even in the national media. She was not absolutely sure, but she didn't think any bishop in this church was married. None of them, to Ursula's knowledge, went home to a woman and children in the evening. She was fuzzy about what they did, but she knew it wasn't family friendly, as she thought of that concept.

Paul Martin Midden

Ursula flashed on what her life would be like without Radko. She would still have the twins; she would still teach. As she reviewed these things in her imagination, she realized the prospect of relief at not being part of this double-life scenario. While she saw Radko's life as generally his problem, she had grown practiced at steering conversations away from his work when she was with colleagues or with friends. She was also pretty good at dodging probing questions from the five-year-old twins, who occasionally wanted more detail about their father's work. Pretty soon they will not be satisfied with answers like "Daddy works in an office." The relief came when she thought of not having to do this sort of thing, at the prospect of telling the simple truth about her life. She would prefer to do that with Radko in her life, but she had a distinct feeling that whether or not that would happen was yet to be seen and was not entirely up to her. She saw a trash container on the street and threw her uneaten lunch into it, took a deep breath, and walked slowly back to school.

CHAPTER 29

Ursula was surprised to see Radko at home when she arrived home from school with the twins. It was early for him—3:30 in the afternoon. After saying hello and giving the twins a snack, she regarded him carefully.

"I think we need to talk," she said in a perfect alto voice.

"Yes, we do," Radko replied.

A silence stood between them. Radko looked at the children devour their afternoon snacks while chattering on about whatever five year olds chatter on about. He was grateful for their noise. In the strained silence, he felt his bond to the two youngsters he had fathered. His heart lurched.

He motioned Ursula to sit in the living room away from the children, but where she could still keep an eye on them.

"This is harder for me than I let on yesterday," Radko began.

Ursula did not speak, but she felt some relief at the prospect that Radko might level with her. It felt like home: his honesty was one of the most compelling things about him. Curious, given the circumstances, she thought to herself. She allowed herself just a touch of hope.

Absolution

"I think I had lost touch with how important the church is to me," Radko went on. "My visit to Rome, but especially dinner with Mueller, reminded me." He paused. "I am not sure what the right thing to do is…"

"This is not about the right thing!" Ursula snapped, sitting up in her chair with unexpected force. "It's about what you want."

"It's about both, Ursy," he replied, switching to his pet name for her in hopes of mollifying her.

More silence. Arguments were rare in the Slopovich household, and Radko was uncertain how to proceed. Usually he just gave in to Ursula.

"You know I love you, Ursy. I need to talk about this. I don't know if you have any idea of the forces at play here." Radko was sitting erect with more fortitude than he normally showed.

Radko went on to describe his visit to Lake Michigan and his thoughts about his future. He shared with Ursula his tangled conclusion that he could not do this without her.

When he was finished, Ursula looked at him doubtfully and said, "Radko, what you want of me, of us, does not seem possible. Except…this feels like the first time you talked me into this… into this situation." She thought for a moment. "You know, as much as we ignore certain parts of our life, the way we live doesn't make much sense. We act like it's normal, but who would choose to live like this, as if having a wife and children were a shameful secret?"

They talked some more but not about the one issue they both feared most. Soon the kids were demanding attention, and neither Radko nor Ursula wanted them to think there was anything different between them. Radko was relieved when Ursula got up to attend to the twins.

But he was too antsy to just sit there, so he got up, grabbed his jacket, and yelled to Ursula: "I'm going for a walk."

CHAPTER 30

Silas pushed himself back from his well-organized desk and stared into the empty room before him. He was thinking of Radko and Ursula and the terrible spot they would soon be in. They are probably already in it, Silas thought to himself. But he knew Ursula to be a woman who would not avoid confronting the conflicts of her life. He doubted that she had ever left the field of battle in her periodic marital wars with Radko. Lucky bastard, Silas thought. He and Radko had been friends for many years, but he liked Ursula the moment he met her. He understood immediately why Radko was so captured by her. He also knew that when Ursula fussed about something, when some conflict arose in her relationship with Radko, she was fighting for the relationship. She believed in being honest and facing things directly. Silas reflected on the paradox of Ursula's life now that she had been participating in a double life that must be taking a toll on her. On the other hand, he knew that Ursula would do what made sense to her. She would do what she had to do. And what she understood.

Silas's attention then turned to the situation at hand. He had just heard from Wolfgang that the next meeting of the Bishop Selection Committee would be four weeks from yesterday and that Radko's

Absolution

name would almost assuredly be on the list of those selected. Silas knew that when Wolfgang said "most assuredly" he meant with absolutely no doubt at all. Silas had to get busy.

His first call was to Fr. Angelo Cassabelli, the Vicar General for the Archdiocese of Chicago. In this post, Fr. Cassabelli was Radko's superior, although neither man had much interaction with the other on a routine basis. For all practical purposes, however, Fr. Casabelli ran the diocese day to day, and because of this it was wise for Radko to defer to him. Angelo was a bright, affable man with an outsize personality who got along with everyone. His memory for faces and his attention to detail were attributes he wore so easily no one noticed them; but they made him very helpful to those in leadership positions who wanted to keep track of what was going on throughout a large organization. Angelo rarely disappointed in the execution of his duties. He knew everyone on staff by name, as well as their birthdays and most of their significant relationships.

When his secretary told him who was calling, Angelo seamlessly excused himself from another phone conversation with the pastor of the largest parish in the diocese and took Silas's call immediately.

"*Buon giorno, mio amico,*" he said playfully as he picked up the phone. Despite his ethnic name, Angelo knew only enough Italian for the merest pleasantries. His cultural heritage was Chicago's dirty south side.

"It's still daytime there, I take it," Silas replied. He had mixed feelings about this call. He and Angelo went a long way back, as both of them were raised on the mean streets of the south side. But Silas did not like Angelo very much; nor he did like the events he was about to put into play.

"Angelo," Silas continued, making his voice sound more official, "I have news about one of your colleagues. It seems that one of them is to be selected."

It was the way Silas said the word "selected"—three long equally accented syllables—that let Angelo know that this was not a social call. In an instant, he reviewed the other men who worked at the chancery. Only one name connected. "Let me guess," he said. "You wouldn't be speaking of Fr. Slopovich, our contrarian Judicial Vicar, would you?"

"Contrarian?" said Silas.

"'Mysterious' might be a better word," replied Angelo. "I guessed him because he is such a hard worker and an intelligent man. Company man, but good with people whose marriages are falling apart." It was really by contrast to his colorless colleagues that Angelo fingered Radko as likely.

"Yes, he's the one," Silas said. "The Committee is meeting in about a month, and the letters will go out to the Pronuncio right after that." Then he paused. "Do you have any objections to this selection?" he asked as if it were a normal part of the process.

Angelo thought for a moment. "No," he said. "My only objection is that he will be hard to replace. I applaud the good sense of the Committee."

Silas felt a small measure of relief. Step one, he thought to himself. He knew that if Angelo thought there would be a problem, he would have said so in a circuitous but unmistakable manner. Such is the language of church diplomacy.

"Good," he said. "As you know, no one is to hear about this until the official announcement is made. That should be in about six weeks."

"Of course, *mio padre*," said the affable priest with the slightest hint of sarcasm in his tone. No one will hear it from me."

After he put the phone down, Angelo wondered why Silas had called him. It was widely known, at least to those who knew about these things, that the Selection Committee did its work in secret. And why had the Committee selected Radko? His Judicial Vicar did good work, but he was more than a tad on the serious side. Bright enough, Angelo thought. Orthodox enough. Almost no pastoral experience, but sensitive and compassionate with the mostly divorcing people he did have contact with. Truth is, no one knows

Absolution

much about him. Lives out of the city, I've heard, but pretty much of a loner. Angelo had tagged Radko as a lifer: a solitary man who was content to do his job, filling in for vacationing pastors occasionally. The kind that would die in his desk chair. Angelo didn't know a single priest in the diocese to whom Radko was close. He wasn't sure exactly where he lived. How did this guy get by me, and right under my nose? Angelo wondered. He saw the blank spaces in the portfolio of his mind. It's my job to know this stuff, he thought; we wouldn't want the Cardinal to be embarrassed. He made a mental note to look into some of the details of Radko's life.

For himself, Angelo's sole ambition was to keep the job he had. He loved his position of power, which was backed up by one of the most important Cardinals in the American church; he loved Chicago, the city that had always been his home. The thought of becoming a bishop was one he dreaded because it would most likely take him away from this gritty but beloved metropolis. That thought made him shiver.

CHAPTER 31

After Silas finished his call to Angelo, he thought about his small but not insignificant role in Wolfgang's scheme to revolutionize an important teaching of the church. Every time he was called upon to do the Archbishop's leg work, he felt an upsurge in his fear that this was a foolhardy, dangerous plan, that real lives were being jeopardized and real careers put on the line. The Archbishop had little to lose, especially now, as he was getting up in years. But to those men who were entangled in his grand but private scheme, their lives, their well-being, even their membership in the church were at risk.

Silas also knew that if Radko accepted what he was about to propose to him, it would be a giant step forward for the whole plan. Up till now, each of the thirteen bishops who were married by secret sanction presided in small corners of the world where celibacy was, to use Wolfgang's understated term, "de-emphasized": One in Somalia, two in Chad, six in Asian countries, three in South America, one in Polynesia. Silas did not know the exact number of priests who had wives. He knew the number of those sanctioned by Wolfgang's plan—three hundred and sixty-two—but that did not include a number that was no doubt much greater, which included men who took common-law spouses and who lived with them in unbothered defiance of standard church law. The thirteen bishops were encouraged to secretly sanction such marriages when they discovered them, but men whose minds were such that they flouted church law so brazenly did not usually seek permission or even disclose their decision to the local bishop.

But Radko's elevation would mean that, for the first time, a secretly sanctioned married bishop would preside over a diocese in the United States. Silas felt the excitement of this development, but he also felt the fear and apprehension that such a risk entailed. If it didn't work, Radko's life in the church would be ruined. But beyond that, the whole plan might be exposed and come to a calamitous end. Silas's own career, and perhaps even that of Wolfgang, was at stake.

Silas allowed his mind to wander back to Wolfgang's original proposal. He and Wolfgang were vacationing together in Slovakia, hiking in the High Tatras mountains, when Wolf started laying out his plan to an incredulous Silas.

"So you want to start a network of married priests and bishops around the world in the hope of changing church teaching about sexuality?" Silas asked his friend.

"Not just the teaching," Wolf replied, "but the attitude as well. How long has the church demeaned human sexuality and how high a price has she paid for her rigid and uncompromising attitudes? Too long and too high are the answers to those questions, respectively." Mueller paused. "And there is no chance that those attitudes will change by bringing it up at some symposium or conference or meeting of the bishops. The whole question of sexuality surfaced during Vatican II, but it was quietly but effectively silenced by conservative elements in the church. And now, with so many more bishops selected because of their conservative views, it is less likely to happen. Something new needs to happen out there where the people live."

"Wolf, who in their right mind would take such a risk?" Silas said.

"Well, so far Bishop Mantu in Somalia and Bishop Chai-Sun in Tibet. Both still seem to be in their right minds. Just ask their wives."

Silas stopped hiking and looked at the archbishop. "Do you mean to tell me that those men are married? How is that possible?" Silas proceeded to raise objections: According to church law, clerics—priests and bishops—could not present themselves for marriage. That's why the church coined the quaint phrase "attempt to marry" if they went through the ceremony because they could not legally do so.

"Illicit but not invalid," replied Wolfgang to his younger friend. "Illegal but still a marriage. There is something in church history called a 'Secret Sanction'. The church has always reserved to herself the right to sanction certain activities that she felt were for the good of the church or of the world, even if these were less than in tune with current Christian teaching or the desires of those in power at the time. Later these were called 'Pragmatic Sanctions' but the concept is similar. And I believe it was Pope Clement who first noted that a cleric's marriage would be illegal but that it would be valid. It may be another story for those with solemn vows, but most diocesan priests can validly marry, even if it is illegal."

Wolfgang scrutinized Silas before continuing. "Before the last two hundred years, individual bishops had a lot more power than they've had since. Since the mid-eighteen hundreds, successive popes have worked hard to consolidate power in the hands of the papacy. Over time, these moves severely eroded the power that bishops have had since Christianity was first organized. The pope is just first among equals, *primus inter pares*. But true power still resides with the bishops, especially when they meet together in council." Another long pause as they resumed walking. "My plan is to use the ancient power invested in a bishop to make decisions apart from the papacy and to invoke the secret sanction tradition. To-

Absolution

gether, these two things give me as a bishop of the church the authority to marry priests and bishops and to keep these marriages secret. Until such time as their number grows and they can safely become public."

He looked at his young friend. "Don't you see, Silas? Not now, not in our lifetime, but perhaps in another generation or another century or so, marriage and sexuality will begin to be seen in a different, more realistic, and more tolerant light. Not as something antithetical to the gospel but something in profound harmony with it. What has happened up till now has been disastrous. For the church, for her priests, and for the mission, we have to make love the priority in the world."

Silas looked out into the distance and tried to focus on what Mueller was saying. He knew in his heart that his friend was right, that the church's attitudes toward sexuality needed to change. But Archbishop Mueller was a Vatican official, and Silas couldn't have been more shocked at what he was hearing than if a tree along their path had called him by name. He was dumbfounded.

They walked along in silence for some time. When Silas finally looked over at his friend, he saw that Wolfgang was smiling. Why is he smiling? Silas wondered. Is he laughing at my discomfort? Silas didn't think so. He had always found Wolfgang to be a gracious, cultured man who would never point out a person's foibles, much less ridicule them. He felt a wave of affection for the older man who had just taken a risk to share ideas with him that could have cost him his job. He did not know what to think.

It was Wolfgang who broke the silence. "Silas, it is not just marriage I am supporting here," he said. "It is changing our view of sexuality and our presumptuous belief that we own it. Or control it. Or that we should. Sexuality in many of its forms is a good and holy thing. Not just for pious souls who only allow themselves sexual release in the hope of having children, but for everyone to express themselves in a way which feels right for them within the limits of respect, of course, and with an eye toward the safety of children. But among adults, to denigrate sexuality is to put ourselves at odds with the vast majority of humans for whom it is the major source of pleasure and satisfaction. That's just wrong."

Silas did not respond, and his breathing became shallow. In a flash, he understood that Mueller was signaling him that he knew about Silas's own activities, his preferences, his inclinations that did not accord with church law either. Not even close, he thought to himself. Silas did not look at Wolfgang, who pretended not to notice.

"Silas, if we can begin a process that will change this unfortunate state of affairs, we will have done the church, society, and the world in general a great favor. We will have helped humans to grow up appreciating their sexual passions rather than trying to check them at every turn. We will have unleashed a force for good upon the world. A force that is there waiting to be used for good that has been used too often for evil, principally because of our efforts to thwart it. In the process, we will make the church a place where adults can come without having to act like children, pretending to have no real erotic life."

As they walked on in silence, Silas felt trapped. Wolfgang Mueller was his friend, even though he was a high Vatican official. He could denounce him to his superiors, but that would destroy not only Wolfgang's plans but his career. It was clear that Wolfgang was taking a huge risk to share with him his intent. He probably took a very carefully calculated risk that Silas would join him. If I don't denounce him, I am already a conspirator. Damn this calculating bastard! Silas thought; but this thought was immediately followed by a sense of closeness and trust that was implicit in Wolfgang's disclosures. If Silas had been more of a risk taker, he would have held Wolfgang's hand.

CHAPTER 32

When Radko returned from his walk, it was nearly dark. He walked in through the side door, which led directly to the kitchen. Ursula was setting the table in preparation for the evening meal.

"How was your walk?" Ursula said, focusing her attention on the table.

"Brisk," replied Radko.

Ursula turned and looked at her husband. "Radko," she began; but then she stopped.

Radko returned Ursula's gaze but did not speak. He walked over to her and put his arms around her. "My Ursy," he said softly.

They stood there for a moment. Radko loved the warmth and feel of Ursula's body next to his. Even through their clothes he could feel her strong but feminine frame leaning into him.

"We'll talk later," he said after a while.

Ursula pulled herself away from him, kissing him gently.

Even the children were subdued during dinner. They seemed to sense that all was not well with their parents. They looked at each other in that surreptitious way that five year olds have, which is far from subtle. Sergei was so nervous he couldn't take his eyes off his mother.

Absolution

"What's the matter, ?" asked his mother.

"No one's saying anything, Mom," he replied, his voice shaking.

When Ursula did not immediately reply, Radko spoke up: "Honey, there are some important things going on at my work, and your mother and I need to talk about them. Things are a little tense right now, but everything will be okay."

"Are you going to get a divorce?" asked Marguerite.

Radko turned to her and said firmly, "No, Maggy, we are not going to get a divorce."

Ursula's eyes widened ever so slightly, but it was clearly visible on five- year-old radar.

"What will happen if you get a divorce?" Maggy asked.

Radko felt his impatience rising. "Maggy, we are not getting a divorce," he said too loudly.

Maggy was quiet, but she looked at her mother with concern. Ursula reached over to her and patted her gently on the head. "Where did you get the idea that we might get a divorce, honey?" she asked Maggy.

"Janey and Rob said that their parents were always quiet at dinner and they got a divorce," replied the perspicacious five year old.

Ursula saw her opening: "Yes, but they were quiet night after night after night. This is only one quiet dinner. Divorce doesn't happen until dinners are quiet for a long time."

Maggy regarded her mother with suspicion. Her mom had always told her that she would never lie to her, so she had to give some weight to what she was saying. She looked over at her brother who was looking at her with wide-eyed anxiety.

"Okay," she said, feeling all eyes on her. "Then, can Sergie and I watch some television before we finish our homework?"

She should run a Middle Eastern bizarre, Ursula thought affectionately, respectful of Maggy's quick turn of mind. "For a little bit."

"Can we do it now?"

"What do you say?"

"May we be excused, please?"

"Yes, you may be excused," Ursula said, grateful that the cloud had lifted a little from their evening meal.

After the kids left the table, she turned to Radko. "We cannot lie to the children, even if they are young," she said.

Radko looked at her with a stony expression. "I did not lie to her," he said. "The last thing I want is a divorce."

They resumed their meal in silence.

CHAPTER 33

Angelo Cassabelli woke up early on Saturday morning with Radko on his mind. Silas's call had been in the back of his mind ever since he got it yesterday, as was his incredulous awareness that he did not have much information about the Judicial Vicar. As he lay in bed and watched the dawn slowly emerge, he wondered how he would fill in the gaps of his knowledge. He could call the Vicar in Baltimore—What was his name? Catsweiler. Slopovich was in the seminary there; Catsweiler probably knows him pretty well. He also thought about other Romani, seminarians who were chosen to study theology in Rome—the cream of the crop—who might know Radko. He would have to make some calls.

As he dragged his large frame out of bed, he recognized that something else was tugging at the back of his mind. Looking at himself in the mirror shaving, he realized that it was the fact that Silas had called him at all. Angelo knew that there were a few sacred traditions of the church involving secrecy. One was the seal of confession, the rule that no priest could disclose what a penitent says to him in confession for any reason whatsoever. Violating this rule was the fast track out of priesthood. But another was how bishops were selected. This process had been honed by centuries

Absolution

of hard-fought experience in leadership and was ironclad in one respect: it was never ever discussed outside of a conference of the people involved. No one ever gave advance indication. The Pronuncio in Washington, D.C., the papal ambassador himself, did not know who was selected until he was officially notified in writing in Latin on official Vatican stationary. A phone call to give a heads-up? Never done! What is Silas up to?

After his morning ritual, he went down to breakfast in the rectory dining room. One of the advantages of living in the Cardinal's residence, besides being so close to the highest authority in the diocese, was that three meals were served each day in the elaborately-appointed dining room by a collection of nuns whose sole desire was to meet the culinary needs and inclinations of those seated around the heavy oak table. Angelo loved food.

On this particular Saturday morning, it was Angelo and the young deacon who was serving his academic year in an internship at the cathedral. A pleasant if rather bland twenty-two-year-old, Jack Peterson was the apparent model of the kind of seminarian the church was looking for these days. Studious, orthodox, well-groomed, orthodox, polite, orthodox. Angelo chuckled at himself. He knew that seminarians had to tow the party line, but he also remembered that in his formation there was a bit more latitude for current trends in thinking, both in the field of theology as well as in related fields of contemporary thought. Now it was a matter of playing I Am More Conservative Than Thou. Tiresome, Angelo thought, but hopefully it would pass in time. He regaled the young man with juicy but unimportant details of Archdiocesan politics.

After breakfast, Angelo retired to the library adjacent to his room. He ran through his rolodex, an exact copy of the one he had at his office, and dialed Thaddeus Catsweiler's private line.

No answer. Angelo hated leaving messages, but he made an exception for this call. He asked Ted to call him back at the earliest opportunity. He did not leave his number because he felt that would be too obsequious and suggest that their relationship was not close. He should be in Ted's rolodex.

Angelo thought for a minute. Whom did Radko study with in Rome? He called a couple of numbers but no one picked up. He thought of driving to the address that was in Radko's record at the chancery, but then he had a better idea. He knew that Radko had a sister who he said that he visited her every major holiday. Back to his rolodex and under Slopovich, Radko was an emergency contact name and telephone number. Gordana Raminski; New York number. He congratulated himself for being so well-organized.

Angelo contrived his cover as he dialed the number. A sleepy female voice answered the phone.

"Ms. Raminski?" Angelo began, unsure of how Gordana would want to be addressed.

"Yes?" replied Gordana, whose sleep was obviously being disturbed by this eight-thirty a.m. Saturday morning call.

"Ms. Raminski, my name is Father Angelo Cassabelli. I work with your brother, Father Radko Slopovich. You are his sister; is that correct?"

"Yes, yes I am," Gordana replied, slightly alarmed that a priest coworker would call so early. She was immediately alert.

"I'm sorry to bother you so early, but your brother has been with the Archdiocese of Chicago for five years now, and he is an excellent member of the administrative team. We were thinking of throwing a party for him to celebrate his time with us and wondered if you and a guest would be able to join us." Good work, Angelo, he thought to himself.

"Oh," said Gordana, instantly relieved. "Yes, I'm sure we would try to make it. When is it, Father?" she asked.

"We have not settled on a specific date, but I think it will be in a few weeks. Could you tell me, please, a little bit about Radko: what he likes to eat and drink; who his friends are. He is a hardworking man, but he is a little bit on the solitary side with us here. As you know, he is not from here. He was trained in Baltimore."

Absolution

They chatted about Radko for a while, Angelo using whatever charm he could muster—and he thought it considerable—to pump Gordana for details about Radko's past, his friendships, and his life in the present. He wanted to know who Radko was close to. As they talked, he made notes with arrows going between contacts he thought might be useful.

By the time he hung up, Angelo felt smug and triumphant. He had some names of Radko's friends; he had established a relationship of confidence with his sister. He felt that he was well on his way to filling in the blank spaces in his mind about his mysterious coworker.

In the midst of these feelings, his phone rang. It was Catsweiler from Baltimore. Goethe was right, Angelo thought, life favors the bold.

It turned out that Catsweiler was not much help. Angelo already had the names of the people that Ted identified as Radko's friends. Ted also, however, explained how, when Radko worked in the Archdiocese of Baltimore, he asked to live alone, ostensibly to be closer to the chancery in downtown Baltimore. Ted also told him that it was widely known at the time that the real reason was that Radko could not stand the people he had been assigned to live with. Ted confirmed that Radko was a hardworking man but a loner who kept his distance from people and who was overall pretty mysterious.

As he chatted with Catsweiler, one thought burgeoned in Angelo's mind, and when he put the phone down, he said it aloud to his empty office: "What is Slopovich hiding?"

CHAPTER 34

Ted Catsweiler was worried. It was clear to him that Angelo was up to something. He was in bloodhound mode, looking for information on Radko. He did not know how much Angelo knew. Containment, Ted thought; it's all about containment.

He looked at the time. 9:00 a.m. Baltimore time; late afternoon in Rome. Ted knew that he had to contact Silas, who would have some idea about how to proceed. He dialed the number he knew by heart.

He got Silas's Italian voice mail. Damn, he thought. Silas, where are you when I need you? He left a message for Silas to call him. Then he went to the kitchen counter in his small rectory and poured himself another cup of coffee. This whole project is just too dangerous, he thought to himself for the thousandth time. But at the same time, his heart ached for Silas, his friend, his lover, his confidant. He cursed the four-thousand-mile divide that separated them, and he wished he had no part in that scheming archbishop's plan.

It was Silas who got Ted wrapped up in this preposterous plan in the first place. Ted wanted to blame him for all the anxiety it had caused him. But Silas was a man to whom Ted was not only enormously attracted, he was also a man for whom Ted had profound respect. Intelligent and well-educated, Silas went after information as if gasping for air after almost drowning in his working-class, south-side Chicago upbringing. He did not meet a problem that couldn't be solved by finding out every detail, every angle, everything there was to be known about it. He had a beautiful mind. In nice packaging, Ted thought.

Ted and Silas met at a gym and began their friendship working out together during their post-ordination training in Rome. It was weeks before they realized they were both priests. Their friendship was a discovery experience, more like encountering a familiar and exciting friend than meeting someone unknown. Their physical attraction was instantaneous, but their subsequent love relationship followed some months later during a ski weekend in the Tyrol, when Ted sat Silas down and explained his feelings toward him.

"So the bottom line is I love you and want to have sex with you," Ted said with eerie and alien candor.

Silas didn't say anything. He got up from his club chair and sat down on the couch next to where Ted was sitting. "What makes you think that's okay with me?" Silas asked with a serious look on his face.

Ted look at Silas sheepishly. "Because you know everything," he said. And he took Silas's hand.

Later, they were lying in bed at the small Alpine hotel where they were staying. Ted was rapturously happy. Silas was not his first sex partner, but he was the first person he had ever fallen in love with. He was the only person he had ever fallen in love with.

Oddly, one of Silas's many attractions was his honesty. Ted shared everything with Silas; Silas for his part never held back his intentions. He didn't want to be an exclusive couple; he valued his relationship with Ted and wanted to keep it. He didn't want to be restricted by it. Harsh terms, but Ted responded to the candor with utter devotion. It didn't matter to him whom else Silas had sex with. What mattered to him was that he had a relationship—a warm, close, passionate relationship—that was utterly honest. Ted did not elect to have sex with other people; he didn't want to. All he wanted was to do his job and to be with Silas when he could. This was a challenge at times, but their times together more than made up for the long fallow periods in between.

When Silas told him during one of their visits that a powerful Vatican official, an archbishop, had a plan to subvert one of the principle moral teachings of the church, Ted thought at first that he was joking. He laughed so hard he almost fell out of bed. But Silas did not laugh. So Ted pulled himself together and tried to take it seriously. He began to ask questions. Pretty much the same questions that Silas had asked of Mueller when the archbishop first proposed the project to him. It took him some time to go from incredulity to belief.

"You're serious, aren't you?" he finally said to Silas.

"Yes, Ted, I am serious. And the more I think about it, the more seriously I take it. You would not believe what Mueller has risked for this plan. It may or may not work. But I can tell you this: If it does work, it will be just as Wolfgang says. In a few generations or a century or two, the teaching of the church on these matters will go from one of control and possession to one of acceptance and tolerance. I believe that with all my heart."

Ted could not respond to that. He had always thought of his peccadilloes as just that, small faults that seemed like harmless pleasures. Like spending a few hours with a particularly good claret and a Cuban cigar. Offensive to the prudish, but a common, delicious, and innocent human foible. Sex, especially homosexual sex, was definitely immoral, but not serious. Until, of course, he met Silas. That seemed less immoral and more serious.

So Ted gradually came to feel like a member of the conspiracy. He did not do much; his participation was limited to gathering information and plugging possible leaks. He never met a married priest or bishop. What did come into focus over time was how well his limited involvement fit into his appreciation of his relationship

Absolution

with Silas. He gradually stopped thinking of that relationship as shameful, and this seemed like a liberating thing. He finally had answers to his conscience when it harped on him that he was violating his promises. Not the promise to love, he answered with a new assurance. He felt like a grown-up, self-possessed and sure of his bonds.

But wishing and dreaming about the past were not luxuries the compromised Vicar General could afford. If Cassabelli stumbled on the truth of Radko's life, it could easily sabotage the first American married bishop; and Catsweiler, while he had no great affection for Mueller or most of the other players in this underground drama with the major exception of Silas, believed with the other conspirators that what they were doing was right. And he was not about to be the one who dropped the ball and brought the whole plan tumbling down.

Switching to more familiar problem-solving mode, Ted reviewed his options. He fully expected Silas to call within the hour, and he looked forward to that conversation. He thought about Cassabelli, a man for whom he had little real respect: he regarded Angelo as an arrogant *apparatchik*, a busybody who used his office to interfere with people's lives simply for the delight in his power to do so. He relished the thought of sabotaging this blowhard's meddling. It was just a matter of how.

CHAPTER 35

Something about her conversation with Father Cassabelli bothered Gordana, but she couldn't quite put her finger on it. She knew Angelo's name because Radko had mentioned it to her from time to time; but always as his colleague or even as his superior, never as a friend or as a person privy to the secrets of his life. Under ordinary circumstances, she would have waited to talk this situation over with her still-sleeping husband, but Gavril had little tolerance for the machinations of the church, including his brother-in-law's, so she decided to call Radko straightaway.

"Good morning," Radko said, obviously sleeping in on this Saturday morning.

"Good morning," Gordana said. She explained the odd call from Cassabelli, but she was uncertain whether to mention the party or not.

Finally, she asked, "Radko, is it usual for the people you work with to have parties for each other, such as celebrating years of service?"

Radko thought for a minute. He remembered a going-away party for the priest he replaced, but that doddering man was on his way to a nursing home, where his dementia would not so readily

Absolution

impede the work of the People of God. Other than that, he could not remember a single event.

"Maybe at the end of their time," he told Gordana.

With that, Gordana proceeded to tell Radko every detail of her early-morning conversation with Cassabelli. Radko was shocked. Why all the fuss? he wondered. What was Fat Angelo up to? The possibilities troubled him.

After he hung up from speaking to Gordana, Radko lay in bed for a few minutes wondering what Angelo knew. He was more than familiar with the Vicar's snooping ways and often thought that Angelo easily went over the line between the professional and the personal. To date, Radko had resisted Angelo's advances, whether these were formal parties—with the exception of the one for his predecessor—or last minute let's-catch-a-drink-after-work invitations.

Radko found Angelo at times intrusive, but he did not dislike him. In fact, he had a warm place in his heart for the affable and outgoing Vicar. For Radko, who was generally quiet and serious, it was something of a relief to be around Cassabelli. Radko didn't have to worry about carrying the conversation because if Angelo could do one thing, it was hold court. Radko admired that in his colleague.

But this morning he was mildly worried that Angelo might have him in his sights. He did not know why that would be. Except for his trip to Rome, nothing out of the ordinary had happened that he could identify. But then he thought of Mueller and the reach of his power. After mulling the situation over for awhile, Radko had to admit that he did not have access to all that was happening. That thought gave him an eerie feeling; it reminded him of his reaction to Mueller's keeping track of him—spying was a good word—for years after he left studies in Rome. There are greater forces at play here, he thought to himself, and got up to go to the bathroom.

After he went into the kitchen for coffee, he saw Ursula, awake and alert. She had made coffee and was reading the morning paper.

Radko realized that he had momentarily forgotten their tense evening after dinner yesterday. He remembered wanting to talk to her, but he really did not know what to say. So after the children were dismissed, he allowed himself to get lost in the domestic details of avoidance, helping with the dishes, perusing the newspaper, reading a half-interesting novel. Bedtime was equally chilly: no conversation, strained looks, eyes downcast. Remembering made Radko feel like a child.

"Good morning," he said to his wife.

Ursula finished a sentence or two of her reading before looking up. "Good morning," she said in a studied monotone.

Radko went over and sat next to her on the couch. "I guess we need more practice at talking about things," he said.

Ursula's eyes blinked in Radko's direction. He knew she was hurt and angry.

He tried again. "I'm sorry, honey, this has been a long week for me." He tried to gauge her reaction as he spoke, but she interrupted him.

"I know it has. For both of us. I think we just need some time to absorb what is happening and what you want to do." She got up and went back into the kitchen.

Radko sat on the couch staring into the empty space left by Ursula's abrupt departure. He had no more idea of what to say this morning than he did last night. He reflected on his resolve to say everything to Ursula he had had when he was staring out into the ocean. He wanted to tell her how torn he was, how frightened he was, how uncertain he was, and how much he loved her. Now those seemed like so many empty words. He was beginning to feel the weight of the situation bear down on him. He felt the heaviness of his own dilemma and of Ursula's as well.

Then he noticed Ursula leaning against the wall that separated the kitchen from the family room, looking down at him.

"I think the truth is," she began, "that you have no idea of what you want and that makes me afraid—very afraid."

Absolution

Radko looked up at her with yearning in his eyes. She was so damned brave, he thought to himself.

"I'm afraid, too," he said finally. "I don't want anything to happen to us: to you and me and the children."

Ursula shrugged. "If that's true, then we should be making some other plans," she said. "I'm not so sure it is true."

Radko looked at Ursula.

"I think you would like us to stay together if there is a way to do it and keep your...promotion."

Smart girl, Radko thought. To Ursula: "It's hard to explain what being selected for bishop means in the Catholic church," he said. "I know you don't understand this, but if I say no to this I have to be very clear about alternative plans.

"Radko," Ursula interrupted, "am I missing something here? How can you possibly say yes to that and hope to remain married?"

"Well, of course, I can't," Radko acknowledged. "But then, that's what I thought about our getting married and keeping my job in the first place. I guess I'm just engaging in wishful thinking."

Ursula turned and went back into the kitchen shaking her head. Who is this guy? she thought to herself. When did Radko become an adolescent?

CHAPTER 36

The party was scheduled for Friday evening on November 9th. Radko couldn't think of a way out of it. Angelo had invited his sister and some old friends, as well as most of the staff of the chancery. In addition, Thaddeus Catsweiler, his former boss, was going to be in town, and even Silas said that he might be able to swing a trip to the U.S. Even though it was two weeks away, Radko was embarrassed just thinking about it.

Angelo had just left Radko's office. He was full of enthusiasm as he told Radko how they—presumably the cardinal and Angelo—wanted to show their appreciation for the Judicial Vicar by hosting a little get-together for him and the staff and a few friends and his sister from New York and maybe some people from out of town if they could fit it into their schedules.

Even with the heads up provided by his sister, Radko didn't know what to say. What could he say? No, I don't want to be appreciated? Please don't celebrate before I retire, which might be sooner rather than later? He was irritated. He was particularly annoyed at himself because he could be so easily taken in by Angelo's infectious if phony enthusiasm. He just sat there as Angelo was talking and waving his arms and smiling; he actually thought for a

Absolution

few minutes that a party would be fun. But as soon as Angelo left the room, Radko pressed his forehead down on the worn walnut of his desk, observed all the life drain out of him, and concluded he was the stupidest and most gullible human on the planet.

A party? I don't even like Little League games. I don't like to talk to more than one person at a time. Maybe I could get sick. Or die. Or better yet, just vanish without a trace.

Radko put these ideas aside. He knew he was overreacting. But he could not ignore the vague feeling that something was going on here that was veiled, something to which he was not privy. He tried to think about what it could be. This has got to be all about Angelo, he thought. What does Angelo want? he asked himself for the umpteenth time, knowing that he didn't have the requisite information even to guess what that could possibly be. But Silas might.

He looked at the clock on his desk. 11:30 a.m. in Chicago; evening in Rome. He picked up the phone and dialed Silas's home number.

Silas answered on the second ring.

Yes, Silas said, Angelo had mentioned the party. As it turned out, he was going to be in the U.S. on business anyway. In fact, he had just been thinking about calling Radko when Radko called him. Silas said it sounded like a good idea and that in church work people were often under-appreciated. He told Radko that he was looking forward to seeing him and bade him a fond good evening.

When Radko put the phone down, he was only slightly mollified. He had no additional information about Angelo's possible motives, and it seemed to him that Silas was acting uncharacteristically like a choir boy. What did Silas care about the church appreciating its workers? he thought to himself. Maybe Silas had had a martini or two by the time I called him, Radko thought.

He looked out his window down at the steps at the entrance of the cathedral. Two elderly women were walking slowly and with apparent pain into the church for a service. Nuns, probably, Radko thought. But he saw himself in those women; or rather, he saw a part of himself that he did not usually acknowledge. His heart went out to those women who in his mind were unquestioningly faithful to their religion. He imagined that they did not put every detail of church life under a microscope; that they did their duty as the church told them what that was; that they had some need to believe or some awareness that there was a point where hardheaded modern rationality could not go. It was about faithfulness. And duty. And being good.

On the other hand, he surveyed his own life—the life of the mind, for the most part. A life that did not accept the impossible; that demanded that beliefs and events make sense; that recognized his humanity, such as it was. A realistic compromise: that was how he thought about the essential bifurcation of his life. It made sense, at least rationally: to respect one's work and to love a woman. As he pondered the events of his life as they were unfolding before him, he feared that he may have been wrong. That what he was now seeing was the incipient wreckage, an accident waiting to happen. A boat about to be dashed upon the rocks of its own, what? hubris, maybe. Or greed. He looked back down at the cathedral entrance. The women were safe inside.

CHAPTER 37

Silas looked across the table at Wolfgang and tried to interpret the look on his face. He had heard Silas's part of the conversation with Radko. His look was neither approving nor disapproving. It was tranquil, accepting, almost serene. How could he possibly be serene at a time like this? Silas thought. A man they both respected and cared about was about to be confronted with a terrible decision. And they were the ones responsible for throwing a monkey wrench into the delicate balance that was Radko's life.

"I'll go if you don't want to," said the archbishop. "I know Radko is special to you. It might be easier for him to consider this situation objectively with me, since we have no close relationship."

Silas thought for a moment. Wolfgang was probably right about that, he thought to himself. Still, he could not see passing on such a job to Mueller or to anyone else. He felt deeply responsible to be the one who would lay out Radko's options for him. Because of their friendship; even though that friendship itself may well be the price Silas would have to pay for delivering the news to Radko.

"No," Silas said. "I'll do it. It might be helpful if you could see him some time after I talk to him. I think it would help him feel more like he is doing something for the church." He paused and

Absolution

then looked over his wine glass at his older colleague, and his eyes twinkled. "You're good at that."

Wolfgang smiled and shrugged slightly. Evidently, I am good at that, he thought to himself.

Then Silas said, "The other issue is Cassabelli. That guy is a dog with a bone. He called Catsweiler in Baltimore to get the scoop on Slopovich. He even called Radko's sister in New York at some godforsaken time early last Saturday morning. This guy needs some attention."

"What did Ted think?" Wolfgang asked.

"That we should have him assassinated," Silas replied, realizing that Ted was only half-joking when he had said that. Then Silas turned serious. "Ted thinks we should respond in full force by attending this party that Angelo dreamed up and fill in any missing blanks in Cassabelli's mind. Angelo is a sucker for what he thinks is inside information, and if Ted and I are both there, we can feed him information that should keep him busy for a couple of months. By that time, Radko will have made up his mind one way or the other and will be out of Cassabelli's circle of influence."

Wolfgang brought his wine glass to his lips and pondered this plan. He always admired what a good team Silas and Ted made. This was useful for Wolfgang's designs, and he was aware that their being together had other attractions for each of them. This was all to the good as far as Wolf could see. It was exactly the kind of pairing that made sense: it was useful, it brought joy to each person, and it served a larger purpose. He nodded toward Silas.

"I concur." Then he turned to the more difficult topic. "What about talking to Radko? Do you think it best that we do this before the party or after?"

"Wolf," Silas said, looking soberly at his friend. "I think it best that we do this as soon as possible. I think Radko is getting edgy. He never picks up the phone and calls me on the spur of the moment. He doesn't do anything on the spur of the moment. I suggest we bring him in as soon as possible, but definitively before the 9th."

Right again, Mueller thought. "All right," he said. "Why don't you make plans to meet with him as soon as you can?" The archbishop paused. "But," he began, "I also want to speak with him. We are taking this plan to a new level by naming a married American bishop. He needs to know that I, as a member of the Curia, am behind him, that I believe this is the best thing."

And that you can pressure him to do it, Silas thought. He did not find the archbishop's manipulations distasteful—in fact, he admired how smoothly Mueller positioned himself exactly where he wanted himself to be—but he had to have some time to think about this. It was a new level for the plan. No one really cared much about bishops in far-off places where there were few Catholics, but a married bishop in the heart of the USA? Now that was news. Silas was not entirely certain that this could even be pulled off. He was sure that he wanted to protect Radko to the extent that this was possible, and he wanted to make sure that Radko was one-hundred percent on board with a decision of his own and Ursula's, of course. But still, he did not like the thought of Mueller pressuring his friend.

"I understand your feelings about this, Wolf," he said in a conciliatory tone. "Let me think about the best way to do it. We'll talk more before I leave."

Once again, Mueller nodded.

CHAPTER 38

After Mueller left his apartment, Silas went to work. He called Ted to tell him about his plans to meet with Radko and to double-team Cassabelli at the party. Ted dreaded the first part, but he delighted in the second.

"So when are you going to meet with Slopovich?" Ted finally asked.

"I'm planning to be in Chicago within the week, Ted, and I'll arrange to meet Radko as soon as possible after I arrive."

Ted didn't say anything. He could sense that Silas was worried about this, and he wondered how he could support his friend. "Is there any way I can help?" he asked.

Silas thought for a minute. Up till now, Ted had never been a part of any actual contact. But he knew Radko and knew him pretty well. He wondered if Ted's presence might be helpful. "What would you think about joining me for this meeting?" he asked Ted.

Again, Ted did not respond right away. He was instantly torn between his desire to do anything he could to help Silas and his distaste for this part of the work. "If you think it is best that I be there, Silas, I will be there," he said finally.

Absolution

"Thanks, Ted. Let me think about it on the flight over. I'll call you as soon as I land in Chicago."

After Silas said good-bye, he held onto the phone for a few minutes. I love that man, he said to himself. He knew just how disagreeable Ted found the actual contact with prospective priests—he had refused Mueller's requests on several occasions that he make contact with men who wanted to marry—so he was filled with appreciation that Ted would even consider joining him for what was no doubt going to be a very difficult conversation.

After this momentary reverie, he turned his attention to other details. He went online to book a flight, and found a reasonable fare two days away. He thought of packing for the trip, but he knew he had time for that. He was anxious. For a few minutes, he did not know what to do with himself. Everything was ready, he thought. And then he realized that he had forgotten to call Radko to schedule a time for them to get together. With the recognition, he sat back in his chair and reached for the nearly empty bottle of red wine that he and Wolfgang had been sharing.

As he sipped the last of a pretty good Chateauneuf, he could think of no more excuses. He picked up the phone and dialed the number.

Radko answered right away. He was surprised to hear from Silas, whom he had just spoken to not two hours earlier. It was early afternoon in Chicago, and Radko had worked hard to bury himself in work to forget about the first part of the day.

"I had company when you called earlier," Silas explained. "Church official, du rigeur: I had to sound upbeat and concerned. He's gone now."

That sounded like a perfectly good explanation to Radko, who was more or less constantly reshaping his behavior to conform to the expectations of those around him. "Oh," he said.

Silas ignored the silence and charged ahead. "The reason I'm calling now is to let you know that I will be in the U.S. this Thursday and would like to see you. We can talk about ways to sabotage that overwrought boss of yours."

This was more to Radko's liking, for while he did not actively dislike Angelo, he was irritated that he had shoved this party idea down everyone's throat. He also loved spending time with Silas, whom he did not get to see very often. Radko knew Silas to be an honest man and a hard worker but also as a man who could let his hair down. They made plans to meet on Friday afternoon after work.

After he hung up he made a mental note to tell Ursula about Silas's visit. He knew Ursula liked Silas also, and Radko finally felt he and his wife had something to focus on besides the strained state of their relationship. Radko couldn't remember when he had felt close to Ursula, although he could place it in his mind as only about a week or so ago. Seems like eternity, he thought.

He looked at the clock. 2:00 p.m. Ursula wouldn't be out of school for another hour. He fidgeted for the next twenty minutes, unable to reignite the work focus he had earlier. He decided to leave work early and drive home. Maybe he and Ursula would get there at about the same time.

CHAPTER 39

Ursula was in no mood to get home early, or even on time. The more she mulled over her relationship with Radko, the angrier she got. She was angry at him, although she had some dim idea that he was in genuine turmoil, that he was torturing himself about the quandary he was in. She was not without sympathy toward her husband or toward the way he was. His passionate ambivalence was a not insignificant part of his charm; she could live with that.

She was mostly angry at herself. She felt she had allowed herself to be hoodwinked, talked into something that was on its face absurd. And she felt trapped: by the agreements and compromises she had made, by the fact that she had two kids, and by her doggedness in staying with something she felt in her heart was just not right. And it was something that would get worse as the children grew older. Her cheeks reddened with anger and shame when she realized how tangled their situation was with her children's future. Had she really thought that she could hoodwink her children forever, as she did herself? It's one thing to do this to oneself, she lectured; it's quite another to require duplicity of your children.

The conviction of her iniquity burned in her. She berated herself all the way to the babysitter's with allegations of her crimes

Absolution

against humanity, in this instance against two hapless five-year-olds whose parents could not face reality. She was filled with contempt for the poor decision she had made. She began to consider ways to remedy it.

When she saw Maggy, all of her uncharacteristic self-doubting ceased. She swept her up and kissed her sloppily on the forehead. Just the way my grandmother used to do, Ursula thought to herself, remembering how she hated it when that old woman slobbered all over her. She did the same to Sergie when he came running up to her. The kids, for a change, did not seem to mind that their mother was being so exuberant. They too felt the strain in their household, and they were happy to allow good feelings to visit them, at least for the moment.

When they collected their things and got into the car, Ursula suggested a snack. MacDonald's, perhaps? Or ice cream? The kids looked at each other incredulously. "Ice cream!" they shouted in unison. "Ice cream it is," responded their mother, and headed for the most extravagant ice cream shop she knew. She felt liberated to do something with the anger she felt.

When the three of them got home, they were all pleasantly sleepy. The kids went to lie down in their bedroom, and Ursula lay on the couch. She was asleep within minutes.

She was still asleep when Radko walked through the kitchen door. He felt a silence in the house: no TV, no chores being done, no dinner being prepared. His heart sank when he saw Ursula asleep on the couch. For a moment he thought she was dead.

"Honey?" he said gently. No response, but he saw her chest rise and fall slightly. Relieved, he went back into the kitchen without waking her.

Then he went looking for the kids. He found them asleep in their beds on top of the covers with their clothes on. He felt like one of the three bears returning home to find the young Goldilocks. He chuckled at the thought and went to find the newspaper.

An hour later, Ursula stirred. She sat up groggily and looked around. At first she did not notice Radko sitting in the easy chair across from the couch.

"Good morning," he said to her with a hint of a smile on his face.

"Hi," said Ursula, still groggy. "Have I been asleep long?"

"I don't know, Ursy, you were asleep when I got home about an hour ago."

Ursula's bleary eyes finally found the clock on top of the television. She stared at it trying to comprehend the notion of time. "You're early," she said.

"I left work early," Radko said. Then he went to make some coffee for his half-awake wife.

When Radko returned with two cups of steaming coffee, Ursula had stood up and stretched. As she took the coffee, she sat back down.

"I was out like a light," she said finally.

"No kidding," Radko replied.

They sat in silence for a few minutes sipping their coffee. Radko waited for Ursula to get awake enough so he could tell her about the party and Silas's visit. As consciousness returned to Ursula, she remembered her conversation with herself earlier that afternoon. She motioned for Radko to come sit by her, patting the couch with her right hand.

Radko almost jumped out of his chair, momentarily startling her. When he sat down, she took both coffee cups and put them down on the table; then she wrapped her arms around him. "I love you," she said to him in a low voice. Then she started to cry softly. "I will always love you."

Radko was thrilled to hear these words, but he was troubled by Ursula's tears.

"What's the matter, honey?" he asked.

"Just hold me for a minute," replied Ursula, feeling the warmth of his body with gratitude and relief.

Absolution

Radko was confused and uncertain. He felt Ursula both close and far away. He did not want the moment of physical closeness to go away, but he had a sense that this was not within his control. He turned to her and said, "I love you, too."

Silence for several more minutes. Then Ursula loosened her grasp and reached for her cup. "How come you're home early?" she asked.

Radko hesitated for a moment and then began telling Ursula about his conversation with Cassabelli and then with Silas. Ursula looked happy when she heard that Silas was coming on Friday. This, in turn, made Radko happy.

"Shall we have dinner here or go out?" she asked.

"I think here. And Silas can spend the night."

Then Ursula put her cup down and looked directly into Radko's eyes. She took his hand. "Radko," she said, "there is something I need to speak with you about." Ursula swallowed hard. Radko could not recall a time when Ursula was so anxious, and he found his own pulse quickening.

"I realized today that I have made some serious mistakes in my life with you," she continued. "Because I love you and because I wanted to be with you, I let myself be talked into something that I cannot...that I can no longer do." She paused and looked at Radko, who was pale and motionless. "I cannot live a lie. No, no; that's not exactly true. I can actually live a lie. But I can't force our children to live a life of duplicity any longer." She looked straight into Radko's eyes. "It's not right for us to require this of our children."

Radko's body did not move, but his eyes broke contact and turned to look downward. He felt the force of Ursula's words. Clear, correct, simply stated, loving. It was her ability to do this that was one of the big reasons he loved her so much. His eyes moved slowly back to Ursula, who was staring into her coffee cup.

"What do you want of me?" he asked her.

Ursula looked at Radko and studied his face. "I want to live openly. I want to be able to tell our children what their father does without shame, embarrassment, or hiding. I want to be free of this duplicity."

This is serious, Radko thought. "You mean, apart from the issue of being a bishop or not?"

"Yes," Ursula interrupted. "No matter what you do. I'm no longer willing to fudge on the truth." She looked away, feeling relieved but also sad.

Radko sat back on the couch and let out a low stream of air. He looked around the room as if seeing it for the first time. He looked at Ursula and thought about the kids asleep in the next room. "I understand," he said quietly.

CHAPTER 40

Later, after the kids woke up, had dinner, and eventually went back to bed, Ursula and Radko were lying in bed holding each other. Each had questions that were too hard to ask, so they lay there in silence, each looking for a way to begin, neither being certain that he or she could.

Radko spoke first. "Do you have a time frame in mind?" he asked.

"A time frame for what?" Ursula said.

"You were pretty clear about what you said earlier. That you are no longer willing to live the way we do. I was wondering if you had any specific plans."

"Plans for …?"

Radko looked at her. "For leaving," he said.

Ursula sighed. No, she did not have plans to leave, she thought to herself. She was not exactly shocked by the question; it was just that it seemed too businesslike for the setting. Also, she wondered about what Radko really wanted. It seemed that he was leaning toward committing himself to the vocation he had.

Absolution

"Radko," she said. "I don't want to leave you. I want us to remain married but to live our lives openly. I don't want to teach our kids to lie about their lives."

"Ursy," Radko said softly. "You've been very patient about my compromises over the years. I know that. I just need a little time to get myself clear about this whole situation." He paused. "I am really glad Silas is coming into town. I can talk it through with him." He thought he sounded more hopeful than he was.

CHAPTER 41

When Silas's plane was coming in for a landing, he looked out the window at the city in which he was raised. Dirty as ever, he thought to himself, not without affection. He didn't dislike Chicago. It no longer felt like his home; he had been in Rome for over a decade, but he had a warm spot in his heart for the vast, sprawling city of big shoulders.

He had been making a list of people to contact. On Thursday, he would pay a courtesy visit to Angelo Cassabelli and perhaps the cardinal. On Thursday afternoon, he would travel to Bismarck, North Dakota, the diocese that Radko was slated for. He reminded himself that it was an American city, a big step forward for the plan, although Tibet might be a tad more user-friendly. In the back of his mind, he was doubtful that Radko would go along with the plan. Not because he didn't want to, but Silas remembered how difficult it had been for Radko to leave the East Coast to settle in Chicago. The thought of a northern outpost close to the Canadian border might be more than he could manage.

This, of course, was probably the smallest obstacle to Archbishop Mueller's ambitions for an American member of his elite club. Silas wondered about Ursula's role in this whole scheme.

Absolution

To date, he had not heard her voice one complaint about living the double life that she and Radko had together. He felt both affection and respect for Ursula. He knew that many women would not even consider such an outrageous arrangement. But Ursula pulled it off with no apparent sign of resentment. Of course, he was not privy to conversations between her and Radko, but he was a good friend of Radko's and thought he would know if it were a contentious issue.

The visit to Bismarck was unannounced and would no doubt surprise the administrator of the diocese, a local priest named Caldwell who was running things until a new bishop could be designated. Caldwell was doing a satisfactory job running the small diocese, but a diocese without a bishop is always in suspended animation. The administrator could make day-to-day decisions and respond to crises, but he could not set the vision or agenda for the diocese overall. For that it was necessary to have a bishop, a man with both the authority and responsibility to set a steady course. A man in a line of succession reaching all the way back to the original twelve apostles, the first bishops. Silas knew that Radko would be excellent for this position. He was intelligent, thoughtful, and steady. He understood how the church worked and knew how to tow the line in terms of orthodoxy. Silas didn't think that Radko would ever allow himself to articulate an unorthodox view in public. His doubts, his real beliefs, were personal and not for public consumption. The way it is with most people in leadership positions that he knew, Silas thought to himself.

On Friday afternoon, Silas would be back in Chicago to visit with Radko. He would probably have dinner with him and Ursula and perhaps spend the night at their home in the west suburbs. Under ordinary circumstances, he would look forward to such a visit and use it to catch up with people who were on his short list of real friends. But this time was different. It would be good to see his friends, but he dreaded the position he was about to place Radko in. Silas's sole consolation was that Radko would have an opportunity to say no and thereby put an end to his participation in this whole mess. It was conceivable that Radko would even reject his selection as bishop, although this was rarely done, and remain in his current position with the Archdiocese of Chicago. In his heart, Silas hoped that this would be the outcome. He knew that Radko was happy in his work and rooted in his relationship with his wife. More than anything, Silas hoped that his friendship with Radko and with Ursula would survive the weekend.

But Silas was a pragmatist, and he knew that outcomes in situations like these could not be predicted with great accuracy. However this weekend went, he would still be seeing Ted Catsweiler next week. It has been months, Silas thought to himself. Telephone contact was frequent, and Silas enjoyed that, but nothing substituted for physical presence, for being with a man he felt was his soul mate. He and Ted would have a couple of days together before they both came to Chicago to deal with Cassabelli at the party the vicar in Chicago concocted.

Silas thought about Ted and how close they had grown over the years. Ted and Silas came from different parts of the country but were in many ways identical. Both came from working-class backgrounds; both worked hard in school; both came out as gay in their early twenties after trying straight sex in their late adolescence. Both dabbled in casual sexual encounters until they met each other. The relationship that ensued changed all that. Much more satisfying being with one person you love and trust, Silas thought, remembering some of the more harrowing moments of his cruising life. Silas thought back to his early declarations to Ted about his need not to be exclusive; to be free to pursue whatever his desires suggested. These seemed like quaint adolescent impulses now to Silas, who had not had another sex partner for years. He was aware that he had never amended those declarations to Ted directly. He and Ted never talked about their relationship, and that suited Silas just fine. He hated talking about relationships. He just wanted to

Absolution

have one, and he did. As the plane landed, Silas was filled with warmth and longing to see his friend.

CHAPTER 42

On Friday morning, Radko was relieved to be going to work. He and Ursula had not spoken much for the previous forty-eight hours, and he looked forward to seeing Silas. They were planning lunch in the city, and then Radko was taking the rest of the day off. He and Silas would eventually make their way back to Radko's house, where Ursula would be preparing a special dinner. On Thursday, Radko had scoured several wine shops looking for Silas's favorite Amarone. Pricey stuff, but worth it for a friend he saw so seldom.

The morning was tortuous. Radko saw Cassabelli briefly and found him unusually businesslike. Radko knew that he had met with Silas yesterday, although he was not privy to their conversation. Radko worked hard to focus on his work so as to make the time go more quickly.

At noon on the dot, Silas appeared at his office door. Radko leapt out of his chair to greet him, giving him a solid Italian *abbraccio*.

"How have you been?" said Radko enthusiastically.

"OK," said Silas, genuinely happy to see his friend.

Absolution

They chatted about nothing for a few minutes: about Silas's flight and Radko's work schedule, about Cassabelli and other people they knew in common, about how lucky it was that Silas would be in town for Radko's party.

Radko stiffened at this last item. "It's not my party," he said a bit too sarcastically. "This is something Cassabelli dreamed up for God-knows-what reason."

"My apologies," said Silas. "I know it's Angelo's thing, but I'm still glad that I'll be here for it."

After a few minutes, Radko suggested lunch. "You must be hungry after doing the Lord's work all morning. How about Carey's?"

"Great," said Silas.

So off they went to the trendy, Chicago-style eatery, just the thing for two guys hashing over old times, current times, and the unmentioned bond between them. Radko felt a wave of contentment that had been eluding him ever since he first got Silas's note weeks ago.

After they had eaten, Silas and Radko sat at the table sipping coffee, both feeling the pleasure of companionship that didn't require any explication. Silas, who grew up in Chicago but had left it decades ago, could not deny to himself how much he cherished everything about this experience: the setting, the friendship, the island of tranquility in the hurly-burly world of the Midwest's largest and most significant metropolis. He was glad to be home.

He was not glad, however, about what he was about to do. In a break in the conversation, he looked at Radko with a plaintive expression on his face.

"Radko," he began, "there's something I need to talk to you about."

Radko looked at him without a trace of guile, either on his face or in his soul.

"What is it, Silas?" he said.

Silas was quiet for a moment. "One of the reasons I'm here is to talk to you about something that is...of great significance."

Radko looked at Silas expectantly. There was no fear in his mind, no apprehension. He loved this moment of peaceful being-together with one of his oldest friends.

Silas looked at him squarely. "Within the next few weeks, there will be a public announcement that you have been named Bishop of Bismarck, North Dakota."

Radko's expression did not change. It was frozen in flight.

Silas continued: "This appointment will be communicated to the Papal Pronuncio in Washington, D.C., and you will receive a letter from the Vatican making it official."

I thought these things were supposed to take time, Radko thought. He thought he had at least six months or a year to digest what he had recognized was a high probability. Faced with it now, he had some trouble breathing.

"You will not be named an auxiliary bishop. The See of Bismarck has been vacant for almost a year, and the administrator, a capable priest by the name of Caldwell, has been running the affairs of the diocese since the former bishop died. You will be the Ordinary, the man in charge."

Radko strained to keep track of what Silas was saying. Okay, he thought to himself: I will be named to a diocese directly. No prep time as an assistant, or auxiliary, bishop in some large diocese. Where the hell is Bismarck, anyway? Did he say North Dakota? The congenial warmth he felt moments before was gone, and Radko was struggling to be attentive while feeling bereft.

Multiple images flashed through his mind. Ursula, the twins, his home in the suburbs, his ordination, his job, Cassabelli, his life as a priest. He thought of Gordana and his parents. His parents would be proud, his sister worried. He felt as if he were in a slow-motion collision. Only it wasn't a car but his life that was at risk.

Absolution

Silas was silent, looking at his friend for some sign of response. Radko's expression had not changed for some moments, and Silas was uncertain of what to say next. He kept waiting.

Finally, Radko let out a breath that he had been holding since he heard the words "public announcement" and "bishop" in the same sentence. He looked down at his coffee cup and slowly returned his gaze to Silas, whose face seemed to be receding rapidly away from him. An errant tear rolled down his cheek.

"Silas," he stammered, "I… I… I…," and then he paused for lack of air.

He tried again. "I don't, I don't think…I don't think …I'm shocked."

Silas looked at Radko with more sympathy than he thought himself capable of. If he were less serious or hardened a man, he would have wept with Radko. Instead, he reached out and held Radko's hand in his. "I know this is difficult for you," he said. "I wanted to be the one to tell you."

They sat together in silence. The tables around them began to empty as people returned to work or to their lives. Silas motioned for the check and handed the waiter a credit hard when he brought it. Within minutes, he had paid. There was nothing to do but leave.

"Why don't we go for a walk?" Silas suggested gently. He stood up and led Radko to the door of the restaurant. He hoped Radko would not faint or fall or begin wailing.

They walked for several blocks before either of them spoke. Radko couldn't take his mind off his conversation with Ursula two days before. The choice that he knew about in his imagination became the choice that now yawned before him, and he felt that his next step could be his last. To lose Ursula was too painful to contemplate. To end his life as a priest in an ignominious refusal to serve as a bishop in the church was equally horrifying. All his posturing, all his tentative dismissal and selective beliefs now seemed paltry, like so much adolescent posturing. If he ever thought he had an immortal soul, he now felt it hanging in the balance. Hell did not seem like an abstract or primitive concept so much as it seemed a real possibility if he accepted either of his choices.

As if feeling his distress, Silas put his hand on Radko's arm. "There's another side to what's happening," he began, "and it's going to take some explaining. Why don't we go someplace where we can talk?"

Radko looked at him incredulously. What more can he say? he wondered. He has just taken a dagger to the fabric of my life, and he wants to talk some more? Damn you, Silas, he thought. But aloud he said "Sure, there's a quiet little pub close to here."

It was in that quiet little pub that Silas laid out Mueller's plan. How for over twenty years now the archbishop has been secretly sanctioning married clergy wherever he could. He named some of the bishops around the world who were married and lived with their wives, some openly but most secretly. He talked about Mueller's vision of the church as the institution that is charged with learning what charity or love really is and how he sees his little project as a step in the direction of increasing respect for and tolerance of affectional bonds throughout the church and the world. He also described Mueller's personal odyssey through the Second Vatican Council and the bitterness that spawned this avocation of his. Finally, he got to Radko's part: how he was to be the first married bishop in the developed world. "I am sorry, my friend," Silas said simply.

Neither spoke for some minutes. Radko's head was swimming. The entire story Silas was laying out seemed so improbable—even preposterous. Radko knew how the church worked, or so he thought, and he could not imagine that Mueller could get away with this stuff, no matter how highly placed he was. He thought back on the effect Wolfgang had had on him during their dinner in Rome a few weeks ago. Potent, he thought: convincing, easy, suave. And manipulative as hell, Radko could see in retrospect. A wave of revulsion ran through his body. He wanted to vomit. He wanted no part of this cockeyed conspiracy. He wanted his wife, his home.

Absolution

The fact that Silas was a part of this conspiracy sickened him further. He thought of Silas as his best friend, the brother he never had, a confidant on whom he could rely. And he was in on the duplicity. He lied to him. He thought back to their meeting in Rome the day before Radko was to contact Mueller. He remembered how Silas listened intently and sipped his drink and ate his food but didn't really say much. It was Radko doing all the talking, and now he realized that Silas was just doing his job, prepping Radko for his meeting with Mueller. He arranged it: It was Silas who gave him Mueller's name.

"Silas," he said finally, "how could you do this to me?"

Silas had no reply.

Radko turned and looked across the room at the handful of patrons who were talking quietly in dim corners of the dark-stained wood tavern. He didn't know what to do. At the moment, he didn't really trust Silas to have his best interests at heart. He tried to clear his mind, stretched his back, and sat up straighter in his chair.

"Look, Silas," he said. "If I understand you correctly, in a few weeks there will be an announcement that I'm being named bishop of some godforsaken diocese in the northern part of the United States. And you want me to believe that I can do this while remaining married to Ursula and raising my children. And this makes sense because there are some rebel bishops in some far-flung corners of the world who are doing this now. Am I getting this right?

Silas tried to ignore the sarcasm in Radko's voice. "Yes," he said.

"And I'm supposed to go along with this because if I don't I will probably have to resign the priesthood altogether and maybe the church and probably have my personal life splattered all over the U.S. media as yet another wayward priest who has been leading a double life? So I can suffer the ignominy of that or I can risk the ignominy of being discovered later to be living a double life when I'm installed as bishop?" Plenty of ignominy to go around, he thought to himself.

"Radko," Silas said, "I understand that this is difficult for you and that there are certain risks involved." He paused and thought for a moment. "I will also understand, and Mueller will understand, if you decide to refuse this selection. We will do what we can to help you go in the direction you want. But don't you see that this is just a way of building on what you've already been doing? How well-suited you are to be the one to make this step? As for the diocese we've chosen..." he caught himself quickly, "that Mueller has chosen, it is a large geographical area with a lot of options for privacy."

"You forgot one thing," Radko said, interrupting this nonsense. "Ursula."

"What about Ursula?" Silas asked.

"Well," said Radko, "apart from the fact that she and the kids would have to live in a cave to remain separated from my work as the bishop of Bismarck, she told me a few days ago that she's no longer willing to carry on this charade. And you know what? I'm not sure I am either."

Silas thought for a while. "The way we envisioned this working," he began somewhat tentatively, "Ursula and the kids would not live in the diocese. You could visit them several times a month, perhaps even weekly..."

"You are not hearing me, Silas. Ursula doesn't want to do this to Maggy and Sergie. She doesn't want to lie to them. And she's right. We shouldn't have to lie to them. I don't see any alternative but to resign completely from the priesthood."

Silas thought for a while. What he thought was that he could convince Ursula to go along with this if given a chance to speak with her. He was unsure how Radko's reaction might alter his plans for the evening. To Radko, he said: "I think you need some time to think about these things. We don't have a lot of time, but we have some. At this point, the selection process is committed, but you'll have the option of refusing when the letter arrives."

Absolution

I could resign before it comes out, Radko thought. He too was wondering about the wisdom of the plans he made for the rest of the day.

CHAPTER 43

Ursula spent the day on automatic pilot. She had so many currents of feeling running through her that she didn't know which ones to focus on. She thought about her declaration to Radko about what to teach their children, and she felt, unfortunately, that she was correct about that. But she also dreaded the prospect that she and Radko would not work out as a couple or that he would be hopelessly unhappy in some other line of work if they did stay married. Either of these could also have a negative impact on the children.

She also thought of Silas. She was fond of him and looked forward to his visit almost as much as her husband. So the thought of preparing dinner and making everything nice for him was a pleasant patch of feeling amid the torrents of scary and unsettling ones she was having. So she went through the day doing what she ordinarily did, trying to keep some of the more distressing possibilities at bay.

As she left the routine of school and went to collect the kids, she felt her insides tremble. Would she really leave Radko? Could she? She knew she could: Ursula did not lack belief in her ability to survive in the world. But she did not want to. At the same time, she was wary of her tendency to think that she could do anything, no matter what the consequences. That was one of the big reasons why she got into this predicament in the first place.

She wasn't so much angry with Radko as frustrated with his dogged devotion to his priesthood. How could this be so important to him? Why couldn't he just join some other church that allows their priests or ministers to marry? She knew that the questions and solutions that were obvious to her were neither obvious nor solutions for her husband. His connection to the church was more deeply rooted in him than that, more a part of his identity that she had recognized in their early years together.

The kids were quieter than usual when she took them to the store to pick up groceries for dinner. They had always been very sensitive to Ursula's mood, and today was no exception. Ursula selected her groceries with intense attention to her list.

Marguerite the Brave spoke first. "Is dinner going to be quiet again, Mommy?"

"No, Maggy," she said, "I don't think so. Daddy's friend Silas is coming to dinner, and I think we will all have a good time."

This seemed to please Maggy. Her parents didn't have visitors for dinner very often, but when they did, she and Sergie got to stay up later than normal. "Goodie," she said.

Yeah, Goodie, thought Ursula, who was realizing the limitations of her explanation about divorcing couples. At this moment, she felt the warmth in her heart that she always felt when her children taught her things like this.

As she drove home, the kids began chattering more freely in the back seat of her small car. Ursula felt strong being with them. If Radko wants to be a bishop, he can do that, she thought to herself. He just can't do it with his wife and children. This saddened Ursula a great deal, but the strength she found in her bond to her children was the more potent emotion. Whatever it takes, she thought to herself.

When the three arrived home, no one was there. This was not unexpected, and Ursula set about taking the groceries in and getting the kids settled. Sergei asked if he could go next door and play with John, another five year old. After Ursula called John's mom, she watched him cross their lawn and knock on the door of the identical house next to theirs. When he vanished inside, she turned her attention to dinner.

A few minutes later, the telephone rang. Ursula picked it up on the third ring. It was Radko.

"Ursula," he began, "I just left Silas at the cathedral rectory, where he spent the night yesterday. I was wondering what you were planning for dinner."

This seemed like an odd thing for Radko to say. He must remember that they discussed dinner plans at some length last evening. Ursula wondered absently if Radko's mind was weakening.

"Radko, we're having all the things we wrote down together last evening. I'm planning on dinner at 7:00 p.m.," she said.

Radko continued hesitantly, "Things have gotten more complicated than even I could have imagined. Silas shared some additional news that we all need to talk about. Are the kids eating with us?"

Ursula put the receiver in front of her face and considered it a moment. The voice sounded like her husband's voice, but she couldn't help but think that perhaps it was an impostor. Or maybe an impersonator.

"Yes, Radko, the twins will be eating with us," she said replacing the receiver to her ear. As they have every time we've eaten together for the past five years, she thought but did not say aloud.

"Okay. I'll call you back later," Radko said. And he hung up.

Why is he going to call me back later? Ursula wondered. She couldn't imagine what news Radko was talking about or why he was concerned about the children being there for dinner. Or why he had called her at all. She shook her head and resumed preparing

Absolution

the dinner that seemed to be getting more complicated by the minute.

When Radko hung up the phone, he felt like an idiot. This would be a lot easier if Ursula and I were on more amiable terms, he thought to himself. He was still agitated after leaving Silas at the pub alone. Radko had declared that he needed some time to think about this whole situation and told Silas he would call him around five at the cathedral rectory. He felt manly leaving the small dark pub and walking out on Silas. It was one of the few times in his life that he had taken a stand about anything. But as usual, he was uncertain what to do next. His senseless conversation with Ursula did not make him feel manly. If anything, he felt confused and uncertain. He knew he wasn't making sense to her. Calm down, he ordered himself. He walked into a Starbuck's and ordered an expresso.

Item number one on his agenda was what to do in the near term, that is, what he was going to do for dinner this evening. Should he go ahead and have that traitor Silas over as originally planned? He thought so, but he was so angry at Silas that he did not know if he could remain calm through dinner. The more he ruminated about this, the more he realized that, though he was mad as hell at Silas, who up until an hour ago he regarded as his best friend, he also recognized that Silas was the one with the information he needed. Silas was part of this ludicrous plot. If Radko could prevail upon Silas to tell him more of the ins and outs of the story, maybe he could think about it more clearly. Right now, all Radko wanted to do was run as far away from anything to do with the church as he possibly could. He had never felt this impulse before. Not during his courtship with Ursula; not when the twins were born; not when his job got frustrating. He slowly realized that he felt shame being a part of an institution that was so secretive, that tolerated stupid conspiracies, and that regarded marriage as a second-rate way of life. Between the bitterness of the coffee and the bitterness in his gut, he almost gagged.

Paul Martin Midden

Radko looked at his watch: 4:45. He decided to go ahead with dinner and called Silas. He said he would pick him up at 5:30 p.m. Silas sounded pleased.

CHAPTER 44

The trip from the chancery to the Slopovich residence was eerie and for the most part silent. Radko could barely breathe as he drove through the heavy traffic toward the west suburbs. He had honked for Silas at the chancery. When he got into the car, all he said was "thanks." Radko made some guttural assent and drove on.

Halfway across town, Silas spoke. "Radko, please, I know this is a difficult situation for you. But I also want you to know that I value our friendship and that I'm not doing any of this to hurt you or to ruin your life." He paused, looking straight ahead. "It would have happened with or without my participation."

Radko gave that some thought. He recognized immediately that he had been assuming that Silas was a prime mover in this series of events, that he was at the heart of the action, and that he was in on all the principle decisions. As removed from his warm feelings for Silas as he was at the moment, he had to acknowledge that he had probably jumped to conclusions. A tiny bit of warmth reasserted itself into his attitude.

"Okay, Silas," he said. "Exactly what is your role in this…this…this conspiracy?"

Absolution

Silas recognized an opening when he saw one. "I was approached by Archbishop Mueller about nine years ago," he began. "We had something of a friendship. We both loved the outdoors and went hiking in the mountains one weekend. It was there that he told me the story of what he was doing. I must admit at first I thought it was lunacy or that he was putting me on. But he was serious. I didn't know it then, but you were already in his sights by that time. You and a handful of his other students from North American College." He paused and glanced over at Radko, who was listening intently.

"Mueller does his homework," Silas continued. "He had me pegged as a safe prospect because of my own, um, extracurricular activities...."

Radko shot a glance at Silas. "What activities?" he demanded.

In a moment, Silas had to make some decisions about how much he should share with his old friend. Discretion had always been his preferred option, and he felt at home with secrecy. But he had a feeling that Radko would pick up any insincerity on his part or any attempt to package the truth in a disingenuous way. He inhaled a sharp breath.

"He knows about the fact that I am gay and that I have a lover."

He does? Radko thought. How did he know that? Silas was supposed to be his best friend, and he just learned two important things about him that he never knew. Radko was shocked. He wondered if a person could overdose from too much information.

Radko noticed his body shaking at the same time that he noticed the sign for a rest stop. Without saying a word, he pulled into the parking area and eased the car into a vacant space. He closed his eyes and put his head on the steering wheel. Silas looked at him intently.

After a minute, Radko brought his head back upright and rolled down his window. He needed air. He undid his seat belt and opened the door, placing his feet on the broken asphalt pavement. He cradled his head with his hands. He thought he might throw up but didn't. He just sat there feeling his life vanishing into a dream, a phantasm, a wish. There was nothing to anchor him into it. He wished it were Ursula sitting beside him.

After some minutes, Radko stood up and walked a few steps. Silas got out of his side of the car and stood up, watching from behind the open car door. He was unsure of what to do, but he was concerned that Radko might be ill. It hurt him to see his friend like this, and he wanted to help in any way he could. He also felt responsible for being the one to lay such heavy stuff on him all in one afternoon.

Finally, Radko turned and looked at Silas. "You're gay and have a lover?" he said incredulously.

"Yes," Silas replied.

Radko regarded Silas askance. "How come you never told me this before?" he asked.

Silas shrugged. "I work in the Vatican. I'm a priest. I know how to keep secrets." Then he looked down at the pavement. When he looked up again at Radko, he said, "I got so used to keeping that part of my life private that I never seriously considered telling you." His face turned dark. "The reason I'm telling you now is that our friendship is in the balance. I don't want to lose you as a friend, no matter what happens with your career."

Despite his uncertain physical condition, Radko felt renewed warmth toward Silas. He knew about secrets. He knew how it was easier to keep a secret from everyone, especially if it was something that could not bear public scrutiny. The outrage that Radko felt moments before dissolved into compassion for the burdens that Silas bore. Silas, who married him, who covered for him, who baptized his children, who had always been there for him. He walked over and put his arms around his oldest friend. "I'm sorry for being so screwed up about all this. Thank you for telling me."

Silas was so surprised by Radko's gesture at first that he tensed, thinking Radko might attack him. When he heard these words,

Absolution

however, his tension eased, and he leaned into Radko's warm embrace. A tear rolled down the cheek of the man who never cried.

CHAPTER 45

The balance of the long drive west held none of the tension of the first half. Radko and Silas spoke about the part of Silas's life that Silas had never discussed with anyone. Radko asked questions gently, trying not to put too much pressure on his refound friend. He listened intently to Silas as he told him about his early exploits, about trying to be straight, about finding his lover. He didn't mention the man's name, and Radko didn't press. By the time they got to Radko's house, the old bond was there again, a bit stronger for the struggle they had just been through.

When Ursula heard the car in the driveway, she turned down the gas on the stove and checked the oven. Walking by a mirror on her way to the back door, she fussed with her hair, making sure she looked okay for her husband's friend. She was looking forward to seeing Silas, but she was wary of seeing Radko, whose behavior on the phone suggested that he was under serious stress. She did not know what to expect.

She opened the door and walked out onto the small back porch. Radko and Silas were just getting out of the car. They both moved with uncharacteristic gentleness and respect and with none of the

Absolution

heartiness they usually displayed with each other. At first she thought that perhaps they were not speaking.

"Hi, honey," Radko said.

Silas greeted her with a hug and a kiss. "Ursula, it's so good to see you. It's been so long. How are you?" he asked solicitously.

Ursula could not put her finger on what was going on. The pair seemed fine, if subdued. Deeper, she thought. Usually they were like high school students on their way to a football game. Nonetheless, she was happy to see Silas and relieved that Radko appeared sane. "Please, come in," she said.

Ursula called to Maggy to come say hello, and Maggy did so with more than compliant grace. She loved the idea of company and, even though she had never met Silas, immediately gave him the benefit of whatever doubts and apprehensions she might have had about meeting a stranger. She also got more attention because her brother was next door. She liked that.

Radko escorted Silas into the living room while Ursula took drink orders. She had the makings of martinis ready and dutifully fetched the drinks. The four of them sat down in the worn but comfortable living room furniture. "Maggy," Silas began "The last time I saw you, you were a little baby. How you've grown. How old are you now?"

Maggy beamed. She liked Silas. "I will be six on my next birthday," she declared with precision.

"Well, you are turning into a beautiful young lady," Silas fawned.

Ursula told Maggy to go next door and get her brother. Maggy pouted mildly, but she would not risk being anything less than a perfect child by disobeying her mother in front of this new friend. She went to get her brother as her mother watched through the side window.

When Sergei came back, he was less than happy. "We were watching *Sesame Street*," he exclaimed to his mother. Nonetheless, he was duly introduced to Silas, who commented on his handsome appearance.

After these formalities, Ursula ushered the twins to the den in the back of the house. She had made them popcorn and told them that dinner would be ready later this evening. She had rented their favorite movie. They both did as they were told, although Maggy balked at being in exile. Throughout the rest of the evening, she found many pretexts for returning and intruding upon the grown-ups' conversation.

After sipping martinis and munching on appetizers, Ursula got up to prepare dinner. Silas looked at Radko affectionately. "She's a wonderful woman, Radko," he said. "You're a lucky man."

At that moment, despite all that had happened in the past eight hours, Radko felt like a lucky man. He was glad that Ursula and Silas hit it off so well, and the bitterness he had felt about his friend a few hours ago was a distant memory. He luxuriated in the moment of intimacy, friendship, and the unhurried consumption of life's gifts. He was happy.

When Ursula was ready, she called for the children, who were glad to be freed from the small den, and for Radko and Silas, who were beginning to rediscover each other. All assembled at Ursula's command.

Dinner was well-orchestrated, of course, with each course coming at the appointed time, each well-selected wine poured at the proper moment, each utensil properly arranged. Silas talked about the gossip from Rome and Radko about the local chancery. For the sake of the children, no titles or offices were spoken; everything was first or last name at such and such office. It could have been a conversation about any major international corporation.

After dessert, Ursula ordered the kids to bed, and with mild protesting they went to get ready. At last, Silas, Ursula, and Radko were alone together.

Absolution

"Silas," Ursula said, "it's wonderful to see you." She had a slightly glassy look in her eyes, the kind that wine makes after a third glass.

"It's wonderful to see you, too," Silas replied. "It's been too long." Silas was clear-eyed.

It was Radko who took the risk. "Silas brought me news of my upcoming appointment as bishop," he said to Ursula.

Ursula shot him an alarmed glance. "So soon?" she asked after a moment.

"It is soon," Silas interjected. "Usually these things take much longer."

Silence hung above the trio. "When will it take effect?" Ursula asked.

Silas explained the process as best he could. How in two weeks the papal ambassador to the United States would be notified by mail and how Radko would be receiving a letter in the week or so after that. Announcements were always made on Tuesdays.

"So just a few weeks," Ursula said.

"Yes," replied Silas. He felt that he was an intruder into intimate territory, but he wanted a voice at this table. "I suppose you two have been talking about this," he said softly.

Radko and Ursula looked at each other as Radko replied to Silas. "Yes," he said, "we've been talking about it."

"But not tonight," Ursula added, turning to face Silas. "Tonight is for friendship."

CHAPTER 46

The next morning, Silas took a taxi back into town. He told Radko and Ursula that he had errands to run before going off to some other American cities on Vatican business. He would be back in Chicago on Friday evening for the party. As he took his leave, he hugged both of them.

"*Corragio*," he said to Radko. Courage.

"*Arrivederci*," he said to Ursula, kissing her gently on the cheek.

After he left, Radko and Ursula walked slowly back into the house. It felt emptier all of a sudden. Ursula poured them each another cup of coffee and they sat facing each other.

"Well," Ursula said, "I suppose the time has come for us to make some decisions."

Radko looked at her with fatigue in his face. Usually he loved her directness, her willingness to tackle any issue at any time in any place. But after yesterday he was tired.

"Yes," he said wearily. "In a few weeks, we shall have to make some decisions."

Then he changed the subject and began talking about Silas and their encounters yesterday. How he had left Silas at the pub and thought about canceling dinner. About his senseless phone conver-

Absolution

sation with Ursula earlier. About Silas's revelations about his sexuality. At that point, Ursula's eyebrows lifted.

"You did not know that he was gay?" she said.

Radko looked at her. "No, I didn't," he said with a quizzical look.

"Hmm," Ursula replied. "I thought everyone knew."

Even though he felt a little bit foolish for not knowing something that Ursula seemed to think was widely known to everyone, Radko was grateful that the focus of the conversation was not on him and his decision about being a bishop or not.

"What do you mean, 'everyone'?" Radko asked.

Ursula broke into a small smile. "Radko, I honestly assumed Silas was gay. In fact, I always thought he had something of a crush on you. You never felt that? When he would look at you or touch you or pay so much attention to you?"

"We're friends," Radko said with a defensive tone in his voice. "That's what friends do."

"Not my friends," said Ursula.

CHAPTER 47

As his taxi drove away from the little bungalow, Silas sighed. He was genuinely happy he had leveled with Radko about his sexual life, but he was frustrated that Ursula was so hard-shelled about talking about Radko's prospects for being bishop. He was unsure if he would have another chance to talk with her about it before he returned to Rome on the 11th. He thought maybe he could postpone that return and try again next weekend. Maybe Ursula would like some company during the party she wouldn't be attending next Friday. Ted could probably handle Angelo, whose importance in this drama was diminishing each moment.

Silas spent a good part of the trip back to town thinking of Ted. They would be together by tonight, and Silas could not wait. He had made reservations at the George Hotel, a small but elegant inn on E Street in DC. Ted was to meet him there at 6:00 p.m. for dinner, and the two would spend the next three days together, sightseeing, talking, and visiting the magnificent institutions of the American Empire: the Smithsonian, the National Gallery, the National Cathedral. They would do so as a couple, not as two solitary celibates living severely compartmentalized lives, but as an affectionate unit, a single whole. He cherished the thought of the next

Absolution

three days. This was why Mueller's plan, no matter how preposterous, deserved his time, energy, and attention. To make this natural arrangement okay, to seize it from the darkness and suspicion that had become so militant in recent years.

Silas pondered the American landscape. He remained an American citizen, but it had been over a decade since he'd called an American city or town home. He felt like a citizen of the world; and, in fact, he shared much of the popular European skepticism of American policy under the Republican administration. He was especially outraged about the constitutional amendment proposed by the administration restricting marriage to heterosexual unions. As if words on paper can stem the tide, he thought to himself. Other developments heartened him: the election of an openly gay Anglican bishop happened here; even the starchy Lutherans were discussing gay rights. These were things that seemed impossible to him earlier in his life. While skeptical of American policy, he saw current political trends as a passing fad and looked forward to a time when the pendulum would swing back to more tolerant values. He was glad he was not involved in elected politics.

Skeptical or not, he loved the U.S. Life in Rome suited his sensitive nature and gave him a sweep of experience that was not so available in the United States, protected as it still was by vast oceans. But European life in general was too narrow, too parochial, and too bureaucratic for his allegiance. He knew that the future of America remained the future of western culture. As an American and as a man, he was proud of that.

Silas told the driver to go straight to O'Hare. He would be back in town later in the week and could collect his things from the cathedral rectory then. For now, even though he had some time at the airport to wait, he would rather be en route to Ted than pretend he had something more important to do at the cathedral rectory. He called the residence and told them that his plans had changed and that he wouldn't be back till Wednesday. Feeling relieved, he began to daydream about the next few days.

CHAPTER 48

Angelo Cassabelli was at the dining table when Silas called, and the dining table was within earshot of the telephone. He heard the nun who took the call thank Monsignor Ranke for calling. She repeated the instructions he gave her: Monsignor Cassabelli was not available. You can always count on foreign nuns to be the most punctilious, he thought to himself, smiling.

He was glad Silas wasn't coming back today. He had some calls to make to ensure that all the principals would be at the party next Friday evening, and he was eager to be relieved of the burden of hosting that effete Romano for the better part of the day. After finishing his dinner, he went to his rectory office and began calling the people on his list.

Two hours later, he was frustrated and angry. Gordana had given him a list of seven people she said knew Radko personally. Catsweiler had given him four of the same names. He spoke with five of them, and not a single one was available for the party on Friday. They knew Slopovich, but they obviously did not regard him as a close friend. He was furious with Radko's sister. She was in on whatever it was that he was hiding, he thought to himself.

Absolution

If this were simply a party given for the reason he had stated, this list would have been a matter of small moment for Angelo. But he was after a specific target: he wanted to learn more about the mysterious Judicial Vicar, whose life was getting more mysterious the closer he looked. Even Silas's sudden absence from the rectory today now seemed part of a larger plan, a plan to keep Angelo Cassabelli off the trail. The trail of what, he did not know; but Father Cassabelli could smell a conspiracy when he ran across one, and the air was pungent.

He fumed for a while and looked out the window. As he swung his chair around, he opened his side drawer and pulled out a package of unopened snack cakes that he kept there for just this occasion: to nurse his frustration, to give him something to do while he thought his way through the options available to him, to feed his omnivorous ego. He munched and munched. The more he thought about the situation, the more he came to recognize that not only was Radko hiding something but that he had friends and relatives who were obviously in on the plot. Well, Angelo had his methods as well, and once again he congratulated himself for devising the ruse of the appreciation party. In that venue, he was on his home turf; he could work people and get information they didn't even know they were giving. Armed with an unrestricted belief in his ability to play people, Angelo turned his chair back around to his desk, grabbing another snack on the way.

CHAPTER 49

Annie Kanne's name was at best unfortunate. It didn't matter that the original version, Anita Kanne, had a certain air of distinction about it. That air was lost somewhere before middle school, when she became for all time Annie Kanne, or, as she thought of it more often, Annie Cannie. She surrendered long ago to pronouncing her name this way, as everyone else did. Now, at age thirty-five, she still responded to suggestions that she do something with those juvenile syllables. "Annie Kanne" translated roughly into "Yes" or "I can do it" or, more precisely, "It can be done by Annie." It was a harmless if pitiably childish usage, but in her job as receptionist at the vicariate office of the chancery, everyone was good-natured about it. While she answered the telephone, actual visitors were few in her department, so it mattered little that everyone treated a grown-up woman as if she were in sixth grade.

They did this despite the fact that it was Annie who kept the department running. She was meticulously organized and obsessive about detail. There was no limit to the paltry nature of her concerns or the banality of her questions. Not a hint of guile or irony ever crossed her face. She often brought mind-numbing, picayunish detail to her superiors. Sometimes Father Cassabelli objected to

Absolution

this, as when he was short with her for asking if she should send a fax now, when he asked, or later, when she had time. But even Father Cassabelli, who was known to be short with people at times, appreciated the clockwork precision with which the office he supposedly managed ran. He knew how important Annie was to the ease of his job. Annie Cannie, indeed. She knew where everything was, how everything worked, who was responsible for what. She was always on time, rarely took time off, and treated the office as if it were her personal domain and personal responsibility.

Annie was surrounded by some of the most powerful men in the archdiocese—Father Cassabelli, the Vicar General; Father Slopovich, the Judicial Vicar; Father Mulligan, the Vicar for Clergy; and the list went on and on. She was largely impervious to the heavy weight of power concentrated in the offices for which she was responsible; her most common response to any request was "Yes" or "Annie Kanne." It was true that the cardinal's office was in another section of the building, but Annie felt the burdens of her job in this office to be the focus of her life. She was no more likely to say no than she would be to insist that someone call her Anita. Or Ms. Kanne. She never did.

Annie was unmarried and lived alone in a small apartment, with her life centering on her involvement in the church. She went to Mass daily; she went to every devotion, every service, and every study group her parish offered. She tithed ten percent of her meager earnings to the church and contributed to every appeal. She was, in short, part of the backbone of the church, that segment of the population that gave of its time and treasure to enable the church to do God's work on earth. She never questioned any of this. It seemed to her the natural thing to do.

It was not that Annie had no personal opinions of her own. She liked some of her overlords more than others. She was actually quite fond of Father Slopovich, who was unfailingly nice to her. She respected Father Cassabelli, but everything about him was too much: his weight, his voice, his demanding temperament. She tolerated him with little real affection.

But it was Father Cassabelli who gave her the job of arranging for the party on Friday. Armed with this mandate, she swung into action. On Monday morning, Cassabelli called her into his office and gave her as much information as an important man such as he could think of: who would be there, what kind of food and drink to serve, how to arrange the space. This kept Annie busy for most of Monday.

When Father Slopovich arrived for work, Annie was an especially cheerful version of herself, pleased to be an important part of the planning for a party for someone she liked. She swore to herself to do the best job that she could do. For Father Slopovich. And for everyone who attended.

Not that Father Slopovich looked very good on this particular Monday. He seemed distracted, burdened by concerns she was sure were way beyond her ability to understand. Even though he forced a smile in her direction, his face seemed lined with worry in a way she had never noticed before. She went out of her way on this dreary Monday in November to do what she could for him. She brought him coffee, put his requests on the top of her list every time he asked her to do something. When she saw that his mood was not improving, her own mood began to falter. She started worrying although she wasn't sure what she was worrying about. She was a little sick to her stomach, and her face was flushed.

When Annie was getting ready to leave at the end of the day, she noticed that Father Slopovich was still working in his office. This was rare; she was invariably the last person to leave the building. It was her duty to close down the office: to turn off the lights, lock up, set the alarm, and prepare for the next business day. Having him there was like a boulder in the middle of her route home.

She didn't know what to do. It was his office; she could not ask him to leave. She did all of her tasks except the ones she thought would be a problem for him when he left, such as locking the door.

Absolution

She prepared the coffee for the morning; she cleared off her desk and the credenza behind it. She peered into Father Cassabelli's office. He had left two hours ago, but there were some wrappers in his waste basket, so she emptied it. She put on her coat and pulled out her gloves. She was leaning against her desk wondering what to do next when Father Slopovich stepped out of his office.

"Getting ready to leave, Annie?" Radko said.

"Yes, Father," she replied, relieved to see him out of his office. She did not move.

"Annie, I'm going to be a while," Radko said. "I'll lock up."

Annie wasn't sure she could remember a time when Father Slopovich locked up the office, so, despite her fondness for him, she was mistrustful of his ability to do so.

"Father," she began hesitantly, "Do you know how? Do you know the alarm code?"

"Yes, Annie," Radko replied, smiling inwardly at the devotion of this woman. "I'll take care of it."

"Well, good night then," Radko said and turned back toward his office.

Annie hesitated. "Good night, Father," she said at last. She slowly turned toward the door. Before she closed it, she turned one final time to look where Radko had been standing. He had returned to his office.

When Radko heard the outer door of the office close, he let out a long sigh of relief. He was fond of Annie, who, he recognized, was a vital part of the office. Even though she drove him crazy at times, he found her dogged devotion to task a valuable trait. In some ways, she reminded him of Ursula with fewer intellectual gifts. If he were to be a bishop, he would ask her to join him.

Radko turned his attention to the yellow pad on his desk. On it were listed the pros and cons of accepting the appointment that he knew was coming his way. He had notes and arrows and more notes and more arrows—too many ifs, too many unknowns. He sat there staring at the blue jumble on the tattered yellow pad. The truth was he did not want to go home. He wanted a sign; he wanted to know what God wanted of him. Or what Life wanted of him. Lately he had begun to think that maybe God was just another term for Life written large and personified. He saw his priesthood and his marriage both to be life-giving things, as big things that gave his little life meaning and substance. He did not know how to choose between them. Despite his bravado with Ursula, he did not know if he could.

Radko envied Annie her simplicity. He longed for an uncomplicated life where duty ruled and where clarity abounded. He cursed his complicated reservations about everything. This was one of the reasons he was drawn to the law. The law was clear and carefully defined. The law knew where to point you; the law was the law. But beyond the law, where most people lived their lives, ambiguity reigned. He hated it. Besides, if the law was so powerful, how come it was so easy for him to flaunt it, to live outside its safe bounds? He cursed his own happiness and his good fortune.

Ursula, Ursula, will you really leave me? Is it so easy for you? Will you not stand by me no matter what, no matter the unsavory consequences? At this moment, the cultural differences between him and his wife seemed vast and irreconcilable. He knew Ursula had not been raised to consider what God wanted for her. She was raised to think about what was good for Ursula. He was suddenly jealous of her upbringing. More clarity, less confusion. Simpler.

Radko reviewed the simple things he knew. Two weeks from now he would have to make a decision, a simple yes or no, to something that should have been an unquestioned good. He felt deeply the responsibility for his choices, which now seemed in the cold light of the present to be selfish, to lack the integrity expected of grown-ups. He was good at self-criticism, he reflected; it was just that he wasn't so good at life.

CHAPTER 50

The week dragged on. The more Radko thought about the party on Friday, the more he dreaded it. Silas was gone and would not be back till Friday, or so Radko thought. Ursula was going through the quotidian tasks of her life as if the sword of Damocles was not hanging above their relationship. Radko tried to do what he thought other people did: he tried to put the unpleasant situation out of his mind. He was only mildly successful in this.

Thursday evening was particularly chilly at home. It had always been the tradition of the Slopovich family to roll with the punches when it came time for Radko to do something business-related. If a normal married man could bring his wife, Radko and Ursula would fantasize about his bringing her and joke about the consequences of this. When the time came, however, there was never any question that he would go alone and play out his public persona of a celibate priest, sometimes grateful for the opportunity to do something out of the ordinary. He would give Ursula a particularly deep kiss at the door before he left, signaling his loyalty to her and to them. She responded in kind, embracing him with special affection and warmth. They were on the same team; this was just part of the deal.

Absolution

On Thursday, that ritual seemed like an ancient artifact, a quaint ceremony enacted by a personage dug up from the desert sands. At the Slopovich residence on this Thursday, there was no warmth or closeness or deep kisses, only silence and tension. The children did not even risk challenging the gloom. They did their chores, had dinner, and vanished into another room, confiding in each other only a little about what might be wrong with mom and dad.

Ursula went to bed early and feigned sleep when Radko joined her. He knew she was awake; she was barely breathing. None of that noisy rhythmic undulation that she did when she was really sleeping. Nonetheless, he did not make an issue of it. If he had known what to say to bridge the gap between them, he would have said it earlier. So he lay awake in the dark, staring alternately at the ceiling and out the window.

On Friday morning, everything looked typical on the surface, except that the twins made no noise and mom and dad did not speak. Same tasks getting ready for work and school: same lunches prepared, same admonitions, same routes taken. Except: no farewell hugs, no special intimacy for Radko to go off and do something that was his to do without his wife.

On his long drive downtown, Radko thought that he should have resigned already. Why go through this charade when, within a few weeks, everyone will know the truth? he thought to himself. He felt like a coward. He felt committed to the party, and that compounded his fractured self-view as a man who could not or would not make a firm decision. He was filled with this kind of disgust as he walked to his office.

Annie was unusually upbeat for a Friday morning. She greeted him with a high-pitched, almost squeaky tone that he found cloying and irritating. He smiled wanly at her but did not pause enroute to his private office.

Radko did what he typically did on especially stressful days. He took a deep breath and forced himself to focus on work. This worked for about two hours, until he took his first break. When he pushed himself away from his desk, he looked up to see Angelo staring down at him.

"Ready for the party tonight?" Angelo asked, grinning from ear to ear.

What Radko wanted to say was, "What party?" Instead he said: "Yeah, sure." He recognized the harshness of his tone immediately and attempted a rebound: "This was nice of you to arrange, Angelo. I am not sure I deserve it."

"Nonsense, Radko," Angelo boomed, apparently impervious to whatever harshness Radko may have perceived in his own voice. "We don't do this often enough. Besides," he added, "everyone here is looking forward to it. I'll see you tonight." With that, Angelo Cassabelli turned on his heel and abandoned Radko's office.

Radko stared at the empty space left by the large man who vanished as if in a flash. He was sure events were out of his control. Maybe this is why the notion of God is so compelling to people, he thought absently. He felt himself detaching from his experience. He would have to remain in character as an actor does just to get through this evening's festivities. He was thinking about that when the phone rang.

"Father Slopovich," Annie said on the intercom, "there is an Archbishop Mueller on the line for you."

Mueller? Radko thought. The Mueller from Rome? He scanned his mind: he did not know any other Archbishop Muellers. He stared at the blinking light on his telephone console. Dare I pick this up? he thought. His hand moved slowly in the direction of the receiver but stopped short. Mueller is the last person I want to talk to, he thought to himself. Then he realized that Mueller was calling from Rome, and he picked up the phone.

"Hello," he said.

"Radko," said the ebullient Archbishop, "How are you?"

Screwed, thought Radko, but he said, "Fine, fine, Arch…I mean Wolfgang. How are you?"

Absolution

"Fine, fine. Listen, Radko. I heard about the party this evening, and I happen to be in Chicago. I didn't want to come without an invitation or at least without letting you know. Would you mind another guest?"

Radko's response to this was the same as if the Grim Reaper had gleefully invited himself to his party. One just doesn't say no to archbishops or to Grim Reapers.

They were beginning to fuse in Radko's mind. To clear his head, Radko knew he had to say something.

"Of course not, Wolf. I would be honored for you to come," he said, grateful for his good breeding.

"Great. I understand it is to be at 5:30 in the back room of the Capitol Grille. Is that right?"

This guy has spies everywhere, Radko thought. "Yes, that's right," he said.

"See you tonight, then," the archbishop concluded.

Radko felt the grip of a conspiracy as if it were a giant wooden cangue locking him into place. He presumed Mueller was here to apply pressure on him. And he was right.

Part Two

CHAPTER 1

His Excellency, the Most Reverend Radko Slopovich, Bishop of Bismarck, dozed for a moment on the couch of his large but sparsely furnished office at the Chancery on Raymond Street in the city of Bismarck, North Dakota. A late spring snow was settling in, the wet, heavy kind beloved by children but cursed by their parents. He had been dreaming of Ursula and Maggy and Sergie, his wife and children. In this dream, a recurrent one, he saw them falling off a windswept cliff into a vast sea and was helpless to save them. He awoke with a start.

Even during an afternoon nap, he thought resentfully. His sleep at night was more or less constantly disturbed by both waking and sleeping images. The former were mostly just mental pictures that triggered strong emotions—grief, loss, anger, rage, helplessness. The latter were nightmares. The one involving a cliff was common.

Radko dragged himself to the small washroom off his office. He had told Annie, his secretary, that he did not want to be disturbed. But Annie had no control over the disturbances engendered by Radko's mind, and he thought that perhaps real people would be easier to deal with than the phantoms he could not control. After splashing some cold water on his face, he returned to his desk,

Absolution

pressed the intercom, and told Annie that he was once again available.

Within minutes, the intercom buzzed, and Annie told him that he had a call from Father Rawles, the pastor of a rural parish that was working to build a new church. Probably wants to talk about fundraising, Radko thought. What do I know about that? He pushed the button on his phone.

"Hi, Bishop," Stan Rawles said in an excessively exuberant tone for a snowy afternoon in March. "I'm calling to bring you up to date on the funding efforts for Saint Matthew's parish." And off he went.

Radko listened patiently, rubbing his temple and trying to focus on the issue at hand. Rawles was a go-getter who could squeeze more than enough money out of his four-hundred-family flock that was spread over thirty square miles. He wondered why this good priest wanted or needed to call him all the time with updates. He is probably bragging, thought Radko, who was still getting used to his newfound power as bishop. People actually went out of their way to get his attention. In all his years in chancery work, he never dreamed that such power could exist on a day to day basis. He thought of his bishops as people whose permission he needed from time to time. But apparently he was alone with that notion. People around him deferred and demurred, rarely told him the whole truth, especially if there was bad news, and put a rosy spin on everything. It left a bad taste in Radko's mouth.

People clamored for his attention constantly. Thank God, Annie had agreed to come with him from Chicago. She was not only efficient, but she protected him like a high-tech sentinel, constantly monitoring possible incoming threats to his time and tranquility. The move from Chicago was not really so difficult for Annie. The characters in her life changed, but its essence did not. She still lived in a small apartment and centered her life around the church. She still attended daily mass and devotions appropriate to the season.

She still gave generously of her income to support the work of the church. She still did her duty as she saw it.

But there was also a difference in her life. No longer did people treat her like a child. No more teasing about Annie Cannie and all that middle-school nonsense. Radko had never spoken about this to Annie, but he resolved in his mind that, if she accepted his offer, he would treat her with the respect due a normal adult woman. No childish nicknames. That simple decision seemed to reverberate positively through Annie's soul. At first he introduced her as Anita, and Annie's spine seemed to straighten. After the first few weeks, Radko thought that she had actually grown a couple of inches. After a few more weeks, she had allowed herself to be called Annie. Just Annie. Annie's transformation was a small ray of sunshine in his otherwise bleak Dakota winter.

Radko sat back in his chair and looked out the window. He was much more pleased with Annie than he was with himself. He only rarely lost touch with the self-pity that set in shortly after his ordination as bishop. He honestly could not distinguish that self-inflicted misery from the other painful feelings that swirled in and out of his body and his mind: the grief, the rage, the sheer sorrow he felt in the face of the sharp and dramatic changes in his life over the past few months. He was running on a belief—some would say a superstition—that somehow the mess he had made of his life would get better, would resolve itself in some sort of redeeming experience, the exact nature of which eluded him completely.

He thought about leaving the office, even though it was only three o'clock in the afternoon. Best to get home before the storm gets any worse, he thought, justifying his behavior the way a middle-manager might. Then he recognized for the thousandth time that there was no one to whom he was responsible, except perhaps the Pope in Rome; there was no one who was there to give him permission or to withhold it, to interfere with the power of every simple whim. He was the only boss he had for at least six thousand

Absolution

miles, and he was fairly certain the Bishop of Rome did not give a damn what he did with his time. So he left.

On the way out, he told Annie that he was leaving and that perhaps it would be best for her if she closed the office early, too, given the storm front that was moving in. Annie shrugged. She would rather be exactly where she was than anywhere else she was likely to go over the next few hours, and her look communicated this directly to Radko without words. But, being nothing if not polite, she said, "I have a bit more work to do, Bishop; then I'll lock up."

Radko nodded and donned his coat, hat, and boots before venturing out into the white-out produced by the storm. A young deacon—Radko thought he had some internship type of job in the chancery—leapt into action, pulling on his coat on the way to the door before him. He is going to clean the snow off my car, Radko realized, and he slowed down his forward movement to give the young man some time to do his good deed. He didn't want to stand by and watch the boy work.

He timed it perfectly. By the time he got to his SUV, the windows were clean, the motor was running, and the young deacon was putting the finishing touches on his snow-removal activity. He stood back proudly and opened the car door for Radko.

"Thank you," Radko said, nodding to the young man whose name was not readily available to him. If he had lived in the parallel universe of normal civil life, he would have tipped him, but Radko knew that tipping was an alien activity to the men in black, and the deacon would not only have refused, he would have felt guilty. Or worse, suspicious. So Radko did what all higher churchmen do in such a circumstance: he got into his car and drove off.

Thankfully, the driving was treacherous. The immediate dangers of swerving off the road or plowing into another vehicle grabbed Radko's attention and cleared his mind. For about twenty minutes, he almost felt like a normal human being.

Once safely ensconced in his garage, he turned off the engine and sighed. For a moment, he thought about going for a drive, so comforting was the ride home, so devoid of the usual depressive torment that passed for his normal state of mind. Thinking that he was probably the only person in a thousand miles who would be having such thoughts, he put them out of his mind, got out of the car, and entered the bishop's residence where he lived.

As he entered the darkened space, he felt the plusses and minuses of leading a small diocese. The minus column was easily cited: few resources, not many people, little money, few conveniences. The plus side was the other side of that poor coin: time alone, no one living in the residence trying to take care of him, solitude. At the moment, Radko held to the weary hope that somehow solitude would save him, that being alone would somehow allow him to heal his wracked soul and give him some comfort or clarity. It hadn't happened yet, but maybe he was just not trying hard enough. Or maybe it was too soon.

After turning on the lights, Radko went to collect the mail and check his voice mail for messages. These seemed like old-fashioned habits to him. He had a cell phone that was always with him. He was not hard to get hold of. He had internet access on his computer; most of his correspondence was via e-mail. But he checked anyway and felt the same vague disappointment rifling through the inane advertisements and credit card offers that filled most of the mailboxes of America. The greatest country on earth, he mused.

He made some coffee and headed for his study where his computer sat waiting. He booted it up and waited while it ran through its multiple self-checks and finally gave him the green light to be connected to the rest of the world.

He went straight to his e-mail. Nothing of interest. He was wondering where to go next when the phone rang. The sound surprised him; calls were rare at home.

"Hello?" he said.

Absolution

It was Annie. "Bishop," she said, "There was a call from Monsignor Ranke. I thought you might want to know."

A speck of delight flashed in Radko's wintry mind. "Did he want me to call him?" he asked Annie.

"Yes," she replied. "He said that he was in the States and thought he might work a trip here if you had the time."

All I have is time, Radko thought. Then he took down Silas's number. It was his cell phone.

"I'll call him," Radko told Annie.

And he did. It turned out that Silas was touring the U.S., interviewing a representative of each diocese to determine how their records and archival material were managed. Rome was considering a new computer system to deal with its own material, and was considering integrating all church records worldwide into one system. It was a long-term, ambitious task. The reason didn't matter; Radko was happy to talk with his friend.

"So you're willing to risk life and limb by coming to North Dakota in the late winter?" Radko said.

"I hear it's pretty this time of year," Silas replied.

"It has a certain charm," Radko parried.

They made plans. Silas was to be in Chicago on the 16th; he hoped to be finished with his business there by the 20th. Radko desperately wanted to ask Silas about Ursula, but he hesitated. They could talk about it in a couple of weeks when he arrived, he thought. But desperation is a very powerful thing.

"Have you spoken with Ursula?" he blurted out.

Silas hesitated. "No, Radko, I haven't," he said slowly. He hated lying to his friend, but he had promised Ursula, whom he had seen the day before, that he would not give out this information to anyone, even Radko. Especially Radko. Nor did he reveal that he had spoken to her in person.

Radko could barely breathe. He had asked a question he felt he had no right to ask. "Do you know how she is?" he finally said.

"It's my understanding that she's okay, Radko," Silas said soothingly. "And I understand the kids are doing as well as can be expected."

Radko let these words stand in his mind for as long as he could hold them there. The mention of Ursula's name out loud, outside the confines of his brain, gave her a reality that dimmed in silence. He felt a spasm of love and longing.

"Thank you," he said.

Silas's heart ached for Radko. He had some idea of the misery his friend was suffering. Radko didn't talk about it much, but the undercurrent of sadness was always there. Silas recognized it as much in what Radko did not say as in what he did. He rarely talked of doing anything fun or interesting or exciting. He spoke in an uncharacteristic monotone. He lacked even a modicum of zest for living. Silas was worried.

CHAPTER 2

Silas was not only worried, he was confounded. *Cui bono?* he thought to himself: To whose good is all this misery? He hung up from his conversation with Radko. Ursula was gone. We do not have a married American bishop except in the most rarefied and technical sense. It was true that Radko was married in the eyes of the church—Silas had seen to that. But no one anticipated the powerful reaction from Ursula, who not only protested being played like a pawn on a chessboard but who declared war on all the combatants. Only Silas had been able to maintain some type of contact with her, and this only because she saw him as a messenger and possibly as a friend, not as a co-conspirator.

Silas still smarted from that Friday in November, when he turned up at Radko's house rather than attending the party for Radko. He called Ursula when he was only ten minutes away to ask if she would like some company. Her voice was measured and careful, but she had said yes.

When Silas got to the house, Ursula met him at the door with a dour look on her pretty round German face. She invited him in, offered him a drink, and poured two vodka martinis, one for him and one for her. They sat down on the couch, and Ursula looked

Absolution

straight into Silas's eyes. "What is going on, Silas?" she asked in a tone that was as close to demanding as one could get in polite company. "I want to know the truth."

Silas, who was accustomed neither to the truth nor to being called to account by a woman, studied his drink carefully as he weighed possible responses. He rapidly played out a number of possible scenarios in his mind, but something about Ursula's earnestness told him that only the truth would do.

Silas mustered his own not inconsiderable strength and returned Ursula's hard gaze. "There is a small group of highly placed churchmen who are plotting to change the church's approach to sexuality by arranging married prelates around the world. Radko has been tagged as the first American married bishop." He paused, then aimed the other barrel. "A high Vatican official has flown in from Rome tonight to convince Radko to go along with this plan."

"Mueller?" asked Ursula.

"Mueller," replied Silas.

The two sat in silence for some minutes. Two strong people at loggerheads. He looked at Ursula as if to ask what she was thinking, but her face showed nothing. He did not speak. Instead he looked around the small room. It was neat and tidy, as if just straightened. Then, on the edge of his mind, he recognized that something was missing.

"Where are the children?" he asked Ursula.

Ursula looked at Silas darkly. "Some place safe," she said.

Silas was more than a little alarmed. What was this woman doing? He tried to think quickly. "Ursula," he said, "what do you mean, 'someplace safe'?"

Ursula looked at Silas with rage in her eyes. "Someplace safe from people like Mueller," she said. And then she looked away. "And maybe from people like Radko," she added bitterly.

Silas wanted to bolt out of his chair, but he did not want the raise any more suspicion. With great effort, he sat in his place, gripping the cool glass of vodka that Ursula had given him.

"Ursula," he said softly, "What has happened here? I thought you and Radko were close…committed…"

"So did I," Ursula interrupted. "But Silas, lately Radko has withdrawn from me. And from the twins. It's clear that he wants nothing more than to be a bishop of the church, and I'm afraid I'm just an obstacle to that." She paused and bit her lower lip. "I can't stand the fact that he chose his career in the church over his family." Tears ran down her face.

For the second time in as many weeks, Silas's eyes moistened. He took Ursula's hand. He had not anticipated this reaction. Neither had Mueller. This felt like something bad, evil, not something that would serve the church the way Mueller and he envisioned it. Even though Silas had always been a good soldier throughout the time he had been involved with this plan, he now began to wonder in his heart if this weren't too high a price to pay. But being the soldier he was, he stayed on task.

CHAPTER 3

It was the weekend before when Ursula was transformed from a devoted and supportive wife and mother into a revolutionary. It was no one thing; it was an accumulation of a lot of different things: Radko's halfhearted statements about his need to resign from the priesthood; his unwillingness to make any decision at all, even when confronted about the importance of doing so by his wife; his lack of awareness about Silas's homosexuality. This last point was not so much a fault as a reflection of how clueless Radko was about basic stuff, she thought, and an indication of just how self-absorbed he really was. Also, she felt lied to. Radko had told her that the church worked slowly in these matters and that they had months, maybe even a year. And then Silas came and told them it was a matter of weeks. This disgusted Ursula.

But mostly, it was the lack of care he showed for her and the children, how the three of them did not seem to count when the heat came down. How could he even think of prolonging what now seemed to Ursula to be a travesty instead of a life? To her, it felt as if encrusted mud had been washed off an ancient marble statue, revealing the cold hard splendor of a newly discovered artifact. On Sunday in the midst of what had become routine silence

Absolution

between herself and the man she married, it struck Ursula that her future lay elsewhere.

So she made plans. She called her old school in Baltimore and told them that her husband was being transferred back to that city and asked if they had any midyear openings for a math teacher. They did. She called Joan, the best friend who had been at her wedding, and explained that she might need somewhere for the children and then for herself to stay for a few days while she got herself settled into a new apartment. Joan was all support and encouragement. Ursula went online to find an apartment in Baltimore she could afford, and had three or four solid prospects by the end of her internet session. She spoke with a real estate agent about selling the little house in the west suburbs of Chicago.

And finally, when everything else was done and she could not put it off any longer, she called an attorney to file for a divorce.

This was the hardest step for Ursula. She knew it had to be done, and her dutiful nature checked it off her long list. But the pain she felt inside exploded slowly within her, and when she put the phone down after making the appointment, the torment burst forth and left her lying on the floor gripping her midsection and wailing at the top of her lungs. She was a wounded animal.

After the paroxysm passed, she lay still on the floor for an unknown length of time. She gazed in silence at the wall and ceilings of the space where she had fallen. There were no thoughts in her mind, just vague awareness of bodily sensations. She looked at the photographs and the paintings and the furniture around her, the physical stuff of a marriage and of a family. Things that she had cherished, that she and Radko and the twins had collected together. Things that suddenly didn't matter anymore.

After a time she got up and called the airlines. She had resolved that the kids would go to Baltimore on Friday morning. It would look like their usual routine to Radko, who would go to work as usual. She knew he wouldn't be home till late, since the party was scheduled for right after work. She vowed to herself that Radko would never see his children again. She realized bitterly that this would fit into his priestly life just fine. She was appalled anew that he could even consider walking away from children. All for a silly, damned job.

On Friday morning, she bundled the children up and went through the rituals of taking them to the sitter. Instead of heading in that direction, however, she drove straight to O'Hare. On the way, she explained to the twins that they were going on a trip by themselves. They were going to visit Aunt Joan. She assured them that she would join them on Saturday. She explained that the three of them were going to be visiting Joan for a few days. She did not want to give the kids more than they could handle.

But even Maggy was scared. Her face was pale and the small facial muscles around her lips and eyes twitched as her mother was explaining these bizarre events. What about Daddy? she wanted to ask but was too frightened to risk it. Ursula's heart broke at the pain the kids were feeling and at the additional pain that she knew was in store for them. There was no way around it. These kids would be from a broken home. She found that American expression especially apt, as she could indeed feel the brokenness of her home. And in all likelihood, they would be raised by a single parent.

When she took the kids to the gate and handed them over to the flight attendant, she almost smiled at the big red tags dangling from their matching coats. But inside she was worried that she might have a replay of the episode on the living room floor of a couple days before. She was barely breathing. She saw the two little people to whom she felt most devoted in the whole world holding hands with each other and waving good-bye to her with their other little arms as they entered the jetway. Ursula did not take her eyes off the plane until it was out of sight.

After the plane was beyond the clouds, she wiped her eyes and took a deep breath. She turned from the large glass viewing window and made her way back through the concourse to the termi-

Absolution

nal. Feeling weak and afraid that she might not make it much farther, she spotted a Starbuck's and went in for an espresso. She sat there sipping her coffee and watching the thousands of people in the terminal: the passengers, the employees, the friends and relatives coming and going. It seemed that this was the entire impersonal universe. It did not feel bad; in fact, she preferred sitting here amid the hubbub—and even drew strength from it—to going back to the house where she and Radko had attempted a life together. What had been her home, her safe place, the focus of love and affection, now seemed like a mausoleum, an empty, desiccated place that was repugnant to her.

After reluctantly getting up and going to her car, Ursula began having thoughts of revenge. She did not figure that this type of thinking was healthy, but she could not resist the allure of playing out at least in fantasy scenarios of retribution. She knew she could easily destroy whatever aspirations Radko might have for his career by going public with their marriage. She had all the documentation she needed. She thought darkly that she could even sell the film rights to a studio; such was the potentially shocking revelation of a married priest who was named Bishop in the Catholic church.

But just now she felt weak and fatigued from the arduous work of rearranging every aspect of her life in a few short days. She felt vaguely ill, mildly nauseous, and even feverish; but she diagnosed herself as suffering from stress and then realized that she was probably hungry. On the way home, she stopped at a small diner for breakfast. She had been so anxious earlier that she had not eaten anything. Food might help, she thought. It didn't; she picked at the food when it came but was so distracted and forlorn she could find no enthusiasm for eating it. After a while, she paid the tab and faced the task of going home. And packing.

She had her suitcases packed when Silas called. She wasn't planning to leave that evening; she was just getting ready for her departure the next day. She had resolved to face Radko directly on Saturday and tell him what she was doing: that she was leaving him and taking the kids. Despite her revenge fantasies of a few hours before, she had no taste for blood; she simply wanted to be gone from this place.

When Silas called, a small window opened in her mind. It was not an opportunity to roll everything back: to call the kids back from Baltimore, to unpack the suitcases, to go back to the status quo ante. It was a chance to get more information, to find out whatever Silas knew about what was really going on. Silas lived in Rome; he was sure to know more than she did.

And he did. What Silas told her shocked Ursula at a time when she thought she could not be shocked anymore. A plot? In the Vatican? A plot to make marriage okay? This sounded like something Mary Shelley dreamed up. Ursula had only a tenuous hold on church attitudes about sexuality, but she had gotten the general message that it was bad. She had no inkling of why it would take a plot to change something like this. Why didn't they just talk about it and change their minds? The whole affair seemed to her dreary and senseless.

But what was clear to her was that she was being played. These people must have assumed that she would go along with their childish pranks. Not once had someone from the church, with the notable exception of Silas, come to her to ask her about how she felt about being married to a priest. No one offered to be of any assistance whatsoever. The whole idea of a conspiracy seemed laughably adolescent to her. She felt sick inside, and what Silas told her confirmed every decision she had made in the previous week.

"Did Mueller think I would just go along with this...this...this outrageous plan?" asked Ursula.

Silas thought for a minute. He could see that Ursula believed that Mueller was the bad guy in this whole mess, and for that he was grateful. But he did not know quite how to respond. He finally decided that some version of the truth would work best.

"Mueller sent me to talk with you about it," he said. "I'm not sure what his exact plans were." He stared into space for a mo-

Absolution

ment, hoping that would cover his disingenuousness. "I think it was his intention to provide support for a decision to remain married. To help you and Radko work out a plan of some sort that would enable the two of you to stay married and allow Radko to be made a bishop."

"Silas," Ursula said, "apart from the sheer gall of this man and his plans, how did he think it was going to work out? Were the kids and I never to go outdoors?"

"Well," Silas said, "It was my understanding that you and the kids would live outside the diocese and that Radko would visit every weekend."

Ursula blushed. She was embarrassed to think that there was someone in the world who thought she could possibly be so gullible, naive, and easily manipulated. She took a sip of her martini and turned back to Silas.

"You said that Radko was to be the first American married bishop. Are there other married bishops in other countries?" asked Ursula.

"Yes," said Silas. "There are about a dozen of them."

"And is that how they live? With part-time wives?"

Silas didn't know where Ursula was going with this. So he thought for a moment before he responded. "No, Ursula, most of them live with their wives fairly openly. But they do so in cultures where celibacy is not so, um, regularly observed."

Ursula was beginning to hate the way church people talked. "You mean where people just don't care if the bishop has a wife or not?"

"That's correct," responded Silas.

"Where are these people? Ursula asked.

Silas told her. "Chad, Mongolia, the Seychelles. Third World countries, mostly."

Ursula blushed again. This time it was more rage than embarrassment that someone in the world thought she was so unsophisticated as to cling to a man no matter what, like some Third World woman who needed to hook up with a man just to ensure a regular supply of food. She reminded herself that this was the twenty-first century, although she was pretty sure she was the only one in the room who noticed.

She took a deep breath. "Silas," she said. "I am leaving Radko. I sent the kids ahead because he and I have some serious talking to do. I have an appointment with an attorney and I plan to file for a divorce as soon as possible."

Silas stared at Ursula, whom he now saw in a completely different light. He had always liked her, but what he felt now was deep respect for the fortitude of this woman. Respect with more than a trace of fear. He was not sure how far she would go. There was no hint of ambivalence in her voice, no sign that this was bravado in the hope of getting Radko back. Silas did not think that she wanted Radko back.

"Ursula," he began. "I'm so sorry to hear this." Silas paused and regarded his shoes. "I know Radko loves you very much."

Ursula thought for a moment. "I don't think this is so much a question of love, Silas; I think it is a matter of choice. From the time this talk of being a bishop came up, Radko has given no real sign that he wanted anything else." Another pause. "I believe it is what he wants. I believe it is what he will choose."

"And if he doesn't?" asked Silas.

Ursula looked at Silas squarely. "It's too late for us, Silas. I've made my own decisions."

That sentence hung in the air for a few moments before Silas spoke. He looked at Ursula and was having some trouble with the phrasing of what he needed to ask.

"Ursula," he began. "Mueller is my boss. He sent me to talk with you about this, but I can see that there are other forces at work that he knows nothing about. I'll inform him of your plans, if that's all right with you." Silas paused. "He will ask me if you plan to go public."

Absolution

Ursula shook her head and rolled her eyes toward the ceiling. Protect your interests no matter what, she thought. "Tell your archbishop friend whatever you like, Silas. You can also tell him I have no plans to go public, out of respect for my ex-husband and for the sake of our children. I have no desire to protect Mueller or the church, but I don't want to distress my children any more because of the evil of these men."

The word evil hit Silas especially hard.

CHAPTER 4

As Silas drove away from Ursula's house that night, he pondered the situation, which he felt was now spiraling into an unpredicted and unpredictable direction. He knew that at that moment Mueller was cajoling Radko with the merits of attempting a plan so improbable that few people in their right mind would risk it. Mueller thought that Radko might go along with it because of the lengths to which he had already gone in his life to ensure his marriage to Ursula while remaining a priest. He could have resigned from the priesthood any time over the past five or six years and did not. Mueller was feeling pretty confident.

At the same time, Silas had just witnessed a powerful and completely unforeseen factor, Ursula herself. She is a proud woman, he thought, and she has the guts and intelligence to back it up. Silas was torn. He had been, if not an unquestioning participant in Mueller's plan, at least a reliable one. He had never done anything to stand in the way of Mueller's plan, and for many reasons. He thought Mueller was basically right, that the attitude of the church toward sexuality needed to change. His own active sexual life was another reason. Besides, he admitted to himself, he rather enjoyed the intrigue of the whole matter. He knew that if the plot were exposed, he could be dismissed from the priesthood, but Silas did not lack confidence in his own abilities, and he thought that this was an acceptable risk.

But now he was confronted with a shadowy side of this whole mess. He saw that the plan had led directly to the destruction of a marriage between two people about whom he cared very much. Though gay, Silas felt a strong emotional bond to Ursula, an almost sensual or maybe even a sexual connection. It was a novel experience for him. But the warmth he felt also left him feeling guilty for contributing to the hurt Ursula was suffering and that Radko was sure to feel when Ursula faced him tomorrow. Ursula's use of the word evil weighed on him. Was he involved in evil acts? he asked himself. He did not think so, but he could not deny that real human beings were being hurt. And a family was being torn apart. As he drove down Highway 90, he made some promises to himself. The principle one was a vow that he would help both of these good people in any way he could. He would not abandon them in any way ever. Driving through the city, he thought maybe he was a decent priest after all.

CHAPTER 5

Archbishop Wolfgang Mueller's last minute inclusion in Radko's appreciation party filled Angelo with satisfaction. Suddenly the field of play widened to include not just the usual players in the internecine politics of the Chicago Archdiocese but a player from the center of power in the church worldwide. Angelo could barely contain himself when Radko told him about Mueller's call.

"You mean Archbishop Mueller from the Secretariat of State?" he asked Radko.

"Yes, Angelo, he said he happened to be in town." Radko replied with no enthusiasm.

Angelo knew what every churchman knew about people at Mueller's level of power: they do not do anything by coincidence or happenstance. Everything is planned out; everything has a motive. But apparently Radko did not know this. Poor guy, thought Casabelli: he will be stuck in some godforsaken diocese forever with no hope of advancement.

After Radko left his office, Angelo tried to clear his mind. It was difficult because he was so excited. He wasn't sure why the archbishop would attend such a low-level event, but he knew it had to be a very significant reason for him to come all the way from

Absolution

Rome to do so. He reached into his desk drawer for the club-size box of Twinkies he kept there. If Mueller's coming, the cardinal will want to know, he thought. But the cardinal was out of town. He'll still want to be informed, Angelo thought. He was glad that he thought of this and that Slopovich apparently had not. Angelo could see his stock going up in the eyes of the cardinal and his star rising even higher in the small firmament of the Chicago chancery. He reached for the phone and dialed the private cell phone number of the Cardinal Archbishop of Chicago, who was in Mexico on vacation.

CHAPTER 6

After informing Angelo about Mueller's visit, Radko returned to his office in a dejected state. He could sense Angelo's glee that he would be rubbing shoulders with a powerful man from the Roman curia. He also knew what everyone knew, that this was most certainly not a coincidence. Radko felt events overtaking him, and he did not like the direction in which they were headed. He played the scenario out in his head. He was supposed to act as if Mueller was a friend and call him by his first name, and all the while Mueller would be pushing him toward accepting his appointment as bishop. Radko did not think he had to make a decision tonight, but he was angry at the prospect of being pressured. One of the few rewards of the evening would be acting like Mueller's friend in front of Cassabelli, who would melt with envy.

With no interest in or capacity for working, Radko called Ursula, who he thought might be home. No answer. He tried her cell phone. No answer. Where is she? he thought absently. It was three thirty, and he had two hours before he needed to show up at the contrived get-together in his name. I used to be so good at dodging these things, Radko thought to himself; maybe I'm getting old.

Absolution

He called Annie and asked her to hold all calls. He went over to the couch in his office with a book he had been wanting to read, and scanned the first few paragraphs. He was no more successful reading than he was at working, so he grabbed his coat and decided to go for a walk before he had to turn up at the Capitol Grille.

He told Annie on the way out that he would see her at the party this evening, knowing that she wouldn't miss it. Radko couldn't tell if she would come because she liked him or because Angelo had asked her to or if it was just another thing on her long duty list. He wondered if she ever did things that were not duty-driven. He would never know, he thought, as he exited his office and headed toward the elevator.

The brisk November wind of Chicago hit him like the welcome anodyne it was from the stuffy office he had just left. He breathed in deeply and headed toward Michigan Avenue, that crowded Mecca for shoppers who were at the top of the midwestern food chain. He didn't really mind the unbridled swell of capitalism and wealth that permeated the boulevard. In fact, he admired it: the furs, the cars, the limousines, and the ambience of the upscale venue. It was so alien to his life.

He had hoped not to think about his life for a little while. He was sick to death of reviewing the details of his situation over and over in his mind. He needed a decision, and he was really the only one who could make it. He knew that, but it was not how his life seemed to him. Or felt to him. Rather, it seemed that his decisions were always filtered through the lenses of other people: Mueller, Ursula, even Angelo and Silas. He used to think this was a good thing, consistent with what he was taught as a child: be of service to others; think of others first. In reality, he looked at his role in his life as a minor one: the person who holds these others together, who steps gingerly in those places where no one else is seriously offended. Small places, he thought; tiny spaces.

But even these thoughts struck him as irrelevant. All the mental gymnastics in the world would not prevent current events from unfolding. If he wanted a voice in them, he had to say so, and then he had to convince everyone that what he wanted was viable.

It was at this moment that Radko faced his desire most clearly. I know what I want, he now saw; it was as clear as could be. He felt sick inside. He did not know if he could pull it off. He thought of all the long conversations he and Ursula had had about getting married and conniving for him to remain a priest. He saw how that worked against all odds, really, especially given the fact that Ursula knew so little about the church. Well, he allowed, maybe it worked out because she knew so little about church matters. But why couldn't he do it again? Why wait for Mueller to pressure him? The archbishop must have some notion of how he saw events playing out in this improbable scenario. Obviously, he believed they could, or he would not have come all the way to Chicago to attend this thinly veiled travesty. I'll take the battle to his territory, Radko thought, and his mood began to lighten.

Radko didn't know how he would convince Ursula to go along with this, but he remembered the heady days when they were courting and thought back to how the sheer enthusiasm of his plans made them seem possible. And they were possible. We did it, Ursy, you and I. We even had our children. It worked once; it could work again.

Beset by more confidence than he had felt in a long time, Radko began walking toward the restaurant where the party was to be held. His mood began spiraling upward for once. He had not felt this good for weeks, and he was relieved that, at least for now, he felt as powerful as the events swirling around him.

CHAPTER 7

When Bishop Slopovich thought of that evening in November of last year, he scowled. He remembered the confidence he had felt within himself as he approached the party. He thought back to how he rose to the occasion, greeting each guest warmly and receiving their accolades and appreciation. He was successful in getting Angelo to burn with envy as he embraced Archbishop Mueller when he entered the room, running fashionably late. He genuinely enjoyed seeing Ted Catsweiler, his former superior, who had come in from Baltimore for the festivities. He was disappointed that Silas was not there, but his friend had called him on his cell phone at the last minute to say that he was tied up with a minor automobile accident on the Daniel Boone. Radko was disappointed, but he did not question Silas's explanation one bit. He wished his friend well and asked him to come later if he could.

As the evening wound down and most of the guests left, Mueller invited him to have an after-dinner drink at the Drake where he was staying. Radko took this in stride. He figured that this was the real reason why Mueller was here, and he felt ready for whatever the archbishop had on his agenda.

Absolution

"So," said Radko, as they were settling into the elegantly appointed Coq d'Or lounge. "I'm glad to see you, Wolfgang. I know you didn't come all this way to pat me on the back. Please let me in on the reason for your visit."

Wolfgang did not demure. "I have come to be of whatever assistance I can as you prepare for your ordination to the episcopacy," he said, looking Radko straight in the eye.

Radko smiled. The waiter came and they each ordered a drink.

"Wolfgang, being a bishop is an honor one cannot easily walk away from. But at the same time, Ursula and I have yet to work out a suitable, um, arrangement."

Then Wolfgang launched into what was clearly his prepared text. He described how, while most married bishops lived openly with their wives, he did not think that was possible at this point in the United States, and that he thought that Ursula and the children should live outside the diocese, perhaps even in Canada, outside the boundaries of the United States, and that Radko could visit them two or maybe even three days a week, given the fact that Bismarck was not so demanding a placement. He compared it to executives who are more or less constantly on the road and in general painted a picture of a slightly challenging but perfectly reasonable way of life that would hopefully change in the coming years to include more time for Radko and Ursula and the kids to be together.

When Radko thought back on this conversation, he shook his head. This was exactly what he had been prepared to hear. He was not shocked. He did not quibble or argue with Mueller. In fact, he took his point of departure from where the Archbishop left off.

"I agree that it would be wise for the family to live outside the diocese," he replied to Mueller. "In fact, I think the idea of Canada is a good one. More separation; more distance built into the equation." He didn't say to Mueller that he could hardly wait to tell Ursula, but that was what he was thinking to himself. Wrapped in the warm wood and leather of the upscale lounge, bolstered by his favorite cocktail, and sitting in the presence of a powerful supporter, all of these plans seemed eminently doable. It was just a matter of bringing Ursula along and helping her see the reasonableness and elegance of the plan.

From the perspective of four months out, however, Radko, now a bishop, judged himself to be a lamb willingly cooperating with his own slaughter.

Radko could not have been more shocked or surprised at the events that transpired when he got home that night. He was hopeful about sharing his conversation with Mueller with his wife, missing the closeness they used to have. It had been over a week since they even touched each other in an affectionate way. That seemed to Radko like a long time.

It was late when he got home, just past eleven. Ursula was sitting in the living room reading a book under a single light. He was mildly surprised that she was still awake, but he was glad. He greeted her warmly and sat next to her on the couch.

Ursula looked at Radko. "How was the party?" she asked.

"Good," Radko replied. "It turned out that Archbishop Mueller from Rome was in town and was able to come."

At the mention of Mueller's name, Ursula's stiff expression hardened even more. She didn't say anything.

Radko felt the temperature drop. This was not going so well, he thought.

"I'm going to check on the twins," he said, and got up to go to their bedroom.

Ursula took in a sharp, rapid breath. "They're not here," she said.

Radko turned and looked down at her. "Not here? Where are they?"

Ursula put her book down and looked at Radko. "Please sit down," she said.

It was then that Ursula told him she had sent the kids away, that she was moving away herself and that she did not believe their

Absolution

marriage worked any longer. She had not planned to tell him late at night like this; she had planned to tell him the next morning. But she couldn't sleep and Radko wanted to check on the kids and she just could not contain herself anymore. Tears rolled down her face as she told Radko that she thought the bond between them was broken. She repeated her bitter disbelief about his desire to be a bishop no matter what impact it had on the children, on her, on their marriage.

Even as Ursula said these things, she felt the tug of her long relationship with Radko. She loved him; she couldn't do anything about that. In her mind, she relented about some of the more hurtful fantasies she had been nursing. Maybe there would be a way he could see the kids sometime; maybe there was some way she and he could even have some kind of a relationship. But not a marriage. Not a committed, come-hell-or-high-water bondedness that would withstand time and whatever ravages it brought. She was leaving him, but she was sure that he had chosen to abandon her first.

It took Radko some time to comprehend what Ursula was saying. Occasional words, phrases, and sentence fragments tore through his mind as his ballooned ego slowly but inexorably deflated. Leaving...seeing the children...broken...abandonment. Ursula was not really having a conversation; she was telling him how things were with her: what she would do; what she did; what she wouldn't do. It was not a negotiation. It was a fait accompli. Nothing Radko said even came close to turning her mind away from the plan she had outlined. It was only after repeated attempts that he prevailed upon her to tell him where she was going and where the kids were. He did not get angry; he did not cry. He was numb.

Finally, in the middle of another abortive attempt to make sense out of what was happening, Radko got up and announced that he was going to bed. Every part of his body was exhausted, and he had no power to continue the baffling conversation he was having with the woman he loved. He walked into the bedroom, removed his clothes, and fell into a deep sleep. His last thought was that perhaps this was all a dream.

Ursula told him later that she did not leave the couch. She sat there all night, at times dozing but as often awake. She wept quietly. She hated doing what she was doing, but she could see no alternative. Even the way Radko bragged about Mueller's coming confirmed in her mind his true intentions. It was also clear to her that she could not make Radko understand that this was not something most people would elect to do. Most people would not willingly enter into a bizarre arrangement where their bond, their emotional connection, their family had to be a dark secret. It was also obvious that he had not given much thought to the effect of such an arrangement on his children. He acted as if everyone could roll with the punches. She couldn't.

So the next morning, during the time which, according to Ursula's original plan, she and Radko were going to face the truth about their relationship, nothing much happened. Ursula told him her plans and where she would be staying. She told him about the practical arrangements she had made: how she had contacted a real estate agent to talk about putting the house on the market. She gave him the name and phone number of her attorney. That was the hard part, the part where she had to force herself not to fall once again on the floor in grief. She didn't. Stolid and thorough as ever, Ursula made sure Radko was clear about all the details. Then she got ready to leave for the airport. She told him that she would be back in a couple of weeks to get her car and drive it back to Baltimore, but first she wanted to make sure she and the kids were settled into an apartment. In retrospect, it was all eerily civil and amicable and efficient.

It wasn't until after she left and Radko was faced with an empty house that he actually began to comprehend that he was losing his wife. In his mind he traced her imagined route to the airport, figuring that now she would be checking her bags, now standing in line,

Absolution

now boarding the plane. He didn't go after her; he didn't call her. He was in shock.

Radko spent the day sitting on the couch where he and Ursula last sat. He touched the spot where she had sat, patted it, at one point even smelled it. He teared up at times, but he remained more numb than sad. It was as if Ursula had turned into someone else. He did not know this person; he wasn't sure he liked this person. He wanted his wife back, his Ursy, his lover. He and Ursula had had spats before but never, ever did he think that they would not be together. It was exposure to a wondrous if terrifying new mystery. He sat on the couch throughout the night and into the next day.

CHAPTER 8

What Radko remembered of the events that followed Ursula's departure was spotty. He dragged himself to work on Monday morning but only stayed a few hours. Annie looked worried about him in a way he had never noticed before. Feigning illness, he left work and returned to what had been his home and to his couch. He tried calling Ursula several times, but she did not pick up. He left a few messages and tried to be what he thought was adult, but he got no response. He tried to call Mueller at the Drake that afternoon only to learn he had checked out. He tried Silas but had similar results. He felt alone: dumped, judged, punished. He was depressed. And he was angry.

From the time Radko was young, it was always some form of work that helped him when his mood plummeted. Well, he had never experienced an episode quite like this—this was a new level of desolation for him—but it was always focusing on some sort of structured activity that helped him lift himself out of the pit. The deeper the pit the more important the work, he thought to himself.

So he worked. He made a list of all the tasks involved in transitioning out of one life and entering into another, even if he could not quite believe what was happening. He called the real estate

Absolution

agent Ursula had contacted and made arrangements for him to come over and appraise the house. He called a moving company to get estimates. He thought of giving most of the furniture away and starting over in Bismarck.

With great apprehension, he called the attorney whose name Ursula had given him. He was relieved to learn that she had canceled her appointment with him at the last minute, but this detail was insufficient to stem the deepening wave of desolation that was sweeping over him. He looked around the house and determined to give the furniture away.

There were two feelings Radko had about this unhappy predicament that he felt bad about. One was a faint but unmistakable sense of freedom. He was released from the burden of having to convince Ursula to go along with Mueller's plan. Ursula had made his decision easy. He thought with no small measure of guilt that it was probably his marriage to Ursula that earned him the bishopric, but he would assume the duties of that office unencumbered. He felt guilty about what looked like his manipulating the situation, and he felt guilty about Ursula's prominent role in this. The other feeling was anger: Ursula made her decision and pulled the plug on the marriage without even consulting him. This enraged him, although that darkness alternated only intermittently with the grief that was building in his soul.

He also began to plan for his move to North Dakota. Looking at the calendar, he realized that the announcement would come within the next ten days, so he had little real time left at his present job. With a little luck, he might be able to wrap that up early. He made more lists of things he needed and things he needed to think about: his staff, a preliminary visit to Bismarck, the details of protocol involved in a bishop's assuming power in a diocese. He was a canon lawyer; this stuff was right up his alley.

So he set off on autopilot. He took care of business; he tried not to think of himself. The more he thought of Ursula, the more available his anger toward her became. He did not know where to put the twins. The fact that they were innocent victims of this situation weighed on him, and he tried to think of ways he could be a father to them. All of these depended upon his dealing with Ursula, who, in his mind at least, had turned into a flaming-sword-brandishing angel who guarded access to his children. He practiced resentment for the power she had.

The actual events of the drama—the announcement of his appointment, his departure from Chicago, his ordination as bishop in the small cathedral in Bismarck, his moving into the official residence and meeting the staff at the chancery—all of these were done as an actor might do them, with a studied and attentive if distanced attitude. Distanced, he hoped, from the internal turmoil that slowly morphed into a chronic, bland, desolate internal landscape. Radko kept putting one foot in front of the other, hoping that, at some point in the future, he would have time to sort things out and come to an improved conclusion of the horrid events of past months.

After Radko arrived in Bismarck, it was easier to focus on tasks outside himself. There was so much he didn't know about the area, about being in charge, about what it actually meant to be a bishop. He forced himself to learn these things. His hope was that he could keep his own misery at bay long enough for it to dissipate.

Radko was so busy focusing on taking care of business that he did not fully grasp some of the things his new colleagues, the priests of the diocese of Bismarck, were telling him. When he was able to peer beyond his gloomy mood, he thought that everyone was being a bit standoffish, maybe even suspicious. They were nice enough—members of the clergy are practiced at being nice, especially to superiors—but there was a note of something that Radko could not quite put his finger on. Anxiety, maybe, or apprehension.

A few weeks after he settled into his new office, he asked Monsignor Caldwell, his Vicar General and the former Administrator of the diocese, about it.

Absolution

"Bruce," Radko said, "some of the priests seemed a little, um, anxious when they first met me." He paused and cocked his head in thought. "Even after several meetings." He looked directly at his vicar general. "What is going on here?"

Monsignor Caldwell looked back at the Bishop with uncertain eyes. This is exactly what I am talking about, Radko thought to himself. What are you so worried about?

Finally, Bruce spoke. "It's your predecessor, Bishop," he began slowly, not taking his eyes off his new boss. "He was a little, um, hard on the presbyterate. Asked a lot of them; did not give them much time." He continued with his eyes locked on Radko's, "When he died, there wasn't much grieving, if you know what I mean."

"Was he that bad?" Radko asked.

Caldwell stared at the bishop for a long while, trying to assess just how far he could go in sharing what he knew to be true about the previous bishop.

Radko, who was listening attentively, picked up on this. "You may speak candidly, Bruce," he said gently. "I'm new at this bishop business, and any information you can give me could be helpful."

Caldwell took a deep breath and began speaking. He described how Bishop Valazquez was more duke than pastor; how he would only meet with his priests when he had to; how he often lost his temper when somebody challenged him; how his interests were dominated by the wealthy members of his flock; and how he valued buildings and bequests over people. There was more than a little bitterness in his voice.

Radko listened. He was actually feeling some relief to be focusing on something besides his sorry state, and he believed that by extending himself just a little to the people and clergy of his new home, he might be able to undo some of the alienation and dissatisfaction that had clearly set in with them; it might also help his own. He wondered absently if he was up to it, but he thought it might be a path out of his personal desolation. Maybe he could find redemption after all.

He shared none of this with his anxiety-plagued vicar. To him, he simply said, "Bruce, I hope we can do better. I don't have much experience with this, but I will do what I can."

Bruce nodded appreciatively, presumably because Radko's response was kind.

After Bruce left, Radko made some notes. He would make the rounds in each parish and be as available as he could. He did not look forward to this kind of work; it was far different from what he was used to, but if he were going to be bishop to these people, he might as well start now.

That was late January, a cruel time to resolve to visit far-flung parishes in North Dakota. Nonetheless, Radko forced himself to keep on task. There were over a hundred parishes in his diocese, and he made plans to visit each of them. Some he would have to visit for sacramental reasons—confirmations mostly—but when he did so he spent a couple of hours at all the other parishes in the vicinity. If there was no confirmation scheduled, he would visit four or five parishes a week. It kept him busy.

Even at this pace, Radko knew that it would take him almost half a year to get around to everyone. But from where he was sitting, time seemed to extend out interminably, and he saw no other options for himself. Besides, he preferred spending time in his episcopal SUV where he was not surrounded by people. He could be alone with his thoughts. He could think of Ursula and Maggy and Sergie. And he could weep.

Radko's desolation ranged from the emotionless void of depression to the heights of self-loathing. Certain pictures from the past were especially violent in his mind: the moment he met Ursula, the time she told him she was pregnant, the birth of their children. When he remembered holding the two small humans in his arms for the first time, shame and longing both descended upon him. It was best for him to keep moving.

CHAPTER 9

The ten days between Silas's call and his visit seemed like more of the same for Radko. He did his job as bishop as he saw fit to do it, often looking to the people around him for direction. He continued the gradual process of acclimating himself to casual power, watching as others deferred to him, made way for him, and withheld bad news from him. He continued to remind himself that, if he wanted the truth, he had to go out of his way to ask for it.

Meanwhile, the depression that had been his constant companion began to seem like normal living. He could not remember ever being depressed before in his life, but his dysphoric mood began to play tricks with his memory. He began to think that maybe he had been depressed for a long time and that he just didn't recognize it. He recalled his dissatisfaction early in his career as a priest when he lived with two men who, if their social skills were added together, did not quite attain the competence of a typical second-grader. Maybe I was just depressed then, he thought. Even the corny commercials on television for various antidepressants began to speak to him differently. Maybe I should try that, he thought.

It was during this acute period of internal haze and external acclimation that Silas finally came to see him. He had arranged to

Absolution

meet Silas at his residence, where his friend would spend a few days.

Silas arrived in the late afternoon. The streets and highways of Bismarck and of North Dakota were still snow-packed, although it had not snowed in a couple of days. Silas was tired from the long drive from Chicago, and he was relieved that he was able to find the bishop's residence without incident. He knocked on the door wearily.

Radko opened the door and smiled at Silas. He hugged him warmly and welcomed him inside. He almost wept at the sight of his friend.

Silas was thunderstruck. Radko was never a big man, but his weight had dropped off precipitously. He was gaunt and pale. Even his welcoming smile seemed wan and lost. And in the hug Silas felt a bony angularity that he had never felt before in an adult human being in the developed world.

"Radko," he said, "What has happened to you?"

Radko shrugged and led Silas into the living room. He gazed at Silas with affection, but he was mildly embarrassed at his appearance. He knew he had lost weight; he just hadn't thought it was quite so noticeable to other people.

"I haven't been eating so much lately," he said. "I don't have a housekeeper and sometimes I just forget." Most of the time, he thought to himself.

Silas frowned. He didn't want to be impolite, but he was anxious about Radko's condition. "I was worried about you when I spoke on the phone," he said, "but now I'm more worried."

They looked at each other for an uncomfortable moment. At length, Radko offered Silas a drink. "Scotch?" he asked.

Silas regarded Radko for a moment before answering. "Yes, of course," he finally said.

Silas watched Radko go into the kitchen to prepare the drinks and looked around. The residence was furnished, but Silas thought that every piece of furniture in the room in which he was standing had been there before Radko arrived. There were some old prints on the wall: poorly executed religious paintings, for the most part. Silas was pretty sure these predated Radko's arrival as well. The whole space seemed hollow. No spark of life or vitality. He shook his head.

"Thanks," he said as Radko handed him his drink. "Nice place."

"Thanks," said Radko. He sat down in a chair that he had never visited before and looked squarely at Silas. "It's wonderful to see you, Silas. And it was brave of you to drive here in this weather."

Silas was rebounding from his initial shock. He felt stupid for expressing his concern for Radko so impetuously. He decided to back off.

"The driving was a challenge, but, you know, it beats sitting in a stuffy archive all day long. That's what I've been doing on this trip."

They talked on for a while about Silas's project and Radko's experience as bishop. Radko managed to share some stories of how people first reacted to his appointment, how the power shifts in the diocese lined up, and how he was slowly learning to be the center of attention.

"You know, Silas," he said. "Being the center of attention is really the hardest part. I don't mind not having a boss, but I'm still not used to people making way for me all the time."

"The perks of power," Silas replied. "I hear it's a bear."

Silas was still thinking of the best way to approach Radko. He thought a gentler approach might be more in order. So after a while, he said in a soft voice: "It has been too long, Radko. This is the hardest part of my job, not seeing friends more often."

He waited. Radko did not respond right away. Silas couldn't tell if he was waiting to ask something or what. Silas, a man who prided himself in his ability to deal with people, was at a loss for words.

The two sat is silence for some time.

After a while, Radko stood up and walked to the window. He looked at the endless white and noticed the heavy clouds gathering.

Absolution

Although he had lived in Chicago, he felt the snow in the Dakotas was relentless.

He turned and looked at Silas. "I don't want to hide the truth from you, Silas; I never have. And the truth is that I feel certain that I have destroyed the best thing in my life." He looked down into his almost empty glass.

Then he continued. "I don't know if it's possible to undo the damage I've done to Ursula or to our children. It's been several months since I've spoken to her, and that was mostly about business—selling the house and stuff like that. She's a very headstrong woman, and I haven't been able to have any kind of extended conversation with her." He hung his head, as if in shame.

Silas did not speak. He was relieved that Radko was talking about what was important.

"I have written her letters, but most have come back unopened. I imagine that she is angry at me—I understand why she would be—but I have no way to resolve it, to bring a better sense of closure to the situation." He paused and looked back out into the fading light. "I would walk away from the diocese just to be near her for a time," he said.

Silas remained quiet. "Angry" did not begin to describe Ursula's reaction, he thought to himself. Enraged, outraged, furious, and militant, hostile: these were closer to the mark. Silas thought that it was only Ursula's concern for the twins that stood between her silence and full media exposure of her relationship with Radko. He was uncertain how long that would last, but he did not think it would be forever.

The two fell back into silence. After a while, Silas looked at Radko. "If I should see her, Radko, is there something you would like me to tell her?" he asked.

Radko looked over at his friend. "Is there a chance you will see her?"

Silas sighed. "Mueller asked me to keep in touch with Ursula to make sure she was being cared for. So I have periodic contact.

You're right, Radko, she is angry. She has refused any kind of support the church through Mueller has offered her. She's a proud woman. On the other hand, she has allowed me to speak with her from time to time. That's how I knew she was doing okay."

Hearing Mueller's name in the same sentence with Ursula's made Radko wince. He cursed his own stupidity and shortsightedness and cursed that of the archbishop. He felt like the fly caught in the wily spider's web and knew, like the fly, that death was only a matter of time. He could protest it, rage against it, bemoan it, but he could not prevent it. This was precisely how he felt, as if he were dying.

He returned to Silas's question. Is there something I want him to tell her? There's a lot, he thought. Tell her I love her and that I'm sorry. Tell her I was a fool. Tell her I made the wrong choice. Tell her I was not worthy of her. He looked at Silas. "Tell her to call me," he said.

Silas nodded slowly. He did not think the likelihood was high that this would happen, but he promised to convey the message if given the opportunity. This was his promise to himself. To help these good, struggling people in any way he could.

CHAPTER 10

The balance of Silas's visit was about food. Radko cooked dinner that first evening, but Silas took advantage of every opportunity he could think of to feed his old friend. He got up early and made breakfast. They went to lunch at a local diner. He volunteered to prepare dinner the next evening and made enough food for twelve. He went to the store to get snacks and stuffed his pockets with them for whenever he had a chance to offer them to Radko. He repeated this on the third day of his visit. He packed Radko's refrigerator with everything he could reasonably think of. Just before he left, he thought that Radko had perhaps gained back a few of the pounds he had lost to the desolation billowing through his life.

Between meals and snacks, Radko showed Silas around the area. He took him to the chancery to meet the staff. They toured the cathedral and other churches of note within the borders of the diocese.

On the morning of the fourth day, Silas prepared to leave. He was driving back to Chicago to catch a plane to Los Angeles. In his heart, he was grateful to be headed toward a more temperate climate. As he and Radko sat at breakfast, Radko sighed and told him he wished he weren't leaving.

Absolution

"Nor I," replied Silas. "It is good to see you, and I look forward to seeing much more of you on my next trip."

Radko smiled, something he had just started doing again during the past few days. "I hope I meet your expectations," he said.

Radko saw Silas to his car and stood in the driveway of the bishop's residence in the cold until he could no longer see his car in the distance. He inhaled the cold Dakota air and went back into the house.

Radko went straight to the kitchen and began clearing the dishes and cleaning up. He felt an injection of vitality from Silas's visit. He was more energized to do things in a way he hadn't been for months. He was still acutely aware of the devastation of the past few months, but he felt a little less run over by it. He thanked the absent Silas out loud as he went about cleaning up the residence. Radko didn"t think he was out of the woods yet, but he began to have a new sense of perspective.

After cleaning up, he went into his study and started making lists of things he had to address. Ursula was on the top of that list. He had to decide what to say to her if she should call, and he thought it was about a fifty percent chance that she would, given what Silas had said.

Next he wrote the names of his children, Marguerite and Sergei. Seeing their names on paper brought an upswell of heaviness in his chest, and Radko took a long slow breath to counteract it. He could not just abandon them, as Ursula would have him do. He had to find a way to make regular contact with them. This was the right thing to do; it was what he wanted to do.

Third on his list was one word: Bishop. With a question mark. He had been avoiding this issue since the night Ursula left. He thought at that time that she made his decision easy, but now he saw how he just used her leaving as an excuse to move up a rung on the power ladder of the church. It did not feel like his decision. He was not sure it was the best thing for him or for Ursula or for the church. He knew that sooner or later he would have to decide to proceed with being a bishop or to make an alternative decision. He did not think he could do this today, but for the first time in months he could envision a time when he could do it. He leaned back in his chair and felt a surge of confidence.

CHAPTER 11

By mid-May, spring was beginning to set in. The days were warmer; there was less snow. North Dakota began to turn green. Or at least partly green. With the coming of longer days, Radko's mood slowly began to improve. He was still weighed down, but the jagged edges of the last six months were not quite so sharp—still very sobering and even serious, but more bearable.

Radko had completed making the rounds of all one-hundred-plus parishes in his diocese, and he knew each priest by name. He also knew something about them. As word spread that he was actually showing some interest, some of the crustier pastors began to thaw in their attitude toward him. He encouraged them to call him by his first name.

He had not heard from Ursula. He had had no contact with his children. There being no one to talk to about this whole matter, he had taken to writing Silas and Gordana long epistles about his thoughts and feelings. Sometimes they responded; often they did not. That did not matter so much to Radko. He recognized his need to express himself, and there being no one at hand with whom he could share the whole truth of his life, he turned to the people he felt he could trust in a way that asked little of them.

Absolution

As the academic year ground to a close, so did much church activity. There were fewer devotions to attend, fewer confirmations, fewer dedications. He was looking forward to taking some time off during the summer and wanted more than anything to leave the diocese and find someplace anonymous where no one knew or cared about what he did. He had not made a final choice, but New York or the Balkans were top contenders. New York because his sister lived there and he could get lost in the city; the Balkans because he thought that perhaps it was time to explore his ethnic heritage in a way he never had. He wasn't too concerned about the specific venue; any place but where he was would have been to his mind more tolerable.

Still, the words on the paper he had written at home continued to torment him. Every once in a while, he would write Ursula to tell her that Maggy and Sergie were their children, not just hers. He would tell her that he continued to believe that he had some role in their upbringing and that he intended not to abrogate his responsibility as a parent. Sometimes he sent these letters; sometimes not. Either way, Ursula never responded. He thought of just going to Baltimore and confronting her, but in his lucid moments he realized just how limiting his position was. What would he say? I'm going to move back in with you? I'll visit every weekend? He knew that, as bishop, anonymity was not easy, and most bishops knew when other bishops were in their dioceses.

So Radko bided his time and got on with the business of running his own shop. He expanded his person-to-person project to learn the names not only of all the priests and deacons in his diocese but the staff members of most of the parishes as well. He knew the financial position of the diocese in detail and just how the resources were being spent. One thing Bishop Valezquez did bequeath him was a financially solvent organization; he was grateful for that. He thought he would spend some time this summer devising a plan for future development; this seemed to him the kind of thing a bishop ought to do.

It was late in May, the 29th to be precise, when Ursula called him. He was on his way home when his cell phone rang. He did not bother to glance at the number on the caller ID screen, and almost ran off the road when he heard Ursula's voice.

"Hello, Radko," she said.

Radko was too stunned to speak, but he was desperate to get words out so Ursula would not hang up. "Hi," finally escaped his lips.

He heard a long breath through the tiny speaker in his cell phone. Finally, Ursula said, "I think we should talk."

About time, Radko thought, angry but not wanting to be. "What do you mean, Ursula?" he said.

Another long breath. Suddenly Radko realized that Ursula was crying. "Oh, Ursy," he said. He pulled his car off the road and stopped.

Ursula continued. "Radko, you know I have been in contact with Silas. And he told me that he visited with you a couple of months ago. And that you wanted me to call you. It has taken me some time ..." her voice trailed off.

"Yes, yes," said Radko too energetically. If Silas had been in the car with him, he would have kissed him. "Ursula, there is so much I want to say to you."

"The kids still ask about you. 'When is Daddy coming home? Where is Daddy'?" She stopped, apparently overcome with emotion.

"How are they?" Radko said earnestly. Tears were running down his cheeks.

Long pause. "Radko, I thought I was ready to do this. I don't think I am. I'll ...call you back sometime." And Ursula hung up.

Radko was stunned for a moment, and then he slammed his palms against the steering wheel. "Damn!" he shouted. He was so angry, he jumped out of the car and walked around the deserted vehicle. Finally, he had a thought and pushed the send button on his cell phone twice.

Absolution

"Hello," the digital voice on the other end said, "You have reached the voice mail of Ursula Fliegendorf. Please leave a message."

Radko stood on the side of the road with the phone at his ear for several minutes. He could not believe that Ursula had gone back to her maiden name. What did she call the children? he wondered. Filled with both rage and disgust, he got back into his still-running car and peeled away from the curb.

He was still raging when the phone rang. This time, he looked at the number on the micro screen. It was Annie.

"Bishop," she said with alarm in her voice, "St. Bridget's Church is on fire."

"What!" said Radko. Annie began to repeat herself, but he interrupted. "I'm on my way," he said.

Radko thought quickly about where he was. St. Bridget's was actually only about three blocks away. He turned his SUV in that direction and stepped on the accelerator. Turning the first corner, he saw smoke rising into the cool spring air. Oh, my God, he thought.

The Bismarck Fire Department was already on the scene when Radko arrived. George Sanbrenner, one of the lay deacons of the parish, came running up to him.

"Bishop, thank you for coming," he said.

"What happened, George?" Radko asked.

"We're not sure, but we think the coal from the incense burner was still burning when it was emptied into a trash receptacle. The server who was assisting at the devotions thinks it was his fault. He's a wreck."

"Where is he?" asked Radko.

"Over in the hall," replied the deacon.

Radko walked off in that direction and surveyed the damage he could see along the way. Not just fire, but a lot of smoke and water damage, obviously. He found the hall and walked into a room of various groups fretting about what had just happened. Tobias Renneke, the parish priest, spotted him and walked over to his direction.

"Toby," Radko began, shaking the priest's hand warmly. "I'm so sorry. Is anybody hurt?"

"No, thankfully," replied Toby. "Everyone was out of the church when it started. Some people, the servers and others who were cleaning up after the service, were just outside. They called the fire department."

"I understand a server thinks he was responsible for this."

Renneke nodded. "Yeah, Tommy Gardner. He may have done it. He's standing over there with his parents," Toby said.

Radko nodded and walked off in that direction. Tommy's eyes widened as he saw the man in black with the big cross walk in his direction. He began trembling.

Radko didn't say anything. He put his arms around the boy and patted him gently on the back. Then he turned to his mother. "Thank God, everyone is safe," he said.

Tommy's parents seemed almost equally anxious. "Bishop," his father began, "We are so sorry..."

Radko interrupted them. "I'm sure that, however this happened, it was an accident and completely unintended," he said soothingly. Then he introduced himself to Tommy's parents, shook their hands, and assured them that no one was pointing fingers. "We have insurance for these kinds of things," he said to Tommy. "Some people will have work. Not all is lost."

Radko took his leave of the threesome, who were smiling doubtfully, and went back over to the priest. "Was there any damage beyond the church building itself?" he asked.

"Not that we know of, Bishop. The fire squad says it will be some time before the building will be back in usable shape, however."

Radko looked at the priest. "What do you need from me, Toby?" he said.

Absolution

The priest looked back at the bishop. "I'm not sure right now," he said "We'll need a place to have mass for a while. I don't know what else."

Radko surveyed the frightened and dismayed looks on the faces of the people.

"Whatever you need, Toby, call me directly." Then he took his leave of the priest and walked around saying hello to the small clumps of humanity gathered at the shrine of the Unexpected.

After Radko had shaken every hand, he walked out of the hall into the brisk air. The fire squad was pulling away. He walked up to the church building and saw the charred remains. He shook his head, blessed the building, and returned to his vehicle.

What a day, he thought to himself.

CHAPTER 12

Presiding at services and praying in public were routine aspects of Radko's job as bishop. He tried to do these things to the best of his ability, but his life before Bismarck had involved very little by way of ceremony. Occasional mass at an unfamiliar church on Sunday when no other priest could be found, but no high ceremony for which the church is so rightly famous. It came surprisingly easy to Radko to do these things: surprising because he had so little experience and because he didn't have what his seminary professors called a "regular prayer life." He had always been uncertain what that meant exactly, but presumed it meant praying on a regular, daily basis. He had long since abandoned the Liturgy of the Hours, the scripted prayers that every priest in the world is supposed to say every day. He was sure he couldn't remember what happened to his breviary, the book he used for that purpose early in his career.

With summer approaching, he found himself missing the services he presided over during the first few months of his appointment. Summer is a slow period for church things: most of the major holidays roughly coincide with the academic year. He spent the early part of June preparing for his vacation in July and August. But

Absolution

still, one of the surprises of his new post was how much he enjoyed dealing with the people of the diocese. Bismarck was among the smallest dioceses in the United States. That was probably why Mueller found it so attractive, he thought to himself with some bitterness. Radko knew a fair portion of his flock by name. He made a point of learning new names every time he went to a parish for some ceremony or dedication.

Even presiding at the confirmation of children, something that traditionally falls to the bishop, began to be a pleasant experience. It hadn't been at first. When he first walked up to a boy about Sergie's age to confirm him, he almost fainted because of the remorse and longing that flooded his mind and sharply restricted his breathing. He spent the rest of that occasion struggling to be civil. When the ceremony was over, he fled to his residence and cried for hours.

But it began to get better. The ritual provides for more latitude on the part of the bishop than most Catholics think, and even in these early months of his episcopate, Radko tried to humanize the whole experience. During the last one he did in May, he was even able to joke with some of the children and their sponsors. He could not put his own children out of his mind, but he was beginning to find their memory less debilitating.

He thought about his children every day. Of all the bonds that had been sundered this past year, it was his connection to his children that he missed most acutely. He missed Ursula on many levels: he missed not having an intimate companion in his life every day; he missed her touch; he missed the love he felt when he was around her, even when they were angry with each other. He even missed simply looking at her, watching her go about her daily routine. But with the children there was all this and more. He was their father; they were his responsibility. It was not so much some forced sense of duty but rather a mission that swelled up from somewhere deep in his biological heritage. In addition to that, he missed seeing them grow and change and cry and be afraid. He wanted to comfort them, to support them, to be a dad to them.

Two things prevented this. One was that Ursula controlled access to the twins and she just would not allow Radko to see them. She had told Silas that it was better for all concerned if the children got used to life without their father. They were young enough not to require much of an explanation, but Radko didn't know what she would say when they were a little older. Radko couldn't bring himself to hate Ursula, but for this he was getting more rather than less resentful.

The other reason was his position. What could he tell the children? That his job was a secret or that they were? To see the children would resurrect the double life, a feature of his past life with Ursula that now seemed like a pathetic teen-age prank. He was embarrassed whenever he thought about it and didn't know how he could have been so blind to the needs of his children, blind to the pressures of living a life of duplicity—yet another reason to be disgusted with himself.

So Radko did not know what he would do next with respect to his children, but he did know that he couldn't just let them go. Another impossible situation, he thought to himself, perplexed by what seemed to be yet another of the irreconcilable issues that were piling up in this messy situation. He thought about it a lot. He even tried to pray about it, but his notions of God and his relationship with him were the fast track to unspeakable shame, so this was of little use. No solution presented itself.

Radko was trying with particular care to find some way to see his children this summer. He knew Ursula's address and her phone number. He could just show up one day unannounced at her Baltimore apartment and demand to see his kids. He would risk a scene that he was pretty sure Ursula would not back down from. Or he could try to get Silas to intervene. As much as he felt that he was already overburdening his busy friend, he thought that this was the wiser option. He sent Silas an e-mail asking for his help.

CHAPTER 13

Silas Ranke and Wolfgang Mueller were pondering the surprising and troubling turn of events over the past months in the matter of what they had hoped would be the first American married bishop. They were sitting on an elevated loggia of the archbishop's house overlooking the city of Rome, sipping aperitifs and enjoying the soft late spring breezes. They both knew that within weeks Rome would be a hothouse, suitable only for American tourists who would suffer any indignity to say they had been in the Eternal City. Even the heat.

Silas was giving Mueller an update on his conversations with both Radko and Ursula. For what seemed like the hundredth time, he was describing how militant Ursula remained in her determination to forge a life without her husband. The only curiosity of the situation was that she had not formally filed for divorce, although she had returned to using her maiden name. The children were still Slopovich.

"So," Mueller said at length, "she has refused every offer of financial, legal, or medical assistance from us." He paused and shook his head. "She is a remarkable woman."

Absolution

Silas nodded. He knew that the archbishop's offers of aid were a combination of charity and self-interest. Mueller would have preferred Ursula to be beholden to him, to use his contacts to arrange whatever legal separation or divorce she wanted, or to go to a therapist or psychiatrist of his choosing. There was the ever-present threat that Ursula would go public with her marriage to Radko or even try to sell the movie rights to a studio for money, blowing the lid off his whole plan. He had never met Ursula personally, but the way Wolfgang saw it, if she were going to go public, she would probably already have done so. She did not strike him as a woman who was given to endless deliberation or rumination about alternatives available to her.

Silas, on the other hand, wasn't so sure. He too knew that Ursula was a proud and decisive woman, but he also thought that she was going through her own process and that the outcome at this juncture was far from clear. He did not hold out much hope—no hope really—for any kind of reconciliation between her and Radko, but he could easily imagine a scenario where she would finally go public, the consequences be damned. He was pretty sure the only intervening factor was her concern about the children, to whom she was fanatically devoted. Even Silas could not understand why Ursula would never allow Radko to see his kids. It didn't seem like her.

"I'm planning a trip to the States in the next few weeks, Wolf," Silas said. "I may have more information then." He paused for and looked at the jumbled beauty that was Rome. "Radko sent me an e-mail requesting my help in seeing his children. I plan to go to Baltimore first and see if I can make any headway with Ursula, but frankly…" He looked straight at Mueller and said, "I'm not optimistic."

This seemed like a small matter to the archbishop. He didn't care very much if Radko saw his children or not; what he wanted was an ordained American bishop, a man who would live out his life respectful of his role in the church and of his emotional commitment to a woman. It did not seem like too much to ask, and he was more than a little irritated that Ursula had not gone along with it. Radko was perfect for the role: talented, devoted, willing to go to any length. He remembered how he seemed almost enthusiastic when they met after his appreciation party in November. Mueller shook his head. "So close," he said aloud.

Silas could tell that Mueller was talking to himself as much as to him, so he gently took his leave and wished Mueller a fond good evening. As he walked away, he thought his friend looked older, weaker. We may have come to the end of this story, he thought to himself as he walked back to his quarters.

Once home, Silas sat down at his computer and reread Radko's message, to which he had not yet responded.

Radko, he began typing:

Thank you for your message. I'll be coming to the U.S. in a few weeks, and I'll see what I can do to accommodate your request. However, I don't want you to get your hopes up.

That's the truth, Silas thought to himself, I don't want to let him believe that I have that much influence when I don't think I do.

But I will do what I can. We'll hope for the best. Let me know when you might have some time during your vacation. Perhaps we can get together.

Warmest regards, Silas

With nothing to add, Silas mournfully hit the Send button. He wasn't feeling very helpful in this matter. In fact, he had begun to question in his mind whether the whole project was worth it. Yes, it did give some meaning to his life, or at least to his relationship with Ted, but if Radko's and Ursula's experience showed anything, it was just how incendiary intimate relationships could be. Maybe the traditional teaching of the church in these matters had more substance than he thought.

He shook his head and put that thought out of his mind. That something is trouble doesn't mean it has no value, he reminded himself. He saw in his relationship with Ted something he didn't want to live without: a grounding, a home, a place to feel con-

Absolution

nected. He saw the same thing with Radko and Ursula, even though it pained him greatly to see it change into something else, something belligerent, combative.

He thought about Ursula. On the one hand, he greatly respected her forthrightness, her honesty, her sheer fortitude in taking a difficult situation in hand. On the other hand, he thought she was being unreasonably harsh preventing Radko from seeing his children and not even allowing any direct contact between herself and her estranged husband. He wondered why she hadn't filed for divorce, although he was also grateful not to have to face that dangerous situation. Maybe he would ask Ursula about it when he saw her.

CHAPTER 14

Across the ocean in the port city of Baltimore in the United States, Ursula was sitting on the patio of her small apartment sipping coffee and pondering her life. It was early on a Saturday morning, and this was the first day of her summer holiday. All she had to do was submit grades for her students, and she would be free until late August.

Ordinarily, this was a happy day for Ursula. She loved teaching, but it drained her, and she had always savored the prospect of two and a half months without the daily burdens of installing mathematical ideas into the heads of twelve-year-old children. But on this day she was not so certain. Truth be told, she was more than a little anxious about having too much time on her hands, given the events of the past months. She thought of getting another job to divert her attention during the long summer break, but she resented having to do something just out of fear. She ultimately decided to protect her free time fiercely, the way she had protected her children since leaving Chicago last November.

Ursula could not think of that long week without shuddering. She had tried not to dwell on it since, but she could not easily put the experience out of her mind. She did not think that she had ever

Absolution

been so angry at any point in her life. It wasn't just anger; it was rage: rage that her husband had equivocated about their life together; that he had casually placed the well-being of his wife and his children in jeopardy; and that he had so easily turned away from her. Even now, almost seven months to the day of this betrayal, Ursula reddened just thinking about it. She had thought she knew him, but she was wrong. She thought of him as a basically good if somewhat immature man, but she was wrong about that, too. She thought he loved her and the children. And in this, too, she was utterly mistaken.

Ursula stood up because she could not have these thoughts and remain seated. She went into the kitchen and poured herself another cup of coffee. She thought of her children sleeping in their bedroom upstairs in their small but tidy townhouse. She knew she was getting too far afield from what she had told herself she would think about, and she slowly returned to the patio. The lovely temperate weather contrasted sharply with the turmoil in her soul, and she thought that maybe for once she should allow nature to do what nature could do to soothe her. She felt the soft breezes on her cheek and inhaled deeply of the early morning air. She could smell the sea.

Despite the rage that rumbled inside her when she thought about her situation, Ursula had told herself that, once she had gotten settled—emotionally, financially, and domestically—she would try to work out a longer-term plan about what to do with the man to whom she had been married. The man who was, as much as she did not like to think about it, the father of the two little people upstairs who were now the unquestioned center of her life.

She had a number of fears. Maybe not fears so much as things that concerned her. Chief among these was whether or not she could ever be so close to another man. Ursula did not doubt that she could carry on with her life; she had proven just how capable she was of doing that these past seven months. But it had taken a toll on her. She found her endless resourcefulness itself a cause of concern. Was it just that she didn't really need a man? While these months had been tough, there was no question at any point that she was capable of pulling off what amounted to a disappearing act. In November she was married and living in suburban Chicago, teaching at a perfectly respectable middle school. In December, she was single and living in downtown Baltimore and teaching in another middle school.

The transition looked easy on paper, she thought. But the reality was quite different. She recalled her early conversations with her friend Joan, the woman with whom she and the twins stayed during the first week back in Baltimore.

"Why did you leave?" Joan had asked, not being a shy or even particularly discreet person.

Ursula thought for a moment and then said "Because he hesitated so long. He wanted his way. Early on, when this issue came up, he used to say that of course he would have to resign the priesthood and of course I and the kids came first. But the closer we got to the announcement, the clearer it was that what Radko really wanted more than anything …" The phrase brought Ursula up short. "More than anything," she emphasized, "was taking that damned job." She looked at her friend severely. "More than us," she said.

Joan nodded. "What a guy," she said. Her own life had not been so successful in the relationship department, and she was jaded about romantic prospects because of a long string of generally unfulfilling relationships with various men. In many ways, she liked men; she certainly liked the ones with whom she was involved. But the distance from liking someone to a longer-term commitment seemed to her perilous, fraught with so many complications that she had always elected to remain unmarried. She was not unhappy with her decision, but she recognized that her expectations for relationships were low.

On the other hand, she admired Ursula greatly for taking the leap with Radko. Joan was more sensitive to the cultural and reli-

Absolution

gious issues involved in that arrangement, having been nominally raised Catholic herself, but to her one set of obstacles and complications was pretty much like another, and she thought the arrangement was so manifestly improbable that it might just work. So it did not surprise her when it did for five or six years. Nor did it surprise her when it collapsed this past fall. She thought the destruction spectacular, way beyond anything she had done to end a relationship. But at base it seemed like inevitable theater to her.

All the same, she knew she had a role in this drama, and she tried to play it with maximum skill. She nodded thoughtfully while Ursula raged. She tsk-tsked appropriately when she talked about what an ungrateful, stupid, blockheaded guy Radko was. She got drunk with Ursula one evening after the kids went to bed and toasted the end of the improbable marriage to which Ursula had given her best shot. On a smaller scale, there had been many occasions in the past where Ursula played this role in Joan's life, so her playbook was clear even if she had to ratchet up the seriousness and intensity of the role.

In the private spaces of her mind, Joan saw Radko as a priest who wanted it both ways. She liked him personally, but she could not shake the impression that Radko was for the years of his marriage to Ursula the triumph of an adolescent dream: to make one decision while not letting go of the mutually exclusive alternative. Nice work if you can get it, she thought grimly to herself; but, as she knew, the piper always has to be paid. Her uncensored ability to mix metaphors in her own mind amused her; after all, no one was watching.

Joan went out of her way to be of assistance to her friend. Ursula had unfailingly been there for Joan, and she was eager to return the favor. She loved Ursula as much as she loved anyone, and the twins would most likely be the closest she would ever come to having children.

For Ursula's part, she was grateful to have a friend like Joan. Ursula thought of her as a nice balance: Joan was spontaneous where she was methodical; Joan was indifferent where she was serious; Joan was devil-may-care where Ursula was overinvolved. She loved her for being what she wasn't.

And more than she had with any other person in her life after the age of fourteen, Ursula came to depend on Joan. She trusted her with the twins that first night; she lived with her for over a week. Since she did not have her car with her during those early weeks, it was Joan who drove her around looking at apartments. When she moved into the townhouse, it was Joan who helped her arrange the move and carry it out. And it was Joan who celebrated the new home and drank the modest Spanish sparkling wine that substituted for the champagne they would both have preferred.

All of this happened like clockwork. Ursula felt taken care of and purposeful. The dark underside of this whole experience was the twins. Even now, seven months later, Ursula was uncertain if she was doing the right thing by them. What she was doing made sense in her mind, but it seemed a little heartless, even to her.

At first, she told the kids that their father had gotten a new job, and that he would not be living with them for a while, maybe for a long time. This was her cover story. Her husband—their father—worked in another part of the country. She thought it was lame but couldn't approach the truth any better. She also knew that it only postponed facing the whole truth with the children, although she thought that it would be some time before they could begin to understand the issues involved. She didn't understand them completely herself, but she was sure the twins couldn't.

At first the kids were scared, and they did not speak much about anything. It pained Ursula to see her two bright and engaging children retreat into silence. Silence individually and between themselves. She seldom heard them talking to each other seriously in the room they now shared, and she was sure that she would hear them through the paper-thin walls of her urban renewal apartment. They fought a lot during the early weeks. Not so much the squabbles that young siblings have with each other but conflicts that were

Absolution

overblown and due more to the heightened sensitivity of each of them, including Ursula, as to any real issue. Ursula responded to these as best she could, but since she was unwilling to tell the kids the whole truth, there was little she could do except enforce discipline.

After a few weeks, there was less fighting and more...Ursula didn't know what to call it. Depression, perhaps. There was a pall over the household, especially around the Christmas holiday. That was rough, Ursula recalled. Each of the three of them tried to pretend that everything was normal, except that one of the major players in the family drama was inexplicably missing. And Radko had loved Christmas. It was he who was the first one up and it was he who handed out the gifts with a joke or a hug or an accolade for each child. Christmas morning that year was a much quieter affair, and, after it was over, Ursula decided that she needed to tell the kids a version of the truth she thought they could understand.

So the day after Christmas, she cleared the breakfast dishes, turned off the TV, and sat the kids down on the couch in the small living room. She sat between them. They looked frightened, as they typically did when Ursula was going to be serious with them. For her part, Ursula was growing accustomed to that tentative look on their faces and took it in stride.

Ursula looked at each of her children and softened her expression as much as she could. The twins were not the only anxious humans in the room.

"There is something I have to speak with you about," she began, reaching for a hand of each of her kids. They were all seated on the small couch.

She paused, took a deep breath, and continued. "Your father and I are no longer together. We are getting a divorce." She did not know how else to put it.

Neither of the twins moved. Their eyes did not leave Ursula's face.

"I know this is difficult for you," she said, "but I want you to know that both your father and I love you very much." Ursula figured that this was probably one of the most inane things she had ever said to a child, given that she had no idea of whether or not her husband loved them. On the other hand, she was sure that she did; that idea reassured her.

The kids were silent. Sergei teared up first; then Maggy; then Ursula. They sat in moist silence for some minutes, holding hands and not saying anything.

At length, Maggy spoke. "Momma," she said, "we knew that."

"You did?" Ursula said without thinking.

Maggy nodded. "Remember when you said that people who were going to get divorced had quiet dinners a lot? Well, you and daddy had quiet dinners a lot."

Ursula smiled inwardly. She did indeed remember saying that, and it delighted her that Maggy was so attentive to the things she said. On the other hand, she was not delighted to be having this conversation.

Then Maggy looked at her brother, who was regarding her anxiously and tilting his head in Ursula's direction, as if egging her on. Maggy took a deep breath to counteract her shakiness. "Did Daddy die?" she finally said.

Ursula's eyes widened as she looked at her daughter with surprise. She looked at her son. They were both looking at her flushed with anxiety. "No, no, honey," she said slowly. "Daddy didn't die." She stared deeply at both her children.

"Then where is he?" she pressed. "How come he doesn't come visit us? How come he didn't come here for Christmas?" Maggy was crying loudly now, and Sergei was joining her.

Ursula didn't know exactly what to say. She put her arms around her children and pulled them toward her. "I am so sorry," she said.

And then she told them the truth. That she and daddy decided to separate in November when they left Chicago and that she

Absolution

didn't think it was good for them to see their father just yet. She could see from the looks on her children's faces that this was the wrong decision, and in the same instant saw her own selfishness and shortsightedness. She was their mother but felt more like an awkward sibling.

Then the inevitable question came, the one that Ursula didn't want to address. "Why did you and daddy get divorced?" asked Maggy. Before she could answer, Sergei added the equally unwelcome "When can we see him?"

Ursula did not reply at first. She thought the first question was really the easier one to address. She had no plans to answer the second.

"It's hard for children to understand why adults make these decisions. Your father and I had some very basic disagreements. We wanted different things. I'll try to explain it to you as you get older."

"When can we see him?" Sergei asked again.

Ursula looked at her son. "I don't know," she replied. "We'll just have to see."

At this, Sergei began bawling and threw himself on the floor. "I want my daddy!" he shouted.

Ursula waited, pretending to have more patience than she had. It was true that she felt that she had been overcautious about the separation from Radko. And she knew that she had to make some kind of arrangement for the children to see their father. But just now, she had no idea of how that would happen, and she was certain she did not want to give in to Sergei's tantrum.

She gave her son a steely look, the one that meant "knock it off." After a few minutes, he did.

Ursula took yet another deep breath. "Right now," she said in a tone that she hoped was more conciliatory, "we have to be brave and go on. We'll be all right." She thought for a moment. "It may be some time before we see Daddy."

She took note of the fact that she used the first person plural but did not ascribe it any special significance. She was still furious with Radko, and she thought it would be a long time before he reappeared on the scene.

Now, sitting in her patio months later reflecting on these developments, she knew she was right. No one dared bring up Radko again. The kids probably did talk about it between themselves, but Ursula could only hear undifferentiated murmuring and whispering from their bedroom. She hoped they were taking care of each other as best they could with the young but potent bond between them.

For her part, Ursula didn't even consider asking Radko back into their lives. She wanted to be more settled, to have enough distance to quell her ambivalence about a decision that sometimes still seemed strident, even to her. Ursula was not given to relentless self-doubt, but she did wonder at times if her hurried exit from Chicago was the fair thing to do to the children. She doubted it, but she didn't have a clear image of an alternative scenario. Stay and torture herself and Radko more? Tolerate his endless covering up of his real intentions? More quiet, disengaged dinners? All these seemed like pointless and painful prospects to Ursula.

On the other hand, she knew there was a big unresolved piece of the kids' life missing, and after a while she began to give more serious thought to contacting Radko. She spoke to Silas from time to time, and she knew that he was lobbying in his respectful way for her to reconsider her walled-off position relative to the man to whom she had been married. Even her friend Joan did not quite understand why it was such a big deal, especially if Ursula didn't love him anymore.

"I do love him, Joan," Ursula finally said to Joan one afternoon in the spring.

Joan looked at Ursula over her low-fat latte. "Oh?" she said.

"Yes," Ursula replied. "I did not leave him because I no longer loved him. In fact, I left him because I loved him but he was not able to reciprocate. Not able to choose."

Absolution

Joan considered this. In her own life, it was usually the loss of that feeling of love that spelled the demise of a particular relationship. When she was younger, she used to think that this was just a sign that the man she was dating was not the "One." Later she came to believe that the experience of falling out of love with someone was probably just the natural course of relationships. It didn't matter to her: she loved being in love and found the humdrum phase of bondedness tiresome.

So she thought she could grasp some of what Ursula was saying. "Do you think of going back?" she asked.

Ursula looked back at her with a mixture of disgust and affection. Disgust attached itself to the prospect of returning to a relationship that she felt was broken, love or no love. Affection for the guileless way Joan asked these impertinent questions.

"I don't think that would be possible even if I did want to go back," she finally said. "Radko is a bishop now. I have followed his career online. Silas says he misses me, but I don't think he misses me very much." She did not mention that she returned his mail unopened most of the time, and that even when she opened it, she could only bring herself to read the first few sentences.

"Have you filed for divorce?" Joan asked impertinently.

"No," replied Ursula.

CHAPTER 15

It was mid-May when Ursula began getting the urge to call Radko. When the idea first popped into her mind, she dismissed it out of hand. Even though it had not been a year since she saw him, it felt like much longer, so different was her life now from a year ago, so settled did she and the kids feel, or at least appear to be on the surface.

But over the following week or so, the notion kept returning to her. Why not? she thought on several occasions. She wanted to speak with him, and Silas had told her that Radko had asked him to ask her to call him, but she hadn't at that time. She didn't feel ready; she didn't want to rock the boat; she got too anxious just thinking about it.

But as the spring progressed, the impulse took shape. She began to think about the conversation with the kids after Christmas, and how much they obviously wanted to see their father. She began to feel guilty about being the one who prevented him from being a part of their lives. She questioned what the best thing for the children was, although she was astute enough to know that her own feelings played into this decision more than she cared to admit.

Absolution

On that sunny afternoon on the 29th of May, she was at home and the kids were with Joan. She found the number Silas had given her in her purse and picked up the phone almost without thinking about what she was doing. Her hands were shaking when Radko answered his cell phone. She remembered stumbling through an explanation and mentioning the kids, but mostly she remembered feeling nauseous and shaky. She quickly terminated the call, breathing heavily and feeling awash with so many contradictory feelings. She just stood there staring at the receiver in her hand. She didn't answer when Radko tried to call back.

It took Ursula the rest of the evening to calm down. She was now beginning to understand why it was so important for her to flee and to avoid dealing with this man. It was just too painful, too overwhelming, too damned complicated. She also realized that this was the reason why she had not filed for a divorce. She didn't want to open up this wound, to relive what was probably the most wrenching and painful event in her life. For the first time in months, Ursula felt the full force of the grief of losing her husband, her marriage, her life.

There was a version of herself that Ursula did not like. It was strong-willed to the point of pigheadedness; decisive to the point of insensitivity; angry to the point of belligerence. She valued the milder versions of these things: she liked being strong and counted on it. She could not imagine being indecisive. She also knew how important it was to put anger to good use. But she shuddered when she thought of the extreme version, and she thought maybe she was there.

So as the evening progressed and the twins returned with Joan for dinner, Ursula resolved to face the situation with her marriage more straightforwardly, less stubbornly, and with greater attentiveness toward all concerned, including her own jumbled feelings about a situation that remained messy no matter how tidy she tried to make it on the surface.

The next day, she sat down and wrote Radko an e-mail.

Dear Radko, she began,

I know it has been a long time since I have responded to you. I want to thank you for being patient with me.

Ursula leaned back in her chair. Now what? she wondered.

I think the time has come for us to bring some closure to our situation. It was very difficult for me to leave you, but I recognize that the children are both of ours, and they want and need a father.

Ursula nodded and felt sensitive.

It is probably best if we could arrange a time to meet and discuss future plans. I am off for the summer and have some flexibility.

Here it comes, she thought.

I also think it would be good for the twins to see you. This will take some planning.

All right, I am being tolerant and respectful, she thought.

Please let me know what you want and what the time constraints might be so that we can make plans.

Ursula thought for a moment.

I think it would be best if we would communicate by e-mail. You may reply to this address.

Ursula.

She did not push the Send button. Not that night. She wanted to give herself some time from the two-minute conversation she had with the addressee of this message.

CHAPTER 16

It was two weeks later when Radko opened his e-mail account, as he did every day, and saw a message from an unknown source. It included the letters "uf," and, even though he thought it was a stretch, he opened it hoping that it would not be another unsolicited pharmaceutical ad.

He caught his breath when he saw that it was from Ursula. He read through the message quickly, fearing that perhaps something bad had happened to the children. Relieved that this was not the case, he let out a long breath and read it again. And again and again.

Radko pushed back in his chair. So she wants to meet, he thought with more satisfaction than he had the right to feel. He was anxious but also euphoric. He leapt out of his chair. Then he wondered if Silas had arranged this, if he had told Ursula to contact him. Then he sat down again. How did she get my e-mail account? he wondered, but as quickly as that thought came he realized that it was on the diocesan website. Did she know about that site?

These thoughts seemed inconsequential to Radko. He was finally going to see his children. He was finally going to see Ursula. He couldn't wait. Suddenly his planning took a more serious turn.

Absolution

Seeing the children changed from a wish to more than a possibility; it was a likelihood. It was going to happen. Feelings of joy and loss washed over him at the same time. He rushed out of his office, telling Annie on the way out that he had some errands to run.

Annie looked askance at the bishop in motion. In the corner of her mind she wondered if he had snapped: he was moving too quickly, smiling with moist eyes, and being entirely too vague. He always told her exactly where he was going. Shaking her head, she went back to work.

Radko drove and drove. He was headed in the general direction of his residence, but he was in no hurry to get there. He stopped and filled his SUV with gas and chatted with the attendant who took his payment. He suddenly wanted to be around people. Not priests or other church people who worked with him but peers. Regular people who were unconcerned about what others thought of them. He thought of driving straight to Baltimore, but even in his agitated state he knew that was a foolhardy plan. He stopped in the parking lot of a funeral home and looked around. There was nowhere in the entire thirty-four thousand square miles of the diocese where he could think to go. This awareness was sobering, and he put his car into gear and drove home.

When he got there, he looked around and suddenly found the rooms of his residence dreary, dated, and alien. It did not feel like his house. His house in Chicago had always felt like home—with furniture and artifacts of his choosing, with things that meant something to him, with noise, with people, with a wife and children. He glimpsed the tidal wave of emotion rise inside him just before it knocked the breath out of him, leaving him curled up on the threadbare couch, filled with desire for the life he had lost.

He lay there for an indeterminate length of time. He could only think of Ursula's e-mail, which he had committed to memory. Just hearing from her was one of the most powerful experiences of his life. It reminded him of when they first met, when they first had sex, when they fell in love. Every cell in his body longed to be near her and with their children. He felt the sterility of his surroundings. The residence was nice enough if a little worn; it was just lifeless. Silas had felt it. It was the perfect place to be depressed.

The imaginings that played out in Radko's mind that evening were almost all fanciful and unrealistic. He would beg Ursula to return to him. He would hug his children for hours. He would walk away from what his life had become. Resign the episcopacy. Forsake his religion. In his mind in his distressed state, these things seemed simple and uncomplicated. It was clear that he had been a fool and had chosen unwisely. Did he not preach conversion: recognizing the sin and turning away from it? He would turn away from this sterile and empty life. He would restore himself to sanity.

It was in the dissociated fog of these kinds of thoughts that he heard a knock on the door. He raised his head off the couch, thinking at first that he had misheard. But there it was again. He never had unexpected visitors. Was someone trying to break in?

Radko pulled himself off the couch and ran his fingers through his hair, trying to make himself presentable. For a burglar? he thought to himself. He took a deep breath and opened the front door.

"Bishop," said a worried Annie standing in the doorway, "Are you all right?"

Radko stared at his office manager, who had never said a personal thing to him during the entire time he knew her. "Yes," he said. Then, "Annie, is something the matter?"

Annie stood perfectly still except for the facial muscles around her mouth. "You seemed upset when you left the office. I tried to call you, but you didn't answer your cell phone. I...I was worried about you." She did not turn to go.

"Oh," said Radko. "Would you like to come in?"

"No...no, thank you, Bishop," Annie replied. "I just wanted to make sure you were okay."

"Why, thank you, Annie; thank you very much," said Radko. And he wished her a good evening.

Absolution

When Radko closed the door, he glanced at the clock on the mantel. He wondered absently why it always had the correct time; he had never set it. But he saw that it was only six-thirty. It felt much later.

Annie's short and unexpected visit had a sobering effect on Radko. He went to great lengths in his life to avoid public scenes or even indications that there was any kind of turmoil going on within him. He hadn't thought that when he left the office there was anything very unusual. Obviously, he was wrong.

He went into the kitchen and made a pot of coffee, thinking about what his next move would be. He recalled the extrapolations of his imagination of just a few minutes before. At the very least they deserve more careful consideration, he thought to himself as the coffee percolated. When it was done, he poured himself a cup and went into his small study, where his computer sat waiting for him.

Waiting for the machine to boot up, Radko began to compose a response to Ursula. He felt his tie to her, and it ached within him. But the welfare of his children was at stake as well as his own ego, so he scolded himself to keep their welfare at the top of his priority list. This was not easy for him.

Dear Ursula, he began,

Thank you for your message. It was wonderful to hear from you. I will have time during July and early August to come to Baltimore for a visit. I'll arrange to stay at a local hotel. Please let me know when the best time for you and the twins would be.

Radko sat back and looked at the blinking cursor. There was so much more he wanted to say. He bit his lower lip as his mind flipped rapidly through the options. His hands returned to the keyboard.

I'm looking forward to seeing you and the children.
Radko

Radko's absent thoughts hung in midair, and he made no motion to send the message. He could hear himself breathing. He reread what was on the screen. After a while, he recognized what was bothering him. This sounds like a business letter, he thought to himself. He deleted the message and started over.

Dear Ursula, he began again,

I cannot express how much your message meant to me, as did your brief phone call a couple of weeks ago. You and the children are never far from my thoughts. I am so grateful that you will allow a visit both with you and with them.

There is much I would like to say to you that should not be shared in this way. Please let me know when you have a few days, perhaps a week, to spend time together talking. We do indeed have some serious planning to do.

It was here that he hesitated.

I love you very, very much,

Radko

He hit the "Send" button and got up and walked away from his computer.

CHAPTER 17

Ursula stared at the message from the man who was about to be her ex-husband. She sighed deeply and knew that her transitional time was nearing its end. If she and Radko met—when they met—it would be time to face the hard stuff. Anxiety and sorrow welled up inside her. She had to admit that up till now, she pretended about certain things. She acted as if Radko had died or was not really a part of her life or the lives of their children anymore. She drew sustenance from seeing herself as a woman cast aside and forced to valiantly if somewhat melodramatically forge a life for herself and her children. Now she had to recognize that the situation was vastly more complicated for everyone. For herself, for her children, even for her husband. She could read in his message that this was not a case of his blithely going off with no regard for her. She was, after all, the one who left, who ran away and made it easy for him. It was she who returned his letters unopened and refused to allow him access to his children. This was not the story of one person; it was a story of four people bound together forever. She hung her head in bewilderment. What was she going to do when Radko came? she thought to herself.

Absolution

She took a deep breath and then took out a piece of paper and started listing her options. See him one time or more than one time; allow him to spend a few hours with the children on one day or several days in a row? He was their father, and there was no reason he couldn't take them for a weekend or some other extended period of time. She didn't think she had to worry about Radko kidnapping his children, as she had read about other fathers doing. He could hardly take them back to his diocese.

Ursula had so many complicated feelings that she didn't think she could manage them all just now. She put the pen down, crumpled up the paper, and got up from the desk where her computer sat. She walked over to the phone and considered calling someone. She could call Joan, as she often did when perplexed. She could call some other friends who were not so close just to distract herself from the conflict inside of her. Or she could call Radko.

She stared at the phone for a long minute. She had to make specific plans with him anyway, she thought to herself. Also, she was haunted by her babbling on the phone the last time she called him, and she thought maybe she could do better in the civil conversation department. Ursula caught a glimpse of her face in a small mirror that hung on the wall in the narrow hall by the telephone. In that reflection, she saw the real reason she wanted to call him. It was not to make plans or to redeem herself; it was to talk to him, to connect with a man to whom she had given herself unreservedly. She took a deep breath and dialed.

She got Radko's voice mail. "Hello, This is Bishop Slopovich. Please leave a message and I will get back to you as soon as possible."

Hearing his title in Radko's own voice made Ursula blanch. She waited for the tone and then spoke with more haughtiness than she intended. "This is Ursula, please call me."

She replaced the receiver and walked into the living room. She was not thwarted from her objective, but she felt angry every time she got a signal about Radko's job. It seemed to her like the bottom line. He was, in fact, a bishop of the Roman Catholic Church, and anything she might think or feel about that did not change that infuriating fact. She tried to calm herself down. He is still the father of my children, she lectured herself. He is still my legal husband. As she sat there, she recognized how painful the next few weeks or months could be.

Her reverie was broken by the ring of the telephone. She picked it up and said hello.

"Ursula?" Radko said.

"Yes?" she replied.

Silence.

"I'm returning your call," he said in an unnecessarily business-like way.

"Thank you," said Ursula, being equally businesslike.

She continued. "Radko, I am sorry. I wanted to call to make plans for a visit, and I… I …I thought it would be better to do this…."

"I'm so happy you called," Radko interrupted. "I'm dying to see you," he added quickly.

Ursula chuckled in spite of herself. Just like Slopovich to say something so corny, she thought. "When do you think you can come, Radko?" she asked.

"The soonest would be the first week of July," Radko replied, hoping that this would work for her. He didn't want to wait a minute longer than he had to.

"Let me see," said Ursula, pretending to look at her calendar. "Do you want to come for the Fourth of July weekend?"

"That would be great," Radko said. Then he added, "I want to see the children."

"Of course," Ursula replied, showing none of the antagonism or haughtiness that was in her attitude and voice earlier. "I'll tell them today that you'll be coming."

Radko felt the softening in Ursula's voice. "Thank you," he said. "I can't tell you how much this means to me."

Absolution

Then the tears came to Ursula's face. She did not say anything for a few minutes. She didn't know what to say. "Me too," she finally said.

"I'll call you when I arrive in Baltimore," Radko said. He thought for a minute and then said: "If something comes up, please call me at any time."

"Good-bye, Radko," Ursula said.

Ursula stood there feeling things that were at once alien and familiar. She had allowed herself no affection for any man since last fall, much less her husband, and found the experience of warmth with Radko unsettling. But at the same time, it was what she had known and lived for seven years now. It was what she anticipated from the first few times she met him as a student before they were married. She had always held her bond to Radko precious and thought it would endure forever. Unfortunately, it might, she thought to herself, fearful that no feeling of warmth could outweigh his abandonment of her.

The telephone rang again. It was Silas.

"Ursula?" Silas said.

"Yes?" Ursula replied, recognizing Silas's voice and wondering how it was that it fell to her lot to speak so often with priests.

"Ursula, this is Silas. I'm calling because I got a message from Radko not too long ago. He wants to see his children and he asked me to check with you to see if there was some way you could possibly see your way clear to allow... "

"Done," interjected Ursula.

"What do you mean, done?" Silas said.

"I just got off the phone with him, and he's coming here the first week of July," she said. "To see me and visit the children."

"Oh," said Silas.

"Silas?" Ursula said. "I'm looking forward to it." She began to cry.

Silas listened intently. He was surprised, and his heart went out to this strong but vulnerable woman. When Ursula did not say any more, he asked "What can I do to help?"

"It helps just talking with you about this, Silas," Ursula replied. "I know I've been angry for a long time, and I'm still angry. But Radko and I, well, we were very close. And sometimes it doesn't seem like it would take much to be close again. Except…"

Silas was silent.

"Except," Ursula continued, "He is still in a job that mysteriously does not allow love between a man and a woman."

That is the problem, Silas thought. Then he said, "Would it help if I were available during the time Radko is there?"

Ursula thought for a moment. Actually, she was not thinking about an answer to his question; she was thinking what a stupid question it was, so patronizing toward her as a woman. Like the good churchman he was, she thought. But she also knew that Silas was just trying to be helpful. "No, I don't think so," she said. "But I may call you afterwards. Thanks for the offer, Silas." She meant that. Silas had gone out of his way to help her.

"Okay, Ursula, but you know how to get hold of me," Silas said.

CHAPTER 18

When Silas put the phone down, he was pleased. Pleased that Ursula was softening, pleased that she and Radko were getting together, pleased that she seemed ready to move forward. He had not seen this softer side of Ursula in many months. He wondered what he could do to be helpful but recognized that much of what was going to happen was between Radko and Ursula.

He opened his laptop and e-mailed Radko that he had spoken to Ursula but that she had beaten him to the punch and already arranged the visit. He expressed his hope that things would go well and assured Radko that he would be here if he needed him.

Then Silas thought about Mueller. He sensed that Mueller had one goal in mind and figured that he had not abandoned that goal just because some obstacles had arisen, even if that obstacle was one of the major players. He considered Mueller a friend as well as a coconspirator, but he was also protective of both Radko and Ursula in their efforts to be the ones who made important decisions about their lives. He believed that Mueller had manipulated these people—with Silas's help—to the spot they were now in. He had some resentment about that and didn't want the Slopovich family interfered with again by Mueller or by anyone else.

Absolution

So he didn't contact the archbishop to tell him about these developments. He thought he had a window of time before anything else of significance changed.

Silas found himself relaxing in a way he hadn't for a long time, probably not since events in Chicago last November. He thought he would call Ted and bring him up to date. Hopefully, they would see each other soon.

So he did just that, and he added another thing to his list about which he was pleased.

CHAPTER 19

Archbishop Wolfgang Johannus Mueller, on the other hand, was not pleased. His first foray into the American church with his plan was stalled. It was almost beyond Mueller's capacity to say that it was lost or that it was a missed opportunity. To Mueller, everything was always in process. Mostly in the process of going his way.

But so far, he had been stymied in every effort to intervene in the situation. He had tried to provide financial support for Ursula in the hope that she would warm to him. He had made offers of professional help—psychotherapy—to help ease the pain. He had even proffered the services of an attorney, although he had mixed feelings when Ursula declined that one. The last thing he wanted was for her and Radko to divorce. But if they were going to do it, he wanted a direct link to the action.

This had always been the archbishop's forte. He had, throughout his career, been able to keep his fingers in various pies, often by simply being nice but as often by being generous. The fact that his family had money and that his own career had been one of such success as to give him access to church funds had made this much easier than if either of those conditions were not true.

Absolution

Still, he thought to himself in the tastefully appointed living room of his spacious Rome apartment, money is obviously not much help in this situation. Neither Radko nor Ursula seemed especially motivated by creature comforts. Too bad, he thought. Sipping his afternoon tea, he was considering ways to ratchet up the pressure, to somehow, in some sufficiently delicate way, nudge the Bishop of Bismarck and the Baltimore teacher back together. The twelve hundred miles between them seemed at times like an insurmountable hurdle, but Wolfgang had always pegged himself as nothing if not resourceful.

He thought of Silas and his untiring role in the various ploys he had attempted over the past year. Silas was almost irreplaceable as a go-between, as a person who could take plans from inception to implementation while making few waves. Wolf valued that in him. But it also seemed to him that Silas was getting a little too close to the protagonists in this little drama, and he wondered if someone else could do the nudging with greater success. With these thoughts, he put his tea aside and walked over to the small corner of his room where there was a small private chapel.

He knelt down on the prie-deux before the small altar. Praying on his knees was something that Wolfgang had done since he was a young boy, and it invariably provided him with a useful combination of just enough physical discomfort and mental clarity to see him through complicated situations. As he typically did, he intoned in his mind the Latin prayers he had learned as a child, invoking the Holy Spirit and asking Him to guide him in this difficult situation.

The archbishop knelt motionless on the bare, worn plank. He was in a type of trance, the kind induced by intense prayer. In this experience, he took leave of his normal, physical self to the point where his aging knees no longer felt the discomfort of supporting his large frame, where the cares of the day, even the thorny situation in America, melted away into a state of calm and peace that seemed to feed his complicated soul. After about forty minutes, he closed with a short prayer spoken aloud, got up, and returned to his couch. He knew the answer he requested would come to him.

CHAPTER 20

Back in America, Radko was making plans. He would be gone from the diocese for over a month, and he made sure that all the significant people in the chancery had his cell phone number and knew they could call him if anything important came up. He then turned his attention to the trip he was to make in a couple weeks.

He thought it best to drive to Baltimore rather than fly. He would have his car while there, and the long journey would give him time to settle into the experience of seeing his wife and children. It reminded him of a drawn-out version of what he used to do in Chicago on the way to and from work. He debated whether to even take any ecclesiastical attire with him. He wondered if he should inform the Archbishop of Baltimore of his presence in his diocese. The answer was no to both of those possibilities, he thought; either of those could make things too complicated very quickly. He would prefer to travel incognito, so much as that was possible.

Radko even gave some thought to creating an alternative identity for himself, but he wasn't sure of how exactly to go about doing that. So in the end, he just decided to go as he was, believing that any attempts to try to be someone else or look like someone

Absolution

else would backfire by adding more anxiety to an already stressful situation.

Should there be someone in Bismarck who would have to know where he was? he wondered. If he told his Vicar or someone in the office, that information could find its way to Baltimore. After all, there were people in that city who knew him. If the chancery in Baltimore found out, protocol would probably require that he make a visit or some kind of contact with the cardinal there. He didn't want any of this; he just wanted to see his children.

On the other hand, it might seem suspicious if he didn't tell anyone where he was going. What could he say? "I'll be gone for six weeks, but you won't know where I am?" That sounded both unlikely and childish. He could tell them he was going to visit his sister back east and leave it vague. He could tell them he was going to California. Or Europe for that matter.

Radko chuckled to himself, the first such chuckle in a long while. This was getting too unwieldy, he realized, so he finally settled on telling Annie that he would be traveling up and down the East Coast, visiting old friends, and that he would prefer not to have to mix in any business or church meetings during this time. He also encouraged her to reach him on his cell phone if something came up.

Annie did not balk at any of this. To her mind, the bishop was beset by too many demands anyway, and she thought that his getting away from it all would be good for him. Especially after the incident a few weeks ago, when she was so worried she went to his residence. She was still a little embarrassed about doing that, but the thought that something would happen to her boss outweighed whatever self-consciousness she had. He obviously needed a rest, and the thought of his having to visit other chanceries or bishops or do formal church activities while on vacation seemed like an unnecessary burden on her already harried bishop. She promised herself that she would protect his privacy in any way she could.

"Do you need me to make any reservations for you, Bishop?" she asked one afternoon after Radko had outlined his definite but nonspecific plans.

"No, Annie," Radko replied. "I will be mostly staying with friends, and if I should need to get a hotel, I'll just find one along the way." He thought for a moment and then added. "If I do need something, I'll call you from the road."

This seemed to please Annie, who fretted about the bishop's well-being and who, even though she thought it was a good idea for him to get away, did not like the fact that he would be somewhere out of range of her vigilant eye. "Anything you need, Bishop," she said.

Radko smiled as Annie walked out of the room. He marveled at how little it took for her to go from an intimidated, overgrown child to a truly useful human adult. Taking her out of Chicago and giving her responsibility helped him enormously. But it also helped her, and Radko was appreciative of the woman Annie had become.

He looked at his calendar. He had nine days until he left, and he did not quite know what to do with the time. There was nothing much scheduled. Kids were out of school, pastors were taking vacations, and the liturgical year was winding down. He decided to make some calls.

His first was to Toby Renneke, the priest at St. Bridget's. Damage from the fire was more extensive than they thought at first, and the entire inside of the building would have to be rebuilt. He asked Toby if he needed any help.

"Thanks, Bishop," Toby replied, "but the people here have been just marvelous. We are temporarily using space at St. Margaret's, which is within an easy drive from here. Fr. Bunshu was very generous. He let us use the church and also the other parish facilities for meetings and such."

"When is the date for the reopening, Toby?" asked the Bishop.

"Should be around the first week of September, Bishop," Toby replied good-naturedly.

Absolution

"Good, good," said the Bishop. "We should rededicate it."

After speaking with Toby, he decided to call Bunshu. Kito Bunshu was a priest from Cameroon who had been in the diocese long before Radko arrived. A large, dark, and imposing man, Kito usually scared people before they got to know him and realized how generous and warmhearted he was.

"Kito," the Bishop began, "How's it going with the added numbers?"

Kito laughed. "Just one big, happy family, Bishop," he replied. "The people from St. Bridget's add a lot to our worship."

Radko knew what he was talking about. Kito was one of those inviting charismatic types whose masses lasted for two hours. Praying, clapping, singing, endless prayers: it was pretty much fun to Radko's mind. And he could only imagine that it was more fun with more people. "Let me know if you need anything, Kito," the Bishop said. "I want you to know how much I appreciate your helping Toby and his congregation with this."

"Thanks, Bishop," said Kito.

Radko got ready to leave for home. As he was walking out through the outer office, where Annie sat guarding his inner sanctum, he felt a sensation of warmth and satisfaction. He loved and respected the people of this diocese, and he would be sad to leave it, even for a few short weeks. This was not a depressing or anxiety-producing awareness; it was simply how it was for Radko. He knew he had some decisions to make, and he hoped that when he saw Ursula and the children those decisions would somehow become clear to him. But just now it did not feel that it was within his control. He was one player among many.

CHAPTER 21

Ursula didn't know what to with herself. She had told Radko that she would tell the children that he was coming, and she did. She didn't look forward to it, so she put it off for several days.

"I know it's been a long time since you've seen your father," she told them, "but he's coming to visit us on the July Fourth weekend."

The kids looked at her with wide eyes, as if they were going to be visited by a ghost. They didn't say anything.

Ursula looked at them and wondered what they could possibly be making of this development. "Um," she said, "How do you feel about this?"

"Fine," said Maggy finally. Sergie nodded. "Fine," he repeated.

Fine? thought Ursula. After being ripped away from him with no notice and no reason, they feel fine? Her guilt required her to have more of a reaction from them.

Ursula tried to regain the momentum. "Your father is looking forward to seeing you very much." She paused. "He misses you."

The twins stared back at her. After a few minutes, Maggy said, "Can we go play now?"

Absolution

Ursula looked at the twins, not comprehending their reaction. "Okay," she said, and off they went.

Ursula sat on the living room couch wondering if she should have said something else or asked them more questions or reiterated the fact that their father had not died, but she didn't.

Instead, she called Joan and described the conversation with her.

"So what do you think?" Ursula asked, after repeating every word she and the twins had spoken just a few minutes earlier.

"I don't think the twins know what to think," said Joan, which was exactly what she thought herself.

"Do you think I should try again?"

"Try what?" replied Joan. "I think this is one of those situations that just needs to play itself out. I think just being available and matter-of-fact about it would be best."

"I guess you're right," said Ursula, who had no idea of what to do instead of that.

Ursula did not move from her spot on the couch after talking with Joan. Okay, so maybe this is fine with the kids. But it may not be fine with me, she thought. Since she had spoken to Radko, she began having memories of their life together before all this bishop nonsense came up. To call them fond memories was an understatement; they were memories of the life she had always hoped for, had always wanted for herself and for whatever children she might have. Close, warm, loving. She had not even come close to any of that with other men she had dated prior to her marriage.

These thoughts frightened Ursula. She didn't want to be beguiled again, to be swept into an impossible situation where she had to lie. That felt like a bottom line to her. She couldn't do that to her children. Nor did she know exactly what to do with the powerful feeling of betrayal that continued to throb within her. Could she ever really trust Radko again? she asked herself.

These thoughts were immediate, compelling, and impossible to resolve. I'll just have to wait and see how this goes when he comes, she decided, and forced herself to get up and go about her daily chores.

CHAPTER 22

Radko left for his vacation early. He decided to drive to New York to see Gordana, who, when he called her to ask if this were okay, was happy to accommodate him. He set out across the northern tier of the country feeling hopeful that his life was finally beginning to move forward after the bleakness and immobility of the past six months. Radko liked to drive, so the two-day trip held the prospect of some pleasure for him.

As he approached Chicago, he thought maybe he could stop by and see some of his colleagues there in the chancery. Then he thought better of it. I don't need any more pressure right now, he thought, with notable regard for himself, a regard that he had not felt much over these past months. Bolstered by the feeling of meaning and significance that comes with making a firm decision, he continued driving east. He hoped to have more feelings like this.

He did, however, want to see more of the city than was possible from the interstate, so he decided to drive though the downtown areas around Lake Shore Drive. Just seeing the thriving metropolis of Chicago triggered feelings of nostalgia. He missed the busy city: not just Chicago, but Baltimore too. He rolled down his windows and breathed in the thick and oily Chicago air. The city was lovely

Absolution

in the summer, at least the parts he could see from the boulevard that passed by the lake. He got off at Columbus and drove up Michigan Avenue, smiling at the hoards of people strolling up and down in front of the expensive shops. He delighted in this hurly-burly world, but he also remembered the night he was last here, the night he felt a surge of confidence only to return home to learn that Ursula was leaving. The pain of that night still had the power to jolt him. In some ways, it seemed like a lifetime ago; but in other ways, it seemed very recent. His life was so different then from now, but the pain of that evening never completely left him. Radko knew that he was only now beginning to recover from the trauma of that awful evening. He cursed himself for being so proud and vain as to miss completely the impact of events on the woman with whom he lived.

He tried to back off from the self-loathing that had become so familiar in his life. If any of us knew all the outcomes of our decisions, we would of course choose differently, he counseled himself. Being immature is not a sin, even at my age.

This mental dialogue got him through the city, and he reentered the interstate to continue his journey. He didn't want to spend the night in Chicago: too many ghosts. He thought that perhaps Cleveland was a more advisable venue. He had never been there and didn't think he knew anyone, and it would probably be easier to find inexpensive lodging on the outskirts. He drove on.

Radko was right. He found an inexpensive Holiday Inn on the western edge of the Cleveland area and decided to turn in early. He went to his room with a small travel bag, got ready for bed, and flipped on the television. He was asleep before the ten o'clock news came on. He woke up in the middle of the night to turn the television off.

The next morning at about six, Radko awoke from a deep sleep. He lay in bed motionless, halfway involved in a dream that was still active. In the dream, he was standing in front of his cathedral explaining to the people why he had to leave the diocese. His voice was choked with emotion, and as consciousness dawned, Radko realized that tears were flowing down his cheeks. Midway through his sermon about the need to heal his own life, he was filled with a crushing sense of loss. Words eluded him, and his speech slowed to a trickle before it stopped altogether and he stood mute before the people of his diocese. He stared at the congregation, who were also silent. It was at this point that he realized it was a dream and that actually he was in a cheap hotel outside Cleveland.

He got up. It may have been a dream, he thought, but it was so vivid and not so far from what might happen. He sat on the edge of the bed with his head in his hands. Nothing about my life is easy, he thought self-pityingly to himself.

He got up and looked in the mirror at the graying, middle-aged man in front of him. I thought being a grown-up was supposed to be easy, settled, he said to his reflection. He felt a wave of dread come over him as he teetered between the depression that had hounded him for months and the delicate new strands of normalcy that he had just been learning to savor. "No!" he said aloud, and the look on the face of the man in the mirror was resolute. "I will not go back there. I will face whatever it is I need to face and make whatever decisions I need to make." He stood motionless for a moment, as if daring the bogeyman of depression to get him. But then he straightened up, walked into the bathroom, and got ready for the rest of his trip east.

CHAPTER 23

Radko liked Chicago and loved Baltimore, but he adored New York. As he drove through the congested streets trying to find his sister's building, he marveled at the colossus that was this city. He was grateful that Gordana had settled here and absently wondered if she were as happy with that decision as he was.

Gordana had told him where to find a parking place, and Radko was lucky to find one without too much trouble. He grabbed his overnight bag and started walking to her apartment on 73rd Street. He found it with no trouble and rang the bell.

Before Gordana responded, his cell phone rang in his jacket pocket. He was startled out of his reverie and fumbled for the phone.

"Hello?" he said.

"Bishop," said Annie, "I am so sorry to bother you, but Father Schwarze has just been arrested."

"What?!" said Radko, alarmed and shocked.

Annie took a deep breath. She dreaded making this call for many reasons. She didn't want to interrupt her boss' vacation; she didn't want to bring him bad news; she didn't want to make his life

Absolution

more difficult. "This morning," she said. "A parent from his parish said he molested her son."

Radko was silent for a long while. He knew a lot about the sex scandals, but there had been no hint of any trouble in his small rural diocese. He knew there was a policy, but he was fuzzy on the details.

"Where is he now?" he finally asked Annie.

Annie paused. "In jail," she said. "He called here first thing." She struggled to continue. "I called the diocesan attorney, Mr. Albecore, and he is on his way to the jail to see him." She finally told Radko the truth. "He told me to inform you as soon as possible."

Radko's mind was swimming. He knew there was a diocesan attorney, but he did not know him. "Who is Albecore?" he asked. He didn't know what else to say.

"He's the attorney the former bishop used. I asked around and found his name. I didn't know who else to call."

Radko thought for a moment. He was glad that Annie had gotten so resourceful. He was uncertain if he would have had the presence of mind to even think of getting a lawyer. But those thoughts were transient. He was more focused on what he had to do at this moment. "What is Albecore's number?" he asked Annie.

She gave him his office number and his cell phone. Radko fumbled around for a pen when Gordana answered the intercom. "Hi, sweetie," said Gordana.

Radko froze. "Hi, Gordana," he said too loudly. He was hoping that Annie had not heard that. He finally located a pen and told Gordana to hold on. He quickly wrote the numbers down and told Annie that he would call her back. The door buzzed, and Radko entered the high-rise building with a sense of urgency and relief.

When he got to the door of his sister's apartment, he had already formulated his initial plans. When Gordana opened the door, he hugged her and tried to explain what happened in the moments after he rang her bell.

"In jail?" Gordana asked.

"Yes," Radko replied. "And I have to speak to the attorney right away." He asked to use their land line, and Gordana directed him to the small study that Gavril had in the rear of the apartment.

Radko got Albecore on the first try. He introduced himself and asked for an update. Albecore knew who he was and gave him what information he knew. Evidently there was an incident in the rectory where a fourteen-year-old boy was helping with some parish chores. He stayed late, and the priest invited him to relax and have a soda. After that, there was some ambiguity. The boy evidently said that the priest massaged his shoulder. The boy panicked and ran out of the rectory. He told his parents, who called the police.

"Why didn't they call Schwarze?" Radko asked.

The lawyer sighed. "A few years ago, they might have, Bishop," he said. "But not in this climate. Everybody knows that it was the civil authorities who forced the church to face this situation." He paused. "No one really trusts the church in these matters," he said bluntly.

Radko thought for a moment. No, they don't, he thought. "How's Schwarze?" he asked the lawyer.

"Not so great," Albecore replied. "He thought he was just being sociable. He says he didn't intend anything by touching the boy on the shoulder. He said he didn't even realize they were alone in the rectory."

Shit, Radko thought. "Any previous history here, Frank?" he asked.

"Not that I know of, Bishop, but I've only known about this for a couple of hours. I'll check on it and get back to you."

"Thanks, Frank," Radko said, and hung up the phone.

Radko stared at the phone for a moment. His personal dilemmas suddenly seemed trivial, even though he knew in the back of his head that they weren't. But in his worst case scenario, he was not looking at prison. He called Annie.

Absolution

"Annie," he began, "I am at my sister's apartment in New York." He paused. "I'll be back in Bismarck in the morning," he said, surprising even himself.

Annie was surprised but pleased. Pleased that he was at his sister's and pleased that he was returning. This situation requires your attention, she thought, although she felt bad about interrupting his vacation.

Radko said: "Could you get me a flight from New York to Bismarck sometime tomorrow morning?" he asked.

"Consider it done, Bishop," Annie said. And he did.

Radko put the phone down and thought about this disturbing development. He could get back to Bismarck and deal with this situation and not interrupt his plans for Baltimore, he hoped. Then he realized he was in his sister's apartment and had not said the proper hellos. He got up and walked toward the living room, looking for his sister.

He found Gordana in the small butler's pantry between the kitchen and the living room. "Hi, Sis," he said.

He hugged Gordana. A long, greedy hug that was almost too much for a sibling. But he was desperately pleased to be with someone who knew him, who knew the truth about his life, and who cared for him.

He slowly pulled away. "I'm sorry," he said to Gordana, "I just got a big problem dumped on my lap. I have to get back to Bismarck."

Gordana looked at him with surprise and some suspicion. "So soon?" she said.

Radko sighed. "Yes," he said. "I'm the only person who can make decisions about this situation, and I have to consult with the attorney, the priest, and the diocesan advisors." He said this with the authority of a man who knew what he had to do.

"But we have this evening," he said to his sister. "I am so glad to see you." He kissed her on the forehead.

Gordana and Radko sat in the living room, catching up on the past six months. Gordana noted how gaunt Radko looked, yet she also saw the passion in him when he talked about what was happening in the diocese, especially this most recent event, which troubled her brother and herself deeply.

"What do you think will happen, Radko?" she asked her brother softly.

"I don't know, Gordana," he replied. "I suspect there will be an investigation and possibly a trial. I don't know this man well, but I don't remember any previous problem."

They sat in silence for a moment. When the door opened, they both jumped a little. It was Gavril returning home.

Radko stood up to greet his brother-in-law, who seemed something of an interloper in the intimate conversation he had been having with his sister.

"How's the priest business?" said Gavril good-naturedly.

"Trouble upon trouble," Radko replied, finding a welcome hint of ease in his response.

"Hungry?" Gordana said to both of them.

"Ravenous," they said in unison.

CHAPTER 24

The next morning, Radko parked his car at the LaGuardia airport and boarded a small plane headed west. He tried to make a list of the things he needed to do, but it wasn't a long one, and he soon fell into that trance that being on an airplane tends to induce.

His mind rewound and fast-forwarded. Back to the diocese that was now his home, forward to his meeting with Ursula, which had, over the past twelve hours, slipped into the second tier of priority in his mind.

Radko could not deny that his energy was directed like a laser on this current crisis. He felt responsible for everyone involved: for the boy, his parents, the priest. It was up to him to address it, to manage it, to put the most responsible face on a situation that might have just been a misunderstanding. But it could have been more, he thought darkly. He regarded his own black mood with disgust, seeing it as a self-indulgence he was ashamed to acknowledge. Easy, easy, he then advised himself. Both situations are important; let's focus on one at a time.

Visiting with the boy and his family seemed like the first order of business. He made a note to call Annie as soon as he landed to

Absolution

get the address and phone number of the family, whose name, he now realized, he didn't know. Add that to the list, too, he thought.

Throughout these thoughts, he held a vision of Ursula and the twins in his mind. In a kind of sacred space. He realized that it was not a matter of trying to fit them in: seeing them was a priority, something he would do no matter what, even if he had to depart Bismarck in the middle of a media frenzy. Don't be so melodramatic, he ordered himself. But the bottom line was still the same: he couldn't justify missing the upcoming visit for any reason whatsoever. He took a deep breath and tried to read the pathetically bland flight magazine. He dozed off.

It was the landing that jolted him awake. He looked at the sparse construction around the Bismarck airport and took a deep breath. As soon as the plane shut down, he turned on his cell phone and called Annie. She had the information he wanted at her fingertips. He told her he was going to the residence to change and call the family; he hoped to see them that very day.

He grabbed his flight bag and made his way to the small terminal. It was windy and chilly in the later morning air, and he glanced at his watch. 11:30. He thought he could see the family this afternoon or maybe this evening if they worked during the day. He grabbed a copy of the Bismarck Tribune on his way to the taxi stand.

Within twenty minutes, he was back at his residence, which still seemed drab and lifeless. He dismissed those thoughts from his mind and sat down at the desk in his study. He took a deep breath and called the Frankley's, Mira and Brent. Their son's name was Brent, Jr. He waited until he got their voice mail. As the cheery greeting played itself out, Radko tried to compose his thoughts. After the beep, he said: "Hello, this is Bishop Slopovich. I heard about the incident with your son, and I wanted to express my concern. I would like to visit with you about this in order to better understand what happened." He thought for a moment. Then he left his cell phone number.

When he put the phone down, it occurred to Radko that he might be the last person this family wanted to talk to. Even so, he thought, it was his pastoral duty to extend whatever resources the diocese had to assist them if there was any lapse on the part of Fr. Schwarze. He called Albecore's number and got his voice mail as well. Then he called Annie.

"Annie," he said. "What's in Fr. Schwarze's file? Is there any indication of misconduct or any trouble?" He didn't know exactly what he was asking.

"No, Bishop," replied Annie. "Since his ordination, there has never been a complaint about him. He became pastor about six years ago, and all accounts are that he is well-liked by his parishioners."

Radko thought for a minute. He needed to call the priest and meet with him. "Where is he now?" he asked.

"Mr. Albecore posted bond for him. He's staying with some friends in a town called Rock Haven, about twelve miles north of here."

"Do you have a number?" Radko asked. Annie gave it to him.

He called the number and an unfamiliar voice answered. He asked for the priest, and the man who answered asked who was calling. When he heard it was the bishop, he called for Schwarze to come to the phone. Before he handed it over to the priest, he apologized to the bishop. "We're trying to screen calls, Bishop; possible media interest."

"I understand," said Radko, wondering if this were going to hit the papers. There had been nothing in this morning's edition.

When Dennis Schwarze came to the phone, he was instantly apologetic. "Bishop, I am sorry about..."

"How are you, Dennis?" Radko interrupted.

The priest took a long breath. "In shock, I think, Bishop. I...I've never even had a traffic ticket, much less been arrested." Radko could hear the anguish in his voice.

Absolution

"Dennis," said Radko soothingly, "I would like to meet with you and talk about this. Would you like me to come to where you are or would you like to come here? I'm at home."

"No, I'll come to you, Bishop," Dennis said.

"Good," said Radko. "I'll see you soon."

After he hung up, his cell phone rang. It was Brent Frankley.

"Bishop," Brent said, after he introduced himself, "I think we owe you and our priest an apology."

Radko was silent. Brent continued: "We panicked when Brent, Jr., came home so upset. We didn't think it through. We called the police and they arrested Fr. Schwarze. We kept Brent home from school today and took him to a counselor. It turned out that Fr. Schwarze didn't rub his shoulder; he just patted it. Brent was tired, he got scared. We believe Fr. Schwarze when he said he didn't even know everyone else had gone home." Brent, Sr., paused. "Dennis Schwarze is a good priest, Bishop. We are so sorry this happened."

Radko collected his thoughts; as well as he could in the light of this new information. "Are you absolutely sure?" he asked him. "We want you to be absolutely sure there is no problem here."

Brent took another breath. "Yes, Bishop, we are sure." Then he continued. "You know, Fr. Schwarze is a little bit, um, effeminate, and the kids talk about that among themselves. So when Brent found himself alone with him, he was nervous. And when he patted him on the shoulder, he just flipped out."

"Oh," said Radko. Then, "Brent, I know this is hard for you and your family. If you are satisfied that all is well, then I am satisfied."

"We have already dropped all charges, Bishop, and we plan to apologize directly to Fr. Schwarze and to anyone else who might be aware of this."

"Blessings on you and your family," said Radko, and then he hung up.

Wow, Radko thought to himself.

Twenty minutes later, there was a knock at the front door of the residence. Radko opened the door to see a pale Dennis Schwarze staring hard at him. "Hello, Dennis," Radko said and motioned for him to enter.

Dennis walked stiffly into a room he had never seen before. He glanced around, but he had trouble taking his eyes off Radko, who was trying not to smile.

"Please, sit down," Radko said, gesturing to the couch. Radko sat on the other end of the long, threadbare piece of furniture.

"Bishop," Dennis blurted out, "I want to apologize…"

Radko waved for Dennis to stop. He didn't want this good man to suffer any more.

"Dennis," he said. "I just got off the phone with Brent Frankley. He now believes that Brent, Junior, overreacted. They saw a counselor, and they want to apologize to you directly."

Dennis' pale face turned ashen. "What?" he said.

"It's over, Dennis," Radko replied. "There are no charges, no allegations, no problems with Brent and his family." He paused and looked at the stricken man. "We are going to proceed as if this did not happen."

Dennis looked down, and Radko could see that he was trying to hold back tears of relief. He leaned forward and took Dennis' hands in his. "It's okay, Dennis," he said softly. "I can only imagine how difficult this is for you."

Dennis fell to his knees and wrapped his arms around the bishop. He cried like no one Radko had ever seen. He didn't know exactly what to do, so he just sat there with his arms locked under Dennis', holding on. After what seemed like a long time but was actually only a few minutes, Dennis pulled away and sat back on the couch. "Sorry, Bishop," he said.

"No need to apologize," said Radko, although now he was a little worried if this hadn't been all too much for Dennis. He wondered if he needed more care and attention.

"How can I help you, Dennis?" Radko asked after a while.

Absolution

Dennis did not respond right away. Radko could see that he was still trying to catch up with events. "I'm not sure, Bishop," he said.

Radko thought for a moment. "I think it might be a good idea if I came to the parish with you and presided at the liturgy this weekend. We can explain to the people what happened in case any of them have questions. I will talk to the Frankleys before then, and they can participate in any way they feel comfortable."

Dennis brightened ever so slightly at the prospect of his not returning to the parish alone. "Thank you, Bishop," he said.

Radko couldn't think of any other business, so he said, "Well, it's set then. I'll call the Frankley's and ask them about Sunday. Why don't we wait until tomorrow morning for your return to the parish? I'll meet you there for morning Mass."

Then Radko blessed the quivering priest and hugged him gently. Dennis could hardly speak as he left the bishop's residence.

After he closed the door, Radko shook his head. He felt compassion and even some pity for Dennis, but he was already formulating his revised plan to get to New York to pick up his car and head for Baltimore.

CHAPTER 25

The weekend was intense and fast-paced. Radko made good on his promises and accompanied Dennis back to his parish the next day. He had called the Frankleys and invited them to the Mass on Sunday to address the issue of the arrest. He also contacted Frank Albecore, the diocesan attorney, to make sure there were no legal loose ends. At the Mass on Sunday, he gave his unqualified support to Dennis as the pastor of his parish.

Only Albecore was not completely on board with this rapid restoration of the status quo ante. He was concerned in his lawyerly way that more investigation might be appropriate to ensure that there was no reason to be concerned about Schwarze's behavior.

"Investigation into what?" Radko asked him.

"Into his background, into how he thinks," Frank replied. "Maybe we should have him evaluated by some psychologists."

Radko sighed. He understood Frank's concern, but this episode came and went so quickly and there was no evidence of any other improprieties in Schwarze's background. He decided against it. "We can watch him a little more closely," he said to the attorney, "but I don't think we should put the guy through any more because of a simple misunderstanding."

Absolution

Albecore nodded as if to acknowledge that it was not his decision to make. It was only his role to advise.

It was Monday, and Radko was back in his office. He still had some days until he was to meet Ursula, and he was eager to get back to the east coast. Annie tried to run interference for him as much as possible, but a bishop in the office was a bishop available, and even she had a hard time keeping up with demands on his time.

Finally, Radko declared that he was leaving, that all business could wait until he got back. Once again, he said good-bye to Annie and to the office staff and, armed with his e-ticket, made for the airport, courtesy of the same eager deacon who had cleaned his car so thoroughly last winter.

Once safely aboard the plane bound for New York, Radko allowed himself some relief. He wasn't unhappy that he had returned to the diocese to deal with the crisis, although the whole experience highlighted to him how tied he was to the new professional role in life. These people certainly need a bishop, he thought to himself.

As he traveled east, farther away from the diocese, Radko was less certain that he was the man for that job. So much of it was so personal, he thought, and he had so little pastoral experience dealing with people. I was a bureaucrat, he thought to himself with some dismay.

Radko thought about the Frankley family and the courageous way they owned up to the truth of the situation. They had not equivocated when Radko told them that he was going to preside at the liturgy on Sunday, and they even volunteered to speak. Radko knew how important this was, given the speed of gossip and rumor in the rural parish where Schwarze was assigned. They were good to their word and described exactly what happened. Dennis was gracious about it, bolstered no doubt by his vested role on the sanctuary and the presence of a supportive bishop. Radko blessed all concerned and left the service with a feeling that the parish and the priest would survive this crisis, perhaps even grow from it. He was grateful for that.

He did not have the same sanguine attitude toward himself or his own life. He remembered the past months of depression and shuddered. During that bleak time, there were few sources of light; but one small one was that he was not leading a double life. Radko looked out the window and recalled the years of his marriage to Ursula. He thought about how he boasted to himself and sometimes to his wife about his ability to deceive other people, essentially to lie to almost everyone he knew about who he was and what he was up to. These recollections filled him with disgust, and he tried to escape momentarily by picking up a magazine. But the glossy rag contained nothing to counter the weight of his own self-judgment. He put the magazine down and looked out the window and at the world below him turning green. It's beautiful here, he thought to himself, thinking that he was probably over southern Canada.

He was aware both of the tentative state of his personal recovery and the fact that he didn't have a clear agenda for his visit with Ursula and the children. Seems like a dangerous combination, he thought to himself: touchy mood and no plan. He was able to manage a smile at his own enigmatic attitudes, and waved for the flight attendant to bring him a drink.

CHAPTER 26

Back in New York, Radko felt a lot more relaxed. This time he was able to greet Gordana in a less desperate, less clingy way. He apologized for the sudden comings and goings and offered to take her and Gavril out to dinner that evening. They agreed. Gordana was happy to see Radko more settled. She had been a little worried just a few days before when he seemed so scared, so needy, and so self-absorbed. She thought maybe he had made the right choice about his life.

But this was not something she would ever say out loud to her conflicted brother. In her own mind, Gordana went back and forth about what Radko was doing with his life. It seemed alternatively foolhardy and sensible—foolhardy because he all but dared the world to find out about him, but sensible in that he had finally made a choice, or at least accommodated a choice that was foisted upon him. After Ursula left, Gordana felt protective of her brother and became a lot more understanding. She knew this ran counter to her critical mindset, but she also thought that Ursula was rash and a little too cunning for Gordana's tastes. Radko's sister judged that Ursula had basically kidnapped their children, and this thought made her more than a little angry. Marguerite and Sergei were, after

Absolution

all, her niece and nephew, and Ursula's actions took the children away from the extended family, as well as away from her beleaguered and not quite ex-husband. No doubt about it: Ursula was a bitch. The fact that Radko's wife had not communicated with her or anyone else in Radko's family was more evidence that she could not be trusted.

But with Radko she worked hard to be evenhanded. She did not know how this situation would play out, and she wanted to guard her relationship with her brother, a relationship that had actually gotten closer in recent years than at any time before in their lives. She loved Radko and wanted to help him in any way she could. She was surprised how many times his actions had escaped bringing the disaster down upon him that she would have predicted, and she thought that perhaps destiny was at play here in ways she did not and could not understand. Thoughts like this made her lightheaded, however, and she soon refocused her attention on dinner plans.

"How about Rudolpho's?" she chirped to the two men in her life.

"Sure," said Radko, happy to have a plan for the evening.

Gavril agreed, and the three trooped off into the Manhattan evening.

Once settled into the restaurant, Radko began describing events of the past week, expressing his appreciation yet again that things worked out so well. Gavril sipped his vodka and listened with all the attention he could muster, but to him Radko might as well have been an eccentric paleontologist with a specialty in pre-Cambrian societies of crustaceans. He searched in his head for a question he thought might be appropriate.

"So, how is this man's behavior your problem?" he finally asked Radko.

Radko did not pause. "Well, as bishop, I'm responsible for each of my priests, for their spiritual and physical well-being." He thought for a moment, looking into his own glass. "And if there is any sign of danger to children, it's my responsibility to take appropriate action to protect their well-being."

"And you think that there's no problem with this man?" Gavril asked, uncertain what spiritual and physical responsibility was.

"I don't think so, Gavril," replied Radko. "The boy went through the situation with a therapist, and the parents realized that their son overreacted. They were willing to stand up in church and take complete responsibility for their actions. It was impressive."

Gavril shrugged. He didn't think this was so settled a situation as Radko seemed to think, but church affairs were not his, and he didn't pursue the matter. He could see that his brother-in-law was pleased with how he handled the situation. Gavril was not an attorney, but he wondered what a lawyer would say to this situation.

"What did your lawyer say?" he said, having tripped over a serviceable question.

Radko thought for a moment. "He was leery," he finally acknowledged. "He thought we should have the man evaluated by some mental health people." He paused and looked beyond Gavril's head. "I didn't see the need, since there was no problem."

While Gavril was not an attorney, he knew enough about the legal system to think that Radko was being dangerously naive. But this had been the case with his brother-in-law from the time when he had met him years ago. He acts like a smart high school student, he thought to himself. Like his wife, Gavril was always at least mildly surprised that Radko's life didn't blow up in his face. But he followed Gordana's lead in not confronting these matters openly. The price of marital bliss, he thought, as he took a longish pull on his drink.

Gordana spoke up. "I think you probably have time to think about that situation, Radko," she said. He thought to himself that he would indeed have to think about it. While it didn't seem to him an urgent matter, he made a mental note to talk to Albecore about the legal side of this more thoroughly.

"Time to order," he said, as the waiter approached.

CHAPTER 27

During the next few days before Radko was to leave New York, he gradually became more unsettled. He was not to meet Ursula and the twins until the weekend of the Fourth of July, and he intended to start driving south on the second. He spent the two days till then spelunking the caves and canyons of Manhattan, window-shopping and breathing in the smells of a city that ordinarily delighted him. But now, he spent most of his time daydreaming about his visit to Baltimore. He stopped by a large toy store to pick up some toys for the kids, and when he went to pay for them, he noticed that his hands were trembling.

The salesperson looked at him solicitously. "Are you okay?" she finally asked.

"Sure," said Radko quickly. He was sweating and his hands were clammy. He left the store as fast as he could.

Out on the pavement in the bright New York sun, Radko thought he might vomit. Buying the toys brought the reality of his fatherhood into sharp relief, and guilt and remorse tore through his body. They are children, he shouted inside his head. They are not disposable. And they are my children. He could hardly breathe under the weight of his sin, of his abandonment of the two humans he brought into the world.

What am I going to do when I see them? he wondered in a self-accusing way.

He looked down the avenue and saw it as cluttered and dirty for the first time. The normally enticing smells of the metropolis suddenly seemed constrictive and foul. He headed back toward Gordana's apartment, trying to get a grip on his emerging emotions.

By the time he reached her building, Radko was out of breath. He wasn't sure what he wanted to do, but he knew that he didn't want to stay in New York any longer than he absolutely had to. He saw no reason why he couldn't leave now. As he rode up the elevator, he began composing the note to his sister and brother-in-law in his head.

Dear Gordana and Gavril,

Thank you for your hospitality. I decided to leave today rather than wait another whole day. I guess I am too eager. Thank you for your hospitality. Hope to see you both soon.

Love, Radko

Short and to the point, Radko thought to himself as he collected his things, locked up the apartment, and headed for his car. He stood at the opened door of his SUV for a moment, looking around him at the city, trying to locate the familiar way he felt about New York, the city he regarded as the height of human achievement and civilization, but he could not grasp it. He shook his head and got in his vehicle, closed the door, and edged into the traffic. It seemed that the drive off Manhattan took forever, and the clogged roads, the construction, the masses of people that filled the space all seemed suddenly noxious to him, an experience he had never had in this city of cities.

Radko didn't know exactly how long the trip to Baltimore would take, but he knew that he would not—could not—stop until he got there. It was already midday on the east coast, and he was unsure how late he would arrive at his destination. But he didn't care. Only one thing mattered now, and that one thing was in the city by the Chesapeake.

On the way south, which was drawn out because of congestion all along Highway 95, Radko could only think of how he had abandoned his children. He thought of Ursula, but not in the desperate way he had in much of the past six months. As if for the first time, he saw his behavior as wrong, as immoral, as contrary to what he should have done. But judgment was focused on his role as father to the twins. They were his children. He admitted to himself with some shame that at first he was relieved that Ursula scooped them up and spirited them away so suddenly. In those weeks before she left, the presence of the children was a painful reminder of how constricted his life was, how limited by their existence. Now driving slowly in stop-and-go traffic, he tried to reason this out, to put his behavior in some context that made sense but respected the immorality of his actions. It was not easy.

He thought back to his own childhood when he was five or six. He didn't have a lot of recollections of those times, but he remembered that he had felt alone and set apart from other members of the family ever since he could remember. He had always attributed this to what he thought of as the "usual suspects": having only one sibling who was outgoing, female, and considerably older than he; having parents who were immigrants to the United States and who spent a lot of time at work; not really minding spending time alone reading or watching television. No one seemed to have any evil intent. His parents didn't abuse him or each other; no one drank to excess; no one was violent or criminal. He always thought he knew why he was so solitary, that this was his lot in life, the way he was and the way things were.

That outlook remained unchanged until he met Ursula. It was she who opened his eyes to another way to be in the world. It was she who broke through his distanced, detached approach to life and showed him that love was more than duty or pious verbiage. In the midst of these thoughts, somewhere around Philadelphia,

Absolution

Radko saw with great clarity the structure of his agnosticism: he saw how the bleak landscape that enveloped him throughout his childhood and adolescent years had left him with little hope that things could be or would be different. He saw how belief in some super being was dangerous, naive, and just served to get his childish hopes up, only to be dashed upon the rocks of his arid, everyday existence. He also saw how he brought this way of thinking with him to his adult life essentially unchanged and unquestioned. It was the one he inflicted on Ursula and his children by finding reasons to abandon them.

The idea that Sergei and Marguerite would feel thrown away by him as their father and left without a word hounded Radko nonstop for fifty miles. He was benumbed: too enraged at his own behavior to cry and too ashamed to have any other thoughts. After a while, he wondered how his action did affect them. Were they depressed? Did they miss him? What did they tell their new friends? He thought that Ursula had probably given them some kind of cover story, but he could not help but wonder what they thought in their young and tender hearts. He wondered if they would ever be able to trust him again.

He was getting impatient with the relentless traffic that stood in the way of his reaching Baltimore, but Radko could not bring himself to stray from the path he was on. He wanted to stop for coffee to clear his mind, to calm down, to center himself in some more realistic perspective. But he kept driving. It was purgatory for his sinfulness.

As he tried to calm himself down in what now seemed like the cramped compartment of his SUV, Radko was suddenly appreciative of his wife as a person quite apart from him. Whatever distress his children were suffering due to his behavior, he was certain that Ursula was doing everything in her power to help them, to nurture them, to be a strong parent for them. He had no doubt whatsoever that Ursula would put her children first and would raise them the way she saw fit, no matter what the obstacles. He loved her for that. That love began to lift his spirits.

As Radko entered the state of Maryland and glimpsed the blue waters of the Chesapeake for the first time, he felt that he was coming home, and this feeling gave him the only solace of the past hundred miles. Of course, he was returning to the place he was raised, the one he had always thought of as home. But this time, it was as if he were returning home for the first time. He had the antennae of a tourist open to new sights and sounds. He could feel the sprawling metroplex that was Baltimore, and his heart leapt when he glimpsed the skyline of the city, which was lighting up for the summer evening. His eyes began filling with tears as he beheld the place he had spent most of his life as a favored son might: with sympathy, affection, and respect. This is my home, he thought to himself; this is where I belong.

CHAPTER 28

Radko began thinking of where he would spend the night. He thought it should be some place close to the city center, so he would not be so far away from Ursula and the children. On the other hand, he didn't want to run into them before his formal visit. He found a small hotel he remembered from his younger days when classmates from Rome would come visiting. He parked his SUV, paused for a moment, and got out of the car to inquire about a room.

Fortunately, there was room at the inn. He registered and went back to his car to get his bags. As he rode the aged elevator to the fourth floor, he began thinking about practical matters. It was 7:30 p.m., probably too late to see anyone this evening. Also, he was exhausted from the trip down, and he thought he was probably poor company in his current condition. On the other hand, he was so close. He decided to call Ursula to make plans.

She answered on the first ring. Radko could hear a television blaring in the background, and he thought he heard Maggy squeal. He suddenly felt like an interloper, a person who perhaps might not be welcome.

"Hi, Ursula," he said. "It's me. I'm in Baltimore."

Absolution

There was a silence on the other end of the phone. Finally, Ursula said, "I thought you weren't coming till tomorrow evening."

"Yeah, well, I couldn't wait," Radko said honestly.

When Ursula did not respond right away, Radko continued: "Look, I just got antsy. And I just got in. I don't want to do anything this evening, but I thought I would let you know I was here and maybe we could make plans." He paused and thought for a moment. "If at all possible, I was hoping we would not have to wait till Saturday."

"I'm glad you called," Ursula said in spite of herself, feeling both her anxiety and her relief rise in tandem.

There was silence on the phone for some minutes, but it was not really an awkward silence. It was the quiet of two souls reconnecting with each other by being together, albeit only through a thin phone line.

Finally, Radko spoke. "We have so much to talk about, Ursula," he said.

"I know," she said.

Radko continued. "I thought we could get together tomorrow morning, just you and I, so we could talk about how to handle things with the twins."

"Yes, of course," Ursula said. "I think I can take them to a friend's house around nine." Then a critical point: "Where would you like to meet?"

Radko took a deep breath. He felt that he was the one with his hat in his hand, and he didn't want Ursula or the children to experience any more discomfort than they already had. "Any place that's comfortable for you," he said. "I'm staying at the Mount Vernon Hotel on Franklin Street."

"Why don't I come pick you up there at about 9:30?" Ursula said, thinking that this was perhaps the safest way to maintain some sense of control over whatever was to follow.

"Sure," said Radko. He couldn't recall ever making an appointment that he looked forward to as much this one. "Well, I'll see you in the morning then," he said to Ursula. Then he paused for a moment. "Good night," he said

"Good night," said Ursula softly.

Ursula put the phone down; otherwise, she didn't move. She was pleased that Radko couldn't wait until the appointed day, but she wondered if this was something for which she was really prepared. How can anyone really be prepared for this? she thought to herself. She had no idea what to expect, but she heard clearly the warmth and respect in Radko's voice. It was then that she saw how much she had missed him. Being brave and bold has its limits, she thought to herself.

What concerned Ursula the most was the warmth and connection she felt with the man she had compelled herself to think of as her ex-husband. She flashed on a scenario in her mind where she and Radko ironed out their differences and got back together, but only fleetingly, so fraught with danger it seemed. It made her shudder, and she took in a breath and forced herself to be realistic.

She called Joan. She explained to her best friend that Radko had come in a day early and they were planning to see each other for the first time in the morning, and could she possibly watch the twins for a few hours while she and Radko decide how to proceed. She crunched up her face like the middle-school girl she felt herself to be and hoped Joan would say yes.

"What time?" asked Joan.

"About nine," replied Ursula, face still crunched.

"Of course," said Joan.

"Thank you," said Ursula.

"Ursula?" Joan said after a moment. "Are you okay?"

"I think so," Ursula replied.

With more relief than she thought she had a right to feel and more pleasure than she thought was good for her or anybody else, Ursula began straightening up the apartment, which was hardly in disarray. She caught herself smiling and tried to think more of the grim thoughts that were so much a part of her for the past eight

Absolution

months so that she wouldn't feel so stupid or vulnerable or childlike. It didn't work very well, so she just let herself smile. In spite of every self-preserving instinct, she was looking forward to seeing Radko.

A few blocks away, Radko plopped himself on the bed of his small hotel room. He felt sure of something, and this experience unnerved him somewhat. He felt sure that he and Ursula could work this whole mess out. It wasn't a surprising realization; in fact, it felt as natural as talking to his wife on the phone had just felt. At the edge of his mind, Radko glimpsed the possible complications of this kind of thinking as well as the spectacular ramifications of any reconciliation. But that was for another time. All he had to do right now was get some solid rest so he could be prepared for tomorrow. And with that thought, he immediately fell into a deep sleep.

CHAPTER 29

Radko awoke at 6:00 a.m. like a shot. He looked around, and it took him a few moments to figure out where he was. He was disoriented by a dream that he was trying hard to remember but which was fading rapidly down into his unconscious whence it presumably came. The sense of urgency that stayed with him was related to someone dying in his dream, and he thought it was he. He was irritated at the prospect that he would expire before he worked out his life and saw his wife and children again, but he was also frightened that he might. The other clear thing about the dream was what seemed like a fated event: that he would be reunited with his family. He drew comfort from the fact that this accorded with his conscious thoughts last evening.

He looked at the clock next to his bed and lay back down. Three hours, he thought; what am I going to do with three hours. His thoughts turned to Ursula. He replayed the conversation he had with her last night and felt again the emotional bond that seemed so readily available. He began to anticipate what the experience would be like seeing his children, and a familiar chill of guilt and shame began creeping up on him. Suddenly, he bolted out of bed. He didn't want to lose the momentum of the moment. So he

Absolution

showered, dressed, and went downstairs to find a place to have breakfast.

Radko perused the newspaper in a small diner he found open, but he had difficulty digesting any of the content. He scanned the headlines and sipped his coffee. He stared out the large window that gave onto the narrow street. The morning was bright and the air felt fresh, so he decided to take a walk along the Inner Harbor. He breathed deeply the sweet morning air and smelled the scents of a great harbor city: salt water, fish, oil. Workers were just going about their morning tasks, setting up stalls and sorting their wares. A few shops were open, but mostly the area was deserted.

He headed toward Harborplace and the activity around him intensified. He loved this simple thing: walking around where the activity was. In his mind, it contrasted sharply with the barren activity of his rural diocese. Surrounded by the growing activity of this bustling market, Bismarck felt like a lifetime ago, a million miles from where his heart was. He found a cafe on a pier and ordered another coffee. He thought about Ursula and thought the unthinkable. What if she says no? What if her life has gone on? Radko wondered if she were seeing anyone else. He didn't think so, but he didn't really know. He kept returning to their brief conversation last night. It was as if he had found the proper medicine for his soul. But, well, she was free to do what she wanted and needed to do, and neither Radko nor anyone else could finally decide for her. He pitied the poor soul who would try.

Looking out over the water, Radko knew that his part in this drama was a limited one. All he had to do was decide for himself where his future lay. He knew that he had made a choice, and he hoped with all his heart that Ursula would be a part of his future. But even if she refused or decided on another course for her life, Radko knew that his real future lay in reassuming the responsibilities of fatherhood for his children. He knew this included resigning from the episcopacy, from the priesthood, and from the whole career track that had been his life. He thought that perhaps this would actually be a small price to pay. He didn't want to return to that life. He didn't want to return to Bismarck; he didn't want to live a life he no longer believed in.

Radko looked at his watch. It was 8:20. He paid his tab, stood up, and began walking back to his hotel. He recognized that he was still torn: he had been a compliant person his whole life, and saying no to the expectations of others or of his work didn't come easily or naturally to him. Nor did a future profession or line of work manifest itself to him. But he also knew there was no real choice. His days as a bishop would soon end. Emotionally, they were already over, and his days as a lay person were beginning. He felt a peace that was only contingent upon taking the actual steps to put his decisions into practice.

When he got back to the hotel, he entered the lobby and saw Ursula standing at the desk. She was early. He walked over to her without hesitation and put his arms around her. She did not protest. The two stood there embracing for several moments.

"I'm so sorry," Radko said finally. He pulled back from the embrace but did not let Ursula go. He looked into her eyes, not so much searching as reuniting.

"I'm sorry, too," said Ursula. She held his gaze.

The two continued to stand wordlessly in the small hotel lobby, impervious to whoever else might be in the room. Finally, Radko asked Ursula if she were hungry, if she would like to eat.

"I don't think I can just yet," Ursula said. "Could we go somewhere private?"

"Sure," said Radko. He considered the options—his room, her apartment, a restaurant. He didn't want to seem presumptuous, and he was a little embarrassed that he didn't have a plan in place. "Umm, how about your place?"

Ursula thought for a moment. She knew she was in trouble. She felt the bond she had been working for months to disassemble reform itself with greater rapidity than she could have imagined. So she thought her apartment was probably not the best place.

Absolution

"Maybe we should go someplace around here," she said.

"Sure, sure," Radko stammered, feeling that he had already blundered in what he hoped was the reconstitution of their relationship. "Wherever you would feel comfortable."

"Let's go find a place," Ursula suggested.

They walked out onto the street in front of the hotel, and the city around them had geared up to full tilt for the day ahead. They walked together down the narrow streets until they found a small restaurant with a fairly private booth in the back. A few business types were scattered at tables around the restaurant, but no one was too close. They ordered coffee and held hands on the laminated tabletop.

After the coffee came, neither spoke for a while, and each retreated to his or her respective cup. Ursula poured two teaspoons of a sugar substitute into her coffee and stirred it reflectively. As she always did, Radko thought. Radko wrapped both his hands around his ample mug. As he always did, Ursula thought.

Suddenly Radko let out a loud laugh, but then he caught himself.

"I'm sorry, Ursy," he said by way of explanation. "I'm so anxious about this visit. I have so many feelings I don't even know where to start." He looked straight at her. "Actually, that's not true. I know exactly where to start." He looked down into his cup for a moment, and when his eyes rose he took in a long breath. "I was a fool. I made a mistake that I think I will regret for the rest of my life." He paused to get a fresh injection of air, but he could feel his face turning pale. "But I don't intend to continue making the mistake again and again and again. I'm the father of our children… "

The air that Ursula sucked rapidly into her lungs made a distinct and audible noise. She stopped breathing momentarily, and her eyes widened. Radko stopped talking and looked at his wife.

"Are you all right?" he said after a minute.

Ursula was quiet and her eyes were moist. She shook her head slowly.

Radko frowned. He thought maybe something was caught in her throat or she was having some kind of attack. He reached across the table and touched Ursula's arm. "Honey?" he said.

Ursula stood up and raised her hand, motioning for Radko to stay where he was. She walked toward the rest room and disappeared behind the brown door with a stick figure of a woman on it.

Safely inside the women's rest room, Ursula leaned against the sink with both hands. She could barely breathe; she thought she might be sick. Her head faced down; she couldn't even bear looking at herself in the mirror. This isn't happening, she thought to herself. This can't be happening. She was too paralyzed to cry.

Slowly, she forced herself to take in deep breaths and lifted her face to the reverse image in the mirror. My decisions were easy when I was the victim, she thought. Now it's time to decide where to go from here. Now's the time to choose. She recognized her past as flawed, but she was also determined not to repeat mistakes from her past with Radko. This relationship is too important, she declared to herself.

Radko waited. He didn't move from the position he was in when Ursula walked away. He was trying to decide if he should intervene further or call an ambulance when the server came by. "More coffee?" she inquired cheerfully.

Radko looked at her is if she had appeared from a parallel universe. He was momentarily unable to place her role in the miniseries of his life. After a moment, he got it and nodded slowly. The young woman dutifully poured the coffee and went searching after other clients.

Radko waited some more. He was just about to signal the manager when the brown door opened and Ursula emerged from the rest room. She reclaimed her seat and looked at Radko.

"I'm sorry," she said, "You just took me by surprise."

"Are you all right?" asked Radko again.

"Yes, I'm okay," Ursula replied, although the color of her skin did not entirely support that statement. "I guess," Ursula paused

Absolution

and looked sideways at the floor, "I guess I have to ask you what you mean." She looked back at Radko.

Radko took a deep breath and began to describe events of the past few weeks, culminating in the experience at the toy store in New York. He told her about how his vision had shifted, how his view of his life had changed. He told her about the drive to Baltimore and how he had essentially reexamined his life going back to childhood, realizing how blind he had been and how he had inflicted his own narrow conception of the world on Ursula and on their children. His speech quickened as he described his desperate need to repair, if at all possible, the damage he had done. He slowed down and hung his head as he told her that he had come to recognize that his love for her and the children was his life and how foolish he had been not to recognize that.

"I know I can no longer remain a priest," Radko said to Ursula. He looked at her and continued. "I don't know if we can repair our life. I want that, but I also understand why you might not want to take that kind of risk." He swallowed hard. "My hope is that at some time we will be able to be together again. But however it goes for us, I cannot bear abandoning my children as I have over the past eight months." A steely look crept over his face. "It's just wrong, Ursula," he said.

Ursula regarded the man sitting across from her with some misgiving. On the one hand, this was the kind of thing she longed to hear, even if she had not allowed herself to face those sentiments within herself. On the other hand, the last eight months did happen. And before that, hadn't Radko lied to her about his true intentions? Fire and water collided within her. Radko's tone, his apparent sincerity, bespoke a process of growing through a difficult experience and coming to a more mature conclusion. But Ursula was scared. She didn't want to trust this man again. Not without action; not without proof of where his loyalties lay.

"So what are your plans?" she asked Radko, sounding harder than she intended.

Radko shrugged his shoulders. "I only have two. And by necessity, three. The first is to resign from the priesthood and the episcopacy, and the second is to relocate to Baltimore to be near you and the children. The third..." he sighed. "The third is to find a job. That one will probably be harder than either of the first two." He looked at Ursula and almost chuckled. "I've never worked a day in my life."

The ends of Ursula's lips curled in a half-smile. "It's not so bad," she teased gently.

Radko and Ursula looked at each other softly for several minutes. Radko felt home again, and Ursula wanted to feel that way also. She shrugged.

"What about the twins?" she asked Radko.

"Well," he responded. "I guess it's time to meet them again." He looked into the distance, trying to picture how this would happen. "You've been with them, Ursula," he said. "I'll follow whatever you think is the best way to do it." Then he had a thought and added: "You told them I was coming?"

Ursula blushed slightly. "Yes, Radko. I told them a few weeks ago that you were coming for a visit this weekend. She paused, bit her lower lip, and continued. "I told them months ago that we were getting divorced."

Radko looked at Ursula. He was surprised although he didn't know why. What else would you say when your mother drags you across the country and your father vanishes?

Ursula then told him about her conversation with the twins the day after Christmas. How they thought that he had died. Radko's heart got heavier as he thought about leaving the kids in limbo.

"I guess," she said, "we'll just have to go see them."

Radko nodded. Without saying anything, he motioned to the cheerful server to bring the check and pulled out his wallet to pay the modest bill. Ursula also said nothing, but stood up and waited until this little ritual ended. Then she and Radko walked out of the restaurant.

Absolution

"Who's driving?" asked Radko.

"I'm parked at a meter," replied Ursula. "I should probably drive." Then she thought for a moment. She didn't want to show up at Joan's house with Radko in tow. "Would you mind if we took two cars?" she asked. "The twins are at a friend's house, and I would rather they meet you at our apartment."

Radko thought about this for a moment and didn't see any problem. It didn't hurt his feelings. He still wanted Ursula to be in charge of this encounter. "Sure, Honey," he said. "Umm, where shall I meet you?"

Ursula laughed a little. "I will pick up the kids and take them to the apartment." She gave Radko the address and made sure he knew where the building was located. "Give me half an hour," she said.

Radko realized how close Ursula's apartment was to where they were standing, and it brought back memories of when they were first dating, how they would go back and forth between their small apartments and stroll up and down the harbor area. A wave of nostalgia washed over him.

"Okay, then," said Ursula with a tone of contrived authority in her voice. She hesitated ever so slightly, and Radko, even though distracted by his inner world, reached over and hugged her gently. She looked at him with big eyes. "I'm glad you're back," she whispered.

"Me, too," replied Radko.

CHAPTER 30

Visiting with the kids was just plain awkward, but only briefly. Radko could not wait a half hour; he did not wait a minute before he walked straight to his car and drove to Ursula's apartment. He was sitting in his SUV with the windows down when Ursula drove up with the children. Fortunately, they didn't notice him—it would have been hard, since he was almost half a block away—and he watched the three other members of his family enter an apartment in an old red brick building on a narrow street. As soon as they were inside, he thought he would give Ursula about five minutes. He checked his watch and realized that the half hour Ursula requested had already gone by.

Radko got out of his vehicle slowly. He looked up and down the street, not so much to check for anyone he might know although there was some possibility that he might meet somebody who knew him; no, it was more because he wanted to savor the moment. He breathed in the humid summer salted air. He was nervous. He didn't know how the kids would react; he didn't know how he would react. He walked slowly to the door where the trio had vanished and knocked gently.

Absolution

The door was thrown open, and Maggy and Sergie bolted through it, throwing their little arms around Radko and screaming "Daddy! Daddy!" They were still jumping up and down when Ursula appeared and shrugged her shoulders above the two delighted children. Radko swooped one up in each arm and entered the apartment. "I have missed you so," he said honestly to his children. He kissed them each twice and put them down on the living room carpet. Then he remembered: "I have something for you! I'll be right back." As he went back through the door, he could hear the sudden sharp intake of breath coming from his children. He turned and said, "Really, give me two minutes." The kids were quiet. "All right, then come with me," he said. The smiles returned, and they ran out the door with their dad.

Radko and the twins walked back to his car, and he retrieved the presents from the store in New York, the one that triggered what he believed to be the most significant transformation of his life.

Once back in Ursula's apartment, the kids sat on his lap for awhile and asked him the kinds of questions six-year-olds ask of parents when the situation is completely beyond their comprehension. "Where did you go? Are you going to leave again? Are you and Mommy really going to get divorced?" And finally, "Can we go play?" So after a quarter of an hour of intense reunion, the twins disappeared upstairs, taking with them the toys and the assurance that their father was not dead.

With the twins safely out of the way, Radko looked at Ursula, who had been standing in the small hall observing the celebration. He silently patted the spot next to him on the couch, and she sat down beside him. "Thank you," he said with tears in his eyes. "Thank you for caring for our children while I was away." He pulled her close and their wet cheeks converged in a kiss neither expected but both desired.

CHAPTER 31

Silas was antsy. After his original reaction to the reunion between Radko and Ursula, when he felt he was able to relax for the first time in months, he had been growing increasingly edgy. He knew it was because he was out of the loop. Ursula had shut down his offers of assistance, and Radko had not asked for help. All he knew was that they were getting together for the Fourth of July weekend, probably in Baltimore. He knew the intentions of neither party.

He thought of ways he could be closer to the action. It would be no trouble to arrange a convenient trip to the U.S. for the holiday, but the thought of just showing up in Baltimore unexpectedly seemed a little forward, even for him. Besides, he already had a trip planned for later in July. He had told Radko that he hoped they could get together. In addition, he thought he heard a complaint about him in the tone of Ursula's voice the last time they spoke: she may have felt pressured by him or intruded upon. He didn't really understand or even claim to understand women, but he thought it best to lie low.

Unfortunately, lying low was not his strong suit. He still had not told Mueller about the reunion, and he was getting increasingly

Absolution

anxious about that. Since he didn't know what else to do, he called on the archbishop at his home in early July on his way home from work.

But when he knocked on the door, there was no answer. The archbishop himself did not answer, which was not so unusual, but neither did his personal secretary, who usually did such chores in Wolfgang's household. Odd, Silas thought, perhaps he is out of town. But Silas had always been privy to Wolfgang's travel schedule. He took out a business card and put it in the mail slot to let Mueller know that he had come by. He thought he would call him in the morning.

On his way home through an early summer Roman heat wave, Silas considered what Radko and Ursula would do. He thought, despite all the evidence that was first hand to him, that there was a small chance that Radko would remain a bishop and reunite with Ursula. This would be Wolfgang's first choice, of course. More probable to Silas's mind was the likelihood that Radko would continue being a bishop and divorce Ursula or that the pair would reconcile and Radko would resign the episcopacy. Silas winced at the potential media frenzy that could erupt if this last situation occurred and were not handled properly. And it was almost impossible to handle it properly, so voracious was the appetite of the American media for scandal in the Roman church.

Silas wondered if there was any way he could be helpful to any of the protagonists in this drama. He thought not, although he could not dismiss the matter from his mind. He had spoken to Ted about it a few weeks ago when Ted was in Rome for a meeting of Vicars. Ted just shrugged his shoulders.

"Silas," Ted had said to him plainly, "you know this whole plan is at base preposterous. And that the possibility of scandal or exposure or reputations being ruined is high." Sometimes Ted could not grasp why Silas was so devoted to the archbishop's plan. Well-intended though it might be, it impacted real people with real feelings.

"I know, Ted," Silas replied. "And, unfortunately, the real people involved are ones I care about. I hate the thought of putting Radko and Ursula through so much hell just to prove a point. But the situation is out of our hands right now." He was referring to his hands and to the hands of Archbishop Mueller. "I keep wracking my brain to see if there is something I can do to help." He paused and thought for a moment. "But I can't come up with anything."

Well, then, just leave it alone, Ted thought. But to Silas, he said "You've done all you can for now, Silas." Then it was his turn to think for a moment. "What does Mueller say?"

At that question, Silas reddened a little. "I haven't told him," he said, looking across the table to Ted in the small trattoria where they were having dinner. "I'm a little protective of Radko and Ursula."

Ted looked at Silas and picked up his wine glass, which he swirled for want of something better to do. Oh, shit, he thought to himself. This is serious. He was considering the implications of Silas, who had a good job in the Vatican, withholding information from Mueller, who had one of the top jobs in the Vatican. He could not imagine that Mueller would look kindly on such a situation.

Fortunately, Silas kept talking. "If they go public," he said, "it could be a huge scandal." He looked down at his own wine glass. "They've suffered enough." He went quiet.

Silas and Ted ate in silence for some time. Then Ted said, "Why don't you come clean with Mueller? It might not be too late."

Silas heard the obvious in his friend's remark: that he had blundered in withholding information from Mueller, who was, after all, the principle architect of this improvident plan. He bit his lower lip in recognition of having made a mess, something Silas didn't do very often. He wondered how he could make this right. It might be that it was time for his involvement in Wolfgang's plan to come to an end. He wondered if that were possible, so implicated did he feel in the plot that had gone on for almost a decade.

CHAPTER 32

Wolfgang Mueller was not one to let the grass grow beneath his feet. Nor was he one to wait around for his prayers to be answered with no action on his part. He had engaged the services of a private investigator in Baltimore to check up on Ursula and to divine if possible her intentions and motives with respect to her estranged husband. In Matthew McDonahee, he thought he had the perfect candidate to do the work he wanted. Matthew, it turned out, had spent some years in seminary formation during his adolescence, and he understood things like discretion and the importance of information. He was also appropriately deferential to those in the church with titles. Finally, he had done some work for the Archdiocese of Baltimore previously and was eager to expand his reputation in church circles.

"So, Matthew," intoned the archbishop, "What have you learned?" The pair were talking in a small booth on the thirty-first floor of the Loews Hotel on Market Street in Philadelphia. They had arranged to meet here to minimize any possible exposure in Baltimore, where most of the investigative work was taking place.

Matthew smiled across the table at the Archbishop, who was dressed in a simple black suit with a white shirt and tasteful striped

Absolution

tie. Looks like a company executive, McDonahee thought absently, as he passed the file across the highly-polished wooden tabletop. "Here's what we know now, Bishop," he said. He could tell from the slightly pained expression on Mueller's face that it was wrong to call him by his ecclesiastical title. Mueller had expressly told him not to do this when he hired him over the phone a few weeks ago, but Matthew found it difficult to call a bishop by name. He tried to recover. "Mr. Mueller, we know where she lives, where she works, all the relevant contact information, such as phone numbers, e-mail addresses and so forth..." he paused briefly. "We also know who she spends time with and the same information about those people. We also know that her estranged husband is going to be visiting her over the July Fourth weekend."

Mueller smiled. He did not ask how McDonahee had come across that last piece of information, but he was glad to hear it. "Thank you, Matthew," he said. "I will call you if I need you again in the future." Then Mueller stood up and extended his hand to the private investigator, who had been expecting a lengthier conversation.

"You're welcome, sir," said the investigator. "Please keep me in mind if there is anything else I can do for you." With nothing else to do or say, he turned on his heel and left the bar.

Mueller sat back down. So this is not dead yet, he thought to himself. He waved for the server to bring him another scotch and opened the sealed envelope the investigator had given him. In it were pictures of Ursula and the children, as well as photographs of her apartment, front and back, the school where she worked, and pictures of the people she spent the most time with, in order of actual time spent with each person. Far and away, she spent most of it with a woman named Joan who worked at the same school with her. Apparently they had been friends since college, and Joan had attended Ursula's wedding in New York six years ago. Wolfgang smiled at the way the circle always seems to complete itself.

For the present, it would be enough for him to know the outcome of the reunion that was to occur that very weekend. He saw immediately that Silas must have known about this meeting and had neglected to tell him. That was probably intentional, the Archbishop surmised. He had been thinking for some months that Silas was too close to the major players here, and the conclusion did not surprise him. He would have to talk with Silas about this when he got back to Rome, but that would not be for some weeks. Right now, he had some work to do.

He reached into his inside jacket pocket for the sleek cell phone he kept there. He dialed McDonahee's number, figuring that the detective was probably not back in Baltimore yet. As he thought, he was still enroute.

"Matthew," said the Archbishop. "I would like everything you can find out about the meeting between Radko Slopovich and Ursula Fliegendorf this weekend." He listened to the investigator's relieved affirmatives. "Could you call me at this number on Tuesday?" he asked. Assured that he would, the archbishop pushed the end key on his phone and sat back to enjoy the drink and the view.

CHAPTER 33

Matthew McDonahee was only partially relieved. On the one hand, he was glad that the archbishop contacted him again after blowing him off at the bar in the Loews. On the other hand, there was something about this whole messy situation that made him wonder what was really going on.

When the archbishop first contacted him by phone from Rome, Matthew was pleased and flattered. He had done some work for church officials in the past, and he saw it as a potential source of regular work in an otherwise hit-and-miss profession. He didn't know why the prelate wanted a dossier compiled on this woman, but he often didn't know the true intentions of his clients. He did his job and let other people do theirs. He learned early on not to ask too many questions. But something about this didn't seem right. Ursula Fliegendorf was as clean as could be. She had arrived in Baltimore after living for some years in Chicago. She was a teacher and devoted mother of twins. She did not date, at least not in Baltimore, and he believed that she had recently separated or divorced from her husband. He could find no records, however, or legal papers attesting to that. He assumed it was true because she

Absolution

appeared back in Baltimore after five years in Chicago and started working at the school where she had worked prior to leaving.

The big surprise came when he found out the name of the man who was coming to visit her this weekend. Radko Slopovich was a Roman Catholic bishop. He was the Bishop of Bismarck, a large but sparsely populated area in North Dakota. From what McDonahee could gather from those who knew Ursula and from his own surveillance of her, this was a man about whom she had very strong feelings. She spoke about him as if they had been married, even as if he were the father of his children. Then he learned that the children's last names were Slopovich, confirming in his mind that the bishop was their father. If this turns out to be true, Matthew thought, he could only imagine what a priceless story he had.

But what was a Vatican official doing hiring a private investigator to look into Fliegendorf's life? Was he going to try to blackmail another bishop? Matthew had worked with some less-than-savory characters before, but never ones who were church officials. High church officials, at that, he reminded himself. McDonahee prided himself on his thoroughness, and he had done some research on Wolfgang Mueller as well. He knew exactly what position he had in the Vatican hierarchy and how important it was. It didn't seem right that he would be getting his hands dirty with this kind of situation unless something had gone wrong. As he drove down I-95, Matthew had to remind himself to keep his focus on the service he was rendering to the client. He easily fell into idle speculation, a habit that had started when he was a teenager devouring mystery novels. He could almost never wait until the end.

CHAPTER 34

For all his rumination about the importance of the church in his life, it didn't take long for Radko to stop thinking of himself as a priest. It was like removing a heavy overcoat that had gotten soaked: you lose the protection but also the weight. You feel lighter. This was how he felt over the Fourth of July weekend, as he reprised his role as father of a family. Starting on the Friday he saw Maggy and Sergie, the Slopovich family was inseparable. They ate together, played together, talked together, and did what families do around Independence Day. They went on picnics; they watched fireworks. They tussled and wrestled around playfully. By Monday evening, Radko felt that his new, lighter coat fit him just fine.

Every night, however, after the kids went to sleep, Radko retired to his room at the Mount Vernon. He would have preferred to stay with Ursula, but they just weren't there yet, and he still didn't think he was in any position to insist. Besides, it gave him some time to think and to try to make sense out of all the emotions that were running rampant through his body. More than anything, it allowed time for his body to unwind. He slept as he hadn't in memory: deeply, soundly, without dreaming. He awoke refreshed, if a bit anxious. And hungry. In fact, he was hungry most of the

Absolution

time. He had to remind himself to watch it more than once throughout each day.

By Tuesday, the world was getting back to work, or as much of it as got back to work in the heart of the summer. Radko and Ursula packed the kids off to Joan's house for the day: Joan promised them that they could swim in the pool at her apartment complex. This made them happy, and Radko and Ursula both felt ready to talk more seriously between themselves.

As she was about to walk out the door, Maggy turned to her parents, and her face darkened slightly. "Are you both going to be here when we get back?"

Radko smiled and tousled his daughter's hair. "Yes, Maggy, we'll both be here when you get back. Now go on and have fun." He watched her face relax with his reassuring words.

After they left, Radko turned to Ursula. "Well?" he said.

"Well, what?" Ursula replied, slipping her arms around Radko's shoulders and putting her face right next to his.

Radko kissed her. A kiss he never wanted to end. But when it did, he did not let Ursula go. He looked into her eyes and then closed his own. "I have missed you terribly," he said.

"And I you," she replied.

They stood in the entry hall of Ursula's small apartment for a while in silence. Holding each other and remembering. And hoping. And trying not to think of the very real obstacles that stood between them and becoming a family again.

"Hungry?" asked Ursula.

"Always," replied Radko, shaking his head at the sheer volume of food he had consumed over the past seventy-two hours.

Ursula led him into the kitchen and planted him on a stool while she began searching for food suitable for brunch. As she busied herself with this ancient domestic chore, she periodically glanced up at Radko, both to maintain the tie she had recently reclaimed and also, she had to admit, to make sure this was not some dream.

Radko did not demur. He watched Ursula cook, luxuriating in the bond that he had taken so lightly not a year before. He shuddered. Then he thought that they might as well plow into the matters at hand.

"Ursula," Radko began, "we have to talk about some difficult things."

Ursula did not stop what she was doing, but she looked over at her husband. "I know," she said. "Why don't you start?"

Radko looked at his wife with steady eyes. He didn't speak right away. Flashing through his mind were remnants of past conversations, some of which were about the predicament they were in and some of which were about the ordinary marital tussles humans endure. He thought about the limitations of words and how they didn't prevent this past disastrous year from happening. He realized he needed more than mere words.

"May I use your computer?" he asked.

Ursula nodded and pointed with her head to the laptop in the corner of the eating area. Radko retrieved it and set it down on the kitchen counter. He opened the word processing program and started typing.

Your Holiness, he began,

I am writing to tender my resignation as Bishop of the Diocese of Bismarck, North Dakota, effective immediately. In accord with Section Two of Canon 401 of the Code of Canon Law, it is my belief that I am no longer suited to exercise the powers of my office.

Respectfully in Christ,

Most Reverend Radko Slopovich, Bishop of Bismarck

Radko sat back and looked at the short missive on the screen. He did a quick word count with the utility built into the software. Sixty-one words. It all ends with sixty-one words, he thought.

Next, he went online and accessed his e-mail program. He copied the file he had just written to an e-mail to Annie, to whom he wrote:

Absolution

Annie, Please check the addressee's mailing address and copy the attached document onto diocesan stationary and get it ready for my signature. Make three copies and send the original to me. Send it to

"Ursula, what is the address here?" he asked.

She gave it to him, and he typed it into the message.

Then he continued.

I would like you to do this as soon as possible. I am not sure how long I will be here, but I would like to have this matter cleared up. Thank you for all your help.   +Bishop Radko Slopovich.

He turned the laptop around so that Ursula could see the text of both messages. She read them quickly and looked up at Radko with a serious, almost stunned expression on her face.

She took a deep breath. "Are you absolutely sure you want to do this?" she asked.

"Absolutely sure," replied Radko without a hint of doubt in his voice. He hit the "send" button.

Ursula did not quite know how to react. Was this some dramatic ploy Radko was using, grandstanding for God-knows-what reason? She studied his face. The collision of feelings in her gut made her realize that, as much as she might want to reconstitute their family, she was mistrustful. She needed time.

Radko's words interrupted her thoughts. "We have had long conversations about our future that were just words. I have misled you. I didn't think I was doing it at the time, but that's precisely what I did. And I set it up so that you left me, allowing me to do something I wanted to do anyway. And in my heart I could blame you. I could point to you and say, 'Look, you left me; what could I do?'" Radko paused. His face was flushed, and he was looking directly into Ursula's eyes.

After a minute, he continued: "I think you and I have a long way to go if we are to get back together. This is what I want. I understand it may not be what you want or what will work. I'm not resigning to impress you. I'm resigning now because, if we are to have any hope, I must be free to deal with you openly, honestly, without subterfuge." He took a deep breath and then continued. "Action is more important than words. I must take action. If we get back together or not, I will not abandon my children again. Ever."

For a moment, neither moved. Then Ursula walked around the counter and put her arms around her husband. "Thank you," she said.

CHAPTER 35

Annie stared at her computer screen without blinking for five minutes. Then the phone rang, and she answered it with none of her ordinary cheerfulness. She took a message and returned her gaze to the screen. He's resigning? The thought finally began to become clear in her mind. She kept repeating this phrase over and over in her head, trying to wrap her mind around it in an effort to subdue it, to make sense of it, to believe it. Or to prove it wrong.

He can't resign, she thought to herself. He's a bishop and a young one at that. Annie wanted to call someone, but she was uncertain of whom to talk to about this. She was pretty sure her boss was counting on her to keep this quiet. So she did something she rarely did. She did nothing. She did not do what the Bishop requested. She turned her attention to other tasks in the hope that maybe this was some kind of mistake or joke.

This tactic only lasted for ten minutes. Then, with hands trembling, she commanded her computer to do what the bishop requested. She copied the letter onto a separate file. She looked up the address of the Holy Father in Rome and entered it in the appropriate place. When it was all centered and perfect, she placed a single piece of diocesan stationary in the printer and pushed the

Absolution

Print button. In under six seconds, she was holding in her hand a document that she was sure would alter her life. Fighting back tears, she took out an envelope and entered the address Radko had given her, unable to imagine where he was or what he was doing.

After she completed these tasks, she opened the e-mail program and replied to the bishop's message.

Dear Bishop,
I have done what you requested.
Annie

Then she collected her things, told the vicar she was not feeling well, and went home.

CHAPTER 36

A half block away from Ursula's apartment, Matthew McDonahee sat in his van, listening to the couple's conversation through the elaborate listening devices that were his prized tools in executing the responsibilities of his job.

So they are his kids, he thought. And Slopovich and Fliegendorf were married. Maybe they are still married, he thought, remembering the fact that there was no record of any divorce decree. The children were about six years old; that meant that the couple were married during Slopovich's time in Chicago. This is a powder keg, he thought. He spent the entire weekend snooping on the conversations, but this was the first confirmation he had from the adults involved that this was a case of a Catholic bishop who had a wife and children on the side. He had heard the kids call Radko "Daddy" all weekend, but he had not heard from his mouth or from Ursula's mouth the confirming words that were just now permanently recorded on his tape machine.

But something had just happened, and Matthew was unsure what it was. It was on the computer, and neither Radko nor Ursula spelled out the action that Radko had taken. McDonahee turned to his computer and started hacking. He did not have Ursula's specific

Absolution

IP address, but he thought he could use the wireless network that covered downtown Baltimore to trace Radko's message. Then he realized that Radko's e-mail account was probably linked to the Bismarck web site, and he quickly found it and scanned. Pleased with himself, he hacked away until he was able to read Radko's last message.

Matthew McDonahee sat back on the small chair that was his command post for surveillance. He's resigning. This must be what the archbishop wanted to know.

I'm done here, he concluded. All that was left was to organize his notes and place a call to Archbishop Mueller, whom he knew would be very pleased with what Matthew had been able to accomplish.

Matthew discreetly disassembled his listening devices and loaded them into his van. He drove away and headed toward his office. He was not happy to have surrendered the better part of the holiday weekend to surveilling these people, but Mueller was a top player at the Vatican, and it was vital for Matthew to give him what he wanted. He was filled with satisfaction that he would be able to provide concrete information, not just speculation about the status of the Slopovich family and Radko's plans.

When he got back to the office, he pulled the archbishop's number from his pocket and dialed the phone. He was excited as he heard the clicks and whirrs on the phone that tagged this line as a secure one. Finally, he heard Mueller's voice. "Yes," the archbishop said.

"Your Excellency," Matthew began, "I believe I have the information you want." He paused and waited, but Mueller did not say anything. So Matthew took a breath and started reporting. He told the archbishop that Slopovich and Fliegendorf were married and had twins about six years old. He told him that Radko and Ursula had evidently been estranged, but now they were planning to get back together. He also told him that Radko had written a letter of resignation to the pope, effective immediately.

When Matthew stopped talking, he listened intently. He heard the archbishop let out a long breath. And then Mueller said, "Thank you, Matthew, I'll be in touch." And the phone went dead.

Filled with satisfaction at the job he had done, Matthew was sure the archbishop would do exactly as he said.

CHAPTER 37

Wolfgang was driving north when the call from McDonahee came. He fully believed that he was living through the answer to his prayers. He was elated that Radko and Ursula were reuniting. We will have an American married bishop after all, he thought to himself with no small measure of satisfaction. He was not so worried about Radko's plan to resign, which of course would render Mueller's own dream temporary. He knew canon law. He knew that a resignation only went into effect when it was accepted by the competent authority, in this case, the Holy Father himself. Wolfgang figured he had some influence there, and to his mind, the situation was going exactly in the direction he wanted. He accelerated slightly on his way to New York.

Wolfgang thought he had a loose end to clear up with his friend Silas. He pondered different ways Silas could or would help him finesse this delicate situation. Silas would most certainly support whatever decision Radko made, and Mueller thought he would be particularly pleased that Radko and Ursula were reuniting. He thought of pressing Silas back into service to help arrange a new living situation for the Slopovich family along the lines of what he had discussed with Radko at the Drake Hotel last November. He

Absolution

was sure that Silas would be more than happy to help, especially if he had been withholding information. Guilt was a common commodity in church circles, and almost no one was immune to its predictable effects.

Mueller took a long breath. He could feel the years in his large frame, and it pained him to sit for long periods. He tried to shift his weight to get more comfortable, but finally he thought it better to find somewhere to stop and stretch. He got off at the next exit and found a nice small hotel with a restaurant that was serving the lunch crowd. He entered and requested a table in the rear, surveying the clientele casually as he was led to the back of the room. He ordered a coffee and small salad and found a newspaper, which he perused without much interest.

He could not get his mind off the fact that his plan was about to take a huge step in the direction he had set for it. Wolfgang Mueller was not above feeling a bit smug about his incipient success, and as he wrapped his hands around the mug of coffee, he smiled to himself. He was filled with gratitude to the God he was sure was directing his hand in this illicit but holy operation.

After a few minutes of sipping his coffee and picking at his salad, Wolfgang checked his watch and placed a long distance call to Silas, who, he figured, was still at his desk in Rome. He was right.

Wolfgang greeted Silas warmly. It had been some time since they had spoken, and Wolf figured that Silas would be relieved to hear from him. He was correct about that as well.

"Silas," Wolfgang said, "I have some news about our friend Radko."

Silas listened intently but did not say anything.

"It seems that he and his wife are planning to get back together. He is now in Baltimore with her."

Silas wondered at the old man's resourcefulness. How did he know this? he thought to himself.

"I think it would be good for you to hook up with Radko sometime soon. I believe you told me you would be in the U.S. later this month," the archbishop continued.

"Yes," said Silas, "I'll be there in two weeks."

"I won't be back in Rome by then, but here is my idea." The archbishop paused to collect his thoughts. "I think it would be a good idea if you met with Radko and maybe even with his wife to pitch the plan we discussed last fall. I think they will be ready for it."

Silas considered this. His instinct told him that if Radko and Ursula got back together, it would not be such a simple matter to continue as if the original plan were intact. Nonetheless, he was so relieved to hear from Mueller that he did not protest.

"I'll talk with Radko about this when I see him later on this month, Wolf," he said. "I'll let you know how he responds."

Mueller said good-bye and clicked off. He put some money on the table, got up, and walked out of the hotel into the balmy east coast sunshine. He stretched and noticed how lovely everything seemed.

CHAPTER 38

Silas shook his head. That scheming Vaticano, he thought. He never lets go. These were observations on Silas's part, not really hostile thoughts. The truth was that he did feel relieved to be reconnected to the architect of the plan in which Silas himself had played such a significant role. But he was unsure, after spending months in contact with the major protagonists of this particular drama, that it would play out as smoothly as Mueller implied. His anxiety about exposure also increased, as it did every time one of these situations moved toward completion.

He decided it was time to contact Radko. He called his cell phone but got his voice mail. He then turned to his computer to compose an e-mail.

Dear Radko, he began,

I'll be in the U.S. the last two weeks of July. I'll be arriving on the 18th. Please let me know your plans so we can get together. Looking forward to seeing you.

Regards,
Silas

Clear and to the point, he thought. He wondered how the weekend with Ursula played out, and as he turned his thoughts to

Absolution

the situation his friends faced, he realized that he was anxious about that as well. In his heart, Silas was glad that Radko and Ursula were willing to give their relationship and their marriage, another chance. Radko had not, to Silas's mind, been happy living as a bishop without her, and he thought it would do his friend good to reconnect with Ursula. On the other hand, he was surprised that Ursula would even consider reconciliation so quickly. But he had to admit that she seemed quite confident during his last conversation with her, quite ready to meet with Radko.

Silas wished Ted were here. The two of them had such a great time when Ted was in Rome in June, and Silas missed him now. Ted was one of the few people with whom Silas could be honest about every facet of his life. He valued that. More than valued it— he needed it. He hoped he could arrange to see Ted when he was in the U.S.

CHAPTER 39

Radko and Ursula spent the rest of Tuesday considering various possibilities. Radko asked her how she felt about the possibility that the media might get hold of this story. Bishops resign, but rarely, and usually for reasons involving scandal. A media storm could not be ruled out.

"Is it really such a news event when a bishop in a small diocese quits?" Ursula asked him.

Radko thought for a moment. "Not necessarily," he said, "but it depends on the reasons I give. If I just quit for no stated reason, it is likely that some media outlet will assign the story to some eager young reporter. If I give a reason, especially if I tell the truth, all hell will likely break loose."

It was Ursula's turn to think for a moment. "I cannot imagine that, even if the story makes the papers, it would be of much ongoing interest." She looked at Radko, and her eyes twinkled. "Not that you are unimportant, Your Excellency."

Joking between the two of them was tentative still on this day, but Radko smiled and squeezed his wife's hand. In the pause between each thought throughout the day, he returned to how lucky—no, more than lucky: graced—he felt to be back in Ursula's

Absolution

presence. And it was that thought that was running through his mind now. He looked at his wife.

"You're right, Ursy," he said. "It could be intense, but hopefully it will be brief." He kissed her on the cheek. "We've been through worse."

Ursula regarded Radko as she leaned against the counter. She forgot what she was cooking. She was marveling at how at home she felt in the presence of this man from whom she had fled months ago and whose presence in her life she had worked so hard to exorcise. She was more than a little mistrustful of these feelings, but mistrustful only in an intellectual way, not in a felt way. When she focused on her emotions, she felt that she was in the right place doing the right thing. Even small things about this situation, such as the fact that they were in Baltimore in the city and not in some godforsaken west suburb of Chicago, felt like the correct pieces of what was admittedly a very complicated and unique puzzle. She wasn't really worried about the future. So Radko's picture appears in the paper in Bismarck or even here: this is America; it will pass. There will be another sensational story right on the heels of it. But she had a chance to put her life with Radko back together in a way that would be better than it was before. She could be free. She would not have to worry about who knew what about whom. That thought felt not just right but pleasurable.

At the same time, she felt that this moment was not going to last forever. A belief was forming in her mind to the effect that, if she wanted a marriage to Radko, this was the time to do it. If this moment passed, her life would go on in a direction that did not include him, or at least did not include him as her husband. If what he was saying was true, and if he continued to act as he had this weekend, Radko's commitment to his children would be a priority. He would therefore be a part of Ursula's life. But if she lost this moment, this opportunity, they would collaborate as two single people concerned about the two small people they had brought into the world, but not as a unified pair, not as a single set of parents. While she could give that arrangement intellectual assent, it seemed to her the less desirable of the two options that played back and forth in her mind.

Ursula straightened up, took a deep breath, and leaned against the refrigerator. She did not take her eyes off the man who was still her husband. What she had been thinking made a lot of sense to her, but she was not quite done with the events of last fall. The effect of those events was to strike a note of warning into what was turning into a happy reunion. She unlocked her eyes from Radko's and looked down at the generic tile of the floor. She had always been sensible. Did she really want to take a risk with a man who betrayed their marriage? You're being harsh, she admonished herself. She looked back up at Radko. Even grown-ups screw up, she thought, and hoped with all her heart that what Radko had done was simply make a mistake. A mistake he seemed very prepared to rectify.

Radko watched his wife in process. He did not know exactly what she was thinking, but he knew her to be an intensely thoughtful person whose respect for reality was enduring. He had seen her in such processes before; and in the past, these episodes had frightened him some. Ursula was unrelenting with the truth and would not equivocate in saying what she believed. She would certainly not get swept away in a torrent of feelings of relief and reconnection. She would decide what was best for her and for her children on the basis of what she believed to be possible.

But today he was not frightened; he was simply respectful. It was clear to him that he wanted to get on with his life with her and with their children, but he fully appreciated the fact that this might not be possible. He, too, felt the weight of the moment. Whether he or Ursula liked it or not, this Tuesday in July in Baltimore was the time and the place of decision. Radko judged that by writing his letter of resignation and directing his secretary to prepare it was a sign of his good faith and a validation of his stated intention. He believed that any further gestures would be cloying and ingratiating.

Absolution

He looked at her across the small galley kitchen with dry, steady eyes.

"What do you want to do, Ursula?" he said.

Ursula returned his steady gaze. "If you are willing to do what you have said you would do and what you have begun," she said, pointing with her eyes to her laptop, "I want to have a life with you." Her eyes broke away briefly. "But only an honest life, Radko, a life our children can talk about and ask about and tell their children about."

Radko stepped toward his wife and put his arms around her. "Thank you," he said, and the tears ran freely down his face.

CHAPTER 40

On the long trip back to Bismarck in early August, Radko thought about the events of the previous month. He felt a calm he had not experienced in months. He wasn't looking forward to what he was facing back in North Dakota, but he knew it had to be done, and he was in no mood to compromise his soul as he had for too many years now.

He thought back to those awkward first days after he and Ursula decided to give their marriage another go. He felt a surge of warmth every time he thought about how they sat their children down in the small living room of Ursula's apartment and told them that their parents were not getting a divorce. Tears came to Radko's eyes as he thought about it, as they did to both Maggy and Sergie when they told them. In fact, the kids did not exactly know how to take this news. It was clear to both Radko and Ursula how deeply they had been impacted by the long separation they had endured. They cried but they were also happy.

"Yippee!" Maggy said, hugging her dad. She wrapped her lanky arms around his neck, and Radko reached out for Sergie with his free hand. The little boy, too, cuddled up to him. They all cried and laughed and cried and laughed some more.

Absolution

Radko and Ursula stayed together that night, mostly hugging and kissing and promising and getting over the surprisingly mild awkwardness of their unadorned bodies. This did not take as long as Radko had feared. He was thrilled to be sexual with Ursula again, and it just confirmed once again the rightness of his decision.

The next morning, the kids awoke first and spied on their parents in their bedroom together, a sight they had not witnessed for what seemed like forever in a six-year-old universe. They peeked around the corner, one after the other, and it quickly became a game. Part of the game was squealing just loud enough to avoid waking their parents, although the thing they wanted the most was for both their parents to be awake. Finally, Radko opened one eye and spied Sergie ducking his head behind the doorway to what was now their parent's bedroom. He waited until he saw the small head reemerge. "Gotcha!" he yelled and startled Sergie so much that the boy jumped. But then he rolled on the floor laughing, while Maggy jumped onto the double bed with her mother and father. Sergie followed suit.

Later that day, Radko checked out of the Mount Vernon Hotel and brought his few things over to Ursula's apartment. It was fortunate that he didn't have much because closet space was limited.

"I guess we'll need a bigger apartment," Ursula observed as she watched Radko try to stuff his few articles of clothing into her already full closet.

Radko chuckled. "We can start looking after I get back from North Dakota," he said.

The mention of that faraway place was accompanied by a two-second pause, in which both Radko and Ursula managed their respective anxieties. For all her recognition of the proper time to make a decision, Ursula felt in her heart that she would feel much better after the announcement of her husband's resignation. To her, that was the unavoidable test.

Radko preferred to pretend that resigning was just another task on his list. He thought about it only occasionally during the weeks of his visit in Baltimore, and mostly he thought that he would simply announce it at a last Mass he would say at the cathedral in Bismarck. The last Mass of my life, he thought to himself. He had feelings about this, but for most of July they were vague and unformed. Some sadness, some relief, some frustration that the situation had come to this. But mostly he focused on the three people he had only lately rejoined and regaled himself at every opportunity with the notion that he had some making up to do with Ursula and with his children. That idea did not make him unhappy.

Silas's visit did cast a shadow over the latter part of July. As Radko drove through the heartland of the country, he frowned as he thought of his friend.

When Radko responded to Silas's e-mail early in the month, he told him that he and Ursula were getting back together. He also told him how excited and relieved he felt about it. He was looking forward to Silas's visit, as he always did, and at first, Silas, who was staying at Ted's rectory, warmly congratulated Radko on his decision and on his good luck. He also embraced Ursula with more warmth than he had ever felt for a woman. He respected her enormously for being willing to give Radko another chance.

Silas was a frequent guest at the Slopovich household. Mostly it felt like old times, good old times that the three of them had shared in the past. Then about a week into Silas's visit, while Ursula had taken the kids somewhere, he turned to Radko and said, "Well, what about Bismarck?"

"What about it?" Radko said, not having to feign indifference.

Silas did not hesitate. "Have you and Ursula spoken about how this is going to work with your being a bishop there?"

Radko looked at Silas for some time. He was trying to think if he had given any indication that he would be returning to Bismarck as a bishop. He didn't think so, since in his mind it was clear that he wasn't. But he also tried to think if he had said anything about resigning. He realized with some surprise that he hadn't. It looked as if now were the time.

Absolution

"Silas," Radko said, "I am only returning to Bismarck to resign and to collect the few things I have left there."

Silas's eyebrows rose slightly. Mueller had not said anything about this. In fact, he had acted as if just the opposite were true. Silas recognized the political, if invisible, hand of the archbishop in the room between him and his old friend. "I'm sorry, Radko," he said, "I had gotten the impression from Archbishop Mueller that you would be returning to the diocese."

At the sound of Mueller's name, a slightly chilly silence swept through the small living room where Silas and Radko were visiting. "You are still in contact with Mueller," said Radko without much feeling in his voice.

"Of course," Silas replied. He was uncertain about what to say next, so he didn't say anything.

Radko looked at Silas. "Did Mueller send you here to get me mixed up again in that outrageous plot of his?" he asked him.

Silas didn't reply. He thought the answer to Radko's question was both yes and no. Yes, Mueller had assigned him a task. No, he did not send me here. I was coming anyway.

"Mueller knew I was coming." Silas said. "He asked me to check with you about your plans for the diocese." Silas paused for a moment; then he lowered his voice and continued: "Somehow, he got wind of the fact that you and Ursula were reconciling."

Radko's face reddened. He was furious at Mueller for his meddling and manipulative ways and had no intention of allowing him to interfere with his life at any level ever again.

"Silas," Radko said, his voice hardening, "Tell Wolfgang that I want nothing to do with his scheme or his plans or him. Ever."

Silas felt his friend's fury. "Okay," he said, "I told him I would ask."

The mention of Mueller's name in the small apartment in Baltimore sickened Radko. There was no way he could keep tabs on me without going out of his way to do it. Then he had the thought that was suddenly obvious. He's thinks I'm still in the game, he thought to himself. He thinks there's a chance that I'll go along with his Machiavellian plot. He was staring into the distance as he was having these thoughts. He slowly turned to look at Silas.

"Tell me everything you know about what this guy is up to, Silas. Everything," he said.

Silas did as Radko requested. But he didn't think he knew a fraction of Mueller's true intent, and he told Radko that as well. He told him that he was to propose to Radko the plan that he and Mueller had talked about last fall, with Ursula living outside the diocese, possibly in Canada, and Radko maintaining regular visits.

Radko listened intently. "Silas, did you hear me say a few minutes ago that I was resigning?" he asked him.

"Yes," said Silas. "I don't know if Mueller knows that or not."

If he knew about Ursula and me, he almost certainly knows about my decision to resign, Radko thought. He sat back in his chair to give himself some space to think about this more clearly.

"If Mueller knows I am reconciling with Ursula and that I am resigning, he must think that our getting back together plays into his hand while the resignation is a mere inconvenience. He must think he can stop me from resigning." He looked at Silas as he reviewed in his lawyerly mind any possible reasons why a simple resignation would not work. "The only reason for a resignation not to be valid," he said aloud, "is for it not to be accepted." It was as he said these words that the light bulb went off in Radko's head. Mueller thinks he can prevent my resignation from being accepted! To Silas he said, "He thinks he can get the pope not to accept my resignation!" Radko started laughing. "The hubris of this guy!" he said.

Silas didn't know what to say. Mueller had not shared with him the full story of what he knew, but Silas was aware that this was a common occurrence on the part of the archbishop and common practice in the Vatican. He felt like a low-level go-between who suddenly had no special allegiance to a man he had regarded as a highly placed personal friend.

Absolution

Silas listened to what Radko was saying, and it made perfect sense to him. He imagined that it was probably exactly what Wolfgang was up to. "What are you going to do, Radko?" he asked.

Radko looked at Silas and said. "I'm not going to tell you, Silas. I'm not sure where your loyalties lie."

Silas inhaled sharply. He felt that he had always been available to Radko and on his side. He had spent hours trying to make this past year as bearable as possible, and he felt judged by the object of those attentions. "That's not fair," he said. "I've done everything I could to help you."

"Everything that was approved by your handler," Radko replied sarcastically.

Silas looked at Radko with a stony expression on his face. He didn't know what to say, in no small part because there was truth in what he had just heard. He stood up and looked down at Radko, who was still seated on an arm chair across from him.

"You might have reason to be angry with me," he said not in a conciliatory tone but more as an announcement. "But I want you to know that I have tried to make everything work as smoothly as possible." He paused as his skin reddened. "It was not I who asked to witness your marriage or baptize your children. It was not I who tried to be married and stay a priest." Silas was having some trouble breathing. "And it was not I whose ambition was so out of control that I abandoned my wife and children." Then he turned and walked out the door.

Radko was stunned. In all the years he had known Silas, he had not once witnessed him lose his cool or even raise his voice. And Silas's last words stung him, all the more because they were true. He could see that now. He could not see it then. This distinction was of no use in assuaging the guilt he felt about it, however. He sat motionless in his chair looking at the doorway through which Silas had departed. He was too angry to go after him. He thought it was probably safer not to be in contact with him for a while.

CHAPTER 41

As Radko drove through Chicago for the second time in as many months, he couldn't help comparing his state of mind then and his state of mind now. Then he had been eager to see Ursula, but he had only recently been on the delicate road to recovery from the depression that had afflicted him throughout the winter months. He had been uncertain what it would be like to see Ursula and was anxious about seeing the kids. The memory of that drive, even though the events were only five weeks previous, seemed like a different time, a different epoch. Now he felt as if he knew exactly what he would do and what he would say. He also knew what he had to do to avoid the machinations of Archbishop Wolfgang Johannus Mueller, a man whose name he had come to loathe.

The way Radko saw it, it was true that canon law required a resignation to be accepted by a competent authority, and in his case that authority would be the pope himself. But once he realized what Mueller was probably up to, he hesitated to submit his resignation, even though it arrived a few days after he had e-mailed Annie to prepare it. Radko thought that Mueller was counting on his

Absolution

compliance with church law. In fact, he thought that Mueller had reason to count on that as well as on Radko's fear of exposure, as that fear had governed much of how he lived his life over the past six years. Every time he thought of this, he felt dismay descend upon him. It was going to be some time before he could forgive himself those adolescent dreams. But despite the dismay, Radko knew something the archbishop didn't, or at least he didn't think he did. What Radko knew was that he no longer cared about canon law; nor did he care enough about exposure to prevent him from doing what he was going to do.

After the confrontation with Silas, an idea crystallized in Radko's mind that had only been vague and unfocused prior to that unfortunate incident. Radko realized that he had been holding onto his career in the church and holding onto the church itself. Mueller might prevent him from having his resignation accepted, but if he announced his resignation to the people and abandoned his post, the Vatican would have no recourse but to declare the See vacant and to appoint an administrator and then another bishop. It was clear that walking away from his post meant walking away from the church. He felt sad about that for all the reasons he had told himself throughout much of his life, but the sadness was outweighed by the devastation and subterfuge engendered by his own duplicity, a duplicity that obscured love and prevented faith. Radko was sentimental, but even he saw in his softhearted way how his future could only be built upon making a firm decision about his life.

Nor did Radko care about exposure. He and Ursula had revisited this issue on many occasions during their month-long visit, and neither he nor she had any qualms about a spurt of admittedly unwelcome publicity. They didn't think it would adversely affect them or their children. When it passed, they would be able to resume their lives with a sense of tranquility that had eluded them in the years before this. They were ready.

So as Radko steered his SUV across the Dakotas at a barely legal rate of speed, his intent was simply to take care of business—to announce his resignation. If he had to name an administrator, he would do so. But then he was leaving the diocese. He calculated the odds of his returning to Bismarck to be near zero. He didn't even care if he ever saw the Midwest again.

It was late when he pulled his vehicle into the garage of the bishop's residence. There were no lights on, and he fumbled for his keys in the dark. As he switched on the light, he was startled by how drab the room and its furnishings were. The walls were a putrid shade of green that had been unpainted for what he guessed was many years. The threadbare furniture bespoke a lack of attention; it reminded Radko of how he felt during much of the time he lived here. He thought of contacting someone to let them know he was back, but then he decided that it was best to wait till morning.

Radko walked into the kitchen and made some coffee. He went around the entire residence and turned the lights on in every room. Even lit up, the space seemed dull and lifeless. He knew his future lay almost anywhere but here. He poured himself a cup of the fresh-brewed coffee, flipped on the television, and pulled out a piece of paper and started making a list of the things he needed to do. He was surprised to learn that all that was his in this building were the clothes in his closet, and there weren't many of them. He thought of packing then and there but decided that he would have time to do that in the morning.

He called Ursula. It was an awkward moment, but it served to bridge the gap between the past and the future that was theirs. After chatting about nothing for a few moments, they said goodnight and expressed their love for each other. After he hung up, Radko had one thought: I can get through the next few days.

CHAPTER 42

The next morning, he called Annie to check for messages and to let her know that he was back. He had not spoken with her since June, and he was sure she had been surprised at his e-mail in early July. But he knew her to be dutiful, and he trusted that she would continue her loyal service until such time as he left, hopefully on Sunday afternoon. He made a mental note to leave her a letter of recommendation.

Even though he was apprehensive, Radko acted as if everything were business-as-usual, and so did his secretary. She listed the calls he had received and told him that his correspondence was on his desk. She asked him if he were coming into the office, and Radko said that he would be in on Friday morning.

"Annie," he said at length, "Thank you for taking care of that matter last month."

Annie was quiet. "Yes, sir," she said quietly.

Radko could tell she was not happy with him. "Well," he said more heartily than he should have, "I'll see you on Friday," and he hung up.

Radko spent the rest of that Thursday morning packing his few possessions and calling some priests in the diocese who had been

Absolution

on his radar screen during his short tenure as bishop. He called Toby Renneke, Kito Bunshu, and Stan Rawles. He also called Dennis Schwarze. Everyone seemed to be doing fine. Then he called Frank Albecore, the diocesan attorney.

"Frank," he said after the normal formalities. "I was thinking on vacation that we should probably do some more investigating in the matter of Fr. Schwarze. You recommended a psychological evaluation at the time and I dismissed it, but I think it would be a good idea—to help him if for no other reason."

Albecore was pleased that the bishop's vacation had occasioned an increase in common sense, and he promised to put the wheels in motion right away.

By three o'clock in the afternoon, Radko had finished with all his chores. He didn't know what to do with himself, so he decided to go to the chancery and check on the amount of mail and other messages that were awaiting him there. He also thought his presence might help cheer up his beleaguered secretary.

A half hour later, Radko pulled up to the chancery building. He was more than a little apprehensive as he walked toward the entrance for what he figured to be one of the last times. Before he opened the door, he looked around and inhaled deeply. The air here was fresh, even in the town of Bismarck. So different from Baltimore or any of the other cities in which Radko had lived. Fresher, but still alien to him. He walked into the building.

When Annie spotted him, she was startled and flustered. She looked down at her desk and pretended to be busy with things. When he greeted her, she could barely look at him.

"I decided to come in early," he said to her with a smile on his face, hoping that this would help quell her anxiety, but it didn't seem to.

Radko walked on and entered his office. There was a sizable stack of mail on his desk, and he was glad he had given himself some extra time to go through it. He had started doing just that when he realized Annie was standing in front of his desk.

"Bishop Slopovich," she said, her voice quivering. "I'm so sorry that you are leaving." She stood there trembling, and her eyes were filled with tears, but she didn't say anything further.

Radko stood up and walked around his desk. He put his arms around his quivering secretary and said, "Thank you, Annie." He held her for a moment, and then he sat back on the top of his desk.

"Annie," he said, "There are some things I need your help with." He paused and looked at her. "Is that okay with you?" he said gently.

"I'll help you in any way I can, Bishop," said Annie.

Radko gestured for Annie to take a seat, and he returned to his own chair behind his desk. He explained how he had not yet submitted his resignation, although he was going to present it to the congregation on Sunday. He also explained to her that the Sunday morning liturgy at the Cathedral would be his last.

"Annie," he said, looking at her soberly. "There might be some publicity about this, maybe not this weekend, but after I announce my plans." He looked at her eyes. "There are things that people will say that may not be so nice. I don't want you to feel that you have to protect me in any way. You can respond or not to whatever comes up, but don't feel that you have to cover for me."

Annie's stare was blank. Radko could as well have been speaking Urdu. "Annie," he continued, but she interrupted him.

"Bishop," she said, "at what Mass will you be making the announcement?"

Radko paused and looked at her closely. "I think the 11:30 Mass," he said.

She looked at him as if to ask if there was anything she could do to help. He couldn't think of anything, so he thanked her again. She got up slowly and walked out of the room.

She's a good person, Radko thought to himself. He wished she could be spared from learning the truth about her boss.

CHAPTER 43

Radko left the office late, thankful that he had gotten a head start on his mail and other paperwork before Friday. He slept soundly that night, and the next morning got up early and went into the office before anyone else arrived. By the time the support staff arrived, he was halfway through the balance of his mail. By the time the rest of the office staff showed up, he was finishing up.

Radko sat at his desk and considered what he needed to do to be sure the diocese would continue functioning in his absence. He had to talk to Fr. Caldwell, his Vicar, and make sure he understood that he would be leaving. He also thought it would be a good idea to talk to the diocesan attorney to make sure he was on board. He was not looking forward to either of these conversations.

Because he couldn't think of anything else to do to avoid it, he called the Vicar General into his office. Fr. Caldwell sat attentively on the other side of the desk.

"Bruce," Radko began, "On Sunday, I am going to announce at the 11:30 liturgy that I am abandoning my office as bishop of this diocese."

Bruce Caldwell didn't say anything, but his head moved slightly. He turned his good ear slightly toward the man behind the desk

Absolution

because he was uncertain if he had heard him properly. He stared intently into Radko's face.

"It's my intention to appoint you administrator of the diocese in my absence," he continued. "I shall be leaving on Sunday afternoon after mass."

The color drained from Bruce's face. He had been administrator before Radko arrived, and he did not relish a reprise of that role. All responsibility and no real authority. All complaints and little power.

"Bishop," he finally said with a look of concern on his face, "may I ask why you are leaving?"

A fair question, Radko thought, but he thought it was best left unanswered. But he had to say something.

"It's complicated, Bruce," he said. "I'm hoping not to have to give much by way of explanation.

Being a chancery official, Caldwell understood the coded message in the bishop's bland response. None of my business. He nodded slowly. "What do you need me to do, Bishop?" he asked obediently.

"Pretty much what you did last time," Radko said. Then he added. "Bruce, I know you to be a good and responsible man. I feel good about entrusting the diocese to you in the interim."

Caldwell got up and walked slowly out of the office.

Radko looked around. "I'm done here," he said, realizing this would be the last time he would visit this space, this place that had almost been his undoing. He sighed deeply and stood up and looked out the window. The day was bright, and he noticed how it made this rural outpost seem pleasant—almost agreeable. He shook his head, gathered up a few things, and walked out of his office. He said good-bye to Annie, but he didn't intend to say his farewells here. It didn't seem appropriate.

CHAPTER 44

The rest of Friday and Saturday Radko spent working on his sermon for Sunday. He was captured by the awareness that this would be his last ministerial act as a priest and bishop of the church to which he had devoted his entire professional life. He wanted his farewell sermon to be a lot of things, and he wanted it not to be a lot of things. He wanted it to be solid and honest and expressive of the sorrow and surety of his decision. He didn't want it to be angry or blaming or self-justifying. He looked at the biblical text of the day. It was the story of Peter jumping out of the boat to walk to Jesus, who was walking on water. How apt, Radko thought.

Radko wrote his sermon in as circumspect a way as possible, while still reflecting a version of the truth. He didn't want to expose his situation if he could avoid it, if only to protect Ursula and the twins from unwanted publicity. Still, he thought in the back of his mind that if publicity doesn't come Sunday, it could easily come the day after.

Radko wondered who would actually be at the liturgy on Sunday. There would be the usual crowd, he thought, the faithful people of the diocese who were the backbone of the church around the world. The same faces, the same families. That was all right,

Absolution

Radko thought; it was important for him to report to the people. It was the people who needed his attention, not the scheming archbishop from Rome. And not his scheming coconspirators, he thought bitterly, the face of Silas flashing across his mind. In the back of Radko's mind, he hoped that he and Silas could be friends again someday, but he knew that day would be far in the future if ever.

On Saturday night, he slept poorly. He wasn't uncertain about what he was going to do the next day, but he was apprehensive. He knew in his heart that what made him anxious was the fact that duplicity had been at the core of his life as a priest, and disclosure, coming clean, was not routinely a part of that life. Not even close, he thought when he awoke throughout the night. He tried to avoid his habit of berating himself, and in fact he took some solace in the fact that he was to face his congregation honestly in the morning. After that, there would be no further need for recriminations of any sort. He anticipated the service wearily.

When he finally awoke on Sunday morning, Radko felt a heaviness in his chest. He went about his morning routine slowly. He felt his life in slow motion. At times it didn't even seem like his life. He didn't call Ursula. He didn't call anyone. He ate a leisurely breakfast, drank his coffee, read the morning paper. At ten o'clock, he decided to go to the cathedral.

He entered the sacristy twenty minutes later. Fr. Caldwell was finishing up the 10:00 a.m. Mass when he arrived. It seemed poorly attended, Radko thought absently. I'll have to ask Caldwell about that. Then he reminded himself that he didn't need to follow up on it at all; he was leaving on this very day.

Sadness began to fill Radko's reconstituted body. The slowness that had characterized his morning seemed to accelerate, albeit imperceptibly. He vested as if in a trance. With each sacramental garment, his movements were ponderous, as if he were praying. He thought that perhaps he was. He took the text of his sermon and put it up the capacious sleeve of his alb so that he could have it readily available when the time came for him to deliver it. He folded his hands in front of the carved oak cabinet that held the vestments for the various seasons of the liturgical calendar.

At eleven twenty, he collected the servers and the deacon who would accompany him to the back of the cathedral so they could all enter in a procession to the main altar, where he would preside over his last liturgical act.

As the door to the sacristy opened and the little troupe began walking along the side aisle to the back of the church, Radko could see that the space was packed with people. He saw some people whose names he knew and many people he had seen before. He saw George, the deacon from St. Bridget's Church, and the Frankleys who had lodged the complaint against Schwarze. He saw Dennis Schwarze himself, as well as a number of other priests of the diocese. They were all dressed in albs and stoles in the first row of the congregation. He realized that most of the priests of the diocese were here. Tears clutched at Radko's throat. Not just reporting to the people, he realized. I am accountable to the people.

The first part of the liturgy went off without a hitch. The responses were strong and the singing loud. But after the reading from scripture, as Radko walked slowly to the lectern to deliver his sermon, he could not stop his hands from shaking.

He stood at the lectern and surveyed the crowd before him. He removed his miter and set it aside. He removed the written text of his sermon and placed it squarely in front of him on the highly polished blond wood surface. This all seemed to him to take a very long time, although he judged that it was probably only a matter of seconds.

Radko looked out over the congregation. He saw Annie and other staff from the chancery. All eyes were riveted on him, and he wondered if he would be able to take another breath.

"My friends," he said. "I honestly do not know why this sacred place is so filled today, but I must humbly say that I am both hon-

Absolution

ored and undeserving." He paused and looked down at the text he knew he would not need.

"I have come here today to share a story with you. A story that ends with a bishop giving up his priesthood." A tear rolled down Radko's cheek. The church was absolutely still.

"For some years prior to my arrival in Bismarck, I was married to a woman with whom I had two children. When I was named to be your bishop, my desire for power and for advancement blinded me to the value of my marriage and led me to abandon the promise I made to this woman and to our children, and we separated. It was a mistake, and I am here today to stand in the long tradition of confession that we Catholics have and to rectify that mistake."

It was then that Radko noticed a cameraman at the back of the church with his lens fixed squarely on him. Oh, my God, he thought, this is being recorded. Public confession was one thing, but confession on the record was something completely different. Nonetheless, Radko knew that he had already crossed the line, spilling out the information he had worked hard to finesse in his written text.

Radko let out a long breath and continued. "For five years before I came here as bishop, I worked in another diocese and lived a double life. I rationalized it by saying that there were two good things that I wanted: one was my family and the other was my work in the church. Over my time here, I was dealing emotionally with the loss of my wife and children." He looked at the people looking at him. "It almost killed me."

Radko was thankful that there was always a glass of water on the lectern, and he took a sip. "I want to tell you how much I have appreciated the goodness of the people of this diocese. I have seen courage and care. Every person I have met has welcomed me with warmth and openness. I, unfortunately, could respond only poorly to all this grace and generosity."

As he was finishing this last sentence, the white-robed priests from the front row of the congregation began filing into the sanctuary. They formed a half-circle around the lectern where Radko was standing, facing out into the congregation. Radko tried to ignore them.

"I have come to realize that I was right on one point: that the church and my marriage were both good things, wonderful things. But I was wrong to avoid choosing, and I have sinned grievously in abandoning my family. It is a sin for which I will seek forgiveness and which I do not intend to continue."

From the corner of his eye, Radko glimpsed the raised hands of the priests who half-surrounded him. Each had raised his hand and was saying something he could barely make out. Then he realized they were reciting in unison the words of absolution, absolving him of sin before God. He could not speak.

After a few minutes, he looked at the hundreds of people in the large church. "I am sorry," he said. "You deserve a better priest; you deserve a better bishop." He took a breath. "Effective immediately, I submit to you, the good people of this diocese, my resignation as your bishop." Radko backed away from the lectern.

Before Radko could make it back to the altar, Brent Frankley stood up in the congregation and said in a loud but shaky voice. "Bishop Slopovich," he began, "I want to say in this public place that you were a good pastor to us. You listened, you reached out your hand, you admitted it when things went wrong. You helped people in trouble, you didn't stand on ceremony. If you made mistakes, well, so have we all." He paused a moment. "And if you love a woman, that part is not a sin in my book." He stood there frozen in the moment when the applause began. Slowly at first, but it gathered steam. People were clapping and started to stand up. Radko tried to motion for them to sit down, but the priests behind him picked up the applause and everyone in the church was on his feet. Radko hung his head.

After a minute, he quit the lectern and approached the priests assembled in the sanctuary, hugging each of them. Then he walked down to the center aisle of the church. He shook the hands of eve-

Absolution

ryone close and hugged as many of them as he could manage. Then he returned to the altar and intoned the first line of the ancient Nicene Creed in a loud voice. "We believe in One God, the Father Almighty," he intoned, and together with the congregation recited the basic beliefs of the Catholic church.

For the balance of the liturgy, Radko was dry-eyed. His quibbles and reservations and criticisms of the church evaporated in the face of the power that was in the large church. He felt the love of the people, as well as their forgiveness. As he approached the final blessing, the last public benediction he would pronounce in his life, he paused and gazed over the throng of people before him. He raised his hand and pronounced the blessings of God upon them, tracing a large cross in the air. He walked out of the church with gratitude in his heart for having this one last chance to be a priest to his people, with his doubts resolved and his faith restored.

CHAPTER 45

Wolfgang Johannus Mueller and Silas Renke were sitting in Mueller's apartment watching the news feed on CNN, which replayed the entire sermon Radko had given in little Bismarck. The station had been replaying it over and over the past few days, and pundits were wading through the meaning of this surprising and improbable story. Wolf smiled wistfully.

"You know, Silas, it was not as we planned," he said philosophically, "but it may be what we intended."

Silas looked over at his aged friend. "Do you think the applause will get the attention of the Vatican?" he asked.

"I will make sure that it does," Wolfgang replied. "I will make sure that it does."

ABOUT THE AUTHOR

Paul Midden is a psychologist who has spent over twenty years working with Catholic priests and religious men and women. He has taught and written about priests in recovery and continues to work in this vital area. He lives with his wife and daughter in Saint Louis, Missouri.